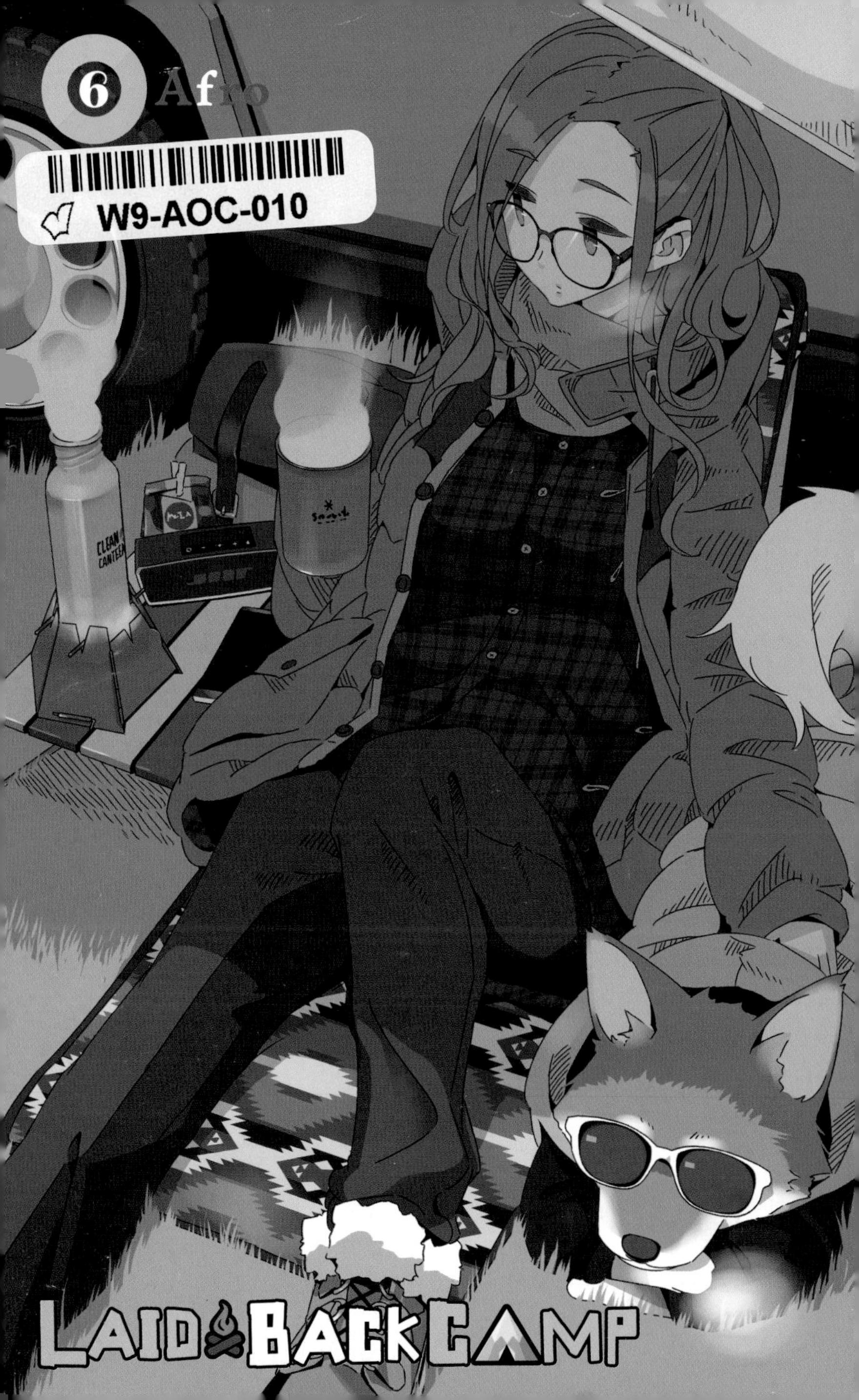
6
Afro
LAID BACK CAMP

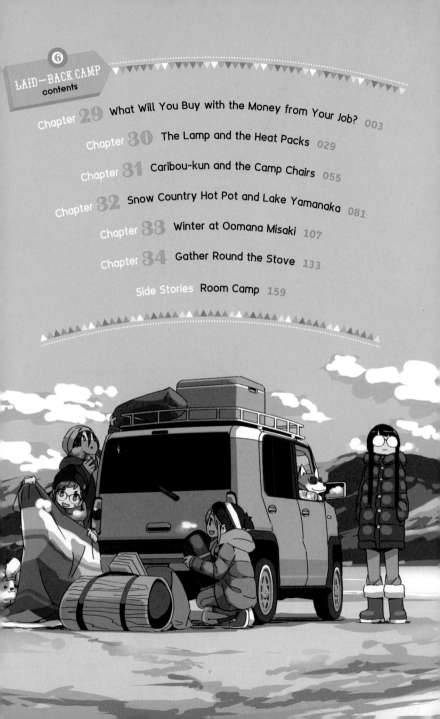

LAID-BACK CAMP
6
contents

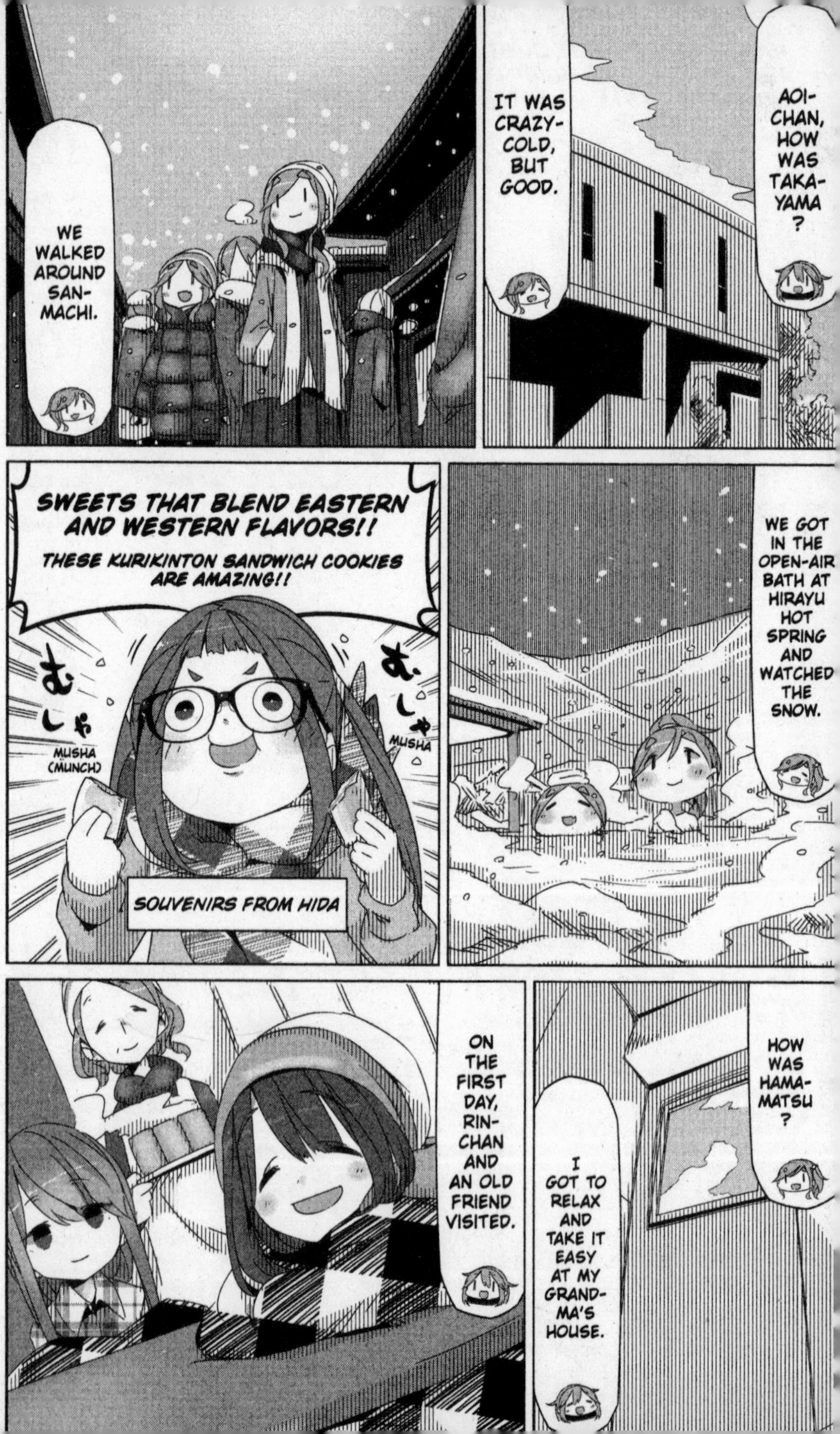
AOI-CHAN, HOW WAS TAKAYAMA?
IT WAS CRAZY-COLD, BUT GOOD.
WE WALKED AROUND SAN-MACHI.
WE GOT IN THE OPEN-AIR BATH AT HIRAYU HOT SPRING AND WATCHED THE SNOW.
SWEETS THAT BLEND EASTERN AND WESTERN FLAVORS!!
THESE KURIKINTON SANDWICH COOKIES ARE AMAZING!!
むしゃ
MUSHA
むしゃ
MUSHA (MUNCH)
SOUVENIRS FROM HIDA
HOW WAS HAMAMATSU?
I GOT TO RELAX AND TAKE IT EASY AT MY GRANDMA'S HOUSE.
ON THE FIRST DAY, RIN-CHAN AND AN OLD FRIEND VISITED.

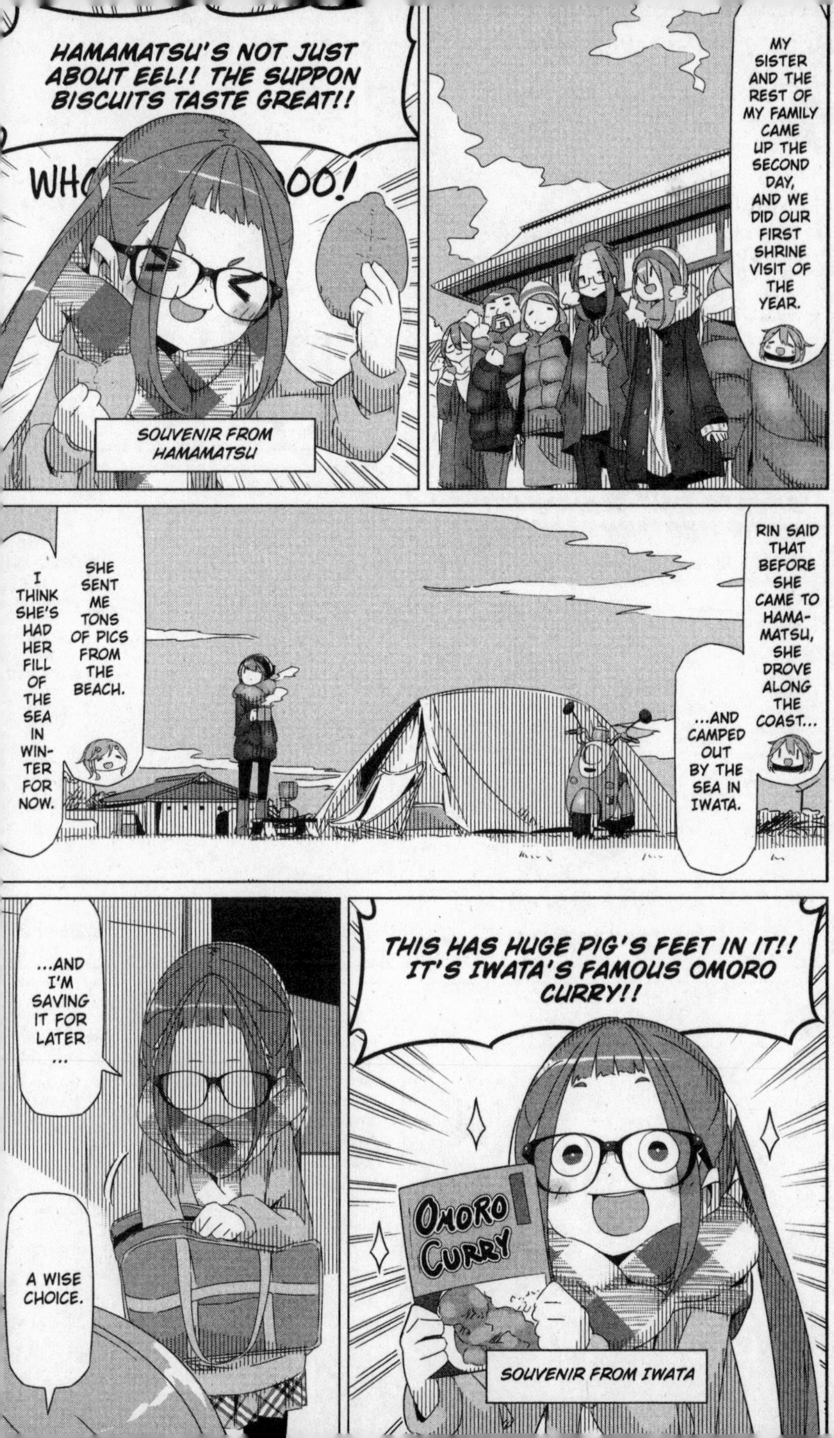
MY SISTER AND THE REST OF MY FAMILY CAME UP THE SECOND DAY, AND WE DID OUR FIRST SHRINE VISIT OF THE YEAR.
HAMAMATSU'S NOT JUST ABOUT EEL!! THE SUPPON BISCUITS TASTE GREAT!!
SOUVENIR FROM HAMAMATSU
RIN SAID THAT BEFORE SHE CAME TO HAMA-MATSU, SHE DROVE ALONG THE COAST...
...AND CAMPED OUT BY THE SEA IN IWATA.
SHE SENT ME TONS OF PICS FROM THE BEACH.
I THINK SHE'S HAD HER FILL OF THE SEA IN WIN-TER FOR NOW.
THIS HAS HUGE PIG'S FEET IN IT!! IT'S IWATA'S FAMOUS OMORO CURRY!!
OMORO CURRY
SOUVENIR FROM IWATA
...AND I'M SAVING IT FOR LATER...
A WISE CHOICE.

CHAPTER 29 WHAT WILL YOU BUY WITH THE MONEY FROM YOUR JOB?

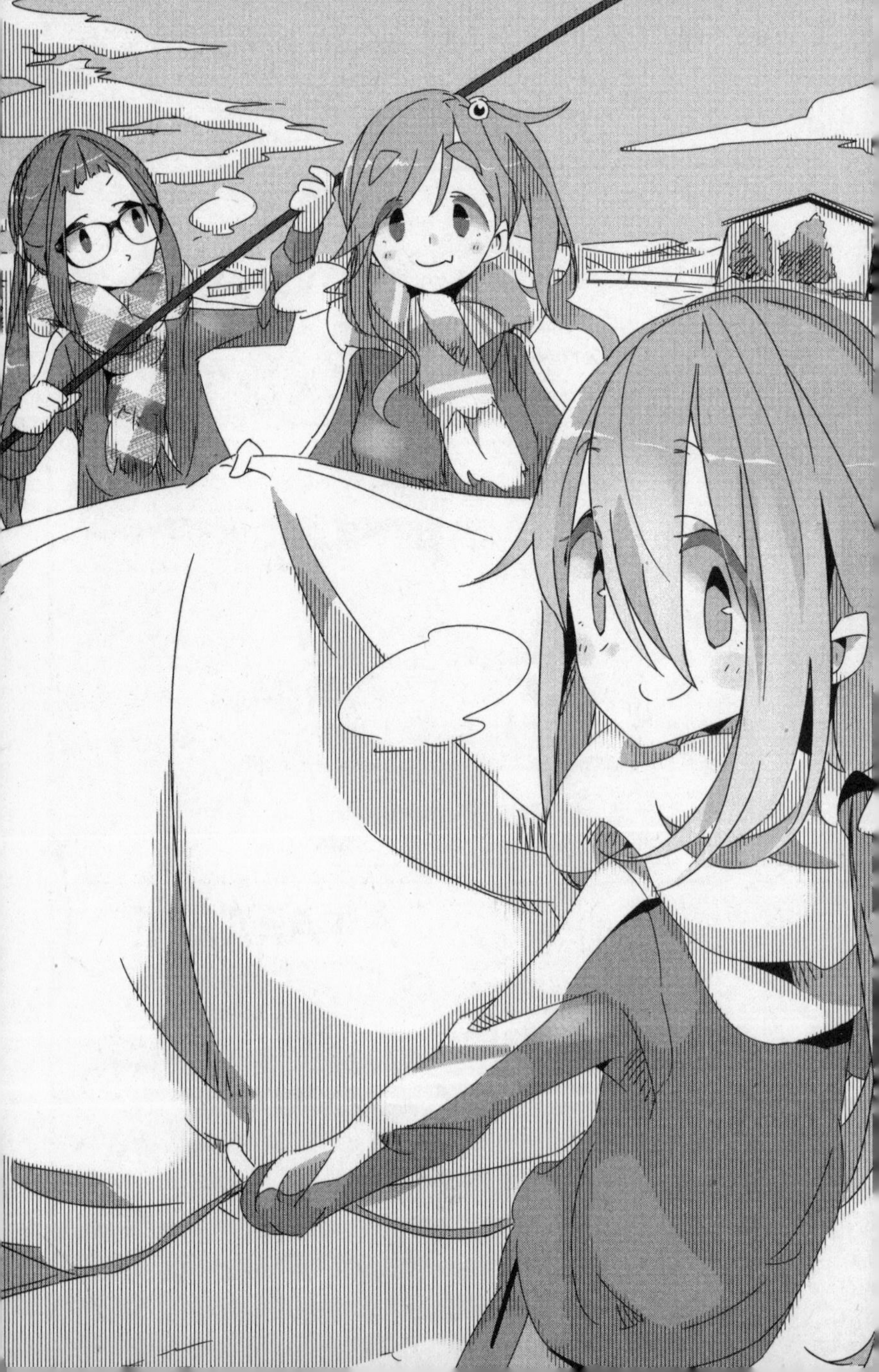

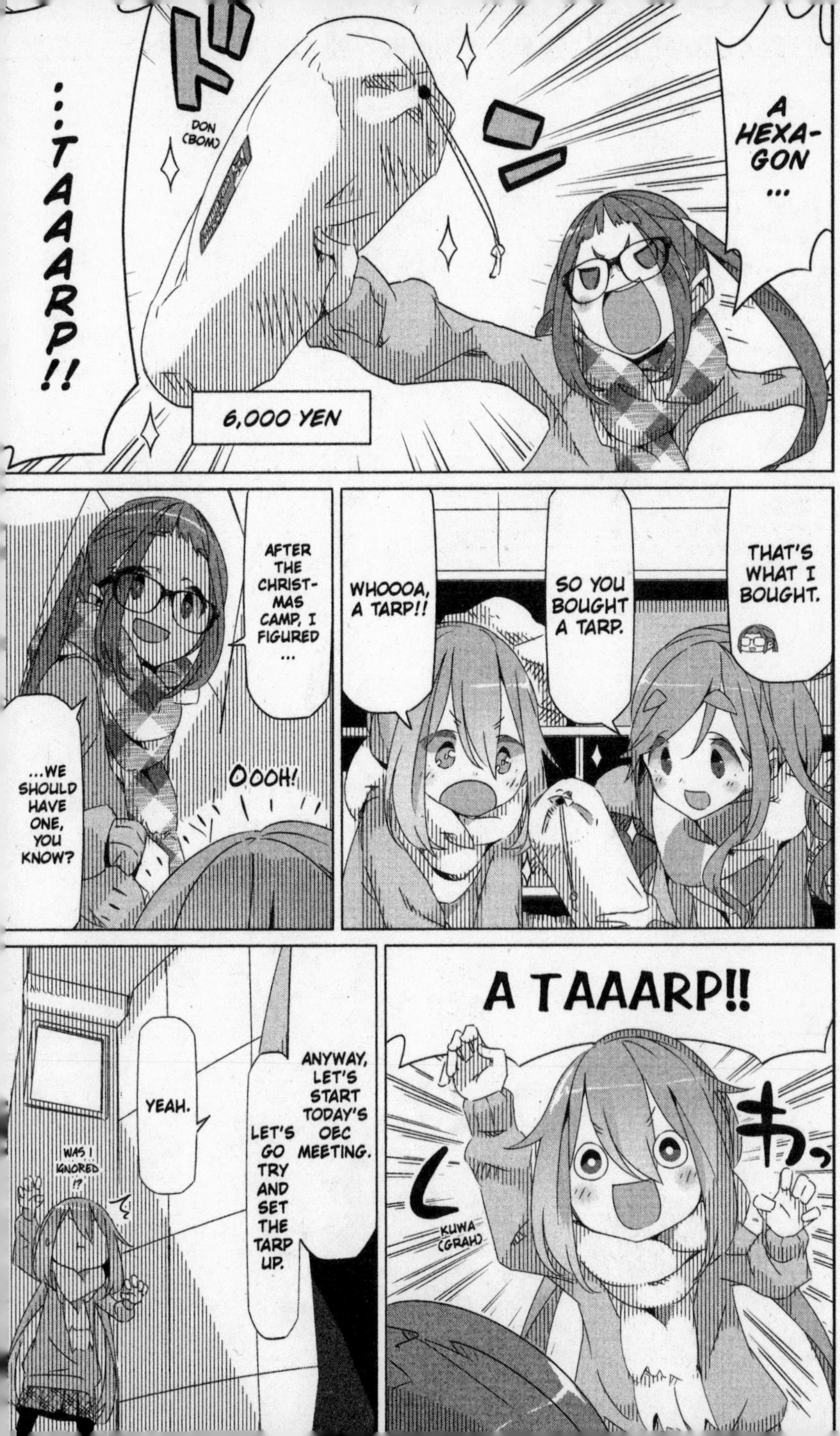
A HEXA-GON...
...TAAAARP!!
DON (BOM)
6,000 YEN
THAT'S WHAT I BOUGHT.
SO YOU BOUGHT A TARP.
WHOOOA, A TARP!!
AFTER THE CHRIST-MAS CAMP, I FIGURED...
...WE SHOULD HAVE ONE, YOU KNOW?
OOOH!
A TAAARP!!
KUWA (GRAH)
ANYWAY, LET'S START TODAY'S OEC MEETING.
LET'S GO TRY AND SET THE TARP UP.
YEAH.
WAS I IGNORED!?

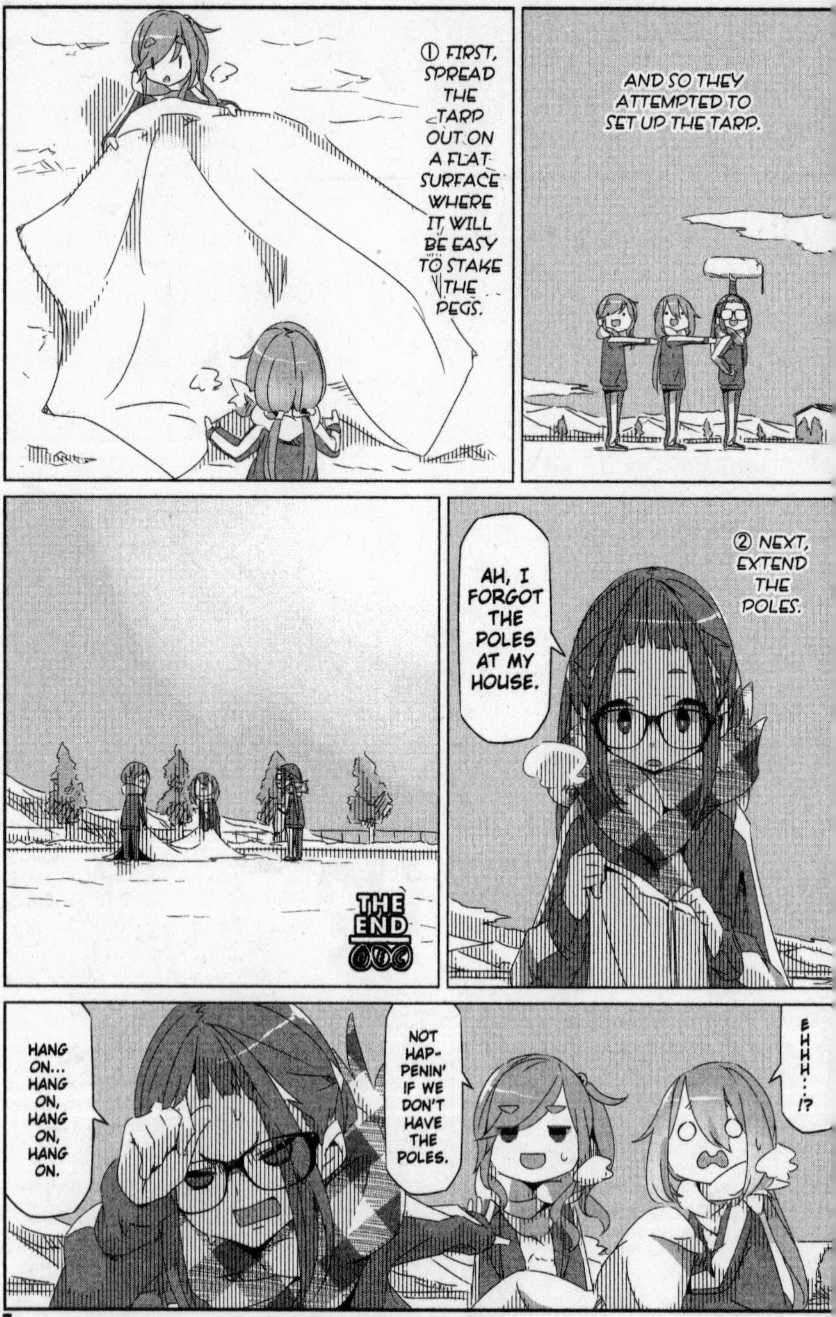
AND SO THEY ATTEMPTED TO SET UP THE TARP.
① FIRST, SPREAD THE TARP OUT ON A FLAT SURFACE WHERE IT WILL BE EASY TO STAKE THE PEGS.
② NEXT, EXTEND THE POLES.
AH, I FORGOT THE POLES AT MY HOUSE.
THE END
EHHH...!?
NOT HAP-PENIN' IF WE DON'T HAVE THE POLES.
HANG ON... HANG ON, HANG ON, HANG ON.

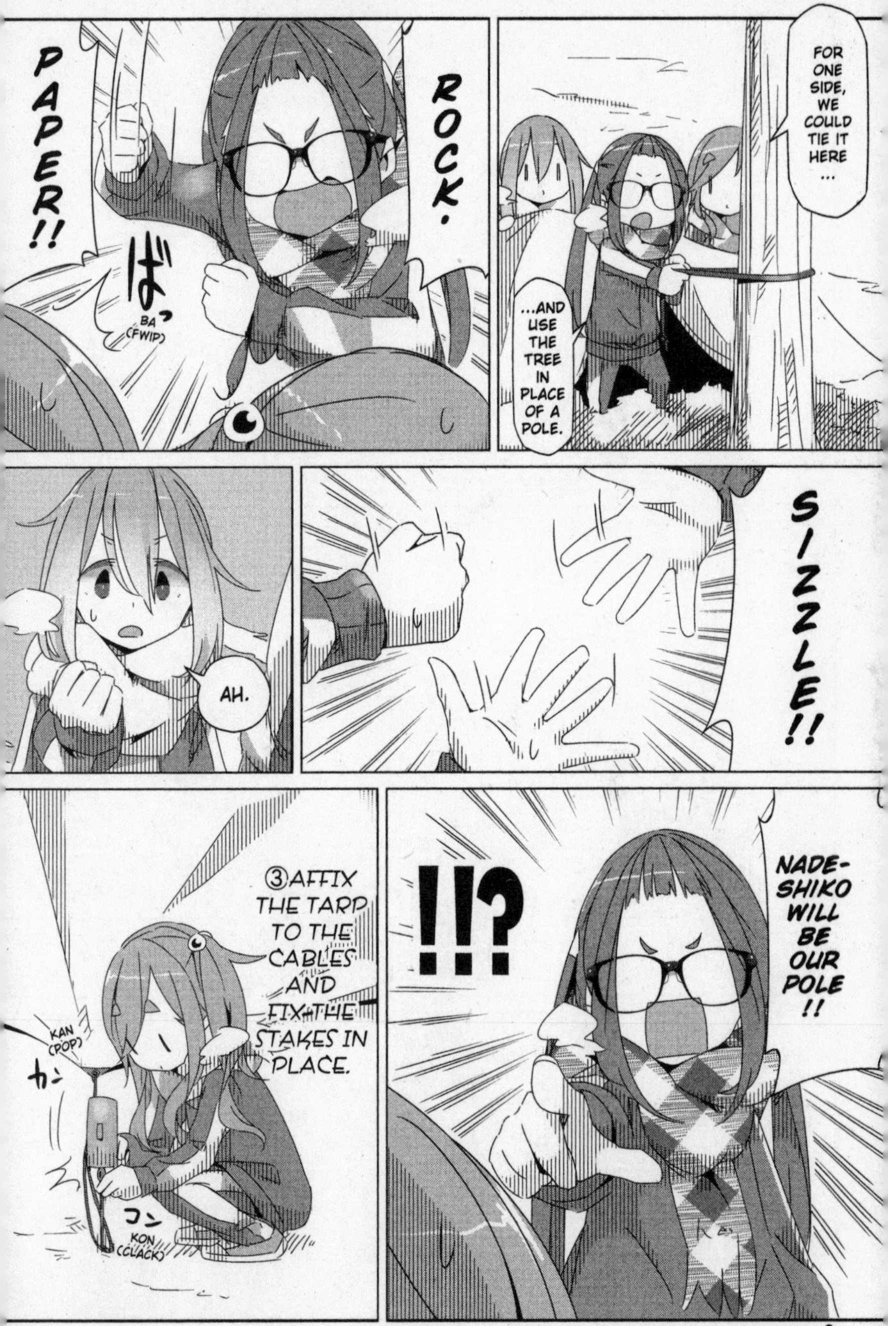

FOR ONE SIDE, WE COULD TIE IT HERE...
...AND USE THE TREE IN PLACE OF A POLE.
ROCK.
PAPER!!
ばっ
BA (FWIP)
SIZZLE!!
AH.
NADE-SHIKO WILL BE OUR POLE!!
!!?
③AFFIX THE TARP TO THE CABLES AND FIX THE STAKES IN PLACE.
KAN (POP)
カン
コン
KON (CLACK)

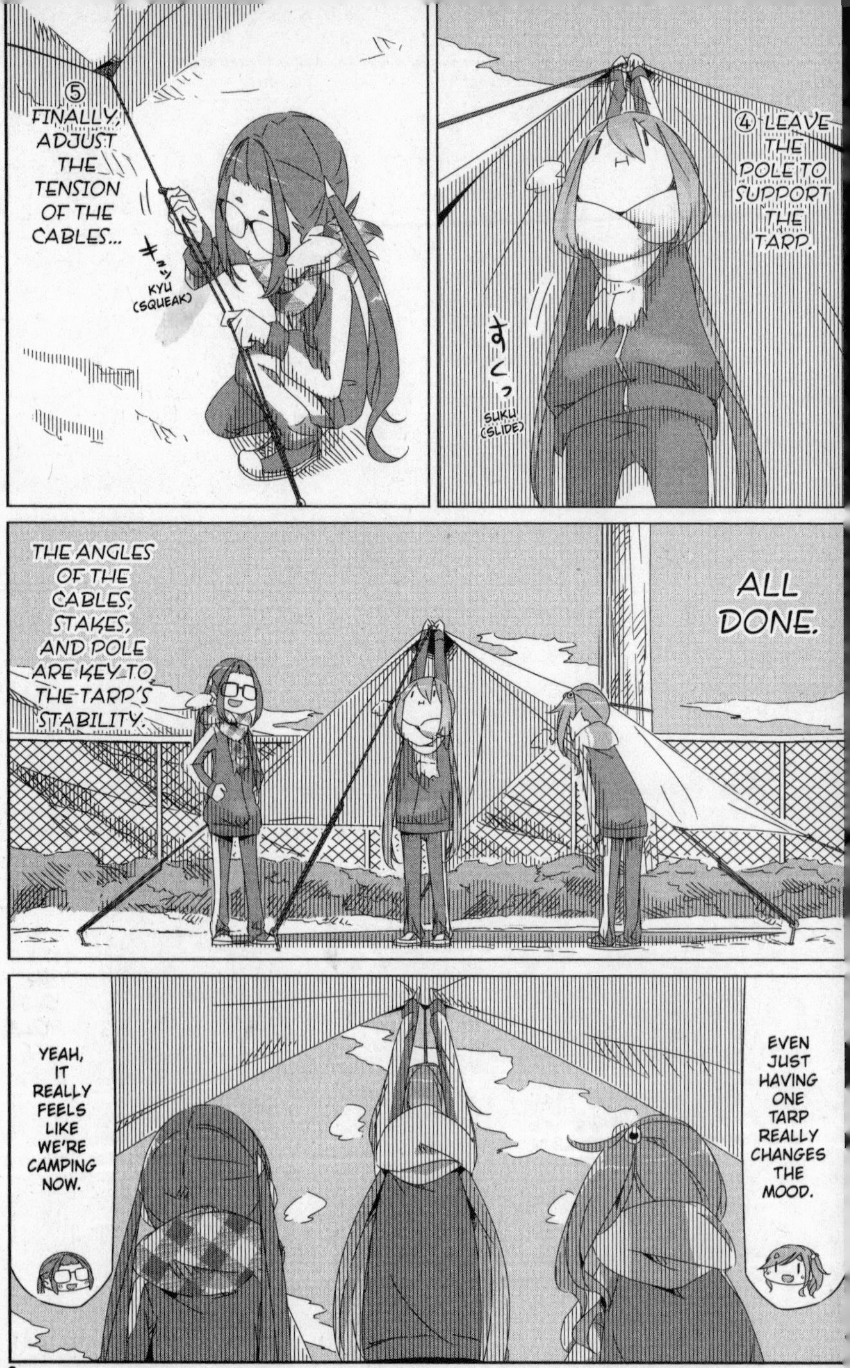
④ LEAVE THE POLE TO SUPPORT THE TARP.
すくっ
SUKU (SLIDE)
⑤ FINALLY, ADJUST THE TENSION OF THE CABLES...
キュッ
KYU (SQUEAK)
ALL DONE.
THE ANGLES OF THE CABLES, STAKES, AND POLE ARE KEY TO THE TARP'S STABILITY.
EVEN JUST HAVING ONE TARP REALLY CHANGES THE MOOD.
YEAH, IT REALLY FEELS LIKE WE'RE CAMPING NOW.

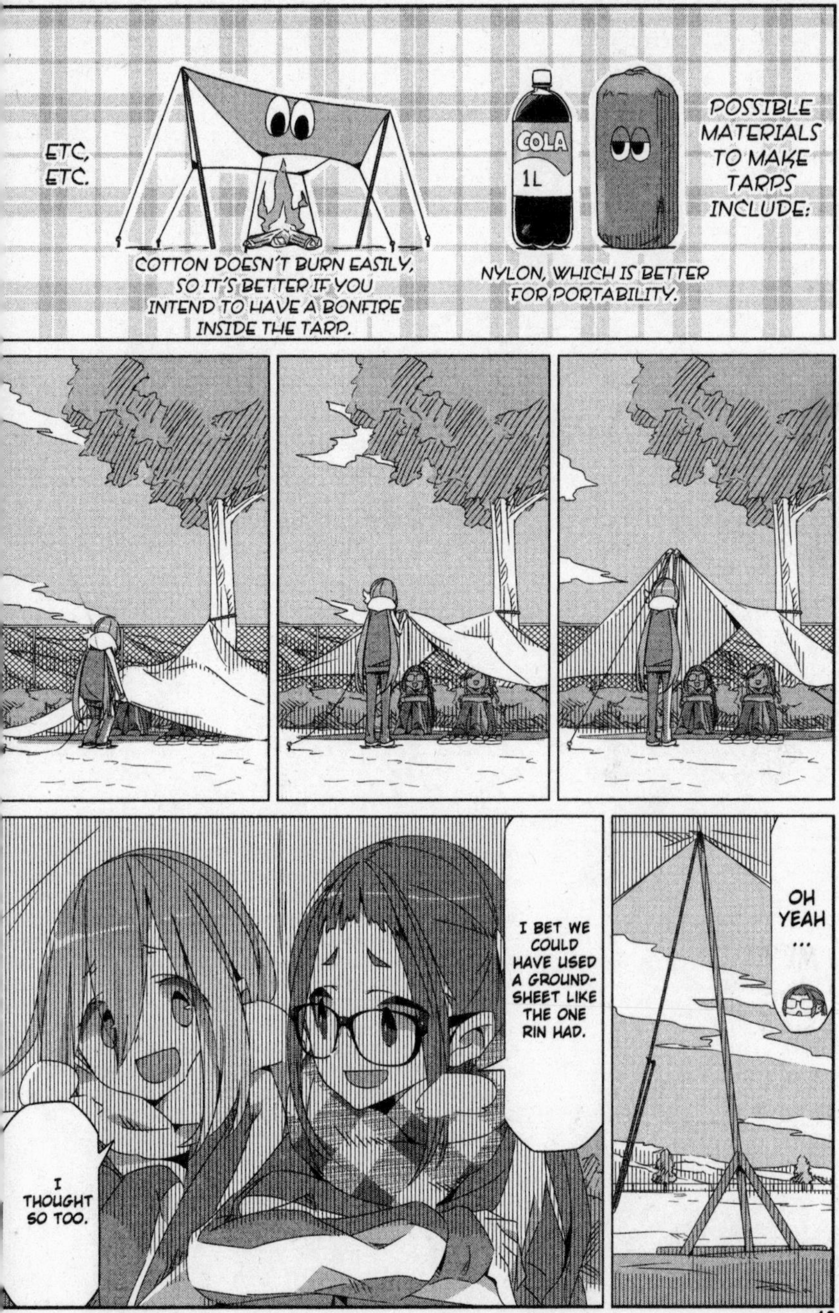
POSSIBLE MATERIALS TO MAKE TARPS INCLUDE:
COLA
1L
NYLON, WHICH IS BETTER FOR PORTABILITY.
COTTON DOESN'T BURN EASILY, SO IT'S BETTER IF YOU INTEND TO HAVE A BONFIRE INSIDE THE TARP.
ETC, ETC.
OH YEAH ...
I BET WE COULD HAVE USED A GROUND-SHEET LIKE THE ONE RIN HAD.
I THOUGHT SO TOO.

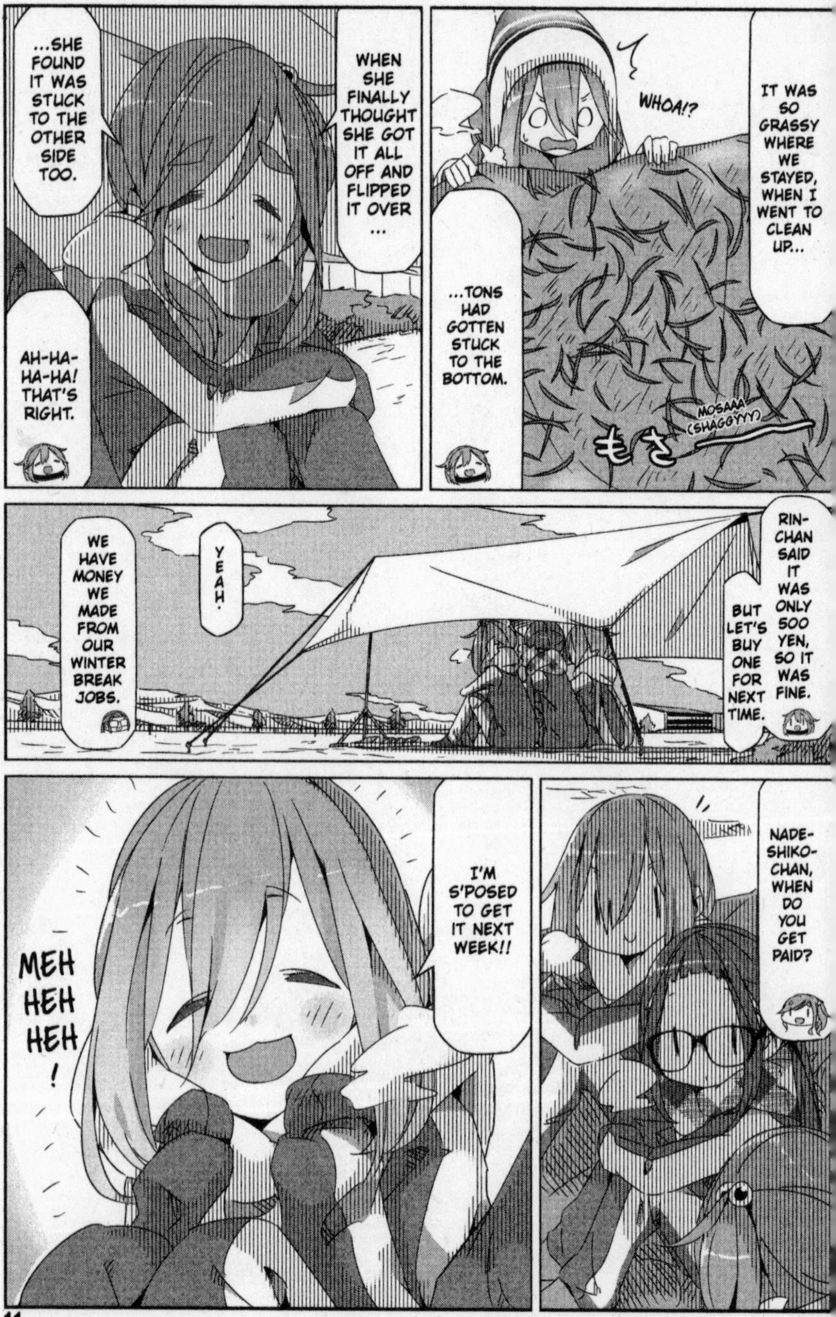
IT WAS SO GRASSY WHERE WE STAYED, WHEN I WENT TO CLEAN UP...
WHOA!?
...TONS HAD GOTTEN STUCK TO THE BOTTOM.
もさ
MOSAAA (SHAGGYYY)
WHEN SHE FINALLY THOUGHT SHE GOT IT ALL OFF AND FLIPPED IT OVER ...
...SHE FOUND IT WAS STUCK TO THE OTHER SIDE TOO.
AH-HA-HA-HA! THAT'S RIGHT.
RIN-CHAN SAID IT WAS ONLY 500 YEN, SO IT WAS FINE.
BUT LET'S BUY ONE FOR NEXT TIME.
YEAH.
WE HAVE MONEY WE MADE FROM OUR WINTER BREAK JOBS.
NADE-SHIKO-CHAN, WHEN DO YOU GET PAID?
I'M S'POSED TO GET IT NEXT WEEK!!
MEH HEH HEH!

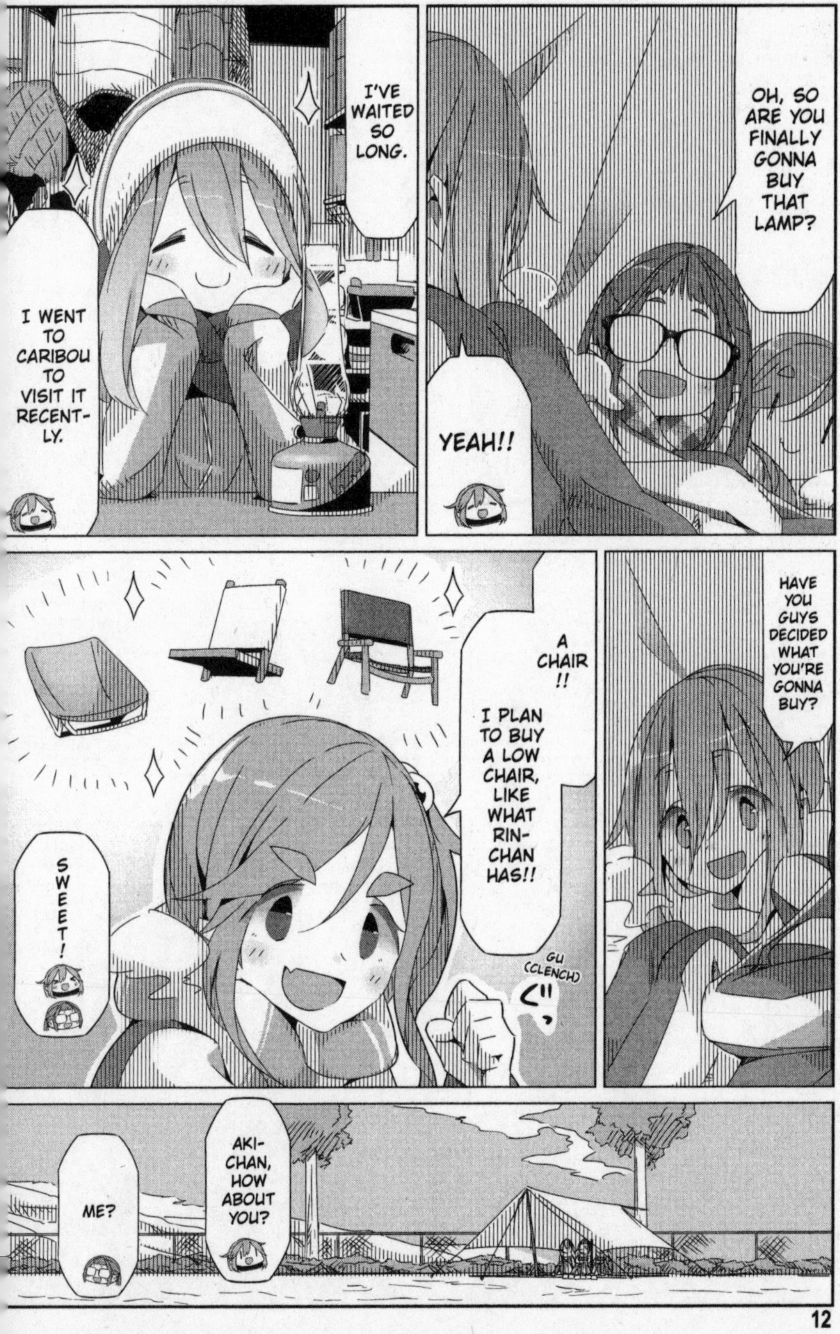
OH, SO ARE YOU FINALLY GONNA BUY THAT LAMP?
YEAH!!
I'VE WAITED SO LONG.
I WENT TO CARIBOU TO VISIT IT RECENTLY.
HAVE YOU GUYS DECIDED WHAT YOU'RE GONNA BUY?
A CHAIR!!
I PLAN TO BUY A LOW CHAIR, LIKE WHAT RIN-CHAN HAS!!
GU (CLENCH)
ぐっ
SWEET!
AKI-CHAN, HOW ABOUT YOU?
ME?

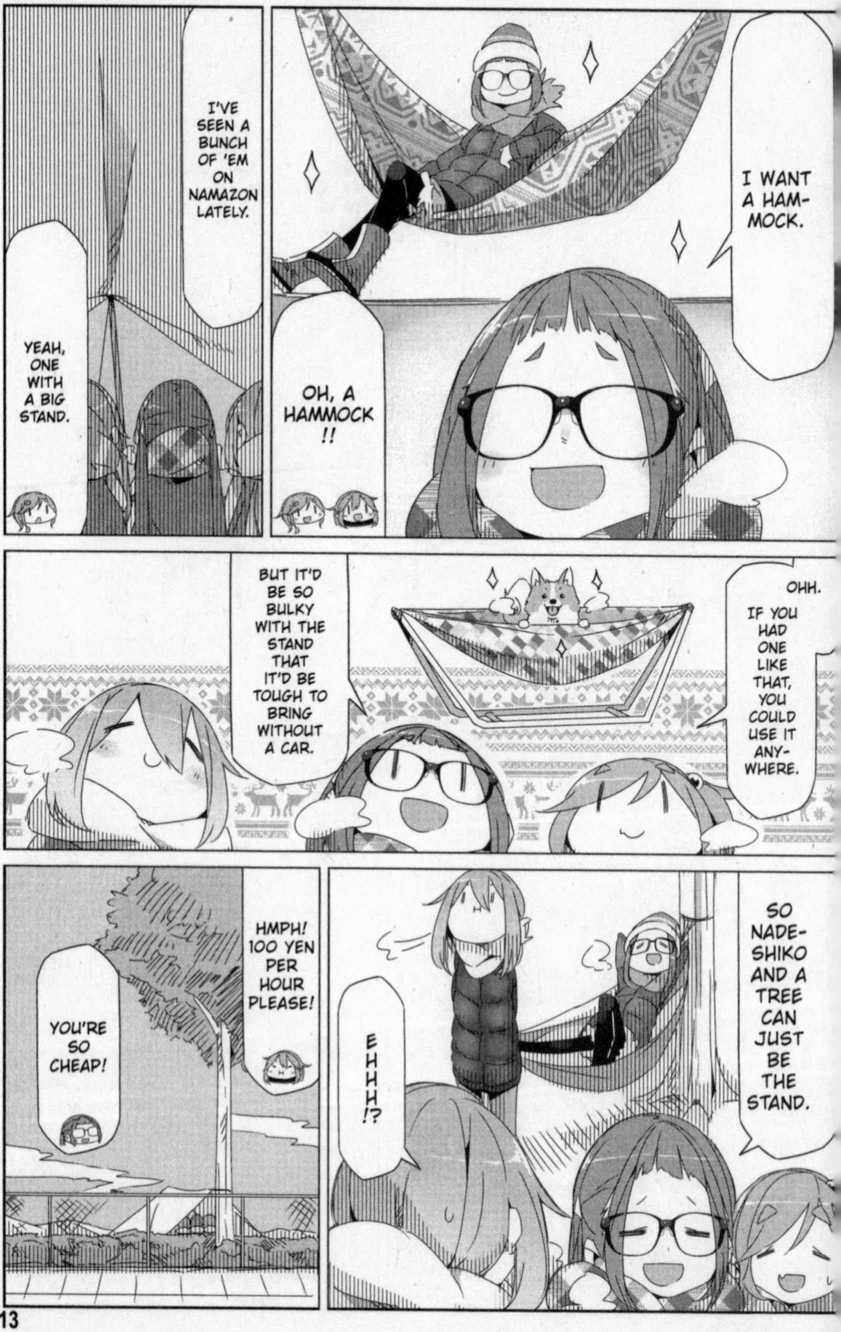
I WANT A HAMMOCK.
OH, A HAMMOCK!!
I'VE SEEN A BUNCH OF 'EM ON NAMAZON LATELY.
YEAH, ONE WITH A BIG STAND.
OHH. IF YOU HAD ONE LIKE THAT, YOU COULD USE IT ANYWHERE.
BUT IT'D BE SO BULKY WITH THE STAND THAT IT'D BE TOUGH TO BRING WITHOUT A CAR.
SO NADESHIKO AND A TREE CAN JUST BE THE STAND.
EHHH!?
HMPH! 100 YEN PER HOUR PLEASE!
YOU'RE SO CHEAP!

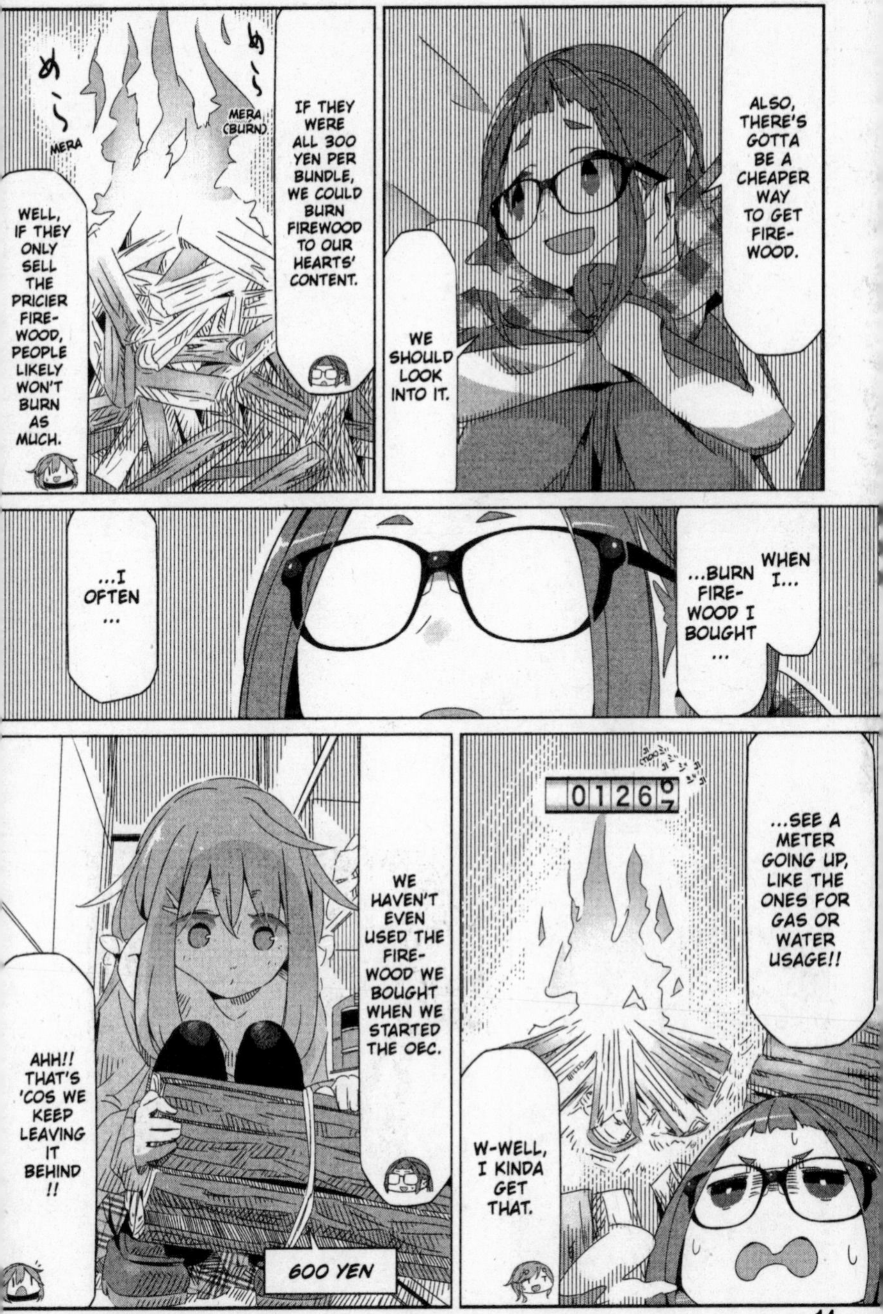
ALSO, THERE'S GOTTA BE A CHEAPER WAY TO GET FIRE-WOOD.
WE SHOULD LOOK INTO IT.
IF THEY WERE ALL 300 YEN PER BUNDLE, WE COULD BURN FIREWOOD TO OUR HEARTS' CONTENT.
めら
MERA (BURN)
めら
MERA
WELL, IF THEY ONLY SELL THE PRICIER FIRE-WOOD, PEOPLE LIKELY WON'T BURN AS MUCH.
WHEN I...
...BURN FIRE-WOOD I BOUGHT ...
...I OFTEN ...
...SEE A METER GOING UP, LIKE THE ONES FOR GAS OR WATER USAGE!!
0126
W-WELL, I KINDA GET THAT.
WE HAVEN'T EVEN USED THE FIRE-WOOD WE BOUGHT WHEN WE STARTED THE OEC.
600 YEN
AHH!! THAT'S 'COS WE KEEP LEAVING IT BEHIND !!

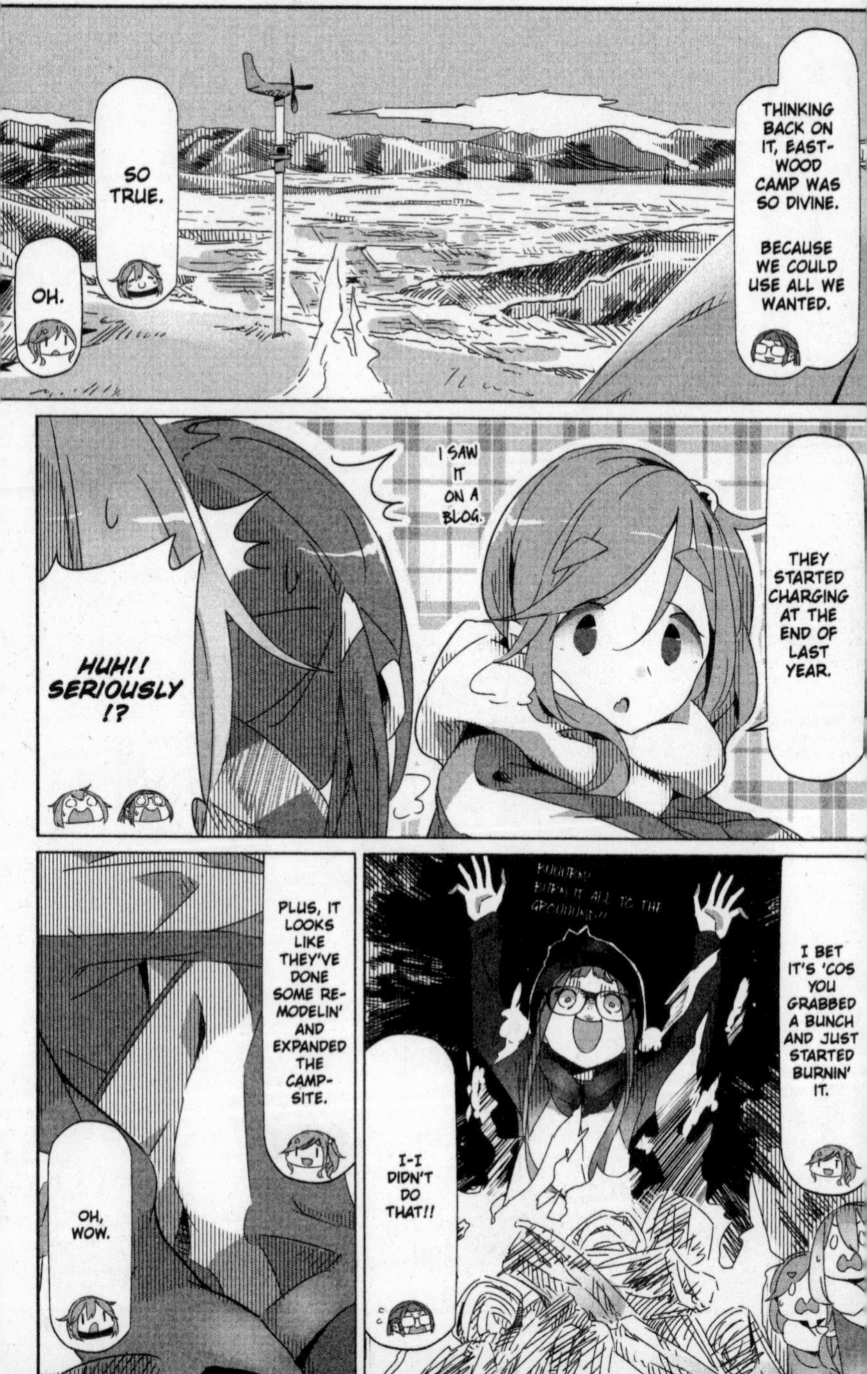
THINKING BACK ON IT, EAST-WOOD CAMP WAS SO DIVINE.
BECAUSE WE COULD USE ALL WE WANTED.
SO TRUE.
OH.
THEY STARTED CHARGING AT THE END OF LAST YEAR.
I SAW IT ON A BLOG.
HUH!! SERIOUSLY!?
I BET IT'S 'COS YOU GRABBED A BUNCH AND JUST STARTED BURNIN' IT.
BUUURN!! BURN IT ALL TO THE GROUUUND!!
I-I DIDN'T DO THAT!!
PLUS, IT LOOKS LIKE THEY'VE DONE SOME RE-MODELIN' AND EXPANDED THE CAMP-SITE.
OH, WOW.

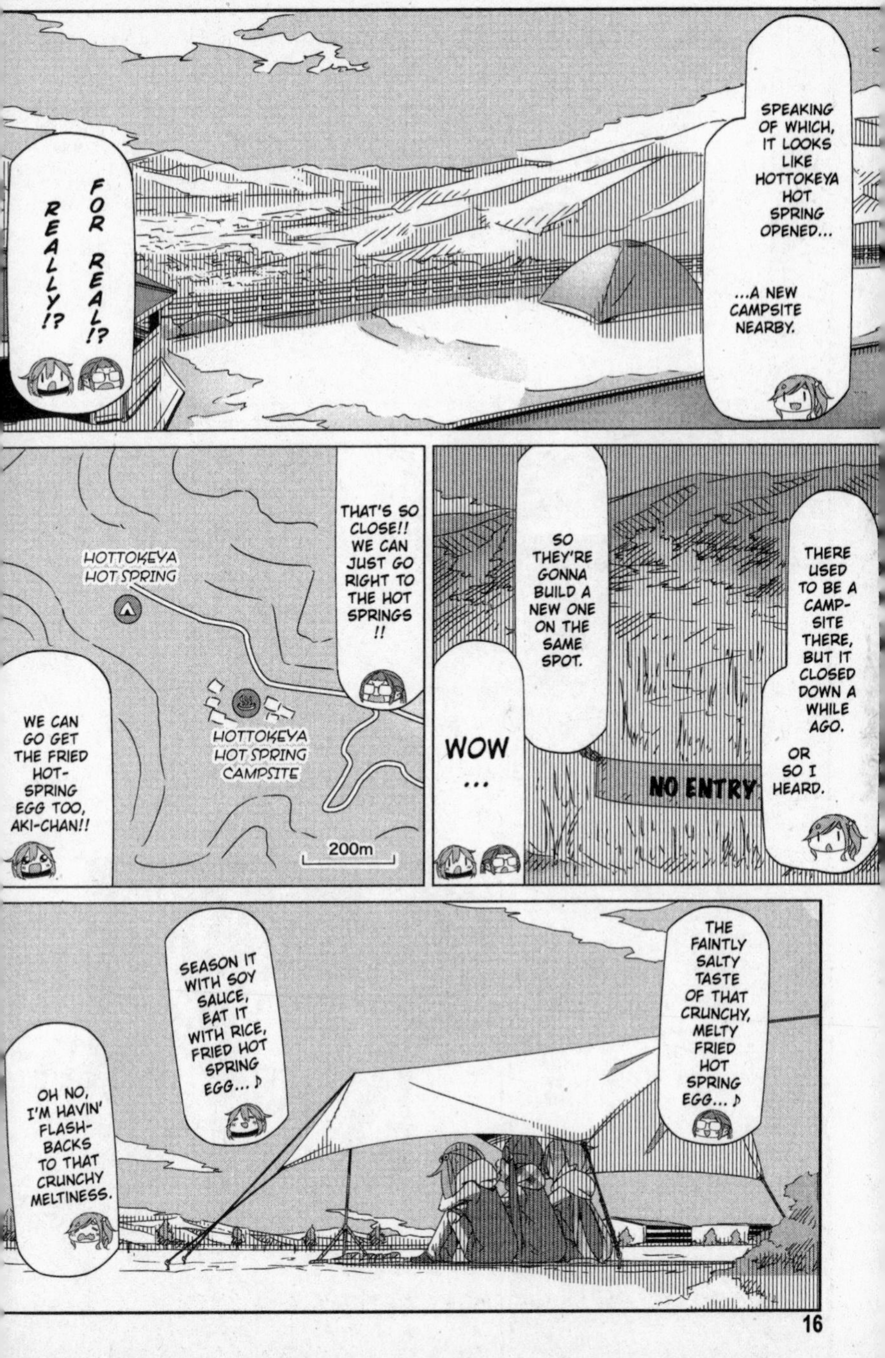
SPEAKING OF WHICH, IT LOOKS LIKE HOTTOKEYA HOT SPRING OPENED...
...A NEW CAMPSITE NEARBY.
FOR REAL!?
REALLY!?
THERE USED TO BE A CAMP-SITE THERE, BUT IT CLOSED DOWN A WHILE AGO.
OR SO I HEARD.
NO ENTRY
SO THEY'RE GONNA BUILD A NEW ONE ON THE SAME SPOT.
WOW...
THAT'S SO CLOSE!! WE CAN JUST GO RIGHT TO THE HOT SPRINGS!!
HOTTOKEYA HOT SPRING
HOTTOKEYA HOT SPRING CAMPSITE
200m
WE CAN GO GET THE FRIED HOT-SPRING EGG TOO, AKI-CHAN!!
THE FAINTLY SALTY TASTE OF THAT CRUNCHY, MELTY FRIED HOT SPRING EGG... ♪
SEASON IT WITH SOY SAUCE, EAT IT WITH RICE, FRIED HOT SPRING EGG... ♪
OH NO, I'M HAVIN' FLASH-BACKS TO THAT CRUNCHY MELTINESS.

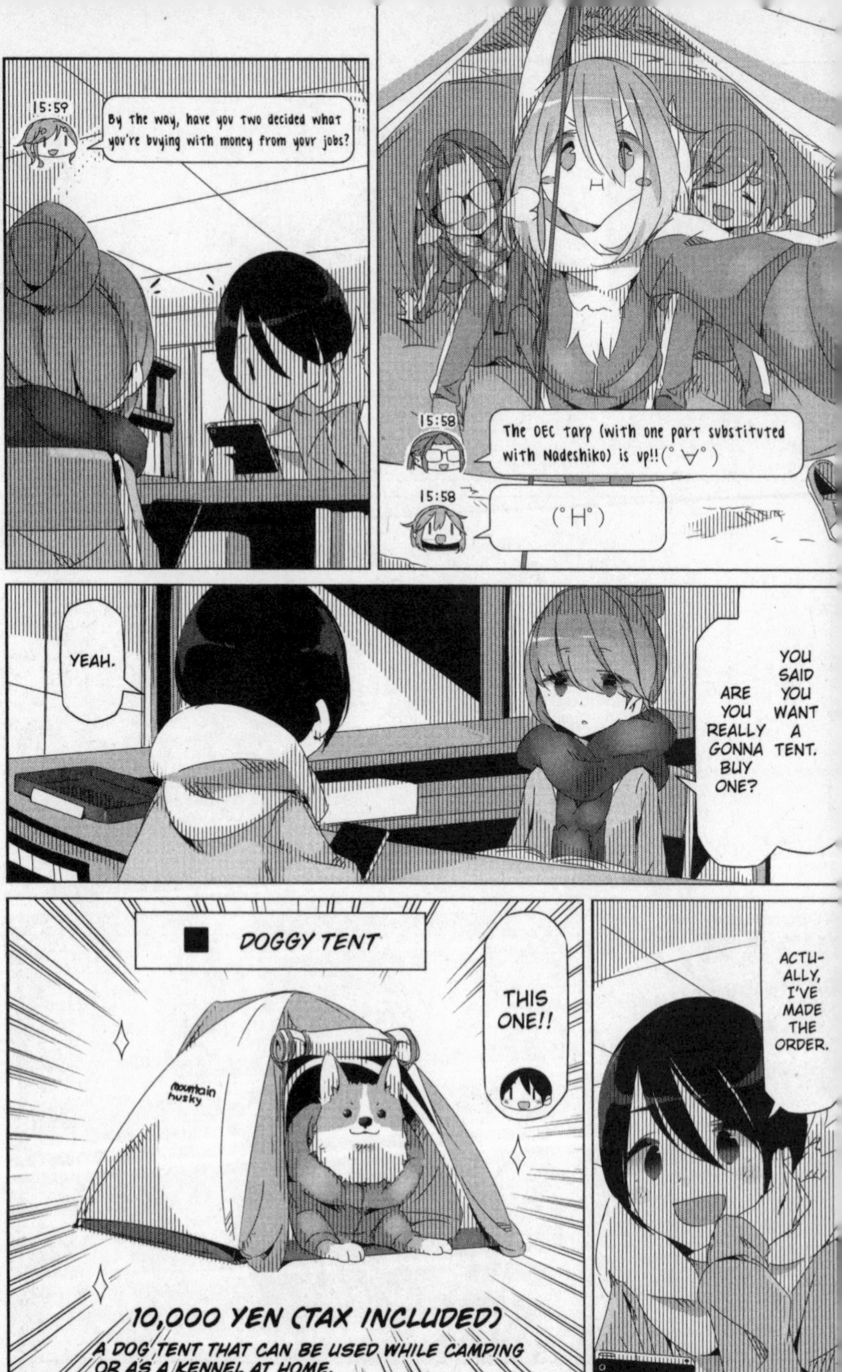
15:58
The OEC tarp (with one part substituted with Nadeshiko) is up!! (° ∀°)
15:58
(°H°)
15:59
By the way, have you two decided what you're buying with money from your jobs?
YOU SAID YOU WANT A TENT.
ARE YOU REALLY GONNA BUY ONE?
YEAH.
ACTUALLY, I'VE MADE THE ORDER.
THIS ONE!!
DOGGY TENT
mountain husky
10,000 YEN (TAX INCLUDED)
A DOG TENT THAT CAN BE USED WHILE CAMPING OR AS A KENNEL AT HOME.

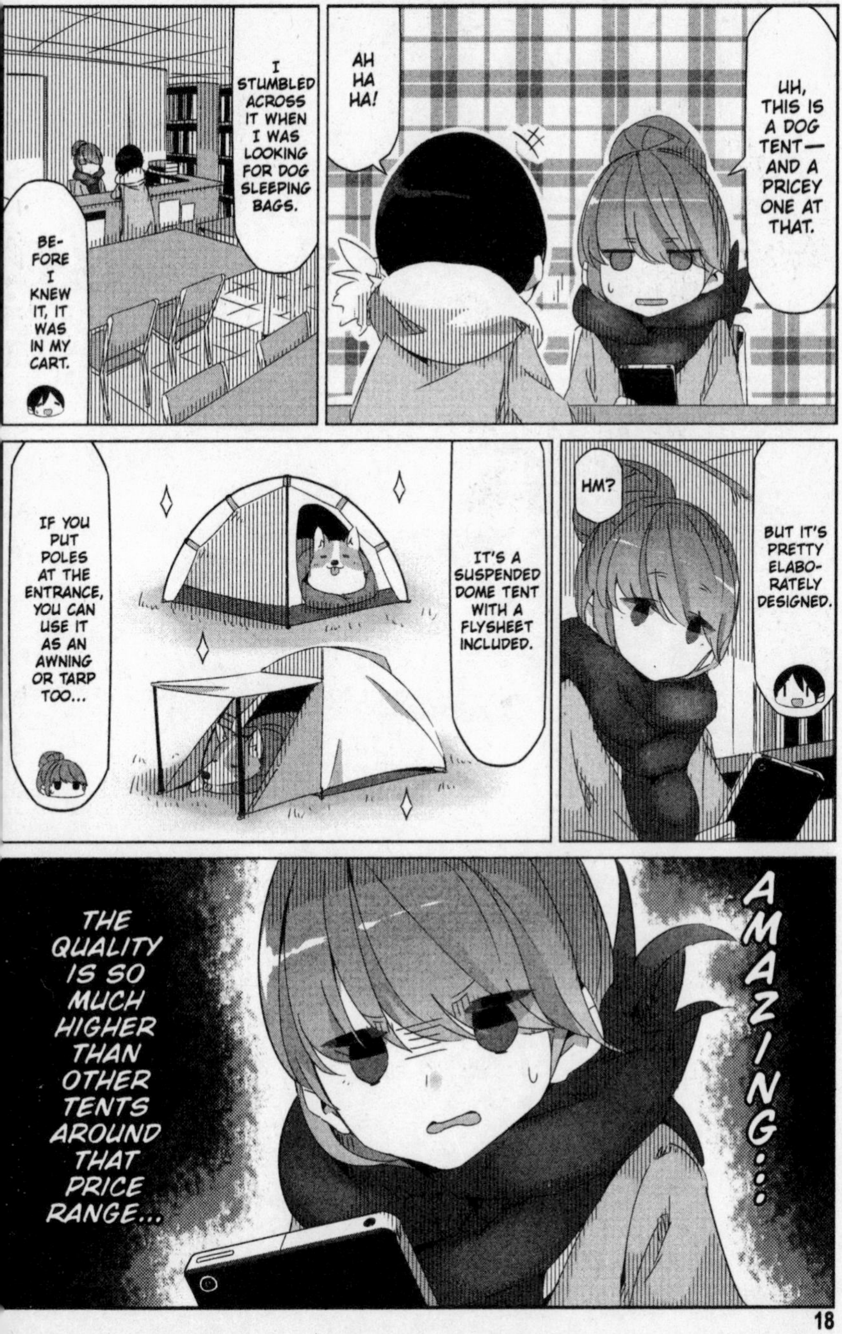
UH, THIS IS A DOG TENT—AND A PRICEY ONE AT THAT.
AH HA HA!
I STUMBLED ACROSS IT WHEN I WAS LOOKING FOR DOG SLEEPING BAGS.
BE-FORE I KNEW IT, IT WAS IN MY CART.
HM?
BUT IT'S PRETTY ELABO-RATELY DESIGNED.
IT'S A SUSPENDED DOME TENT WITH A FLYSHEET INCLUDED.
IF YOU PUT POLES AT THE ENTRANCE, YOU CAN USE IT AS AN AWNING OR TARP TOO...
AMAZING...
THE QUALITY IS SO MUCH HIGHER THAN OTHER TENTS AROUND THAT PRICE RANGE...

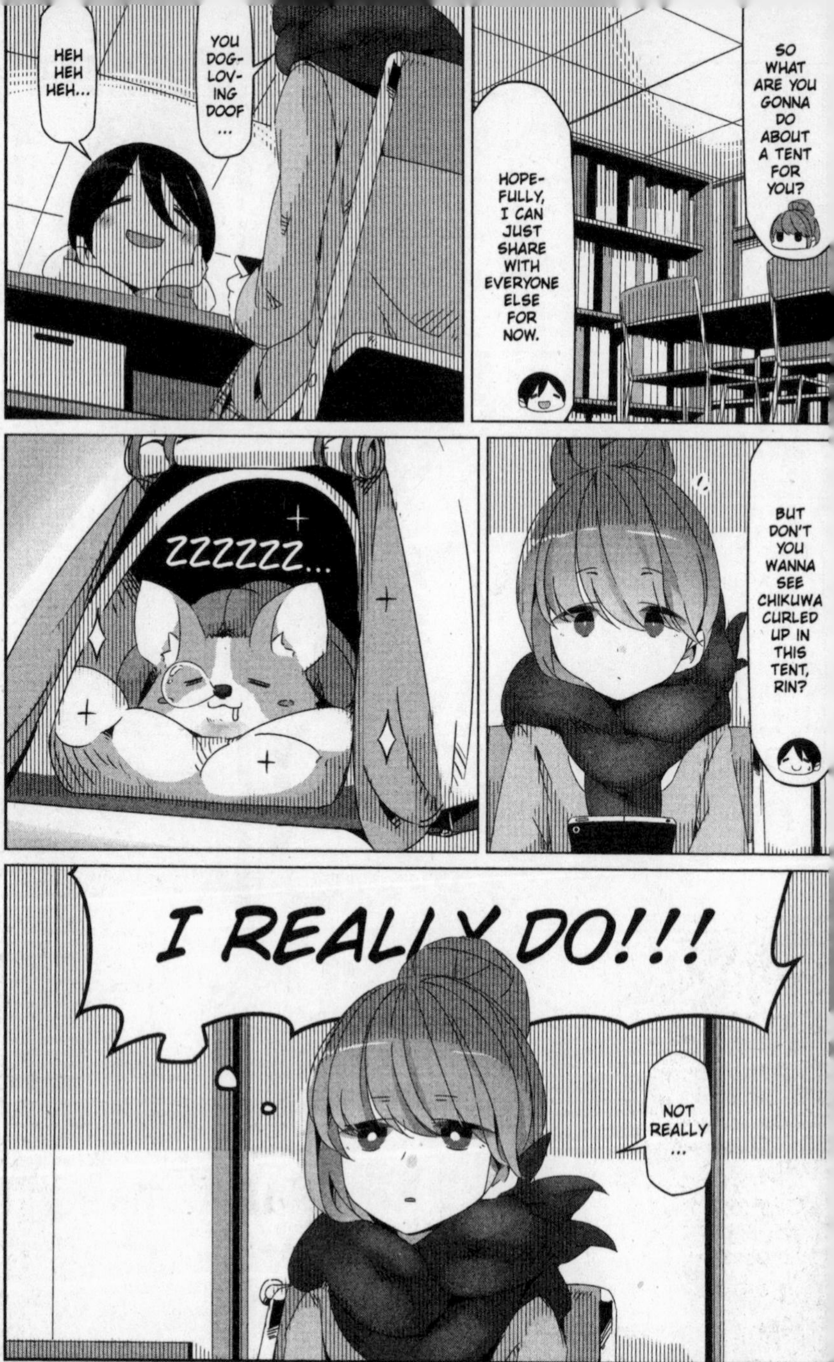
SO WHAT ARE YOU GONNA DO ABOUT A TENT FOR YOU?
HOPE-FULLY, I CAN JUST SHARE WITH EVERYONE ELSE FOR NOW.
YOU DOG-LOVING DOOF...
HEH HEH HEH...
BUT DON'T YOU WANNA SEE CHIKUWA CURLED UP IN THIS TENT, RIN?
ZZZZZZ...
I REALLY DO!!!
NOT REALLY...

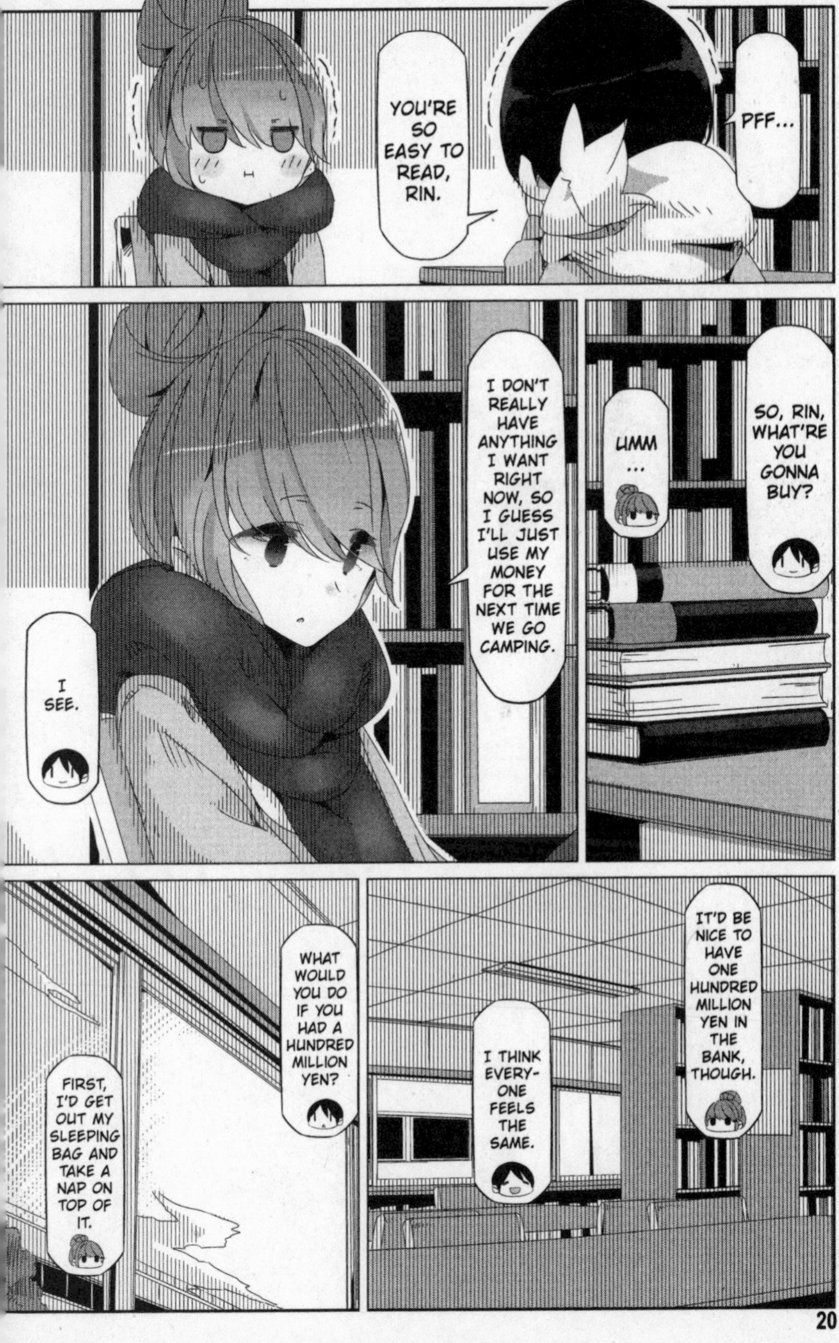
PFF...
YOU'RE SO EASY TO READ, RIN.
SO, RIN, WHAT'RE YOU GONNA BUY?
UMM ...
I DON'T REALLY HAVE ANYTHING I WANT RIGHT NOW, SO I GUESS I'LL JUST USE MY MONEY FOR THE NEXT TIME WE GO CAMPING.
I SEE.
IT'D BE NICE TO HAVE ONE HUNDRED MILLION YEN IN THE BANK, THOUGH.
I THINK EVERY-ONE FEELS THE SAME.
WHAT WOULD YOU DO IF YOU HAD A HUNDRED MILLION YEN?
FIRST, I'D GET OUT MY SLEEPING BAG AND TAKE A NAP ON TOP OF IT.

STAFF ROOM

BYE, SEN-SEI.

BYE.

NIGHT.

HAVE A GOOD NIGHT.

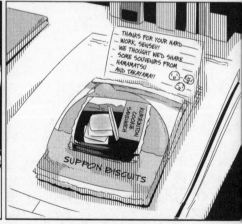

THANKS FOR YOUR HARD WORK, SENSEI!! WE THOUGHT WE'D SHARE SOME SOUVENIRS FROM HAMAMATSU AND TAKAYAMA!!

KURIKINTON COOKIE SANDWICH

SUPPON BISCUITS

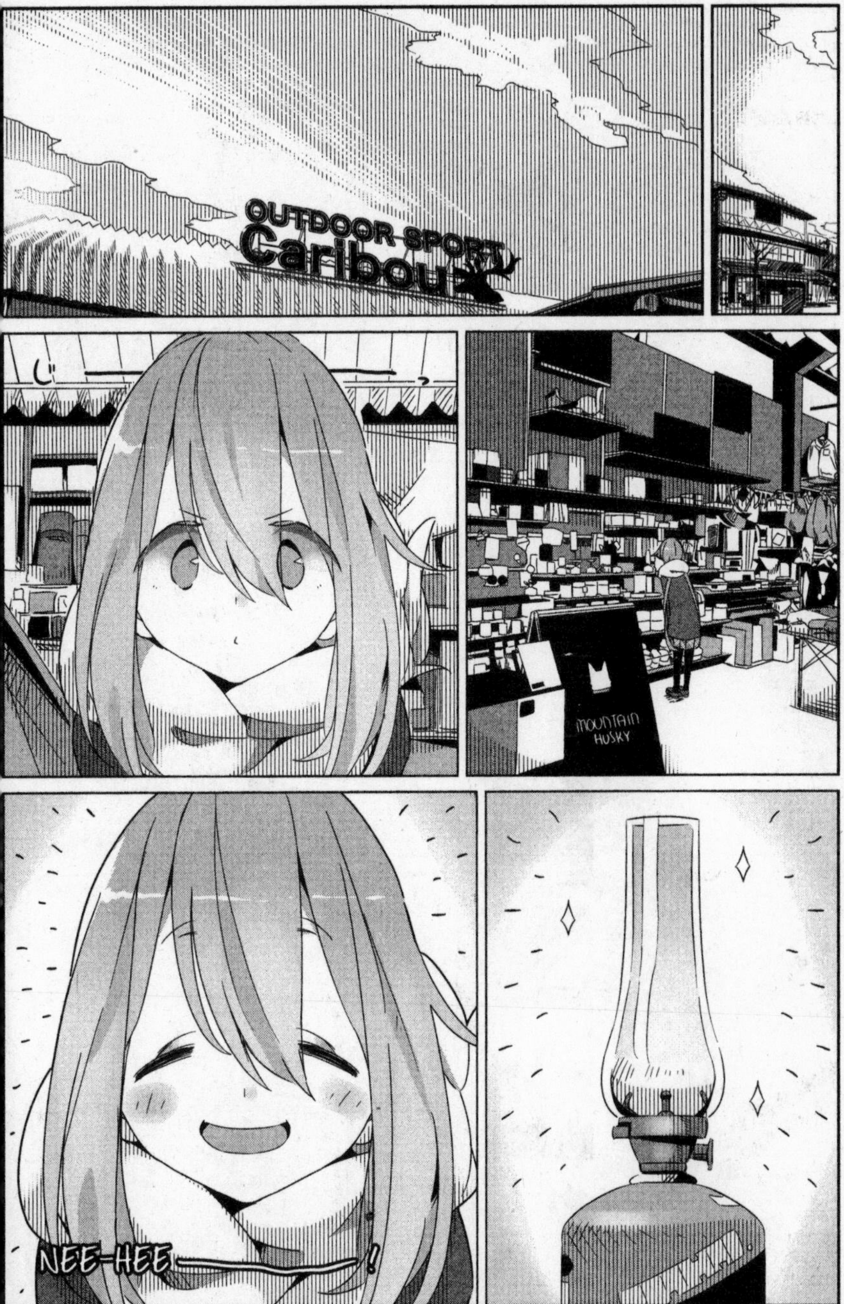
OUTDOOR SPORT
Caribou
MOUNTAIN
HUSKY
じ—
NEE-HEE—!

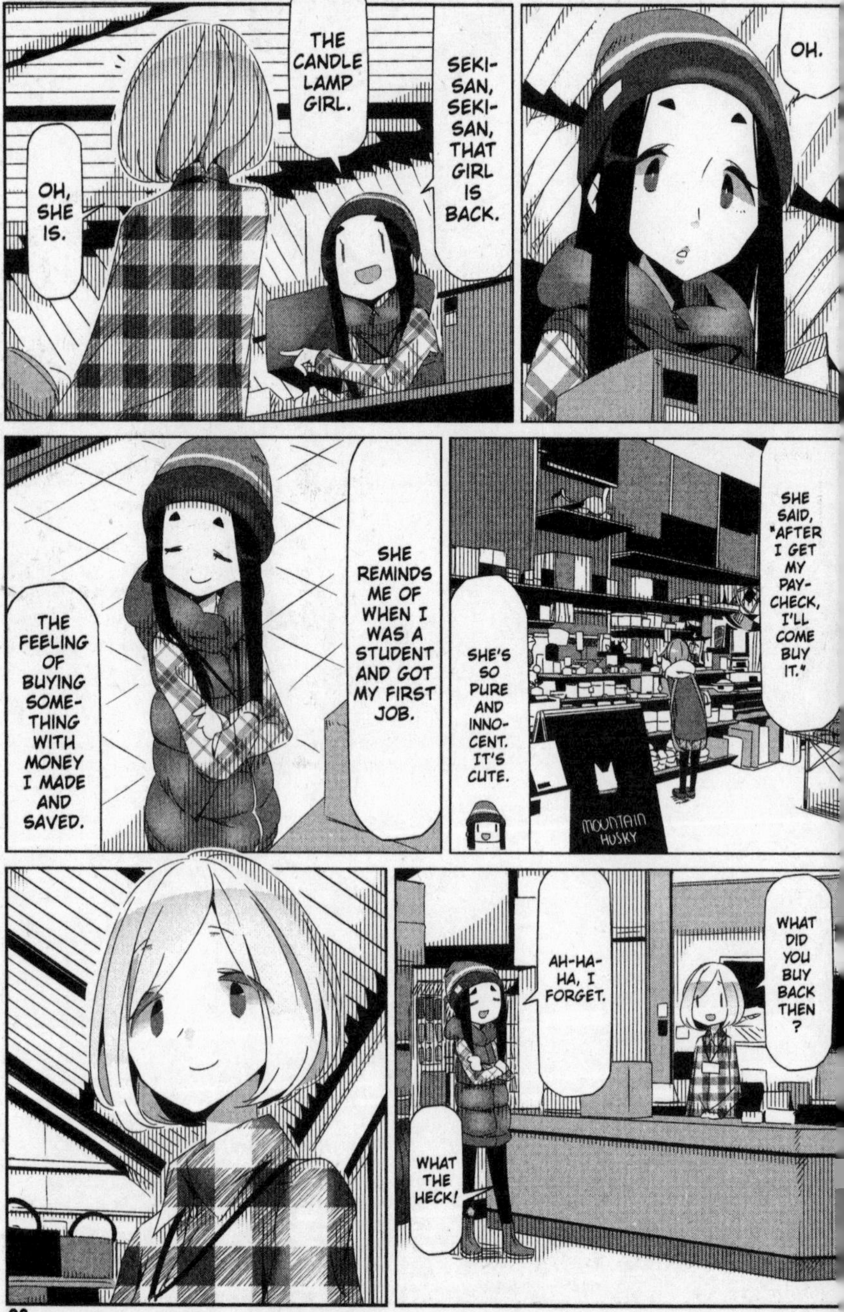
OH.
SEKI-SAN, SEKI-SAN, THAT GIRL IS BACK.
THE CANDLE LAMP GIRL.
OH, SHE IS.
SHE SAID, "AFTER I GET MY PAYCHECK, I'LL COME BUY IT."
SHE'S SO PURE AND INNOCENT. IT'S CUTE.
MOUNTAIN HUSKY
SHE REMINDS ME OF WHEN I WAS A STUDENT AND GOT MY FIRST JOB.
THE FEELING OF BUYING SOMETHING WITH MONEY I MADE AND SAVED.
WHAT DID YOU BUY BACK THEN?
AH-HA-HA, I FORGET.
WHAT THE HECK!

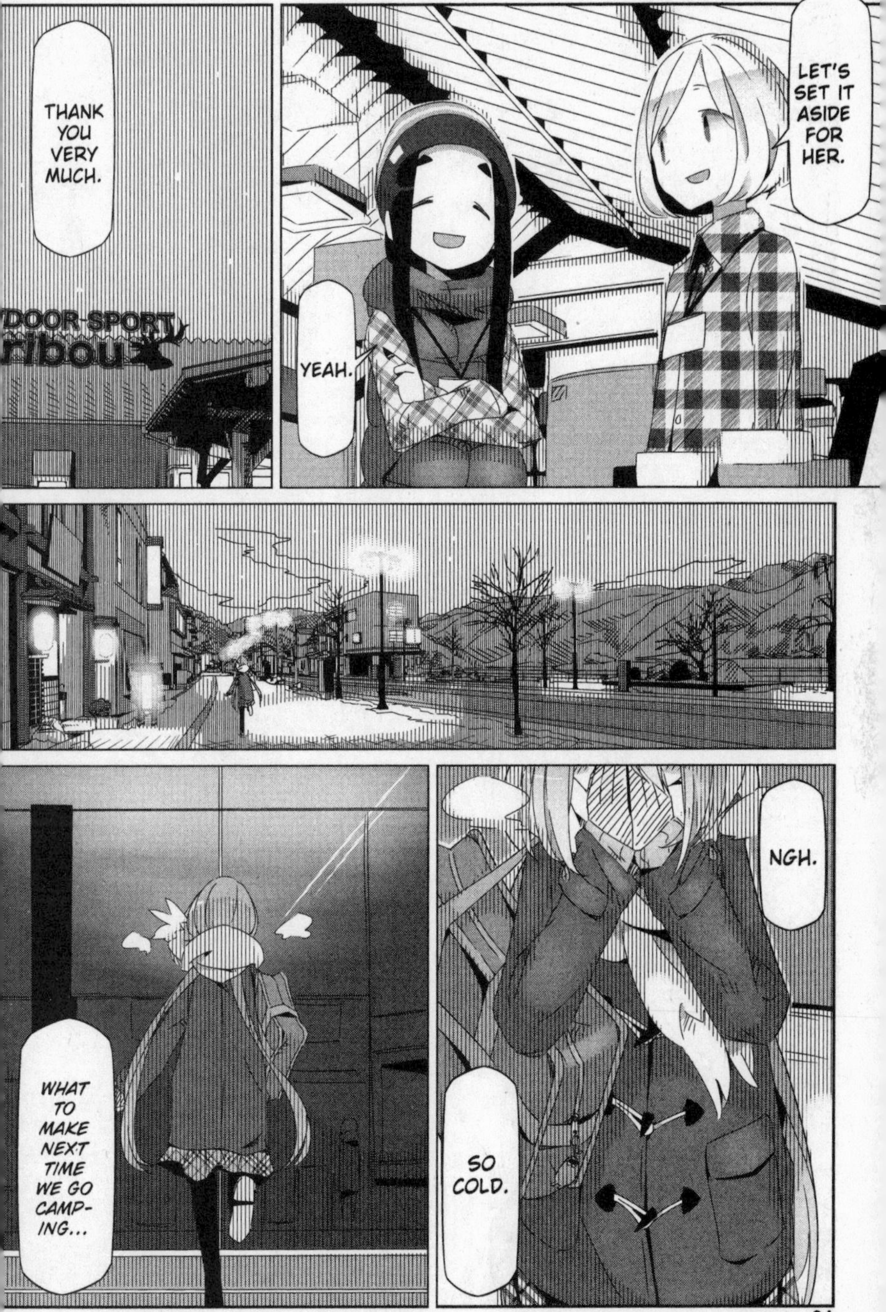
LET'S SET IT ASIDE FOR HER.
YEAH.
THANK YOU VERY MUCH.
DOOR-SPORT
ribou
NGH.
SO COLD.
WHAT TO MAKE NEXT TIME WE GO CAMP-ING...

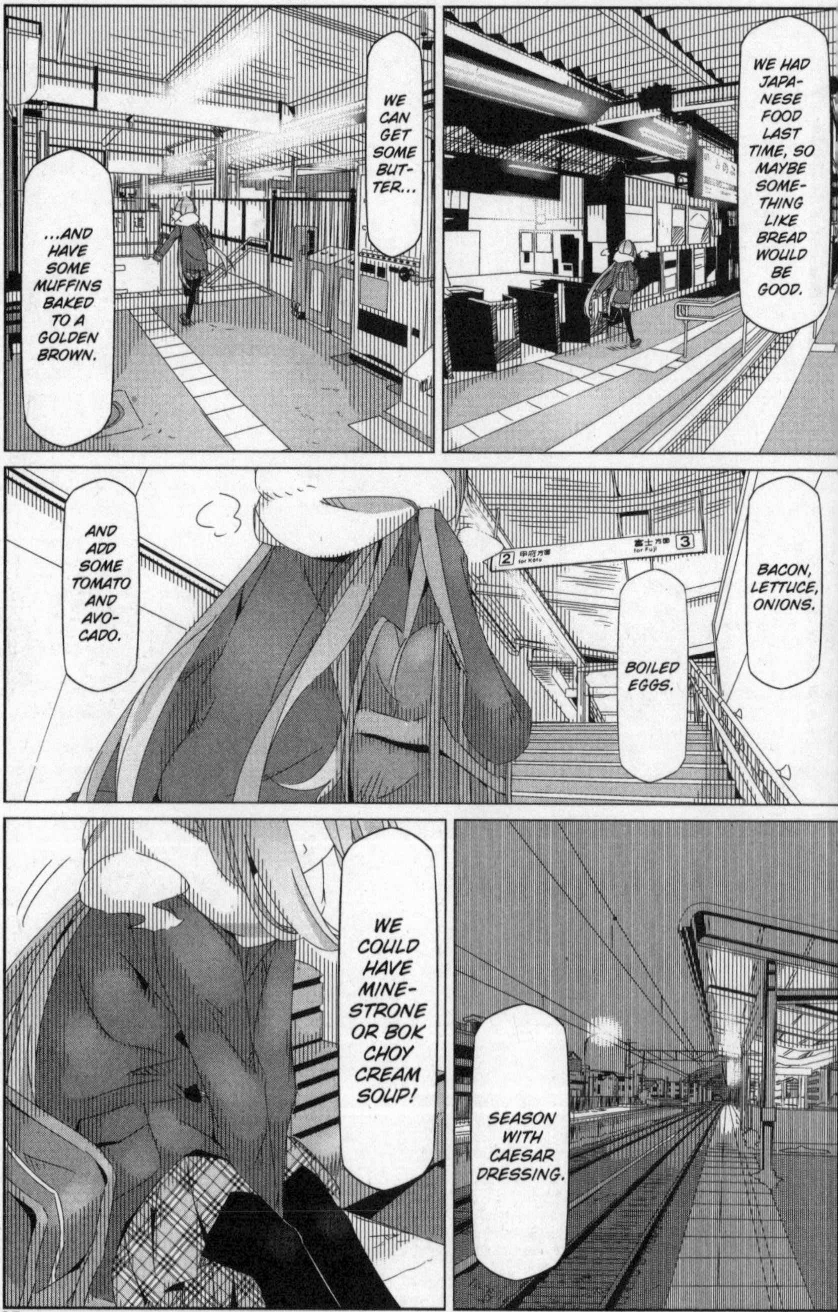
WE HAD JAPANESE FOOD LAST TIME, SO MAYBE SOMETHING LIKE BREAD WOULD BE GOOD.
WE CAN GET SOME BUTTER...
...AND HAVE SOME MUFFINS BAKED TO A GOLDEN BROWN.
BACON, LETTUCE, ONIONS.
BOILED EGGS.
AND ADD SOME TOMATO AND AVOCADO.
SEASON WITH CAESAR DRESSING.
WE COULD HAVE MINESTRONE OR BOK CHOY CREAM SOUP!

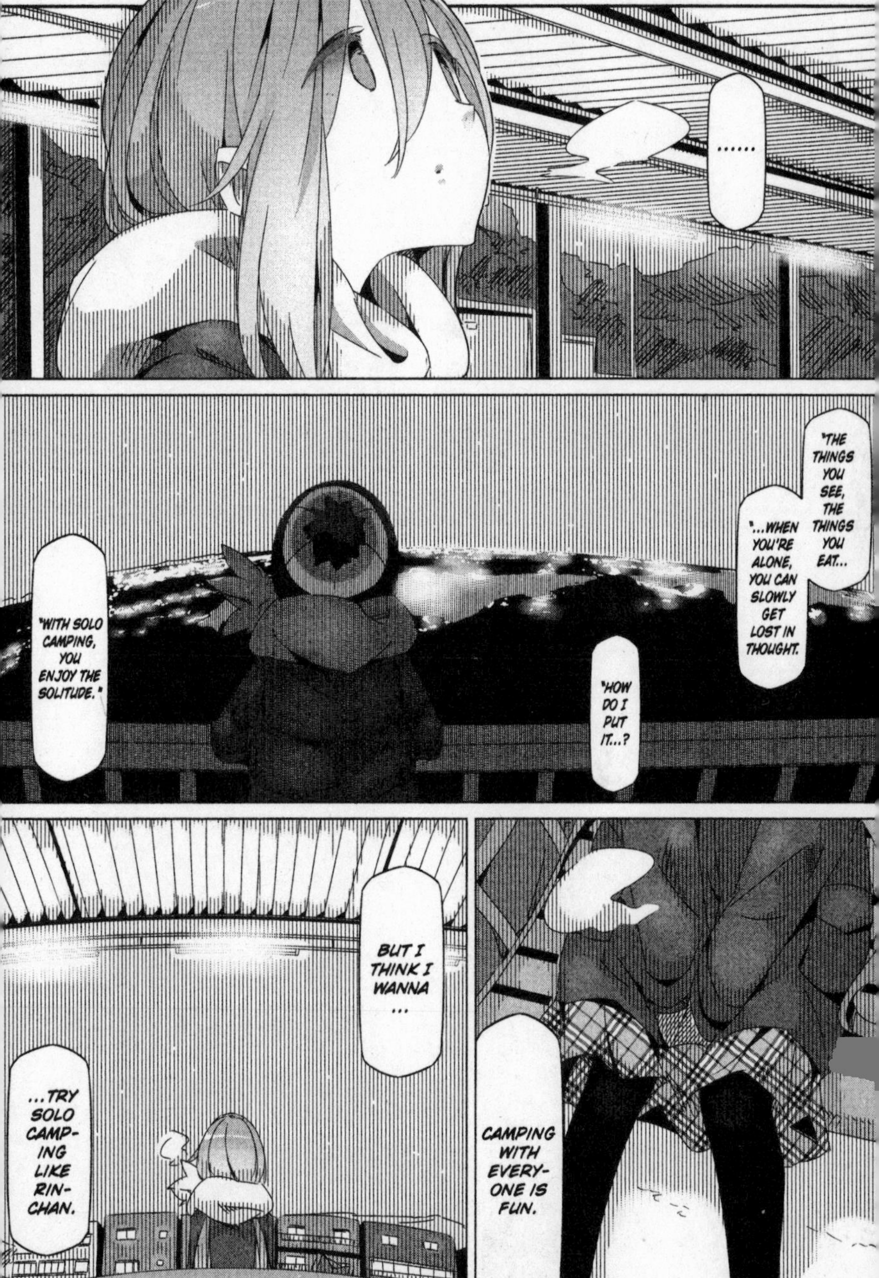
......
"THE THINGS YOU SEE, THE THINGS YOU EAT...
"...WHEN YOU'RE ALONE, YOU CAN SLOWLY GET LOST IN THOUGHT.
"HOW DO I PUT IT...?
"WITH SOLO CAMPING, YOU ENJOY THE SOLITUDE."
CAMPING WITH EVERY-ONE IS FUN.
BUT I THINK I WANNA ...
...TRY SOLO CAMP-ING LIKE RIN-CHAN.

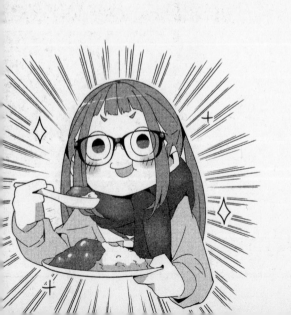

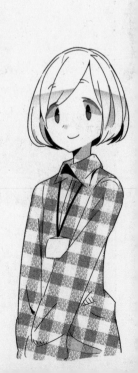

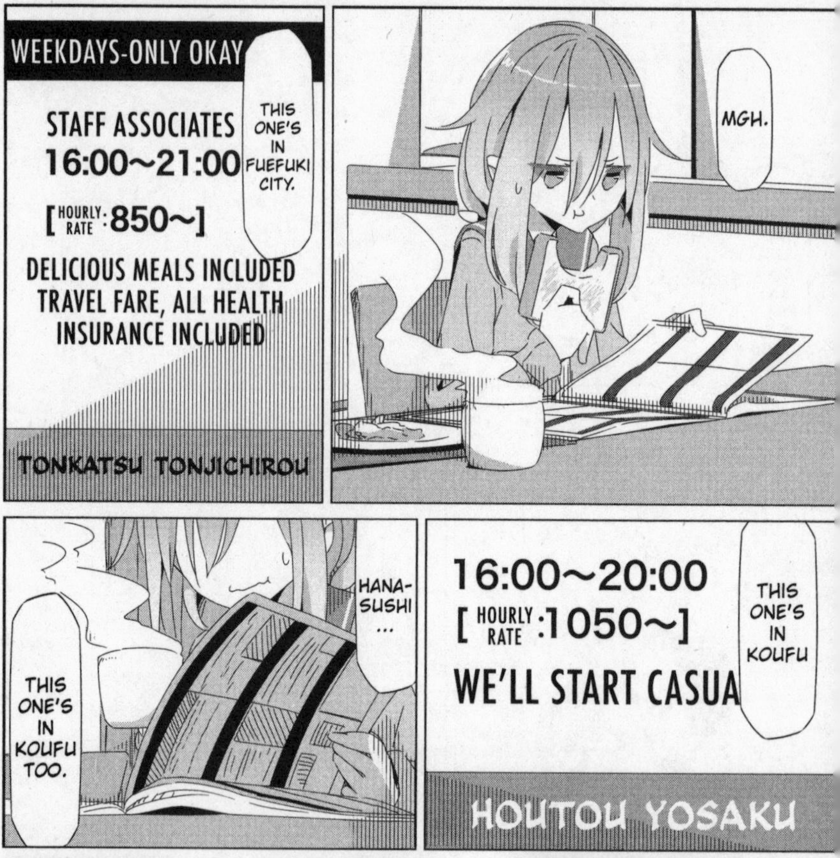
MGH.
WEEKDAYS-ONLY OKAY
STAFF ASSOCIATES
16:00~21:00
[HOURLY RATE :850~]
DELICIOUS MEALS INCLUDED
TRAVEL FARE, ALL HEALTH INSURANCE INCLUDED
TONKATSU TONJICHIROU
THIS ONE'S IN FUEFUKI CITY.
16:00~20:00
[HOURLY RATE :1050~]
WE'LL START CASUA
HOUTOU YOSAKU
THIS ONE'S IN KOUFU
HANA-SUSHI...
THIS ONE'S IN KOUFU TOO.
NEAR MINOBU STATION
ERS WANT
OH, MINOBU!!
SERVICE AREA / NEAR MINOBU STATION
BUS DRIVERS WANTED
UR MORE POSSIBLE
E + OTHER BENEFITS
ROVIDED ON LOAN,
EQUIRED.
A BUS DRIVER.
THAT'S NOT A PART-TIME JOB, THOUGH...

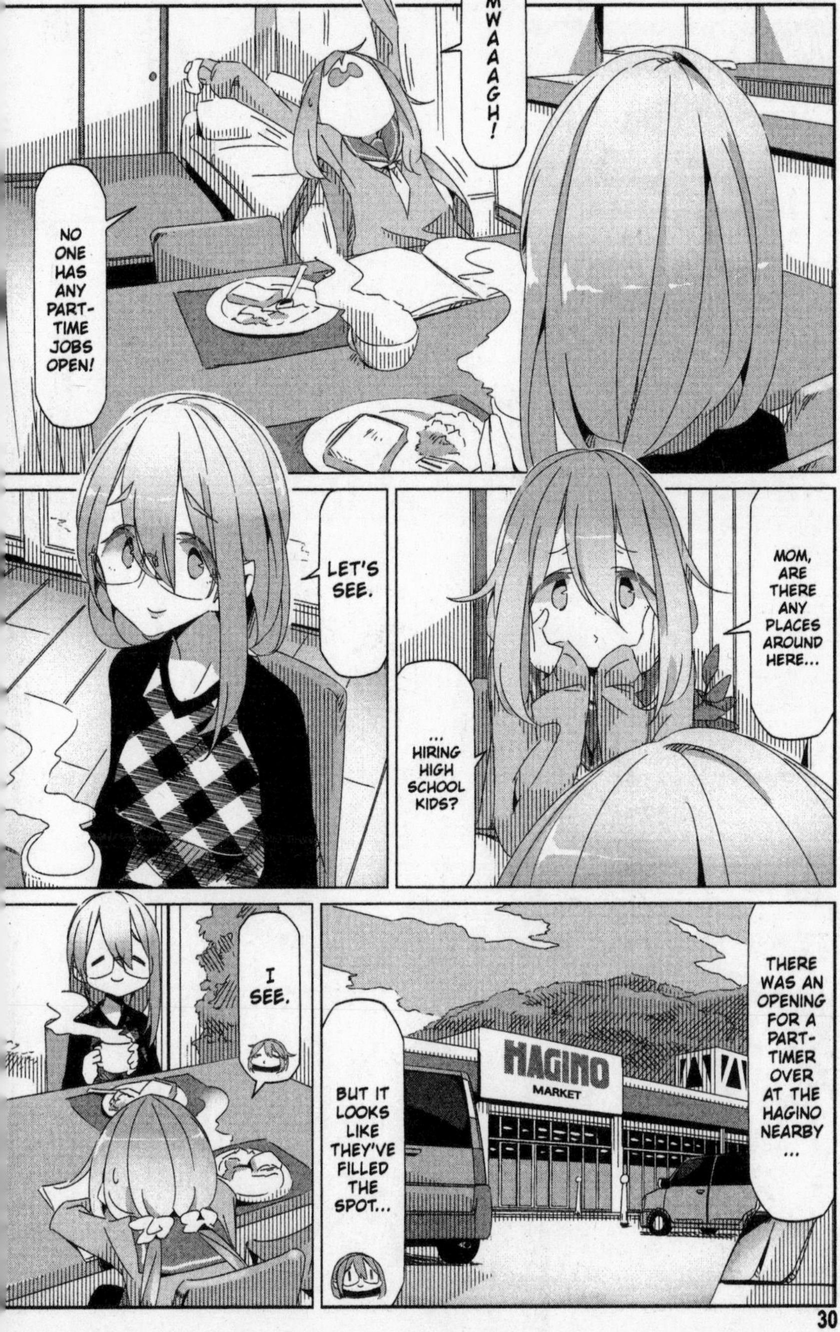
MWAAAGH!
NO ONE HAS ANY PART-TIME JOBS OPEN!
MOM, ARE THERE ANY PLACES AROUND HERE...
...HIRING HIGH SCHOOL KIDS?
LET'S SEE.
THERE WAS AN OPENING FOR A PART-TIMER OVER AT THE HAGINO NEARBY...
HAGINO
MARKET
BUT IT LOOKS LIKE THEY'VE FILLED THE SPOT...
I SEE.

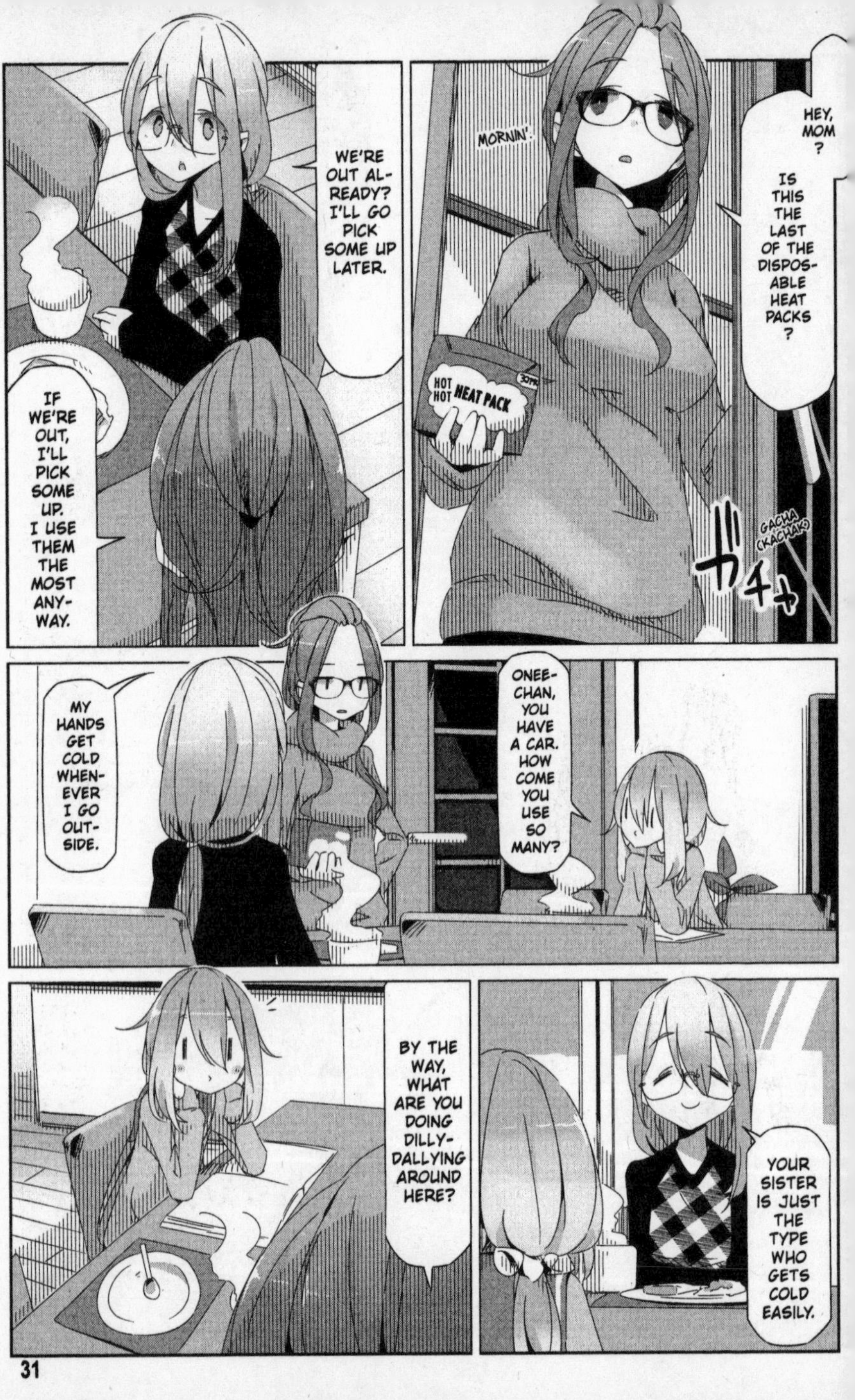
HEY, MOM? IS THIS THE LAST OF THE DISPOSABLE HEAT PACKS?
GACHA (KACHAK)
MORNIN'.
HOT HOT HEAT PACK 30PK
WE'RE OUT ALREADY? I'LL GO PICK SOME UP LATER.
IF WE'RE OUT, I'LL PICK SOME UP. I USE THEM THE MOST ANYWAY.
ONEE-CHAN, YOU HAVE A CAR. HOW COME YOU USE SO MANY?
MY HANDS GET COLD WHENEVER I GO OUTSIDE.
YOUR SISTER IS JUST THE TYPE WHO GETS COLD EASILY.
BY THE WAY, WHAT ARE YOU DOING DILLY-DALLYING AROUND HERE?

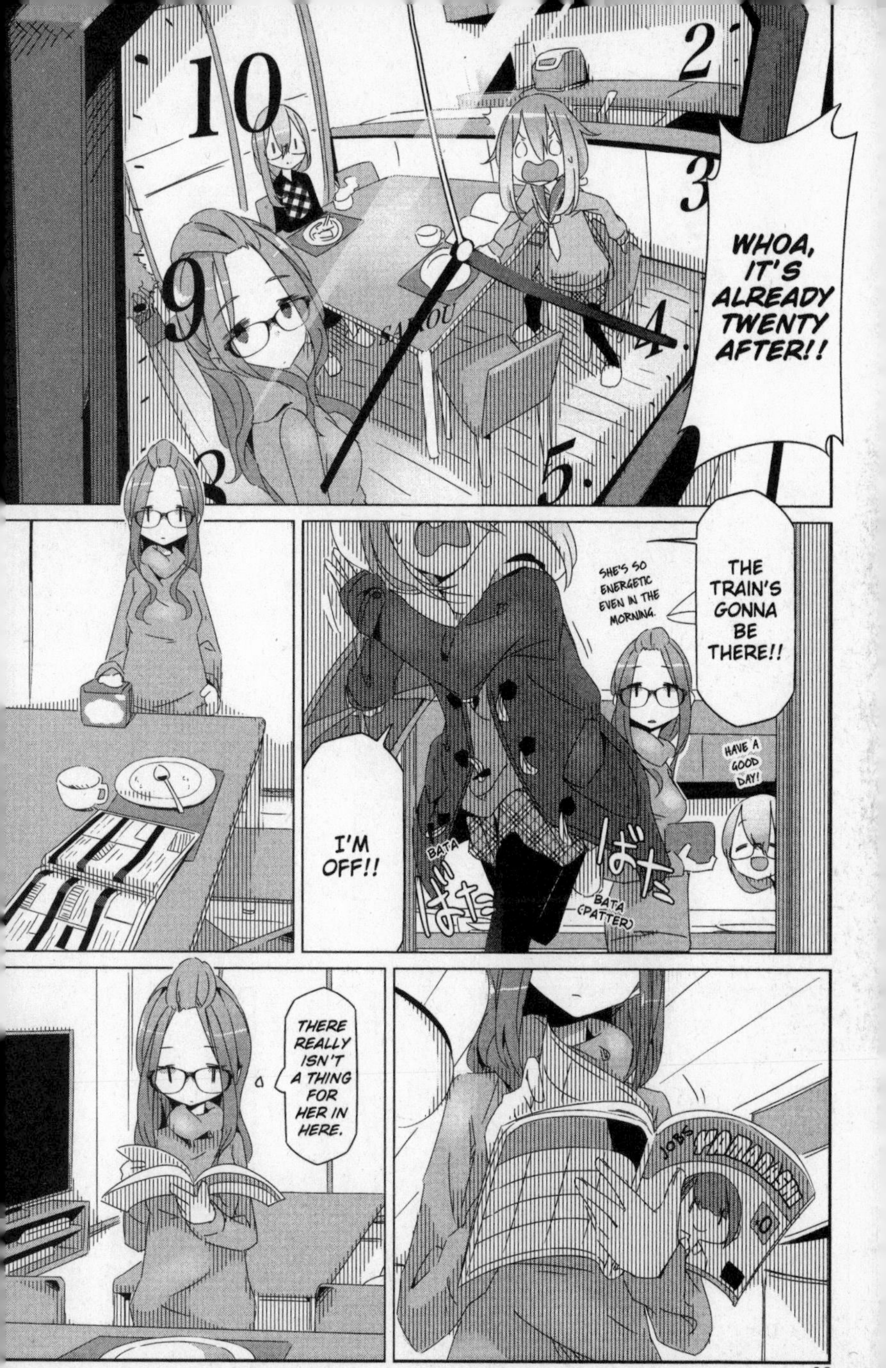
WHOA, IT'S ALREADY TWENTY AFTER!!
THE TRAIN'S GONNA BE THERE!!
SHE'S SO ENERGETIC EVEN IN THE MORNING.
HAVE A GOOD DAY!
I'M OFF!!
BATA
BATA (PATTER)
JOBS
THERE REALLY ISN'T A THING FOR HER IN HERE.

CHAPTER 30 THE LAMP AND THE HEAT PACKS

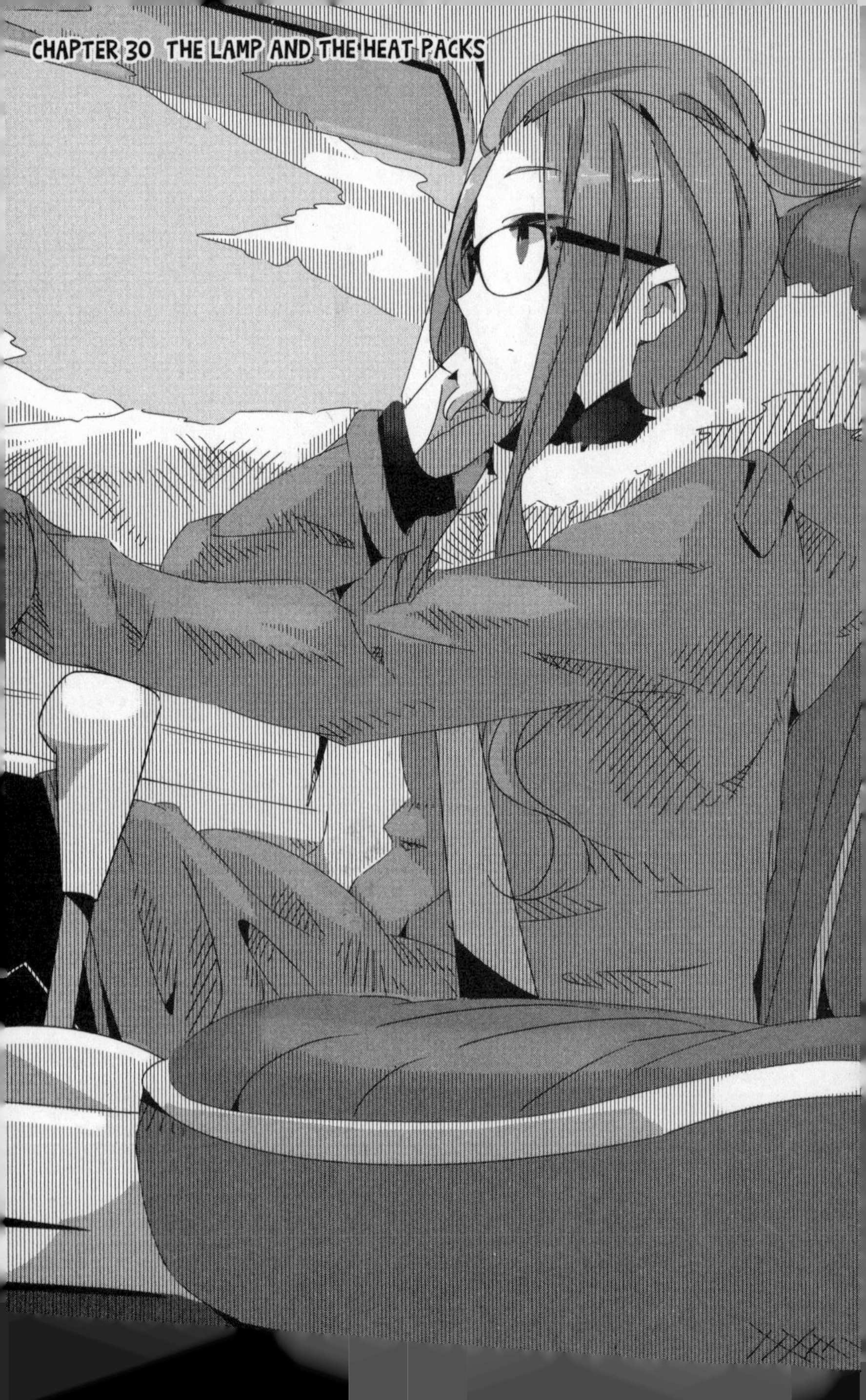

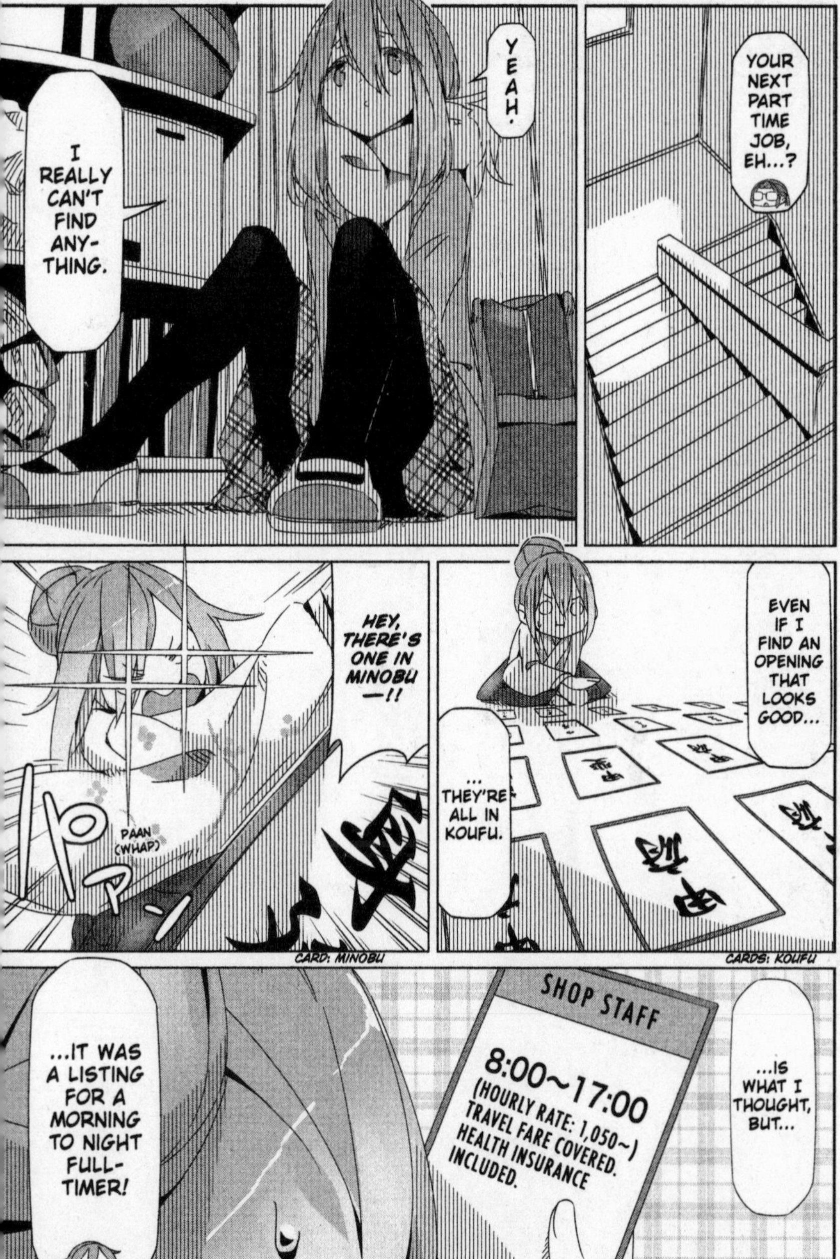
YOUR NEXT PART TIME JOB, EH...?
YEAH.
I REALLY CAN'T FIND ANYTHING.
EVEN IF I FIND AN OPENING THAT LOOKS GOOD...
...THEY'RE ALL IN KOUFU.
CARDS: KOUFU
HEY, THERE'S ONE IN MINOBU—!!
PAAN (WHAP)
CARD: MINOBU
...IS WHAT I THOUGHT, BUT...
SHOP STAFF
8:00~17:00
(HOURLY RATE: 1,050~)
TRAVEL FARE COVERED.
HEALTH INSURANCE INCLUDED.
...IT WAS A LISTING FOR A MORNING TO NIGHT FULL-TIMER!

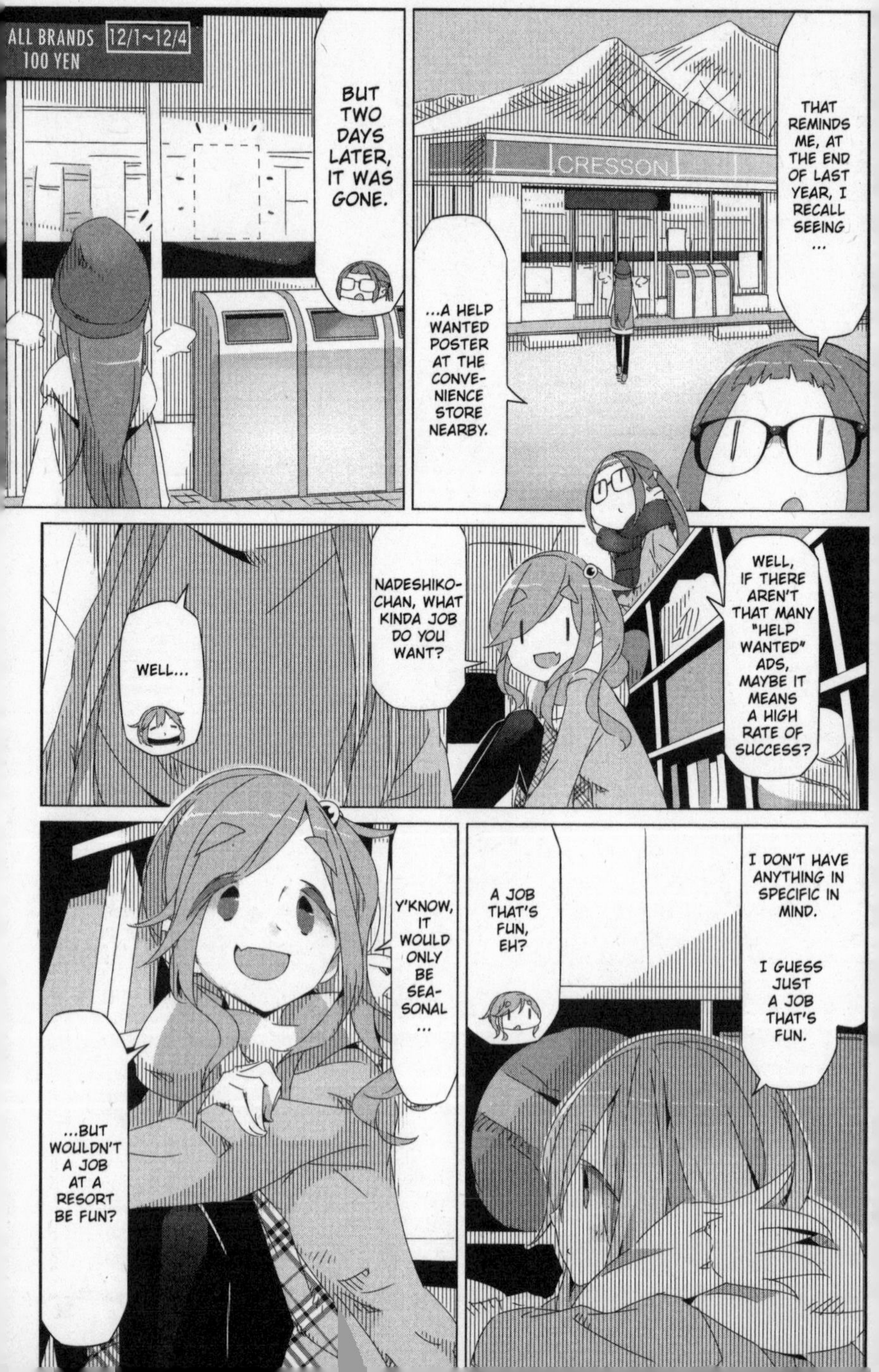
CRESSON
THAT REMINDS ME, AT THE END OF LAST YEAR, I RECALL SEEING ...
...A HELP WANTED POSTER AT THE CONVENIENCE STORE NEARBY.
ALL BRANDS 12/1~12/4 100 YEN
BUT TWO DAYS LATER, IT WAS GONE.
WELL, IF THERE AREN'T THAT MANY "HELP WANTED" ADS, MAYBE IT MEANS A HIGH RATE OF SUCCESS?
NADESHIKO-CHAN, WHAT KINDA JOB DO YOU WANT?
WELL...
I DON'T HAVE ANYTHING IN SPECIFIC IN MIND.
I GUESS JUST A JOB THAT'S FUN.
A JOB THAT'S FUN, EH?
Y'KNOW, IT WOULD ONLY BE SEA-SONAL ...
...BUT WOULDN'T A JOB AT A RESORT BE FUN?

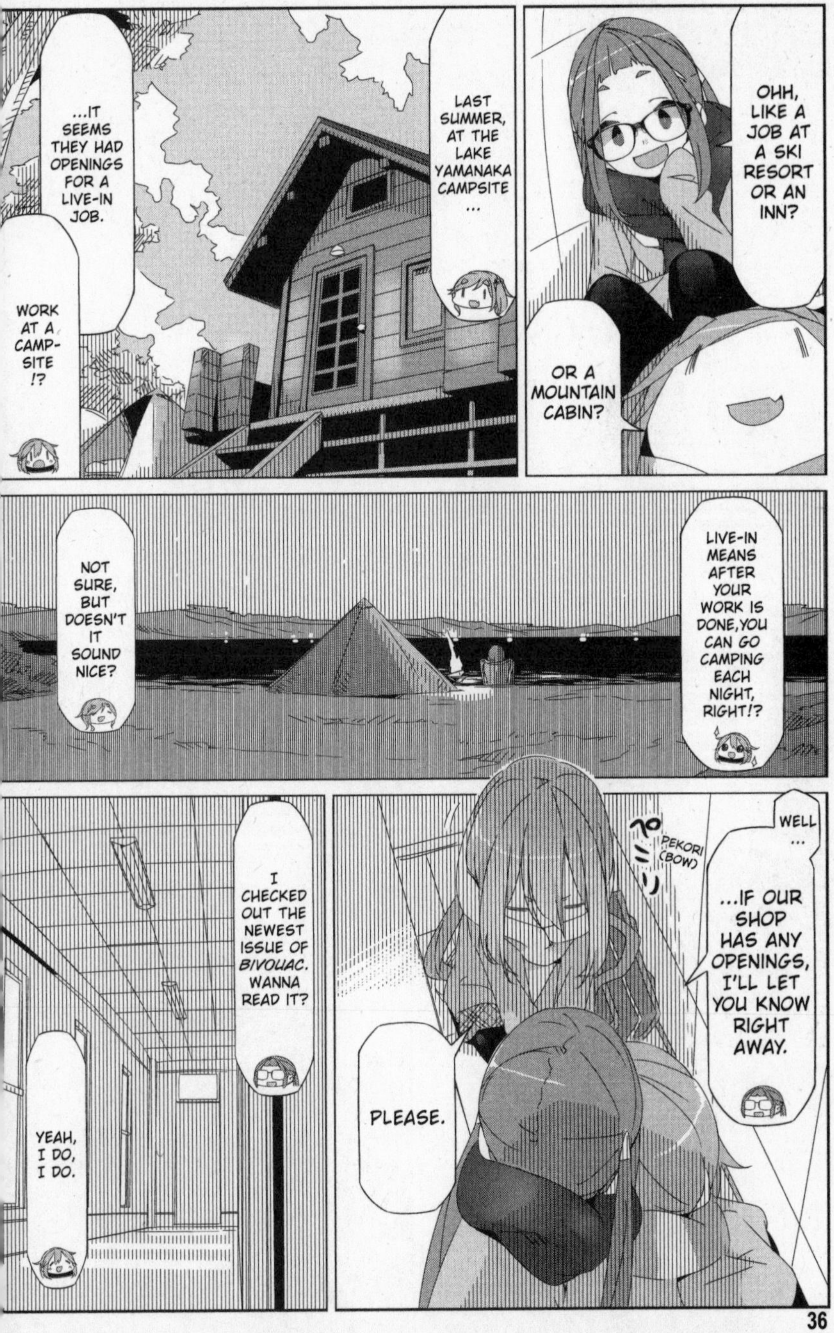
OHH, LIKE A JOB AT A SKI RESORT OR AN INN?
OR A MOUNTAIN CABIN?
LAST SUMMER, AT THE LAKE YAMANAKA CAMPSITE ...
...IT SEEMS THEY HAD OPENINGS FOR A LIVE-IN JOB.
WORK AT A CAMP-SITE !?
LIVE-IN MEANS AFTER YOUR WORK IS DONE, YOU CAN GO CAMPING EACH NIGHT, RIGHT!?
NOT SURE, BUT DOESN'T IT SOUND NICE?
WELL ...
...IF OUR SHOP HAS ANY OPENINGS, I'LL LET YOU KNOW RIGHT AWAY.
PEKORI (BOW)
PLEASE.
I CHECKED OUT THE NEWEST ISSUE OF *BIVOUAC*. WANNA READ IT?
YEAH, I DO, I DO.

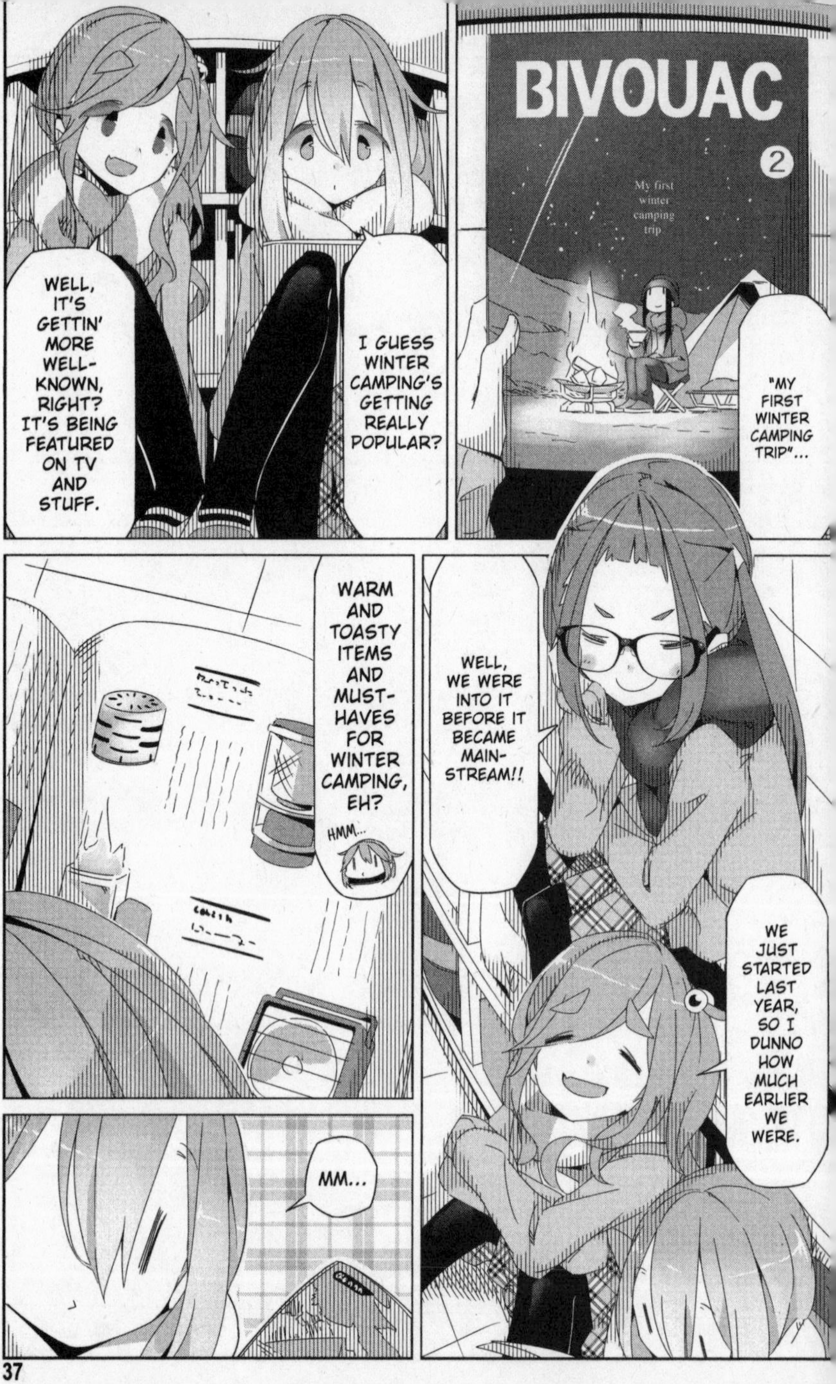
BIVOUAC
2
My first winter camping trip
"MY FIRST WINTER CAMPING TRIP"...
I GUESS WINTER CAMPING'S GETTING REALLY POPULAR?
WELL, IT'S GETTIN' MORE WELL-KNOWN, RIGHT? IT'S BEING FEATURED ON TV AND STUFF.
WELL, WE WERE INTO IT BEFORE IT BECAME MAIN-STREAM!!
WE JUST STARTED LAST YEAR, SO I DUNNO HOW MUCH EARLIER WE WERE.
WARM AND TOASTY ITEMS AND MUST-HAVES FOR WINTER CAMPING, EH?
HMM...
MM...

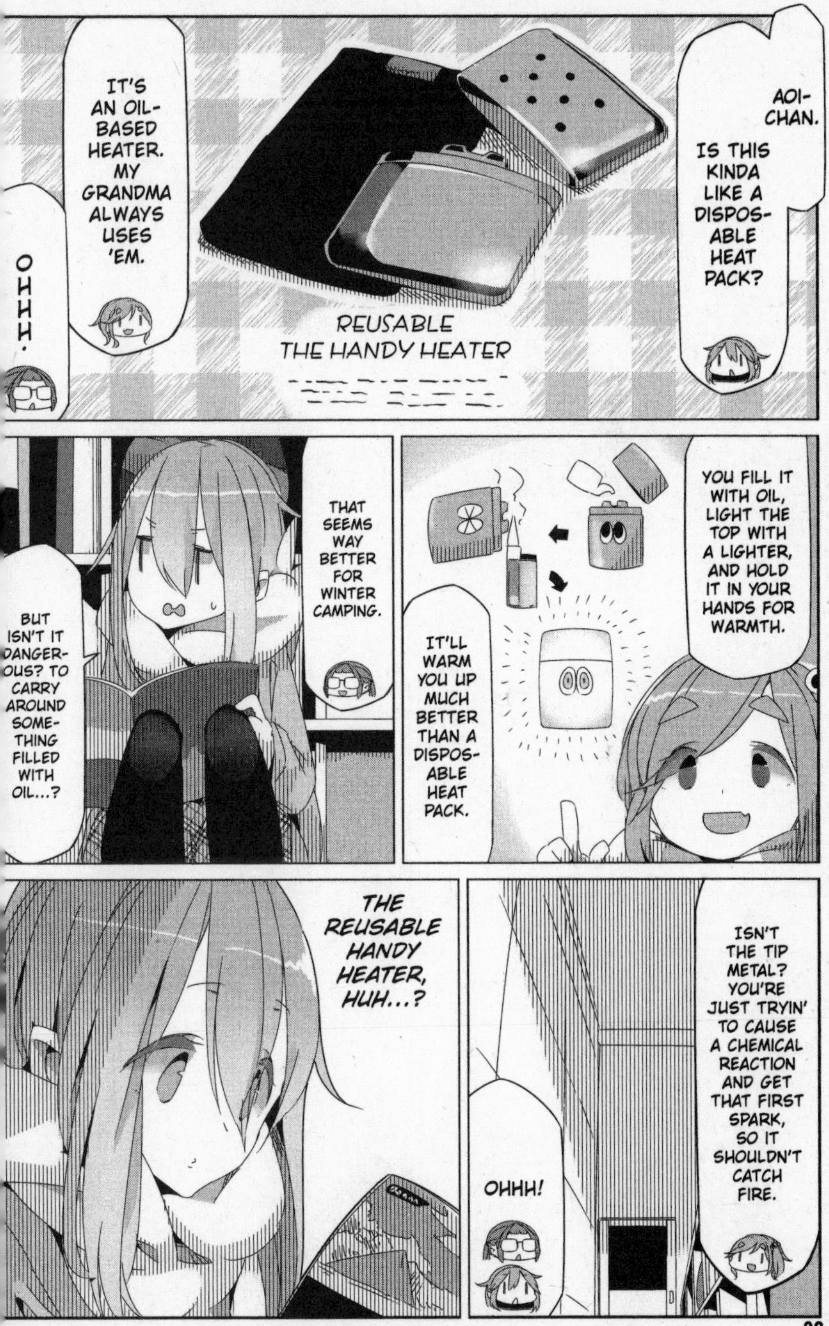
AOI-CHAN.
IS THIS KINDA LIKE A DISPOS-ABLE HEAT PACK?
IT'S AN OIL-BASED HEATER. MY GRANDMA ALWAYS USES 'EM.
REUSABLE
THE HANDY HEATER
OHHH.
YOU FILL IT WITH OIL, LIGHT THE TOP WITH A LIGHTER, AND HOLD IT IN YOUR HANDS FOR WARMTH.
IT'LL WARM YOU UP MUCH BETTER THAN A DISPOS-ABLE HEAT PACK.
THAT SEEMS WAY BETTER FOR WINTER CAMPING.
BUT ISN'T IT DANGER-OUS? TO CARRY AROUND SOME-THING FILLED WITH OIL...?
ISN'T THE TIP METAL? YOU'RE JUST TRYIN' TO CAUSE A CHEMICAL REACTION AND GET THAT FIRST SPARK, SO IT SHOULDN'T CATCH FIRE.
OHHH!
THE REUSABLE HANDY HEATER, HUH...?

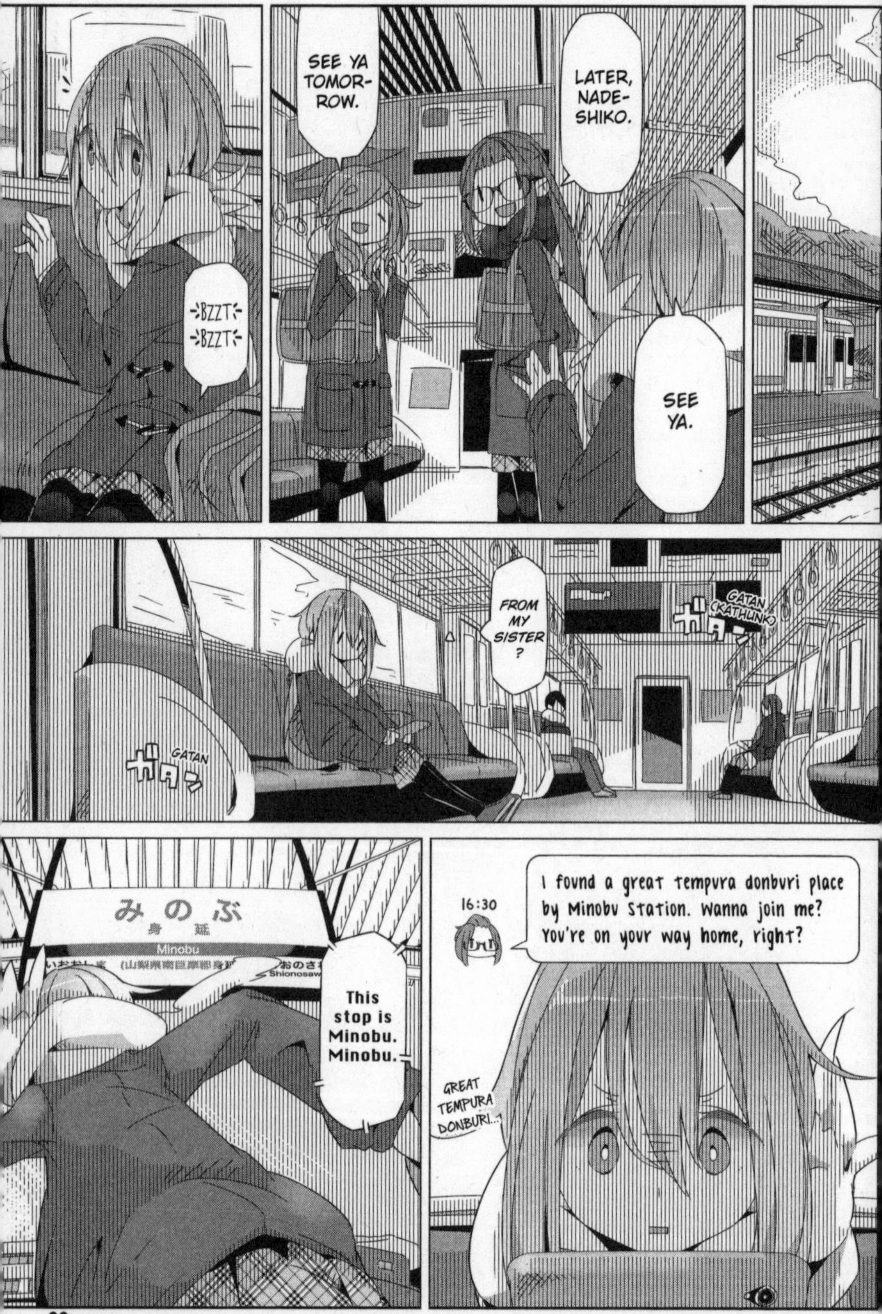
LATER, NADE-SHIKO.
SEE YA TOMOR-ROW.
SEE YA.
BZZT BZZT
GATAN (KATHUNK)
FROM MY SISTER?
GATAN
16:30
I found a great tempura donburi place by Minobu Station. Wanna join me? You're on your way home, right?
GREAT TEMPURA DONBURI...
みのぶ
身延
Minobu
Shionosawa
This stop is Minobu. Minobu.

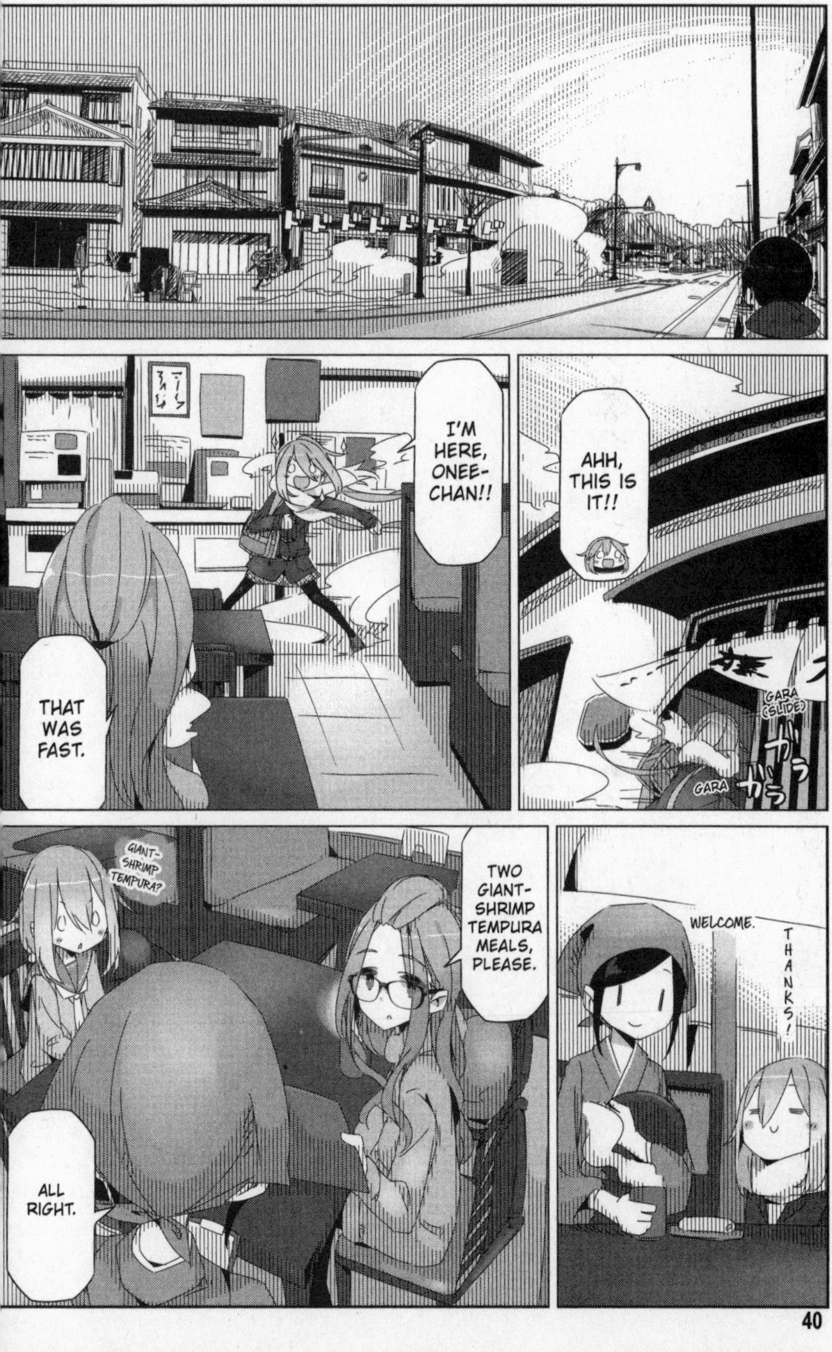
ドドドドドドドド
AHH, THIS IS IT!!
GARA (SLIDE)
ガラ
GARA
ガラ
I'M HERE, ONEE-CHAN!!
THAT WAS FAST.
WELCOME.
THANKS!
TWO GIANT-SHRIMP TEMPURA MEALS, PLEASE.
GIANT-SHRIMP TEMPURA?
ALL RIGHT.

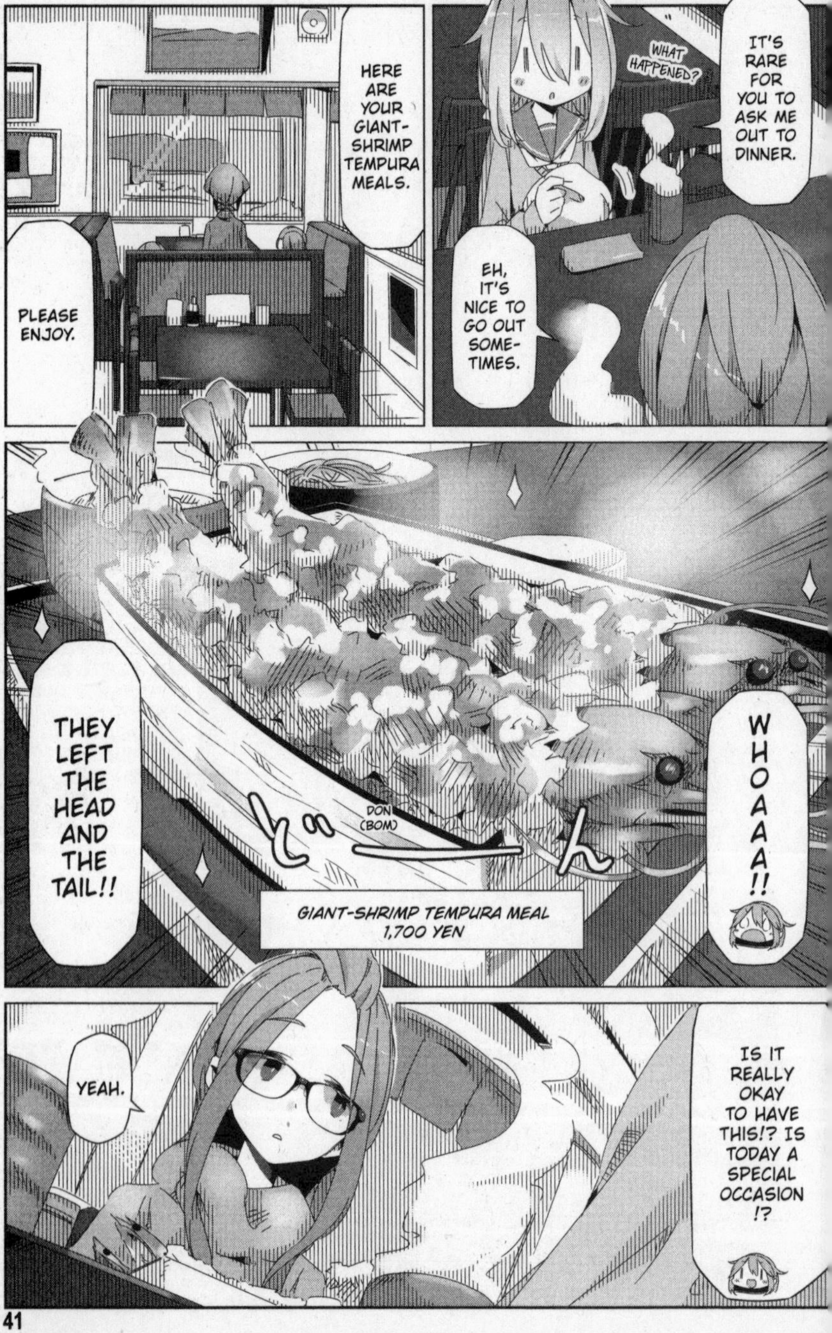

IT'S RARE FOR YOU TO ASK ME OUT TO DINNER.
WHAT HAPPENED?
EH, IT'S NICE TO GO OUT SOMETIMES.
HERE ARE YOUR GIANT-SHRIMP TEMPURA MEALS.
PLEASE ENJOY.
WHOAAAA!!
THEY LEFT THE HEAD AND THE TAIL!!
どーん
DON (BOM)
GIANT-SHRIMP TEMPURA MEAL
1,700 YEN
IS IT REALLY OKAY TO HAVE THIS!? IS TODAY A SPECIAL OCCASION!?
YEAH.

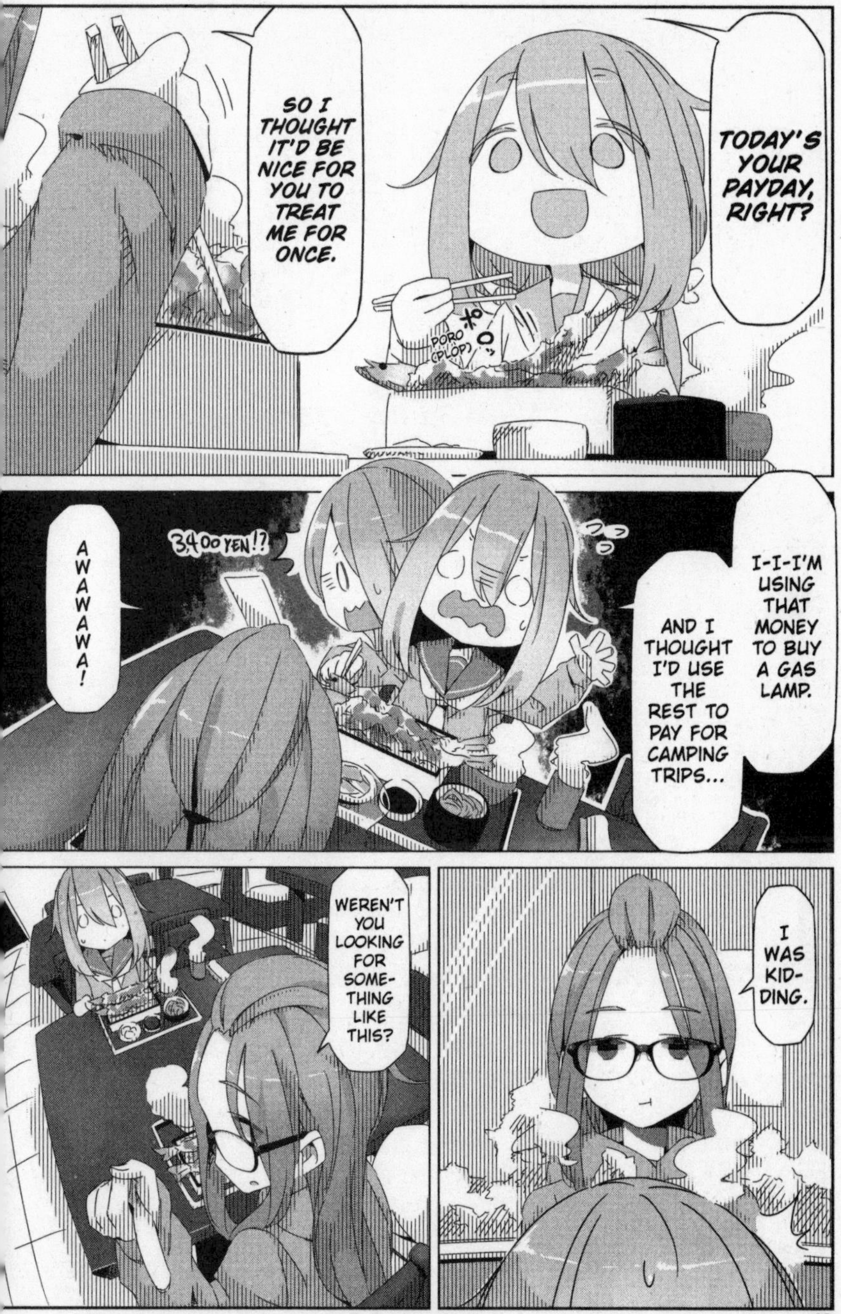
TODAY'S YOUR PAYDAY, RIGHT?
SO I THOUGHT IT'D BE NICE FOR YOU TO TREAT ME FOR ONCE.
PORO (PLOP)
I-I-I'M USING THAT MONEY TO BUY A GAS LAMP.
AND I THOUGHT I'D USE THE REST TO PAY FOR CAMPING TRIPS...
3,400 YEN!?
AWAWAWAWA!
I WAS KID-DING.
WEREN'T YOU LOOKING FOR SOME-THING LIKE THIS?

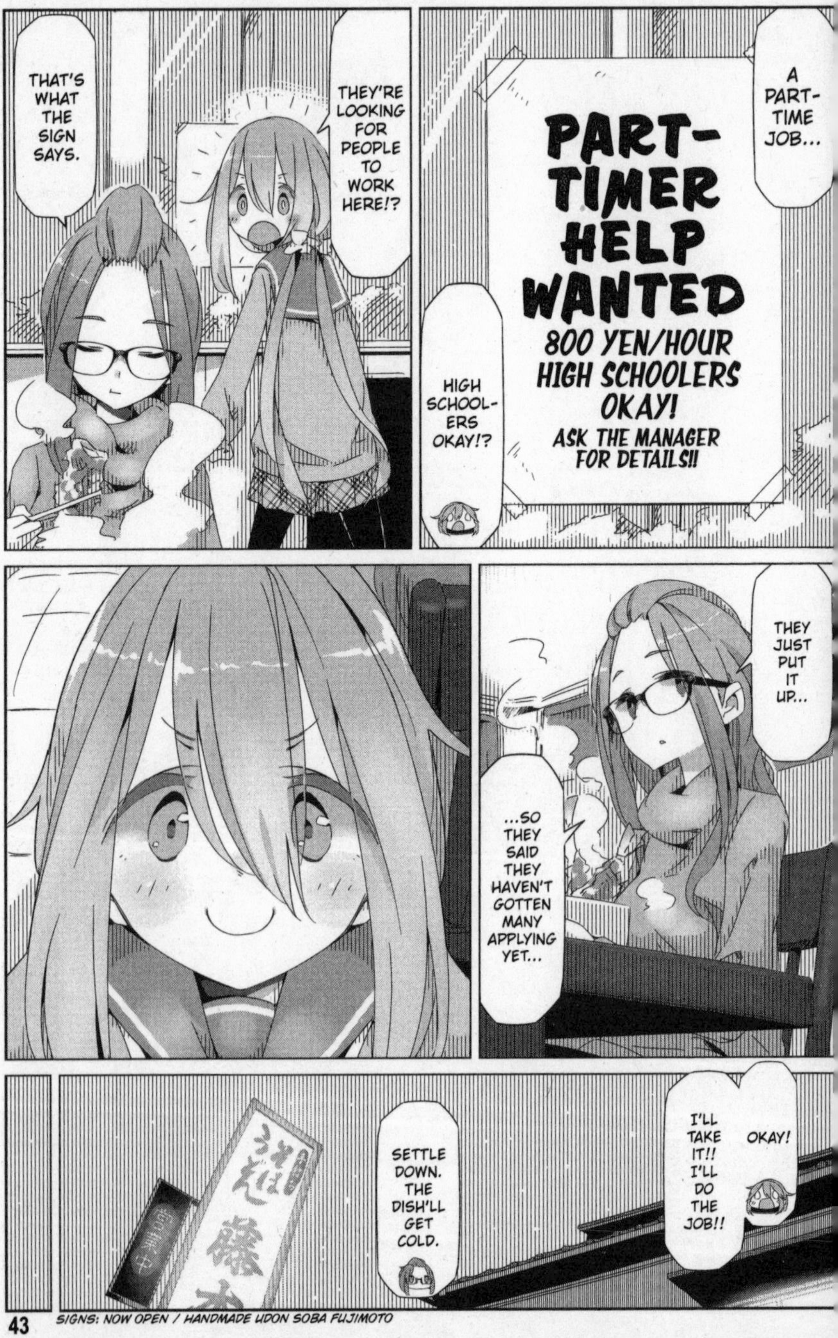
A PART-TIME JOB...
PART-TIMER HELP WANTED
800 YEN/HOUR
HIGH SCHOOLERS OKAY!
ASK THE MANAGER FOR DETAILS!!
HIGH SCHOOL-ERS OKAY!?
THEY'RE LOOKING FOR PEOPLE TO WORK HERE!?
THAT'S WHAT THE SIGN SAYS.
THEY JUST PUT IT UP...
...SO THEY SAID THEY HAVEN'T GOTTEN MANY APPLYING YET...
OKAY!
I'LL TAKE IT!! I'LL DO THE JOB!!
SETTLE DOWN. THE DISH'LL GET COLD.

SIGNS: NOW OPEN / HANDMADE UDON SOBA FUJIMOTO

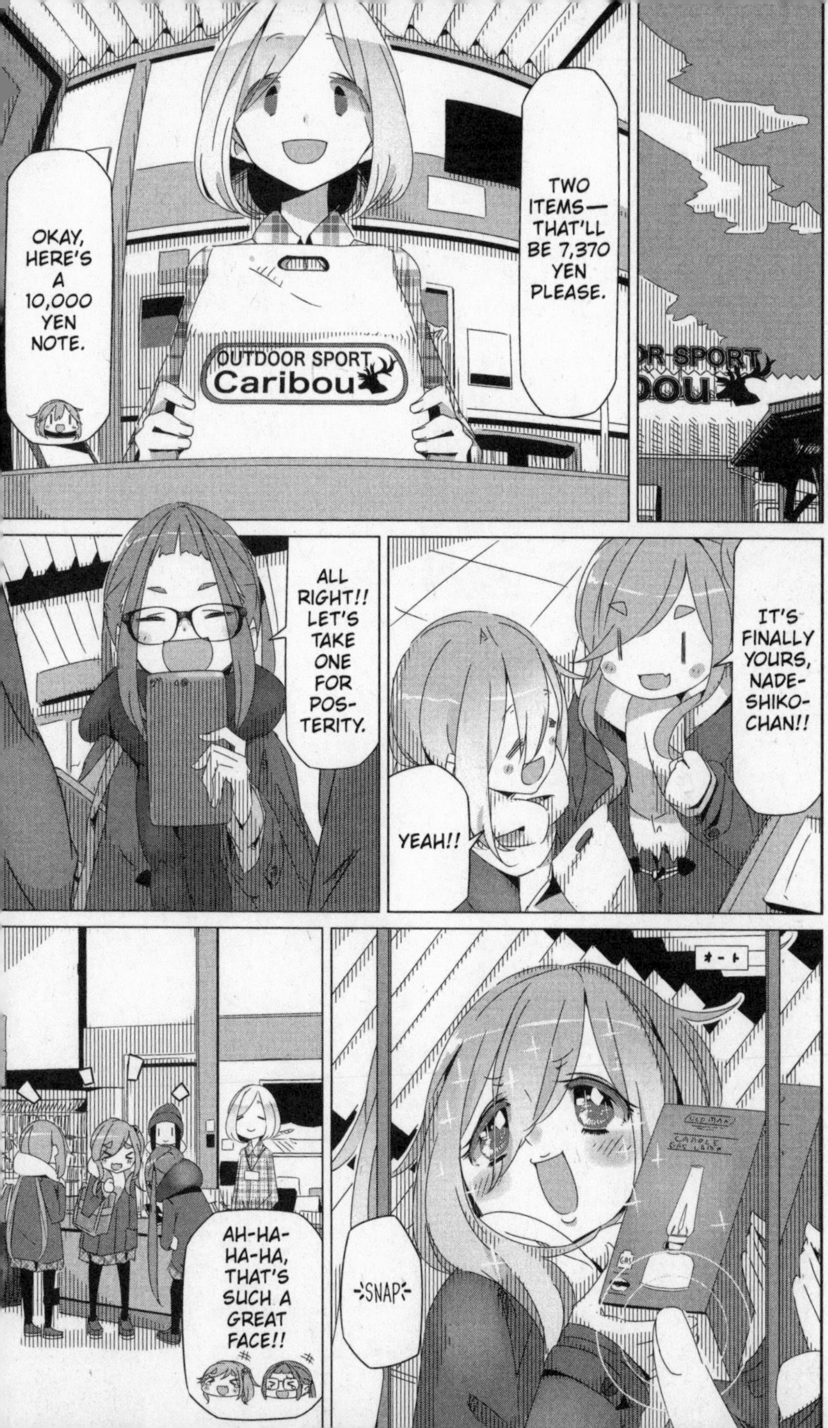
TWO ITEMS—THAT'LL BE 7,370 YEN PLEASE.
OUTDOOR SPORT Caribou
OKAY, HERE'S A 10,000 YEN NOTE.
IT'S FINALLY YOURS, NADE-SHIKO-CHAN!!
YEAH!!
ALL RIGHT!! LET'S TAKE ONE FOR POS-TERITY.
オート
SNAP
AH-HA-HA-HA, THAT'S SUCH A GREAT FACE!!

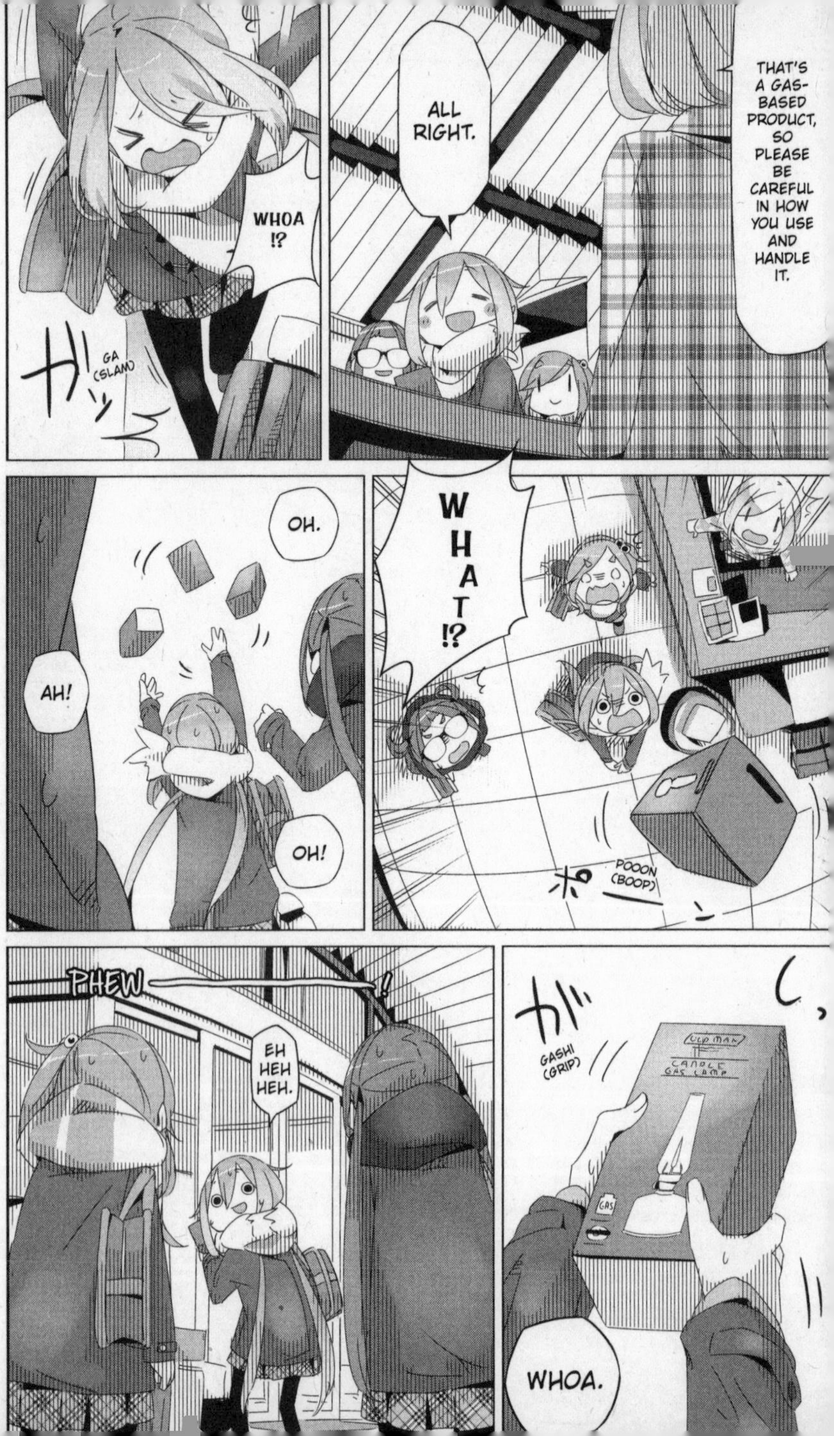
THAT'S A GAS-BASED PRODUCT, SO PLEASE BE CAREFUL IN HOW YOU USE AND HANDLE IT.
ALL RIGHT.
WHOA !?
GA (SLAM)
WHAT !?
POOON (BOOP)
OH.
AH!
OH!
GASHI (GRIP)
OLD MAN
CANDLE GAS LAMP
GAS
WHOA.
PHEW—!
EH HEH HEH.

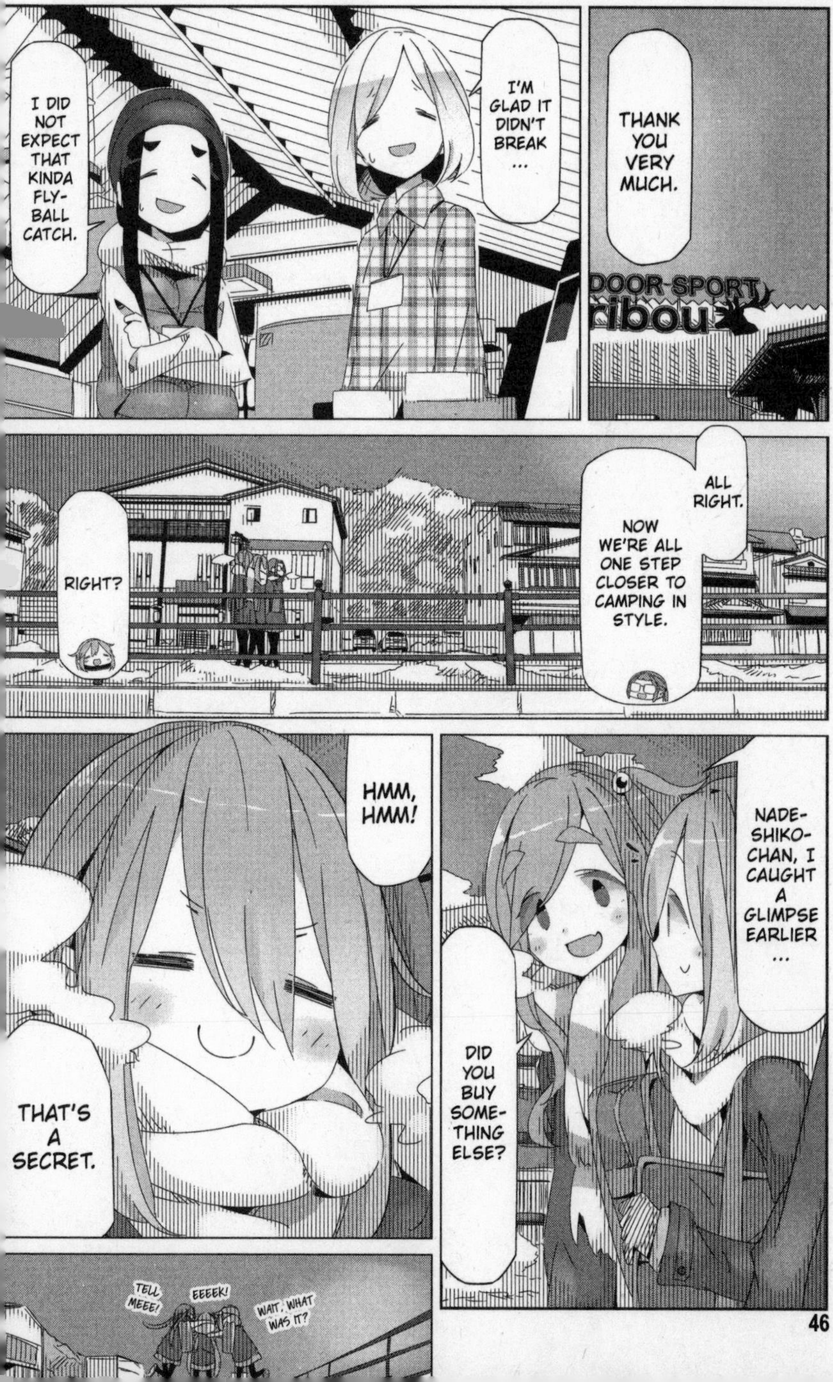
THANK YOU VERY MUCH.
DOOR-SPORT
ribou
I'M GLAD IT DIDN'T BREAK ...
I DID NOT EXPECT THAT KINDA FLY-BALL CATCH.
ALL RIGHT.
NOW WE'RE ALL ONE STEP CLOSER TO CAMPING IN STYLE.
RIGHT?
NADE-SHIKO-CHAN, I CAUGHT A GLIMPSE EARLIER ...
DID YOU BUY SOME-THING ELSE?
HMM, HMM!
THAT'S A SECRET.
WAIT, WHAT WAS IT?
EEEEK!
TELL MEEE!

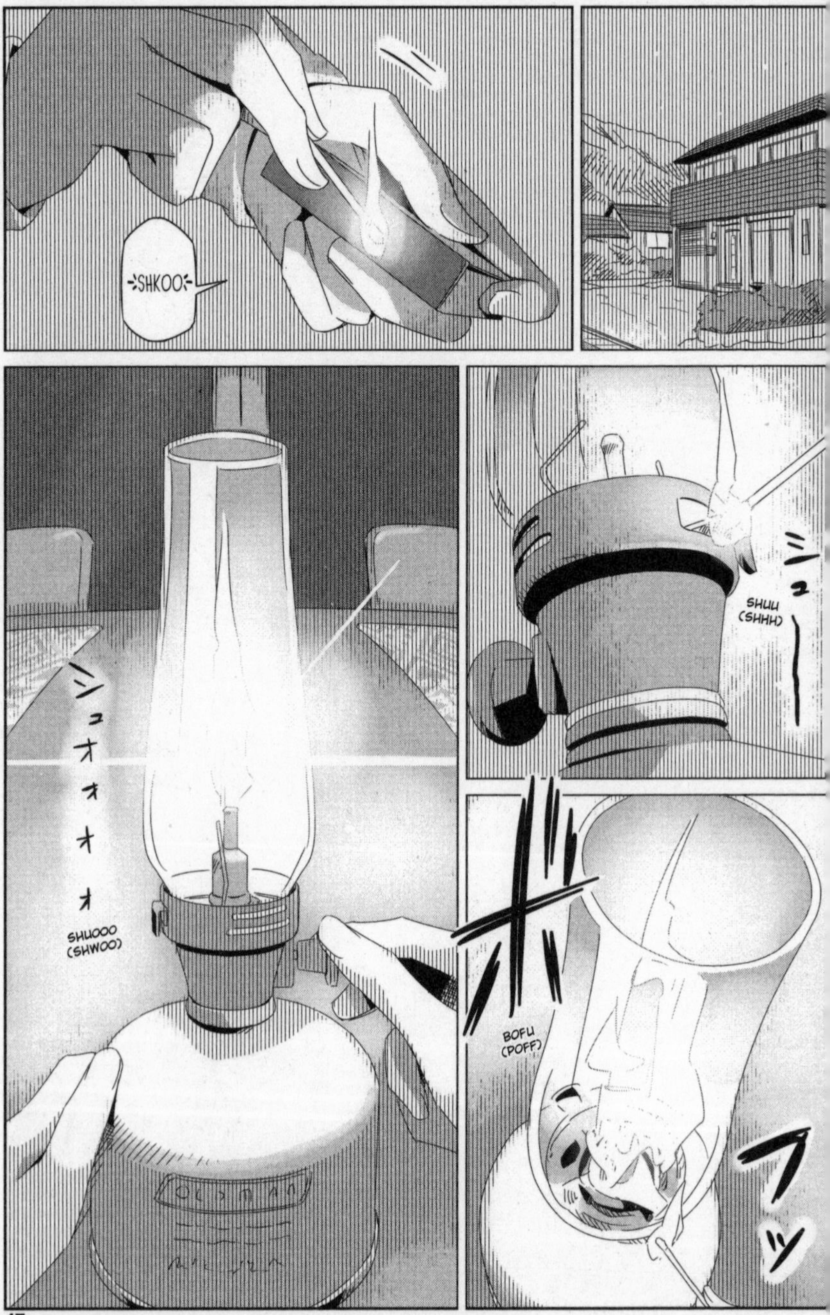
SHKOO
SHUU (SHHH)
BOFU (POFF)
SHUOOO (SHWOO)

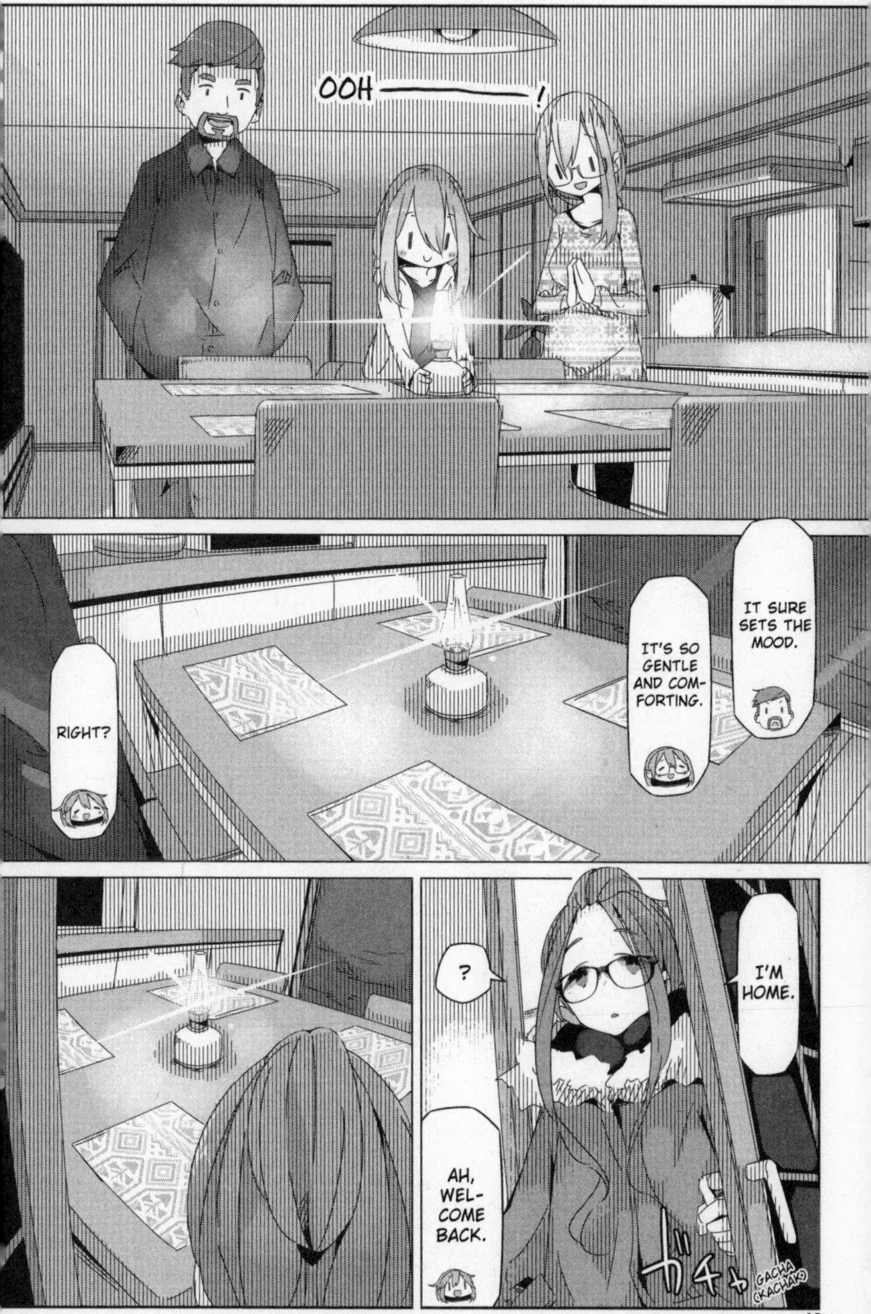
OOH——!
IT SURE SETS THE MOOD.
IT'S SO GENTLE AND COMFORTING.
RIGHT?
I'M HOME.
?
AH, WELCOME BACK.
GACHA (KACHAK)

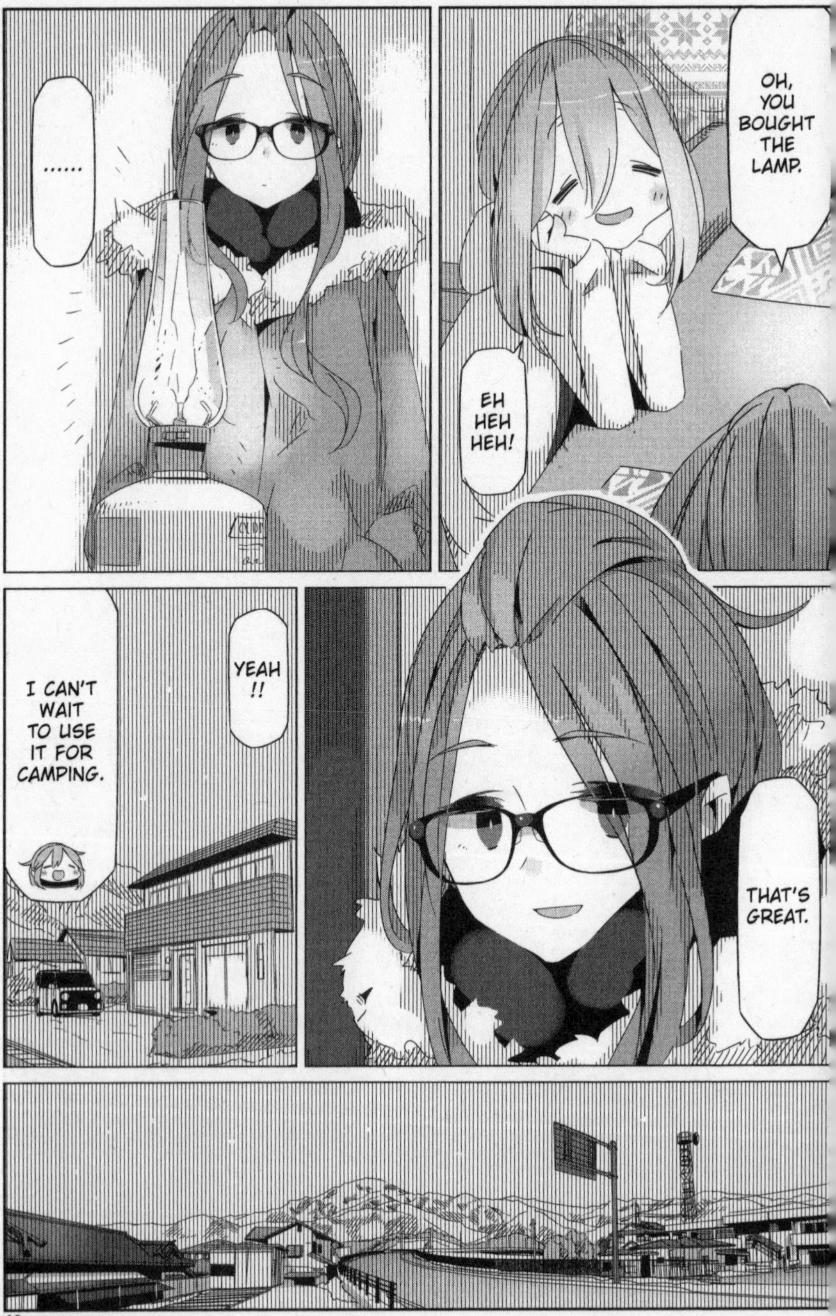
OH, YOU BOUGHT THE LAMP.
EH HEH HEH!
......
THAT'S GREAT.
YEAH!!
I CAN'T WAIT TO USE IT FOR CAMPING.

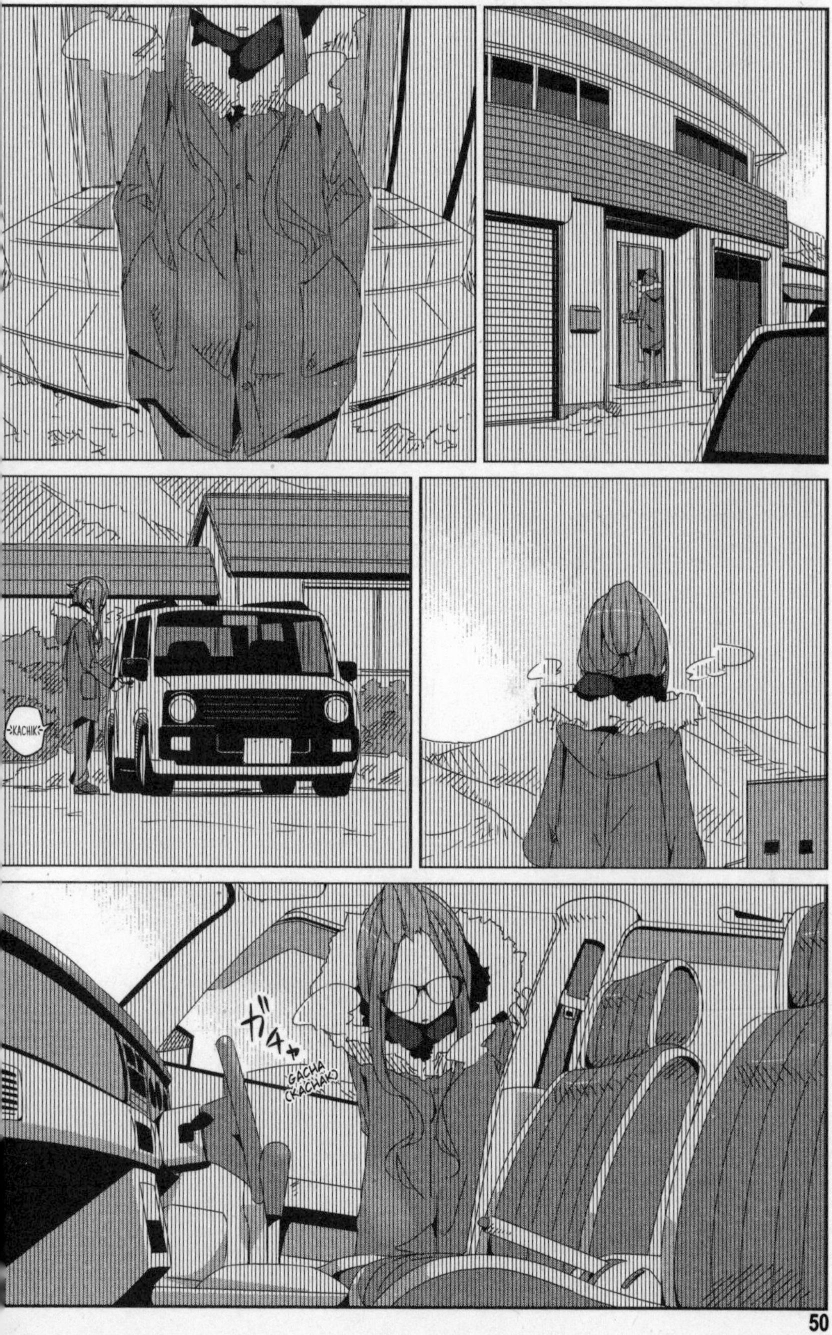
KACHIK
ガチャ
GACHA (KACHAK)

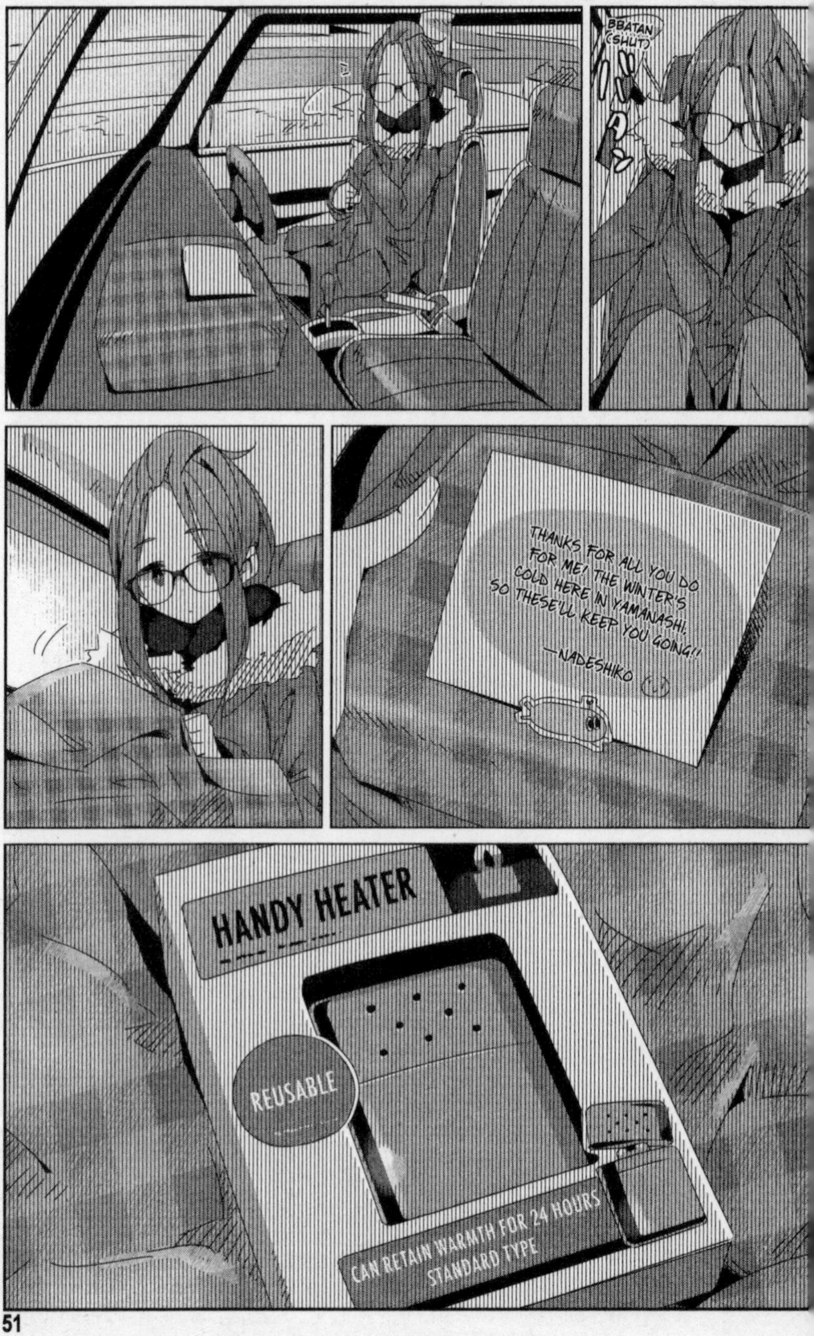
BBATAN (SHUT)
THANKS FOR ALL YOU DO FOR ME! THE WINTER'S COLD HERE IN YAMANASHI, SO THESE'LL KEEP YOU GOING!! —NADESHIKO
HANDY HEATER
REUSABLE
CAN RETAIN WARMTH FOR 24 HOURS
STANDARD TYPE

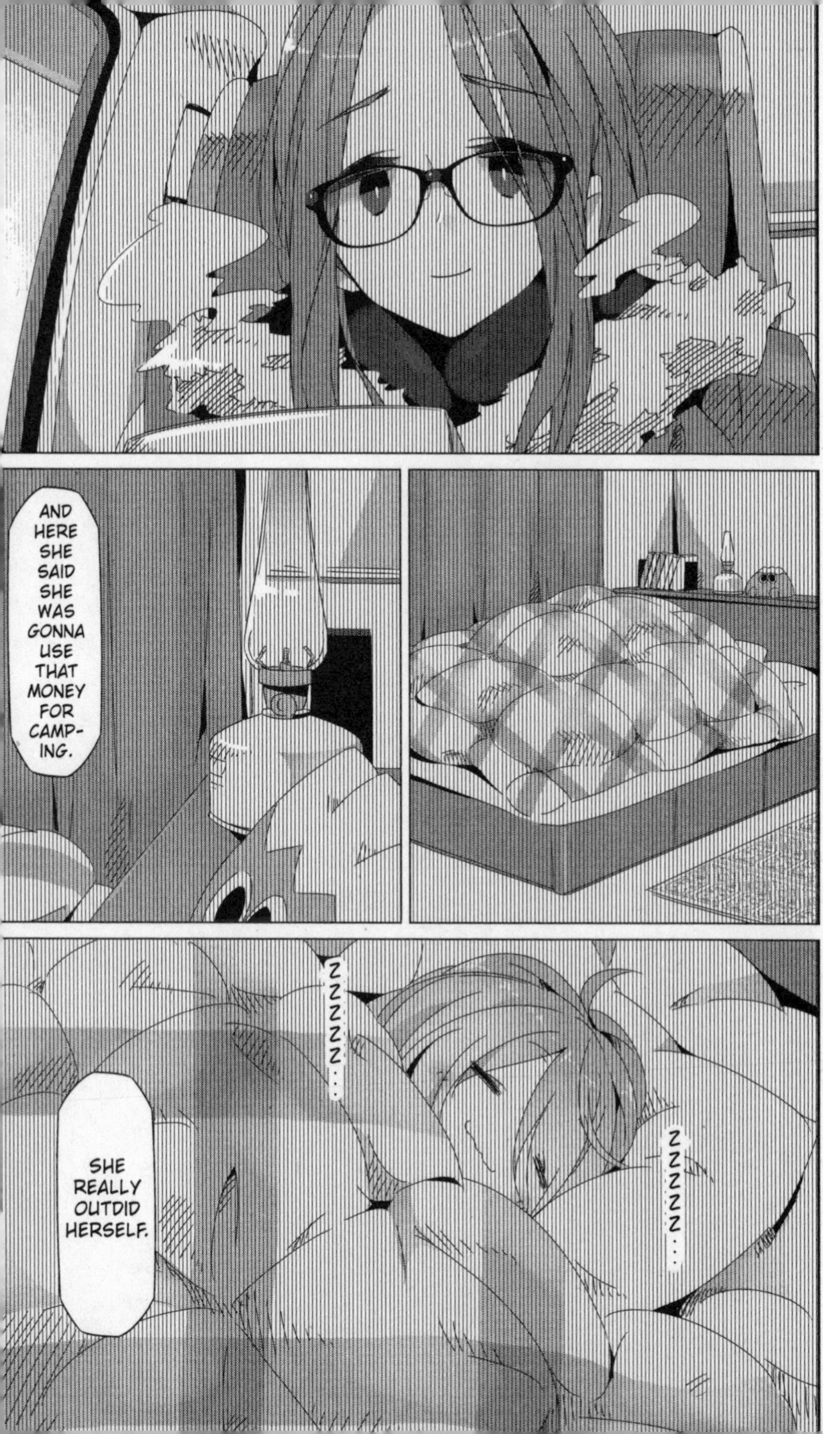
AND HERE SHE SAID SHE WAS GONNA USE THAT MONEY FOR CAMP-ING.
ZZZZZ...
ZZZZZ...
SHE REALLY OUTDID HERSELF.

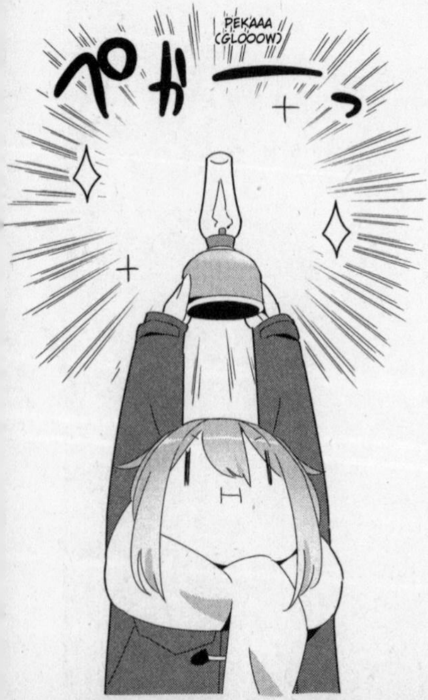
ぺかーっ
PEKAAA
(GLOOOW)

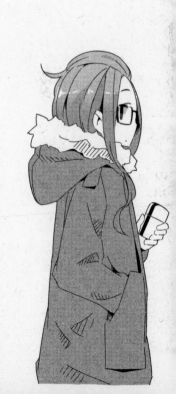

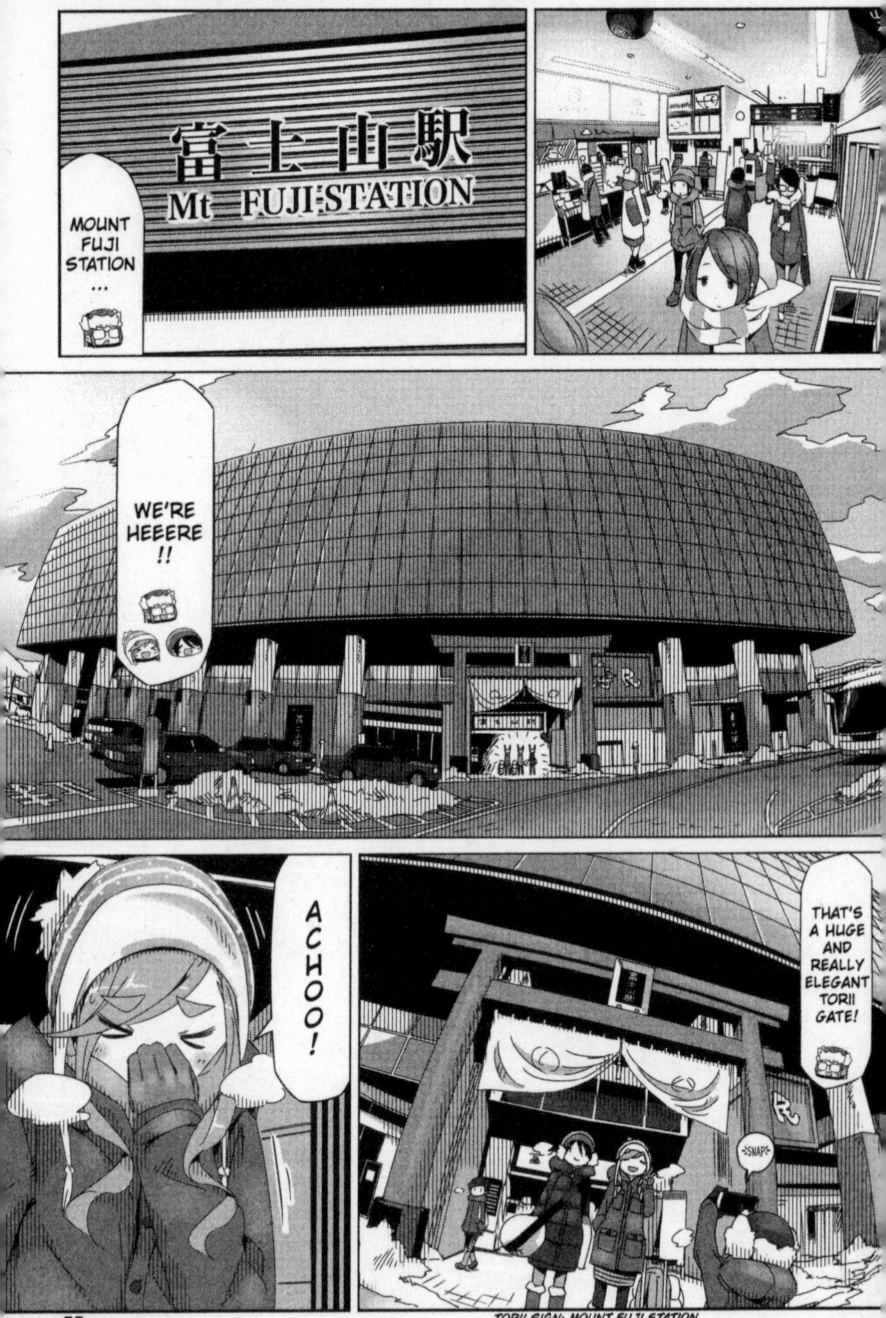
富士山駅
Mt FUJI STATION
MOUNT FUJI STATION ...
WE'RE HEEERE !!
THAT'S A HUGE AND REALLY ELEGANT TORII GATE!
SNAP
ACHOO!

TORII SIGN: MOUNT FUJI STATION

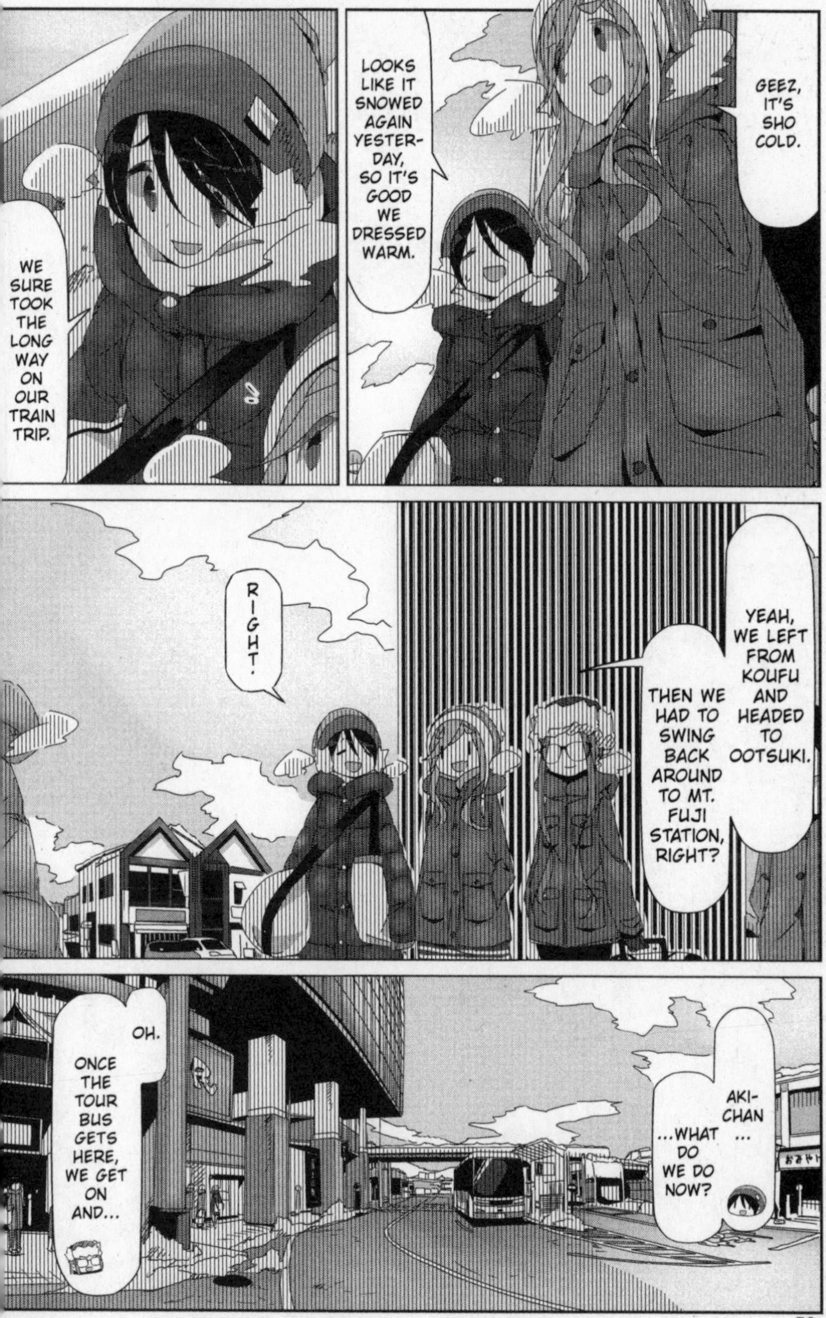
GEEZ, IT'S SHO COLD.
LOOKS LIKE IT SNOWED AGAIN YESTER-DAY, SO IT'S GOOD WE DRESSED WARM.
WE SURE TOOK THE LONG WAY ON OUR TRAIN TRIP.
YEAH, WE LEFT FROM KOUFU AND HEADED TO OOTSUKI.
THEN WE HAD TO SWING BACK AROUND TO MT. FUJI STATION, RIGHT?
RIGHT.
AKI-CHAN...
...WHAT DO WE DO NOW?
OH.
ONCE THE TOUR BUS GETS HERE, WE GET ON AND...

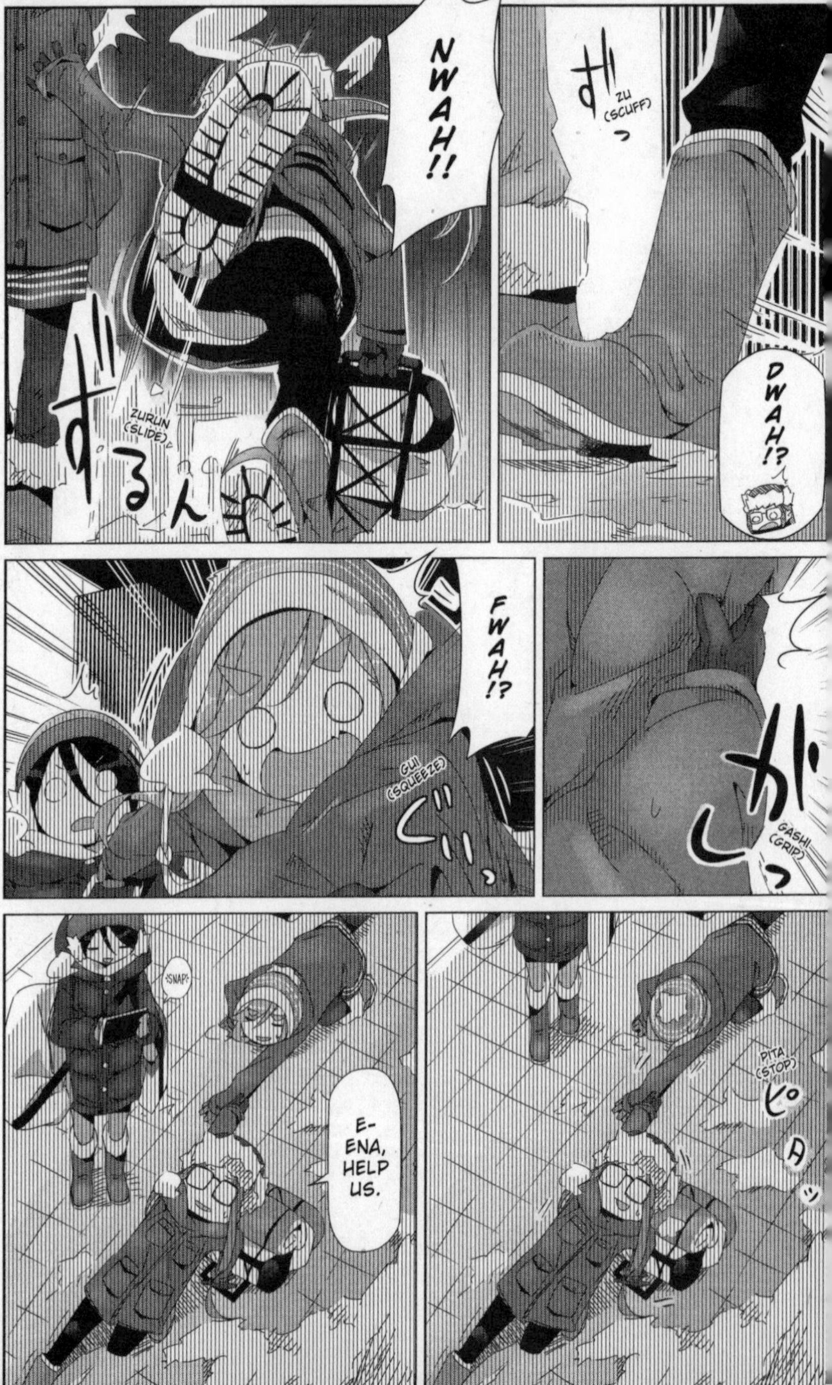
すっ
ZU (SCUFF)
DWAH!?
NWAH!!
ずるん
ZURUN (SLIDE)
がしっ
GASHI (GRIP)
FWAH!?
ぐいっ
GUI (SQUEEZE)
PITA (STOP)
SNAP
E-ENA, HELP US.

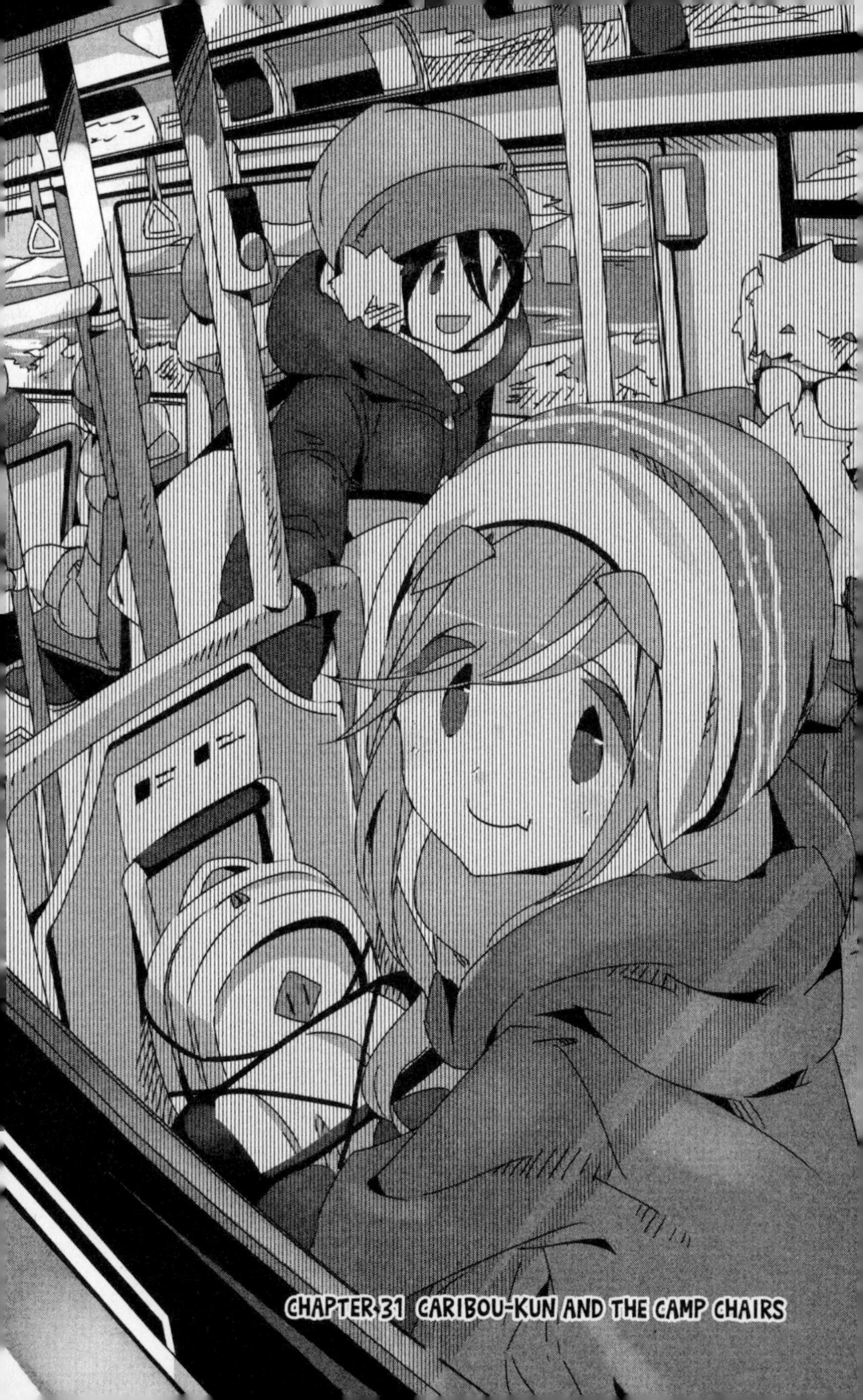

CHAPTER 31 CARIBOU-KUN AND THE CAMP CHAIRS

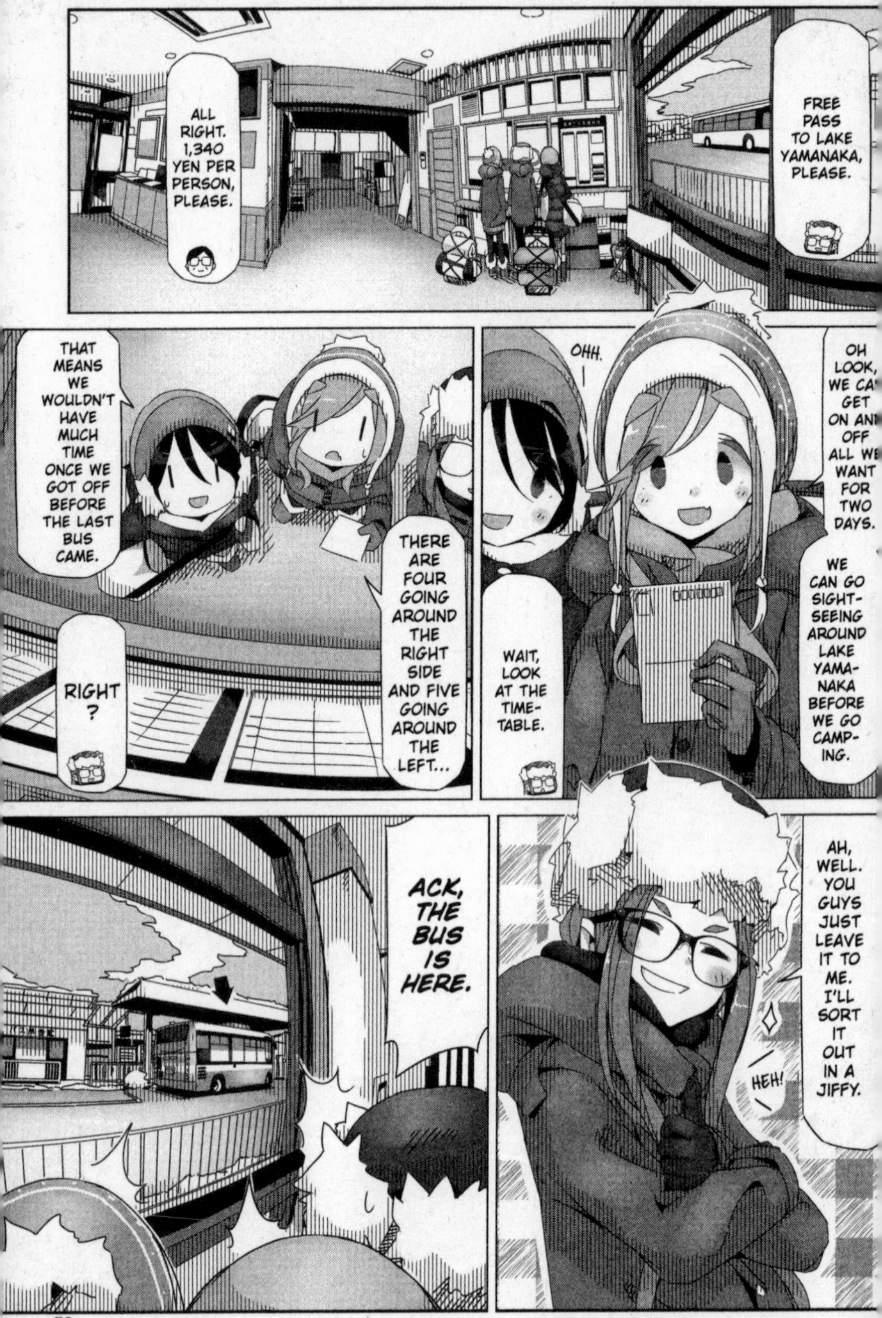
FREE PASS TO LAKE YAMANAKA, PLEASE.
ALL RIGHT. 1,340 YEN PER PERSON, PLEASE.
OH LOOK, WE CA GET ON AN OFF ALL WE WANT FOR TWO DAYS.
WE CAN GO SIGHT-SEEING AROUND LAKE YAMA-NAKA BEFORE WE GO CAMP-ING.
OHH.
WAIT, LOOK AT THE TIME-TABLE.
THERE ARE FOUR GOING AROUND THE RIGHT SIDE AND FIVE GOING AROUND THE LEFT...
THAT MEANS WE WOULDN'T HAVE MUCH TIME ONCE WE GOT OFF BEFORE THE LAST BUS CAME.
RIGHT?
AH, WELL. YOU GUYS JUST LEAVE IT TO ME. I'LL SORT IT OUT IN A JIFFY.
HEH!
ACK, THE BUS IS HERE.

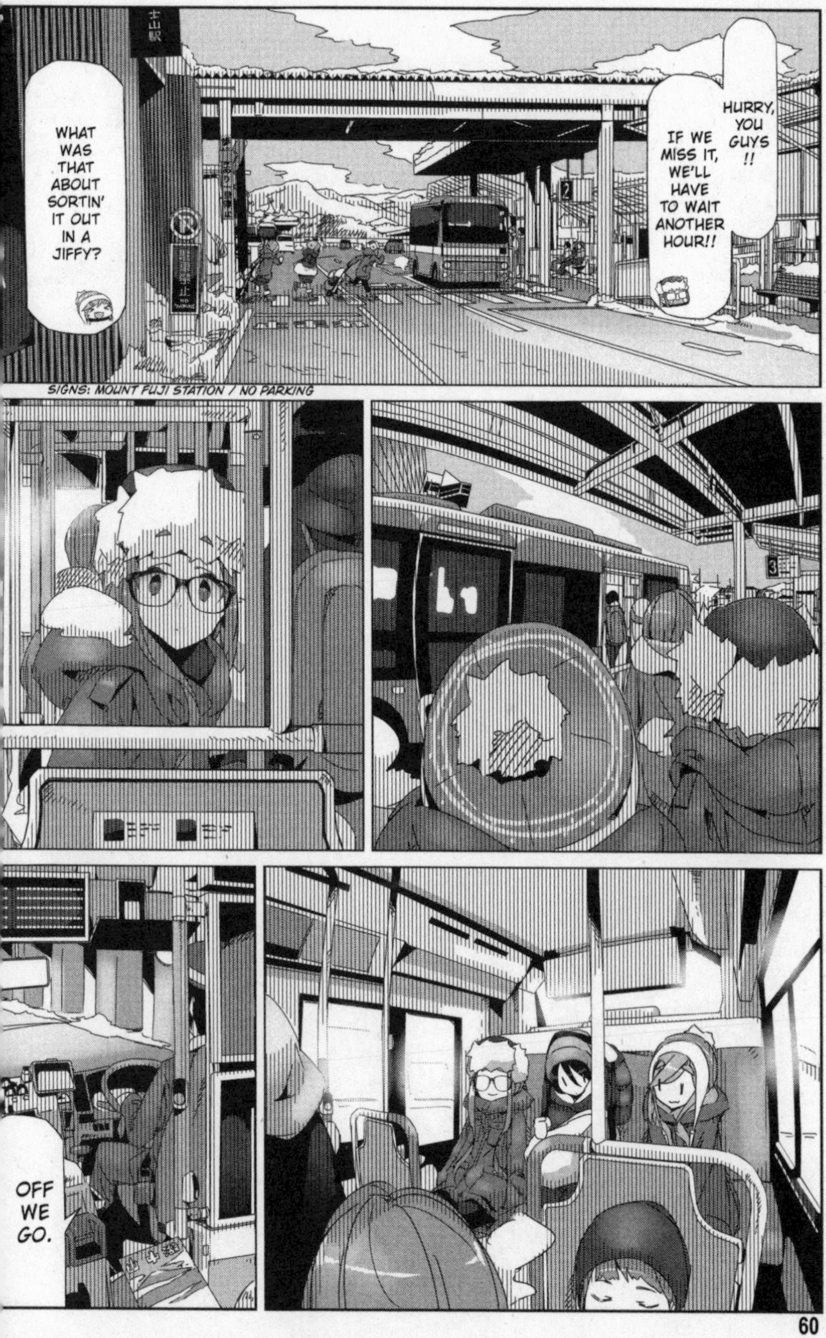
HURRY, YOU GUYS!!
IF WE MISS IT, WE'LL HAVE TO WAIT ANOTHER HOUR!!
WHAT WAS THAT ABOUT SORTIN' IT OUT IN A JIFFY?
SIGNS: MOUNT FUJI STATION / NO PARKING
OFF WE GO.

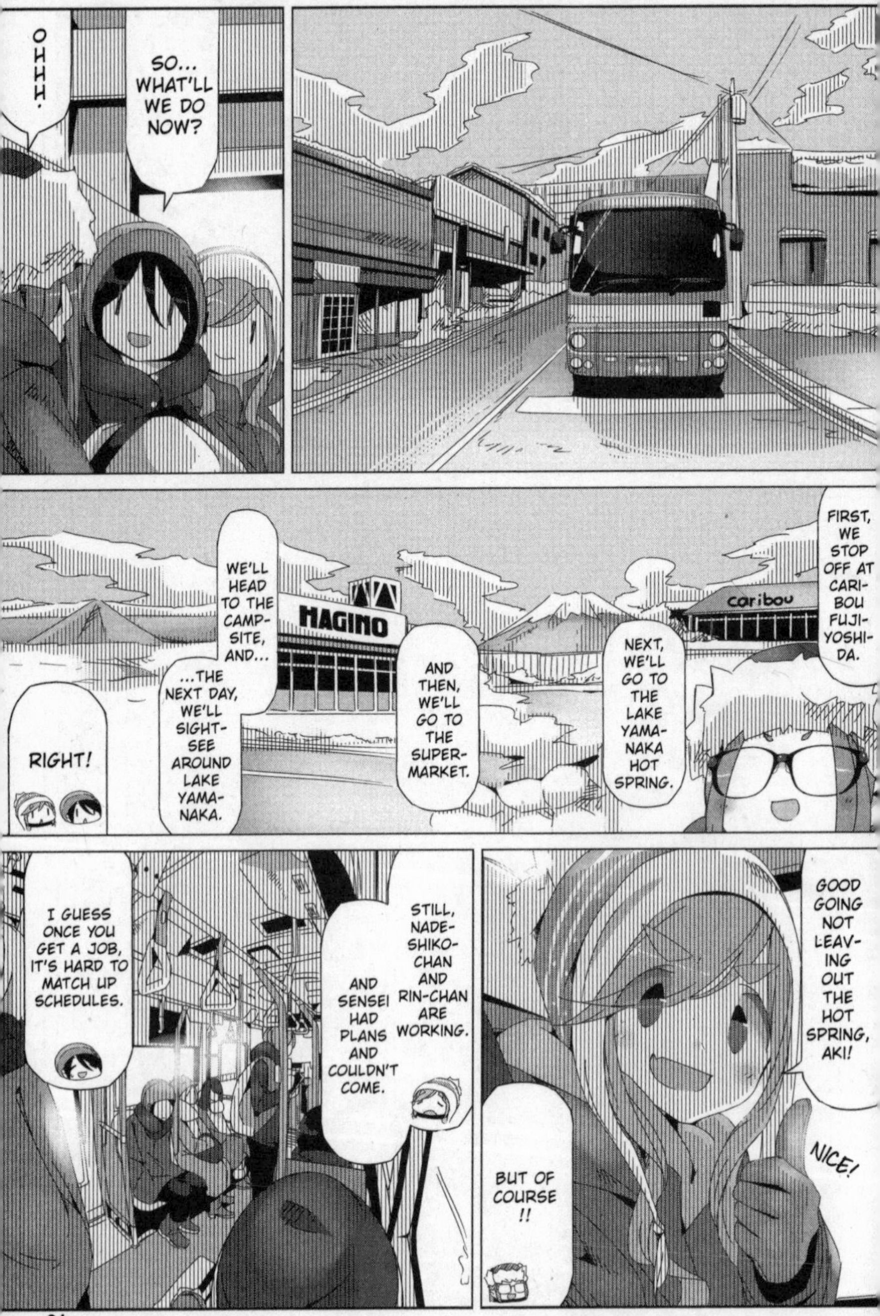
SO... WHAT'LL WE DO NOW?
OHHH.
FIRST, WE STOP OFF AT CARIBOU FUJIYOSHIDA.
caribou
NEXT, WE'LL GO TO THE LAKE YAMANAKA HOT SPRING.
AND THEN, WE'LL GO TO THE SUPERMARKET.
HAGINO
WE'LL HEAD TO THE CAMPSITE, AND...
...THE NEXT DAY, WE'LL SIGHTSEE AROUND LAKE YAMANAKA.
RIGHT!
GOOD GOING NOT LEAVING OUT THE HOT SPRING, AKI!
NICE!
BUT OF COURSE!!
STILL, NADESHIKO-CHAN AND RIN-CHAN ARE WORKING.
AND SENSEI HAD PLANS AND COULDN'T COME.
I GUESS ONCE YOU GET A JOB, IT'S HARD TO MATCH UP SCHEDULES.

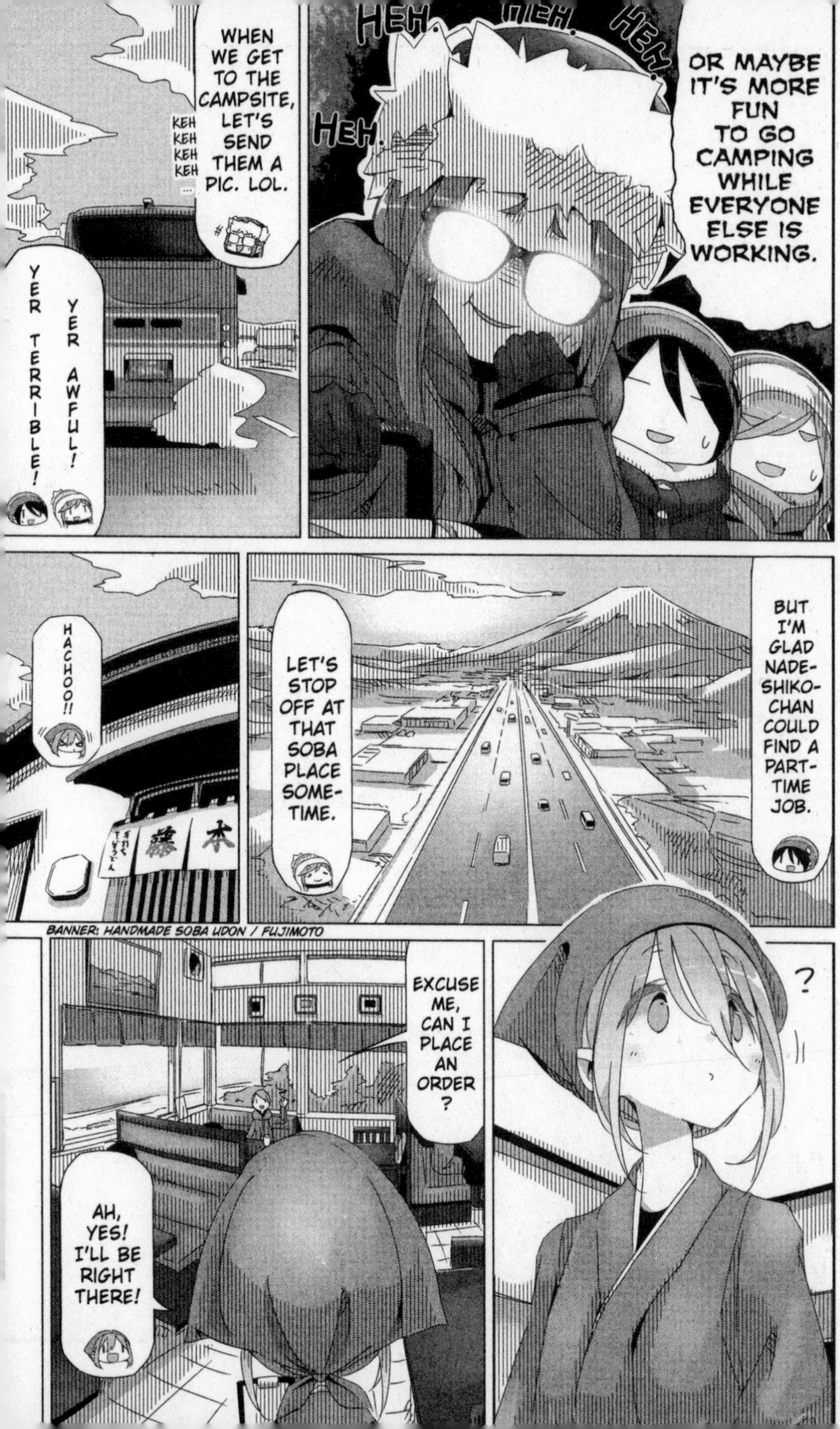
HEH. HEH. HEH. HEH.
OR MAYBE IT'S MORE FUN TO GO CAMPING WHILE EVERYONE ELSE IS WORKING.
WHEN WE GET TO THE CAMPSITE, LET'S SEND THEM A PIC. LOL.
KEH KEH KEH KEH...
YER AWFUL!
YER TERRIBLE!
BUT I'M GLAD NADE-SHIKO-CHAN COULD FIND A PART-TIME JOB.
LET'S STOP OFF AT THAT SOBA PLACE SOME-TIME.
HACHOO!!
BANNER: HANDMADE SOBA UDON / FUJIMOTO
?
EXCUSE ME, CAN I PLACE AN ORDER?
AH, YES! I'LL BE RIGHT THERE!

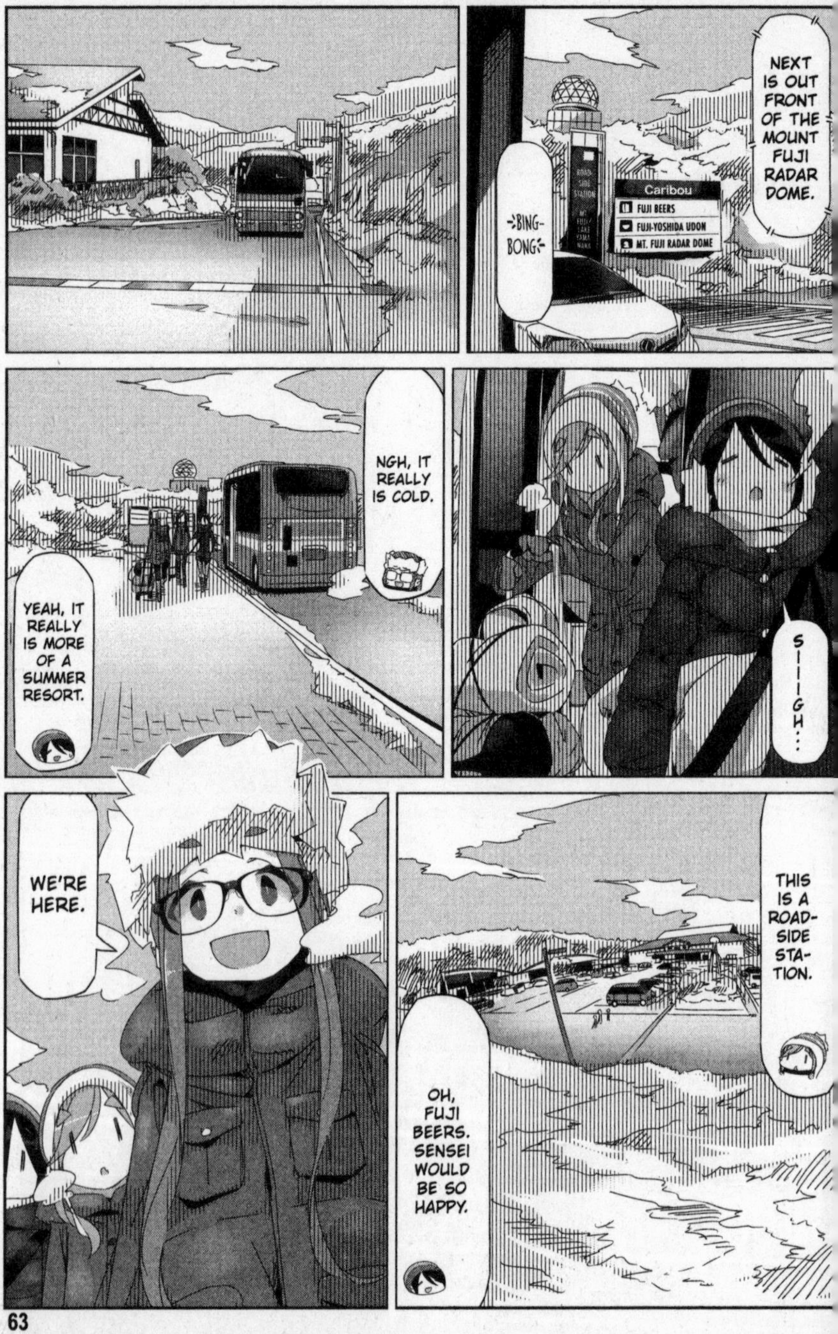
NEXT IS OUT FRONT OF THE MOUNT FUJI RADAR DOME.
Caribou
FUJI BEERS
FUJI-YOSHIDA UDON
MT. FUJI RADAR DOME
-BING-BONG-
S I I I G H . . .
NGH, IT REALLY IS COLD.
YEAH, IT REALLY IS MORE OF A SUMMER RESORT.
THIS IS A ROAD-SIDE STA-TION.
OH, FUJI BEERS. SENSEI WOULD BE SO HAPPY.
WE'RE HERE.

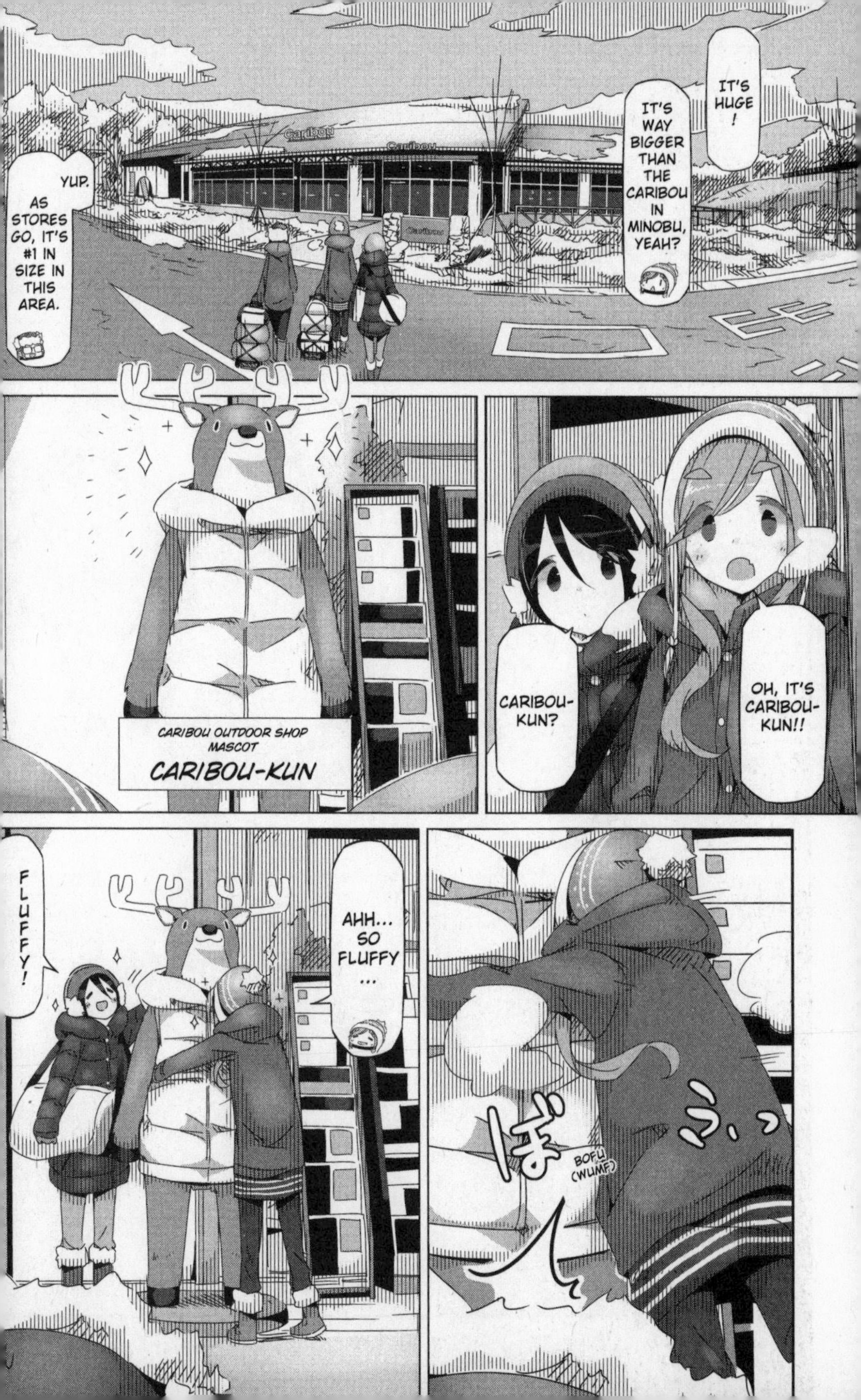
Caribou
IT'S HUGE!
IT'S WAY BIGGER THAN THE CARIBOU IN MINOBU, YEAH?
YUP. AS STORES GO, IT'S #1 IN SIZE IN THIS AREA.
OH, IT'S CARIBOU-KUN!!
CARIBOU-KUN?
CARIBOU OUTDOOR SHOP MASCOT
CARIBOU-KUN
ぼふっ
BOFU (WUMF)
AHH... SO FLUFFY...
FLUFFY!

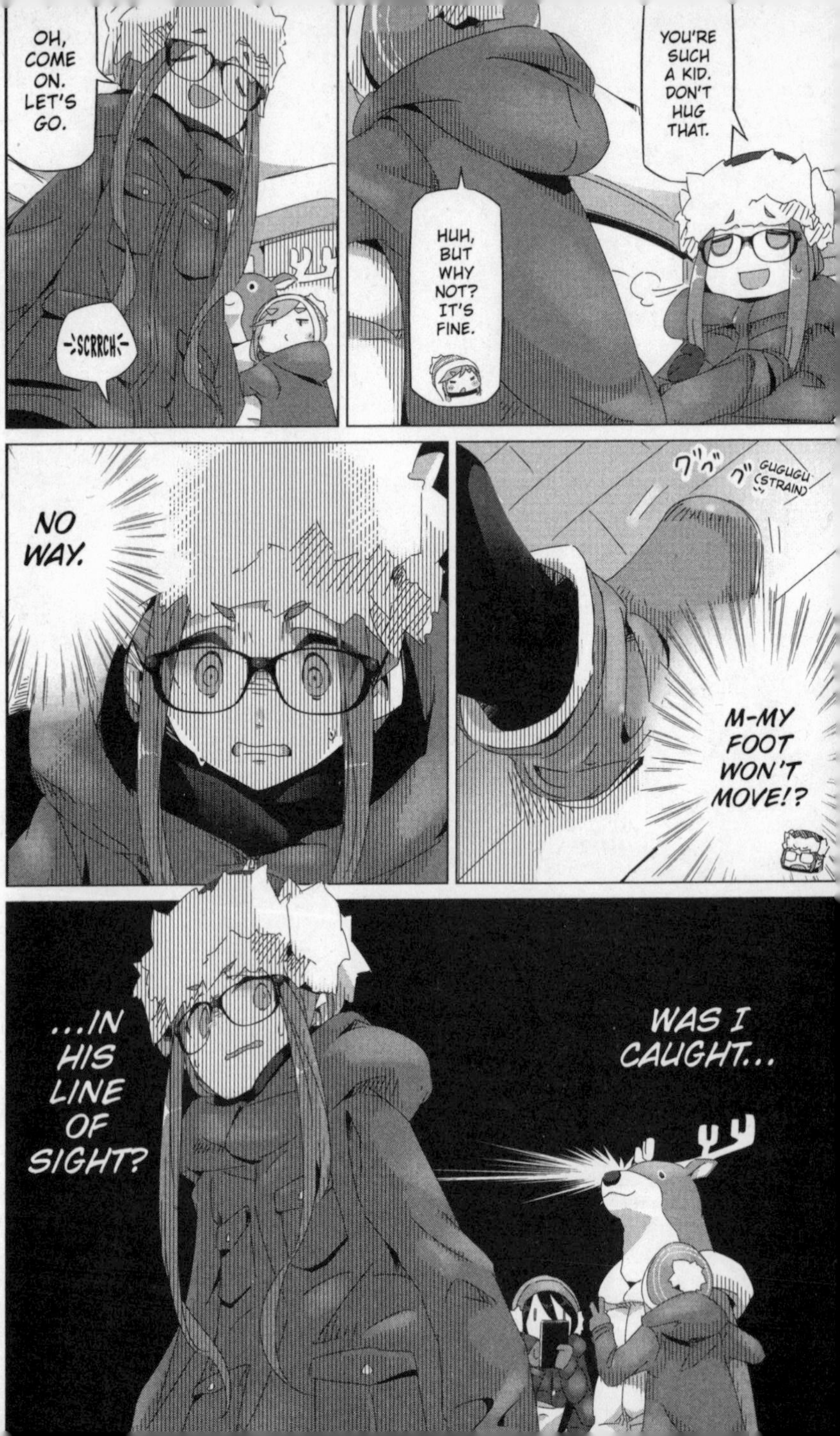
YOU'RE SUCH A KID. DON'T HUG THAT.
HUH, BUT WHY NOT? IT'S FINE.
OH, COME ON. LET'S GO.
SCRRCH
GUGUGU (STRAIN)
M-MY FOOT WON'T MOVE!?
NO WAY.
WAS I CAUGHT...
...IN HIS LINE OF SIGHT?

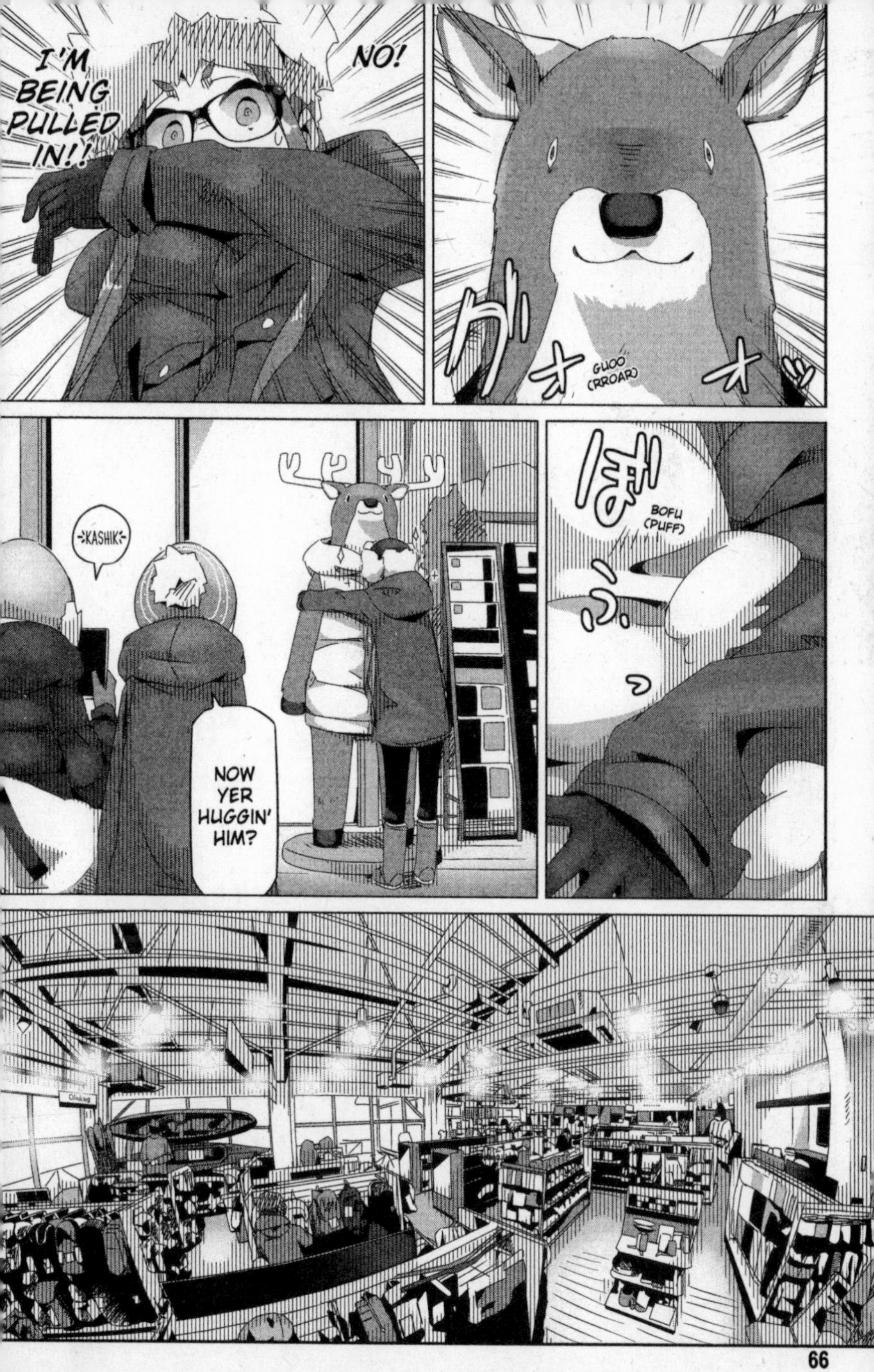
ガォォッ
GUOO (RROAR)
NO!
I'M BEING PULLED IN!!
ぼふっ
BOFU (PUFF)
-KASHIK-
NOW YER HUGGIN' HIM?

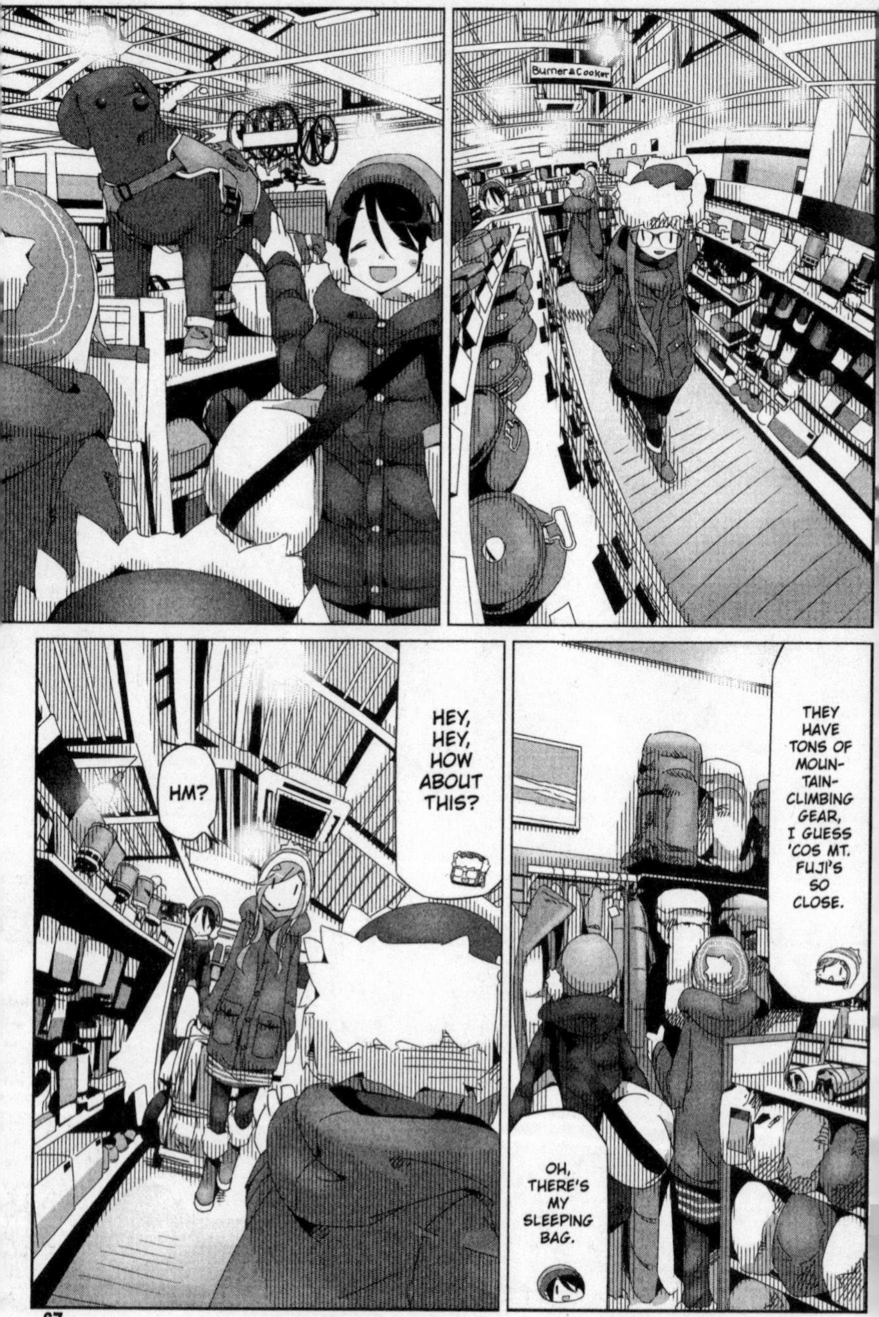
Burner&Cooker
THEY HAVE TONS OF MOUNTAIN-CLIMBING GEAR, I GUESS 'COS MT. FUJI'S SO CLOSE.
OH, THERE'S MY SLEEPING BAG.
HEY, HEY, HOW ABOUT THIS?
HM?

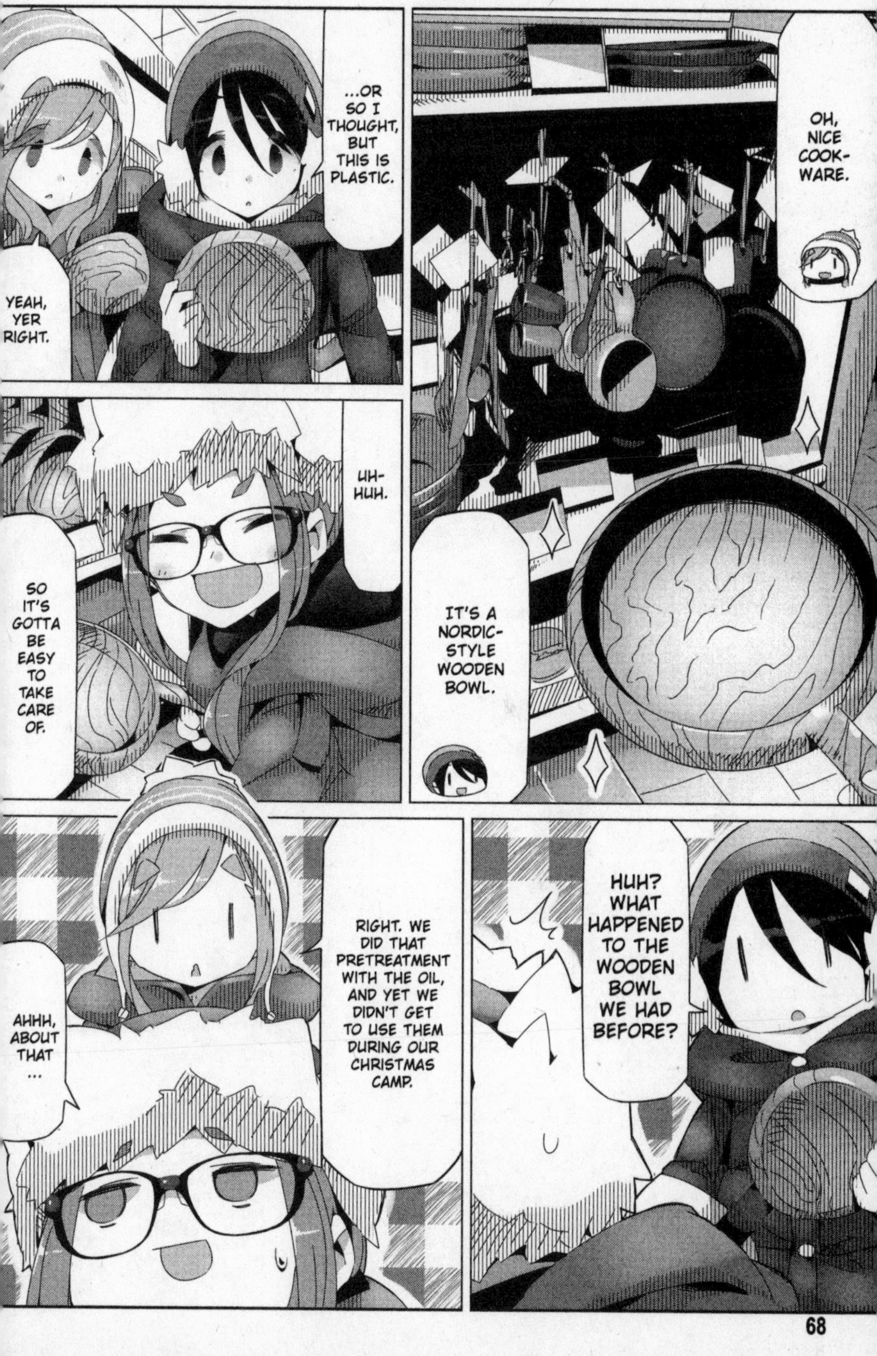
OH, NICE COOK-WARE.
IT'S A NORDIC-STYLE WOODEN BOWL.
...OR SO I THOUGHT, BUT THIS IS PLASTIC.
YEAH, YER RIGHT.
UH-HUH.
SO IT'S GOTTA BE EASY TO TAKE CARE OF.
HUH? WHAT HAPPENED TO THE WOODEN BOWL WE HAD BEFORE?
RIGHT. WE DID THAT PRETREATMENT WITH THE OIL, AND YET WE DIDN'T GET TO USE THEM DURING OUR CHRISTMAS CAMP.
AHHH, ABOUT THAT ...

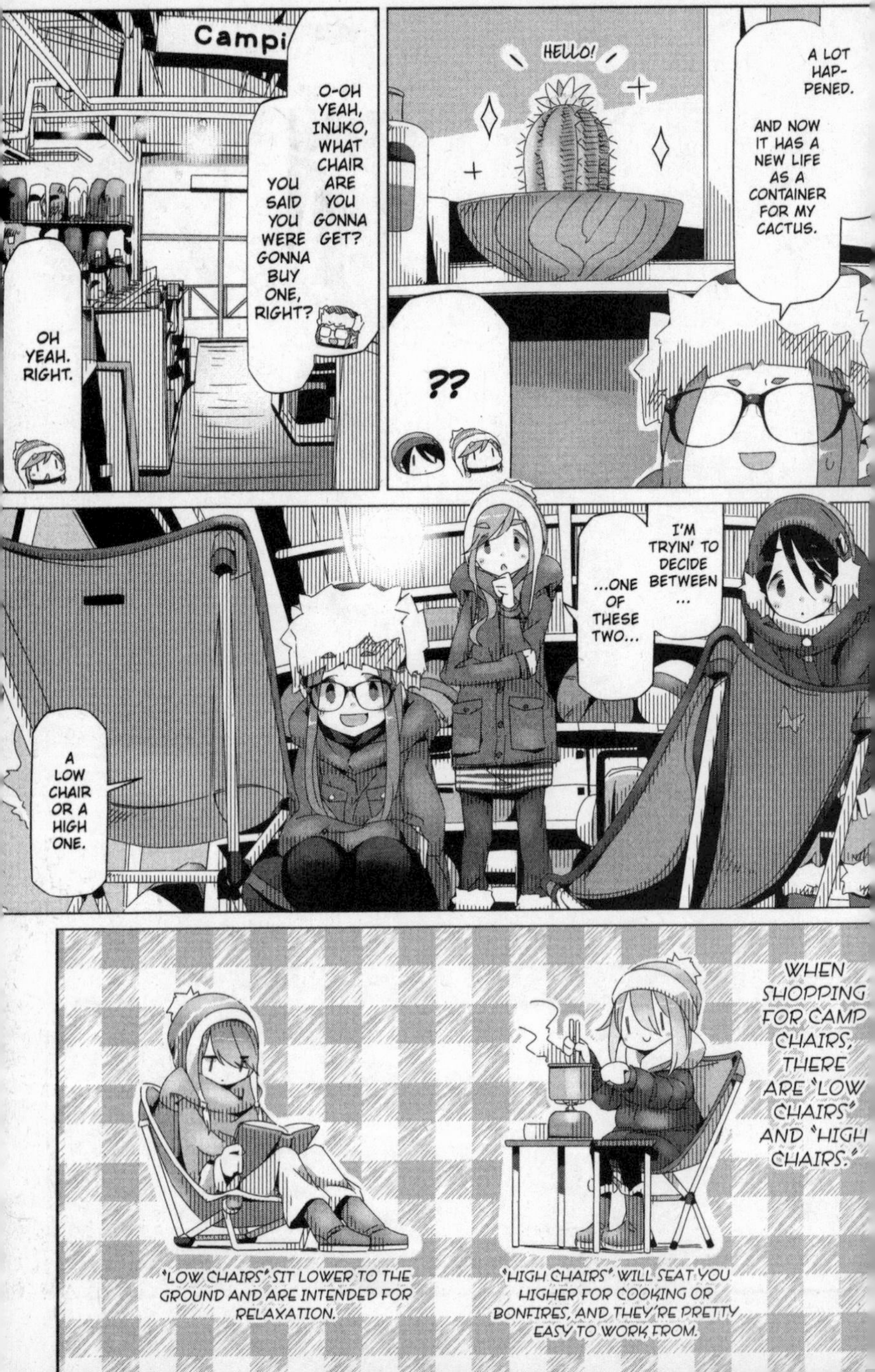
A LOT HAPPENED.
HELLO!
AND NOW IT HAS A NEW LIFE AS A CONTAINER FOR MY CACTUS.
??
Campi
O-OH YEAH, INUKO, WHAT CHAIR ARE YOU GONNA GET?
YOU SAID YOU WERE GONNA BUY ONE, RIGHT?
OH YEAH. RIGHT.
I'M TRYIN' TO DECIDE BETWEEN...
...ONE OF THESE TWO...
A LOW CHAIR OR A HIGH ONE.
WHEN SHOPPING FOR CAMP CHAIRS, THERE ARE "LOW CHAIRS" AND "HIGH CHAIRS."
"HIGH CHAIRS" WILL SEAT YOU HIGHER FOR COOKING OR BONFIRES, AND THEY'RE PRETTY EASY TO WORK FROM.
"LOW CHAIRS" SIT LOWER TO THE GROUND AND ARE INTENDED FOR RELAXATION.

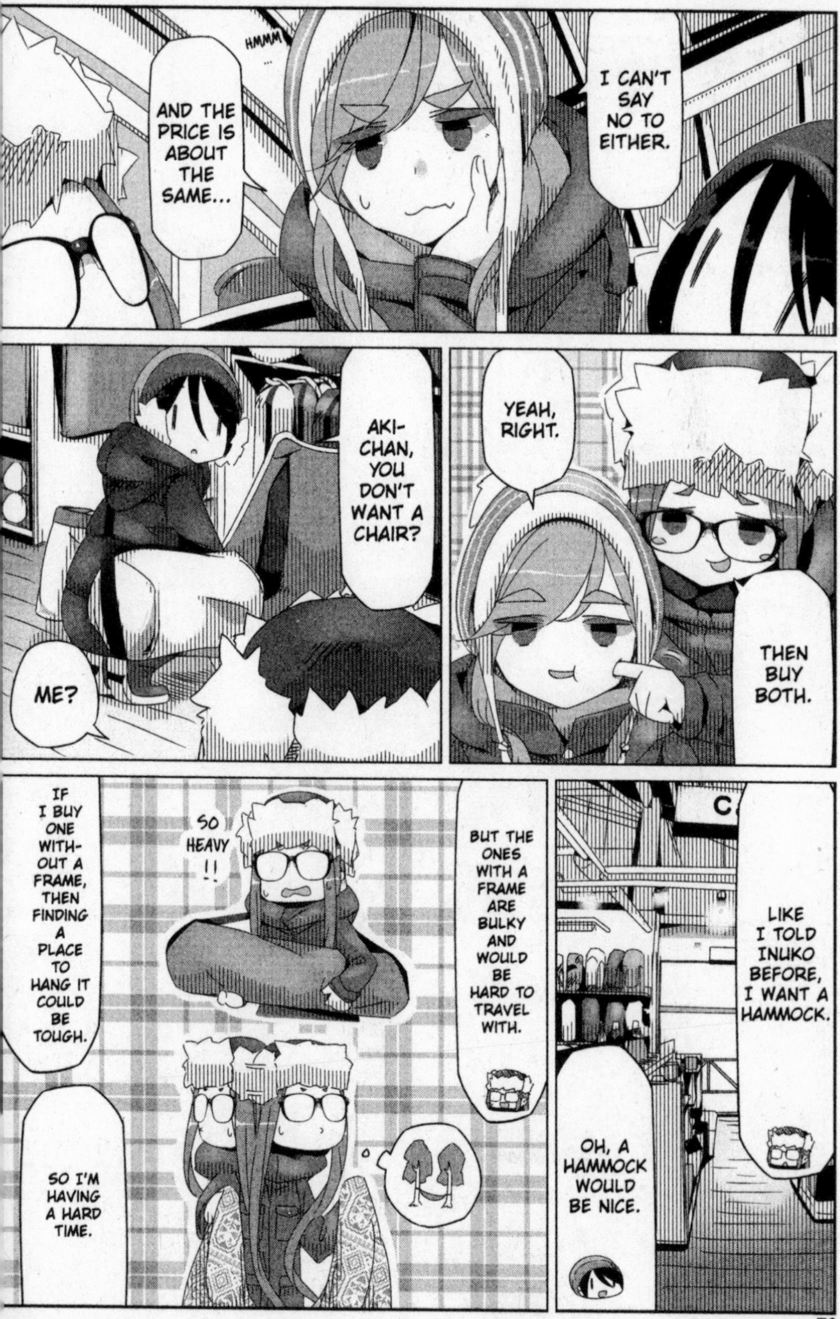
I CAN'T SAY NO TO EITHER.
HMMM...
AND THE PRICE IS ABOUT THE SAME...
YEAH, RIGHT.
THEN BUY BOTH.
AKI-CHAN, YOU DON'T WANT A CHAIR?
ME?
LIKE I TOLD INUKO BEFORE, I WANT A HAMMOCK.
OH, A HAMMOCK WOULD BE NICE.
BUT THE ONES WITH A FRAME ARE BULKY AND WOULD BE HARD TO TRAVEL WITH.
SO HEAVY!!
IF I BUY ONE WITHOUT A FRAME, THEN FINDING A PLACE TO HANG IT COULD BE TOUGH.
SO I'M HAVING A HARD TIME.

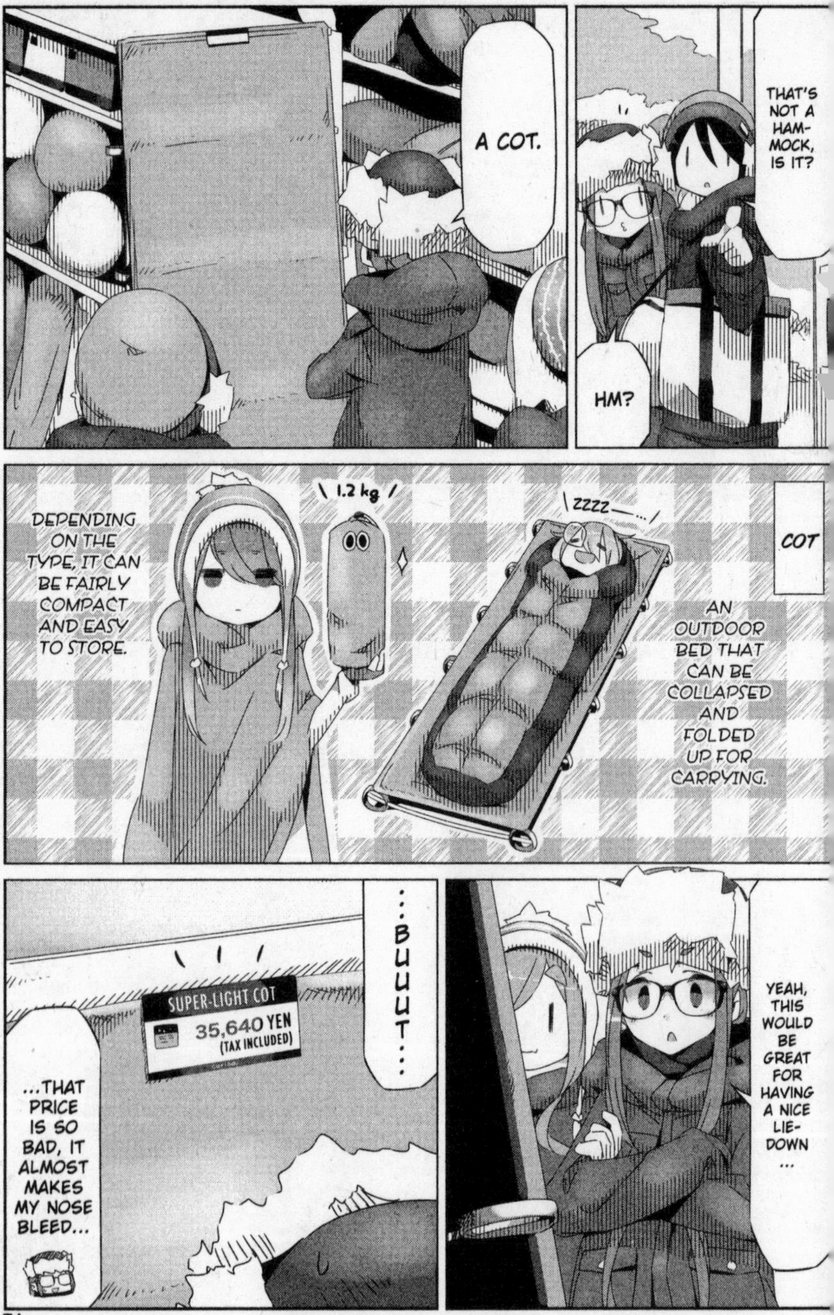
THAT'S NOT A HAMMOCK, IS IT?
HM?
A COT.
COT
ZZZZ——...
AN OUTDOOR BED THAT CAN BE COLLAPSED AND FOLDED UP FOR CARRYING.
1.2 kg
DEPENDING ON THE TYPE, IT CAN BE FAIRLY COMPACT AND EASY TO STORE.
YEAH, THIS WOULD BE GREAT FOR HAVING A NICE LIE-DOWN...
...BUUUT...
SUPER-LIGHT COT
35,640 YEN
(TAX INCLUDED)
...THAT PRICE IS SO BAD, IT ALMOST MAKES MY NOSE BLEED...

CAN I HELP YOU FIND SOME-THING?
I'M HAVING A HARD TIME PICKING A HAMMOCK.
(YADA YADA.)
(BLAH, BLAH.)
A HAM-MOCK THAT'S LIGHT BUT FREE-STANDING...
AND ONE THAT COSTS UNDER 10,000 YEN, IF POSSIBLE ...
OUR LIGHTEST IS THIS ONE, AT SIX KILO-GRAMS.
DON (DUN)
SIX KILO-GRAMS IS A BIT MUCH...

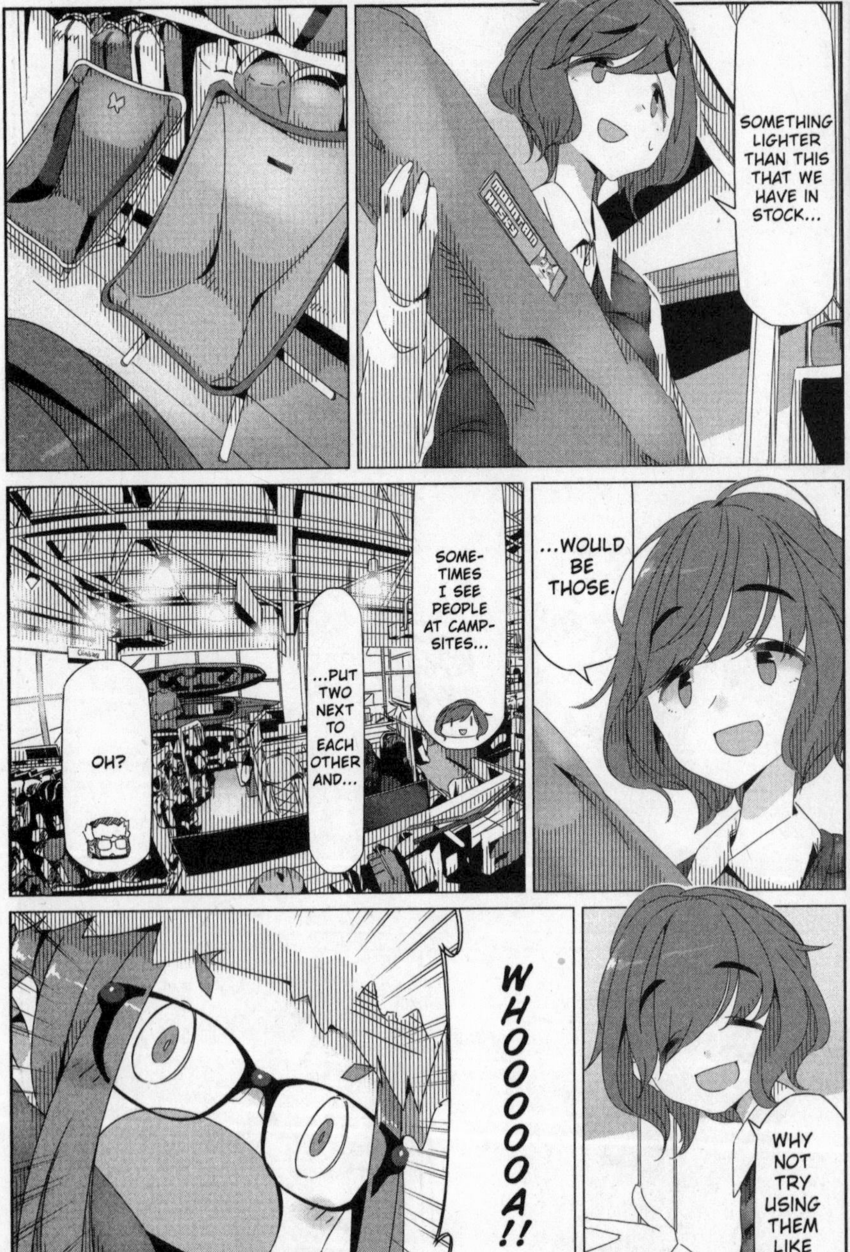
SOMETHING LIGHTER THAN THIS THAT WE HAVE IN STOCK...
...WOULD BE THOSE.
SOMETIMES I SEE PEOPLE AT CAMPSITES...
...PUT TWO NEXT TO EACH OTHER AND...
OH?
WHY NOT TRY USING THEM LIKE THIS?
WHOOOOOOA!!

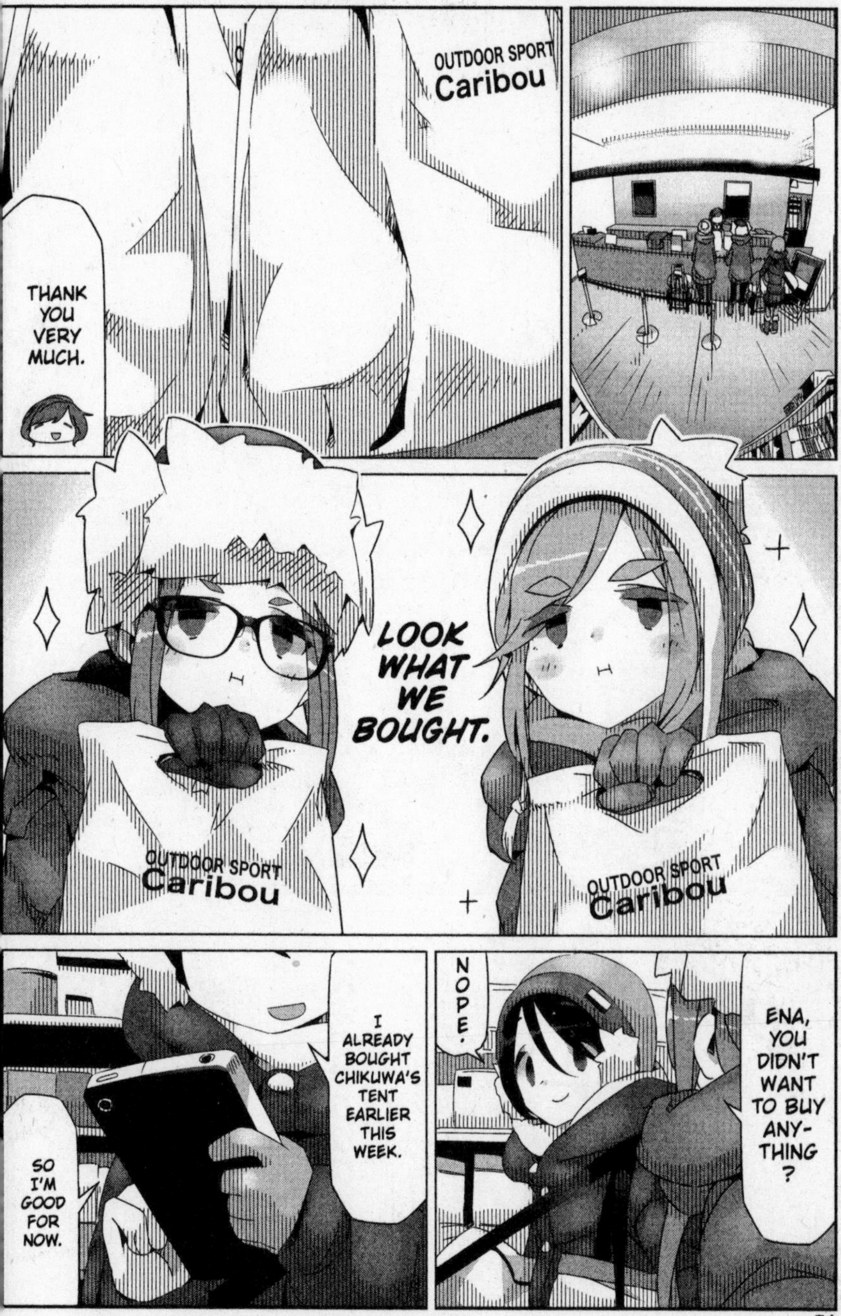
OUTDOOR SPORT Caribou
THANK YOU VERY MUCH.
LOOK WHAT WE BOUGHT.
OUTDOOR SPORT Caribou
OUTDOOR SPORT Caribou
ENA, YOU DIDN'T WANT TO BUY ANY-THING?
NOPE.
I ALREADY BOUGHT CHIKUWA'S TENT EARLIER THIS WEEK.
SO I'M GOOD FOR NOW.

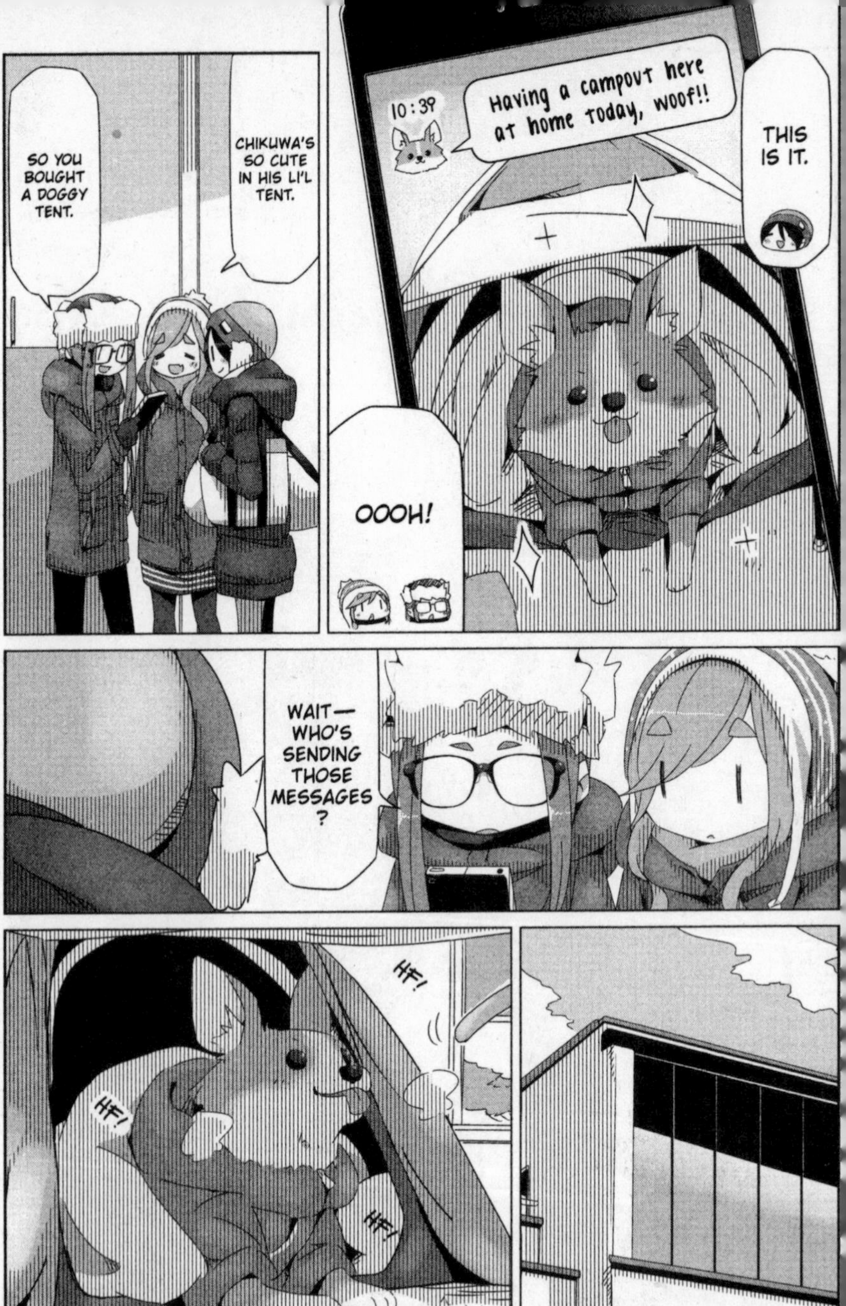
THIS IS IT.
Having a campout here at home today, woof!!
10:39
OOOH!
CHIKUWA'S SO CUTE IN HIS LI'L TENT.
SO YOU BOUGHT A DOGGY TENT.
WAIT—WHO'S SENDING THOSE MESSAGES?
HF!
HF!
HF!

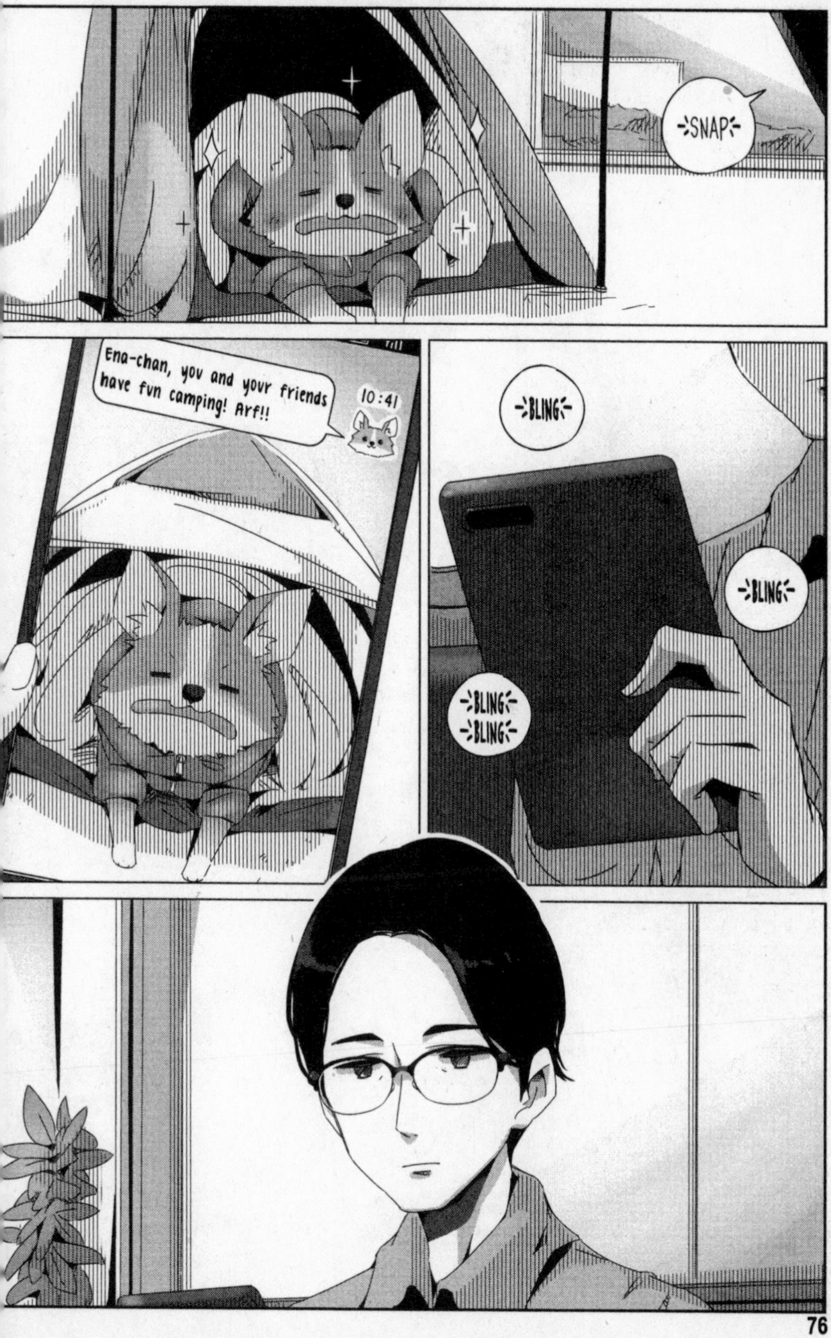
SNAP
BLING
BLING
BLING BLING
Ena-chan, you and your friends have fun camping! Arf!!
10:41

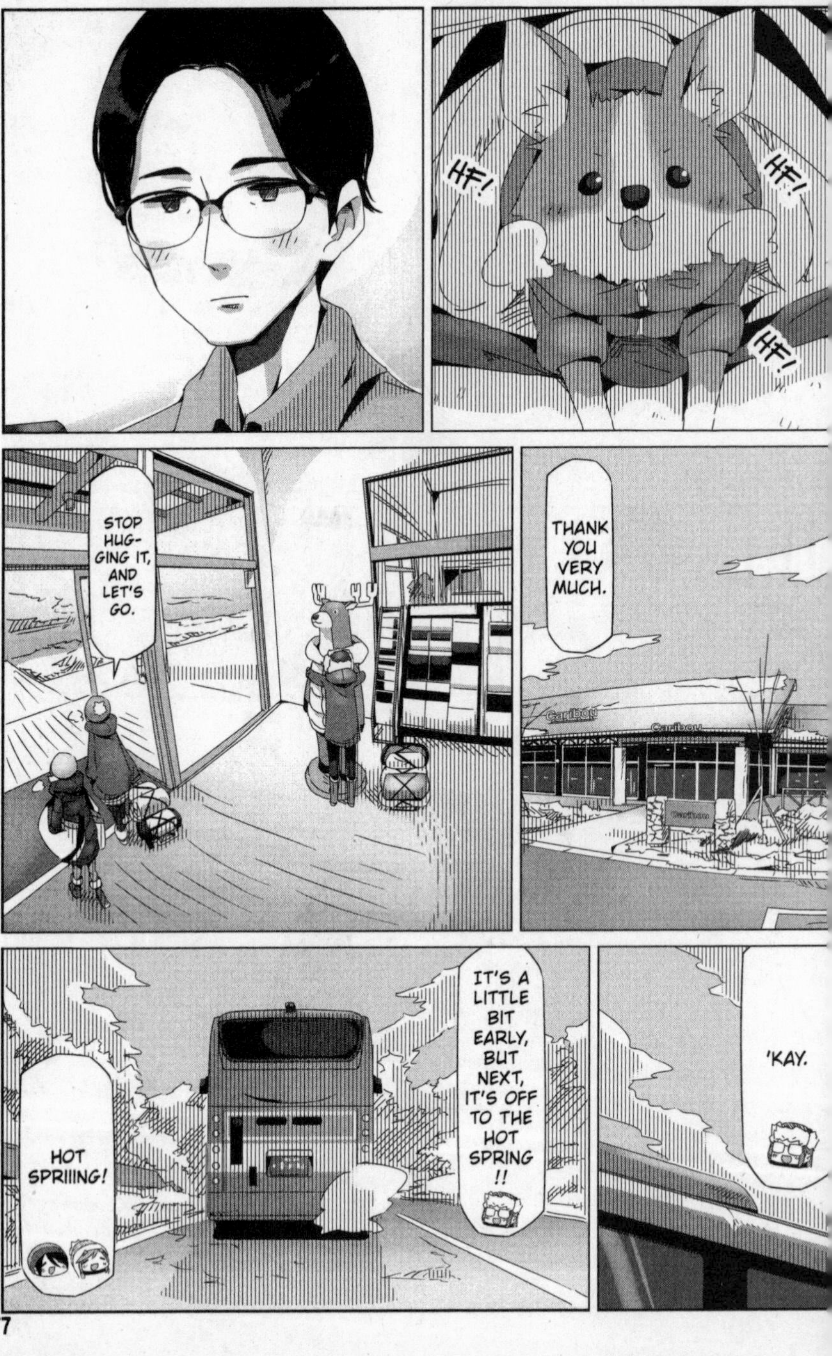
HF!
HF!
HF!
THANK YOU VERY MUCH.
STOP HUG-GING IT, AND LET'S GO.
'KAY.
IT'S A LITTLE BIT EARLY, BUT NEXT, IT'S OFF TO THE HOT SPRING!!
HOT SPRIIING!

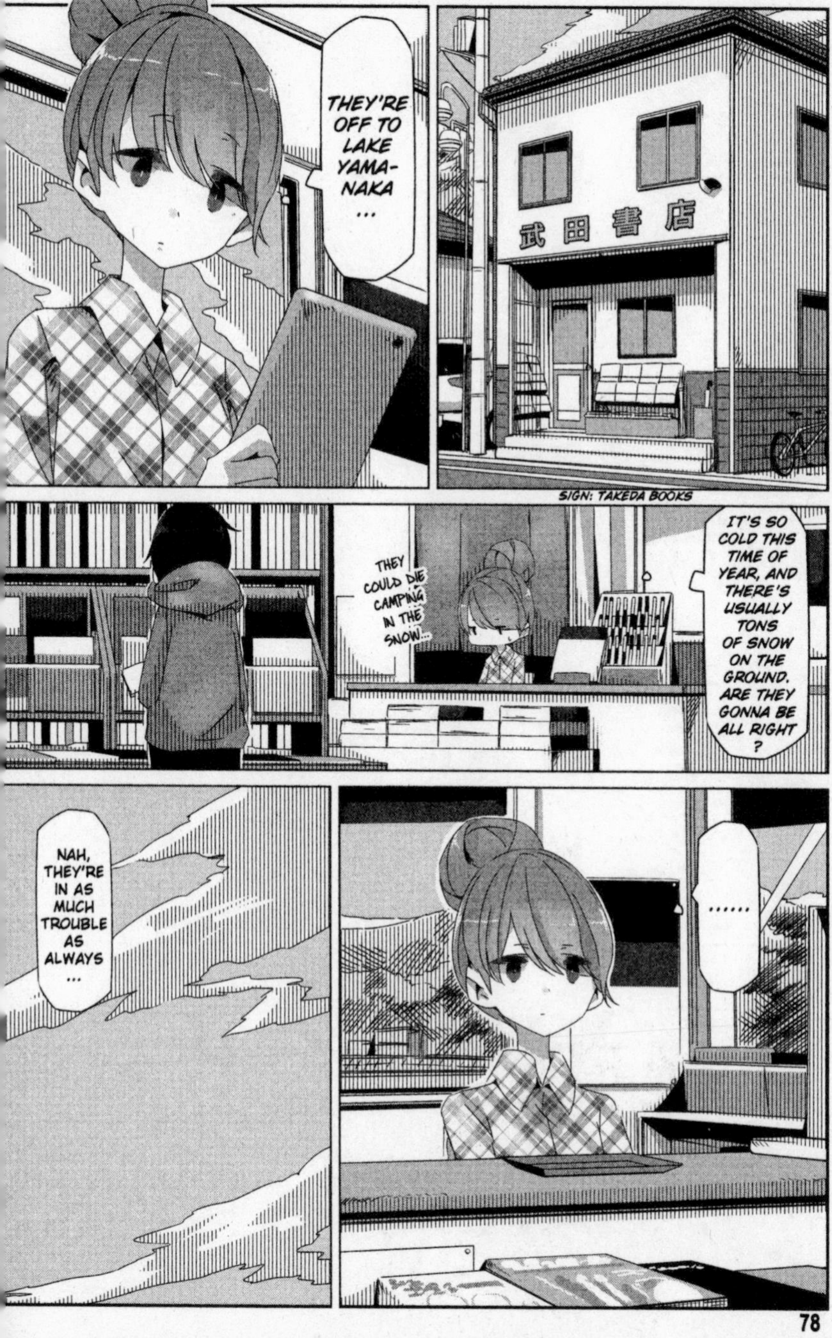
SIGN: TAKEDA BOOKS
THEY'RE OFF TO LAKE YAMANAKA ...
IT'S SO COLD THIS TIME OF YEAR, AND THERE'S USUALLY TONS OF SNOW ON THE GROUND. ARE THEY GONNA BE ALL RIGHT?
THEY COULD DIE CAMPING IN THE SNOW...
......
NAH, THEY'RE IN AS MUCH TROUBLE AS ALWAYS ...

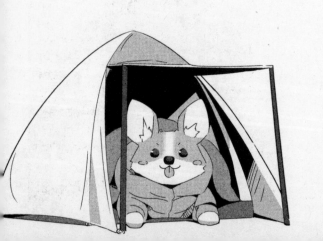

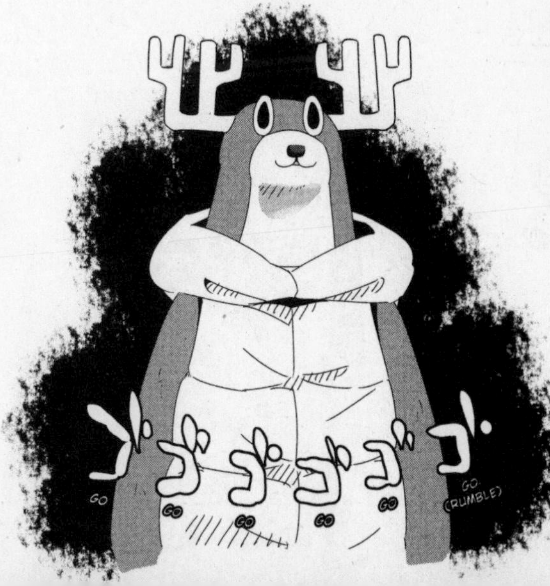

GO
GO
GO
GO
GO
GO (RUMBLE)

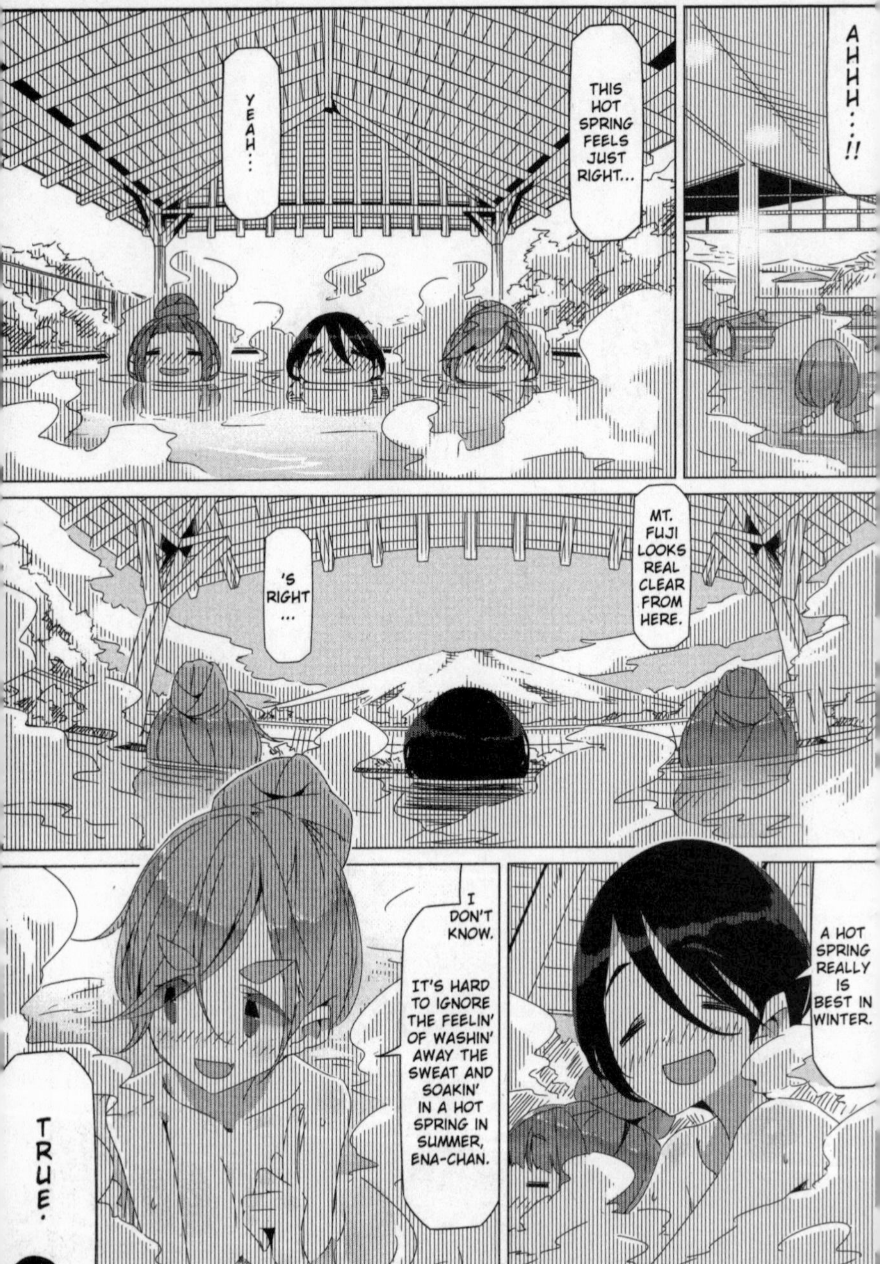
AHHH...!!
THIS HOT SPRING FEELS JUST RIGHT...
YEAH...
MT. FUJI LOOKS REAL CLEAR FROM HERE.
'S RIGHT ...
A HOT SPRING REALLY IS BEST IN WINTER.
I DON'T KNOW.
IT'S HARD TO IGNORE THE FEELIN' OF WASHIN' AWAY THE SWEAT AND SOAKIN' IN A HOT SPRING IN SUMMER, ENA-CHAN.
TRUE.

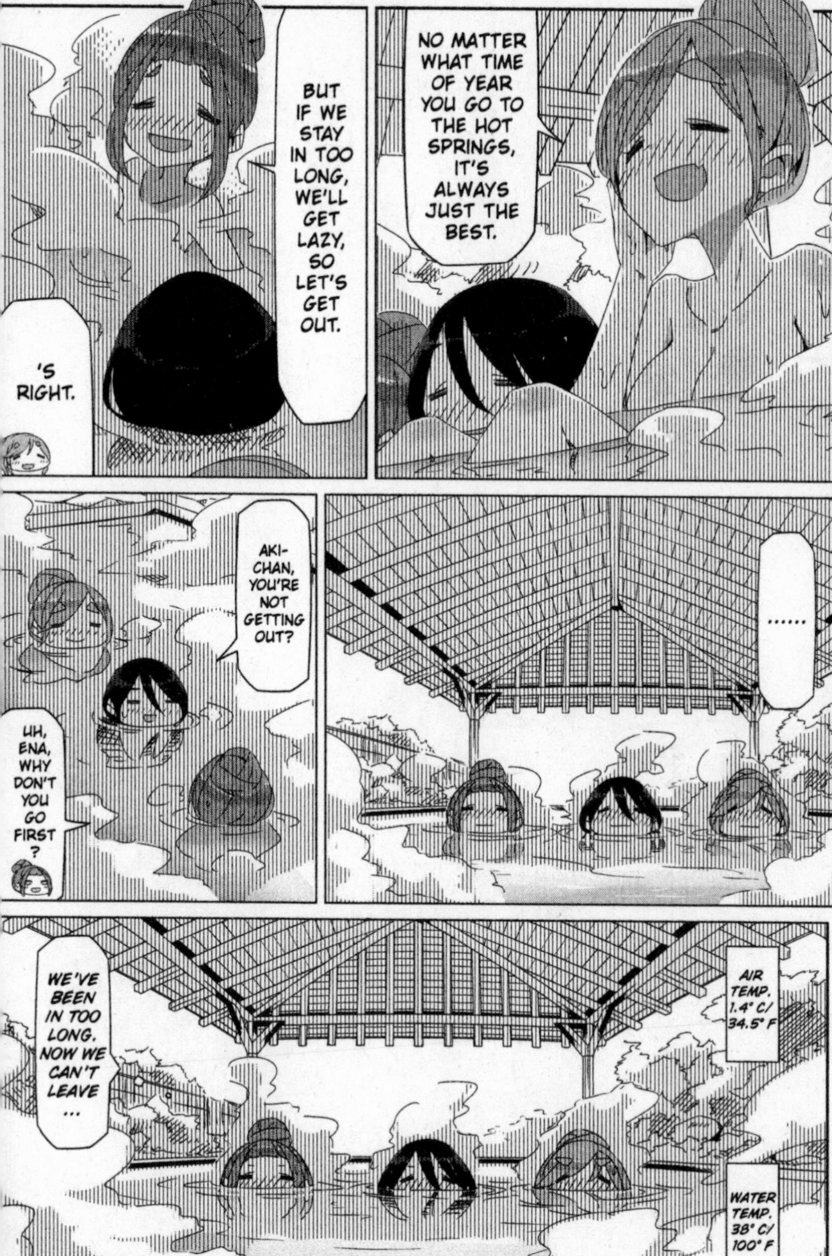
NO MATTER WHAT TIME OF YEAR YOU GO TO THE HOT SPRINGS, IT'S ALWAYS JUST THE BEST.
BUT IF WE STAY IN TOO LONG, WE'LL GET LAZY, SO LET'S GET OUT.
'S RIGHT.
......
AKI-CHAN, YOU'RE NOT GETTING OUT?
UH, ENA, WHY DON'T YOU GO FIRST?
AIR TEMP. 1.4° C/ 34.5° F
WATER TEMP. 38° C/ 100° F
WE'VE BEEN IN TOO LONG. NOW WE CAN'T LEAVE...

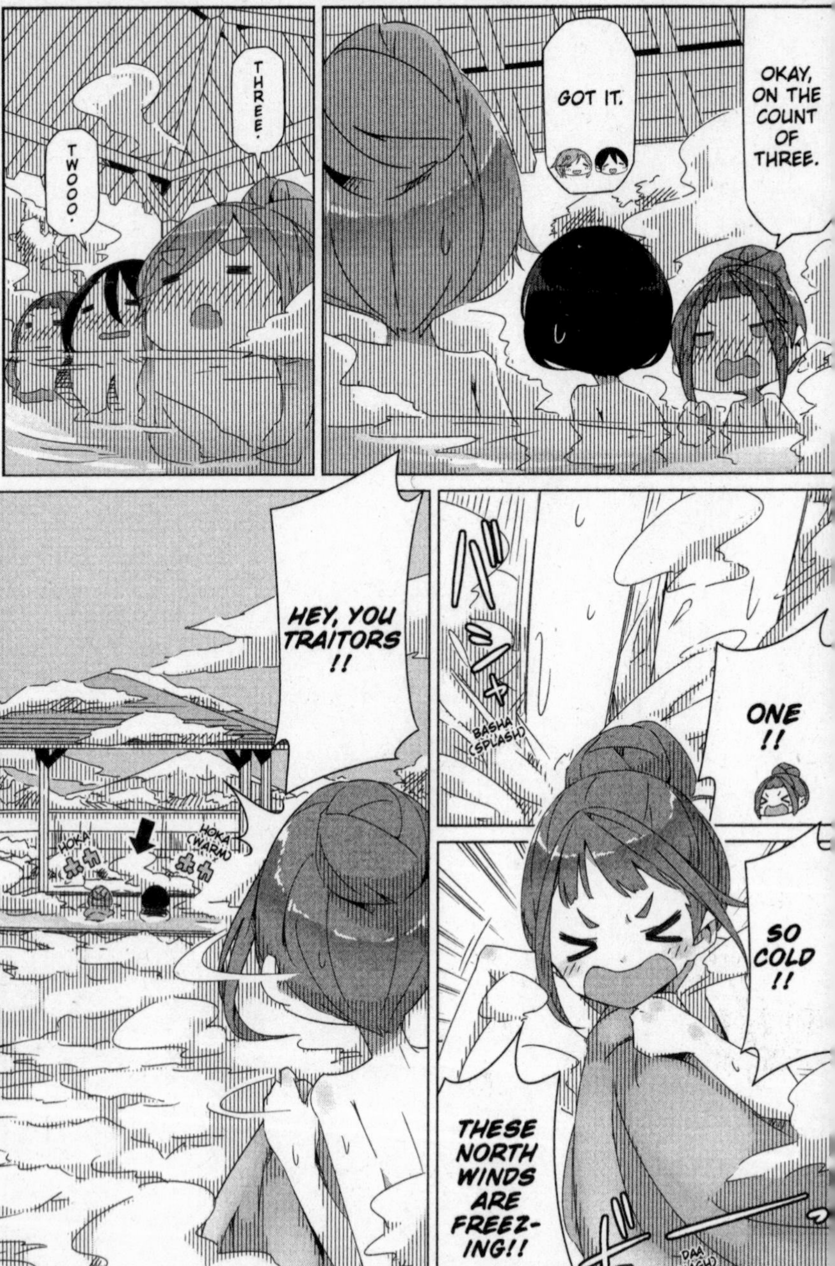
OKAY, ON THE COUNT OF THREE.
GOT IT.
TWOOO.
THREE.
BASHA (SPLASH)
ONE!!
SO COLD!!
THESE NORTH WINDS ARE FREEZ-ING!!
DAA (AAGH)
HEY, YOU TRAITORS!!
HOKA (WARM)
HOKA

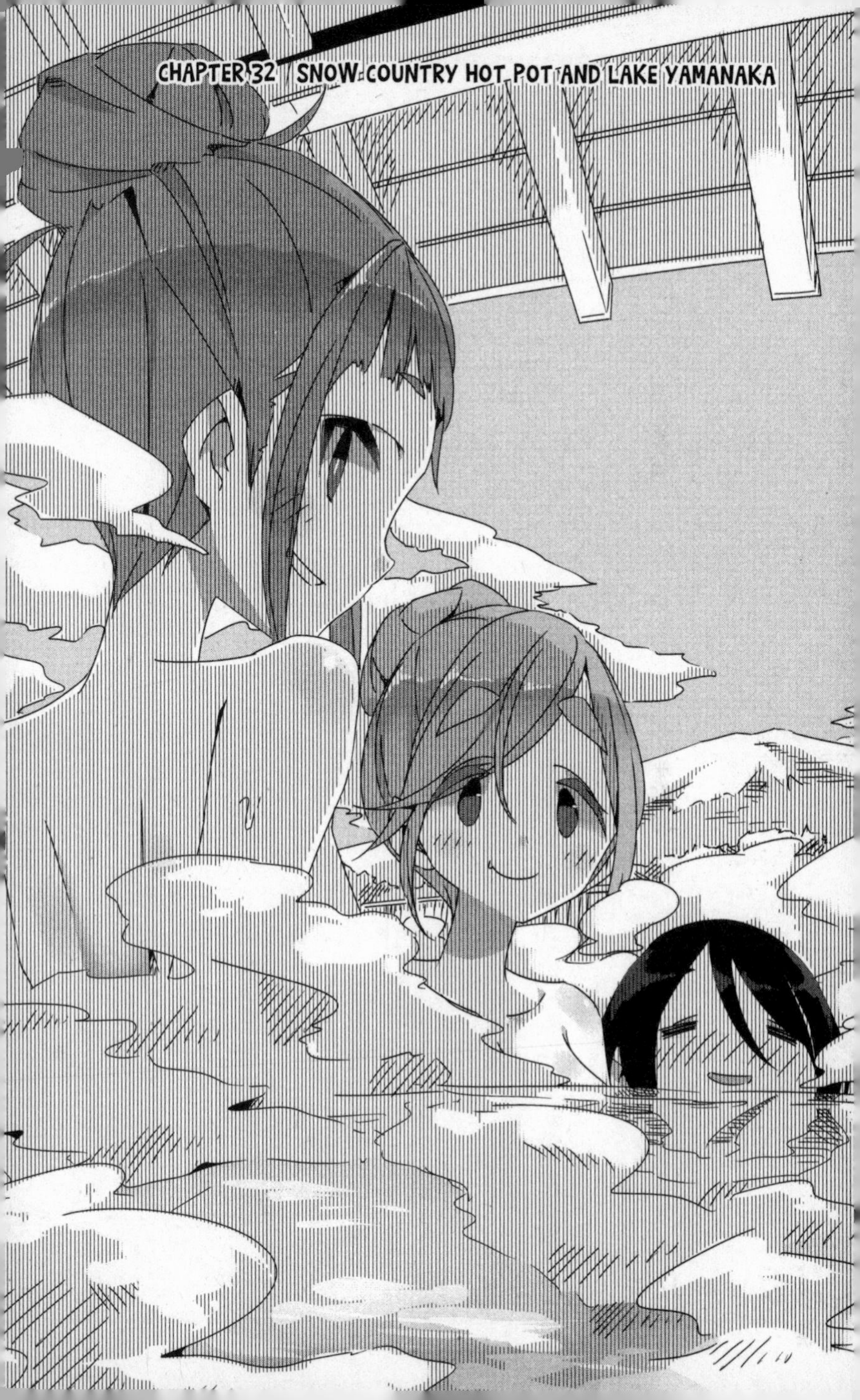
CHAPTER 32 SNOW COUNTRY HOT POT AND LAKE YAMANAKA

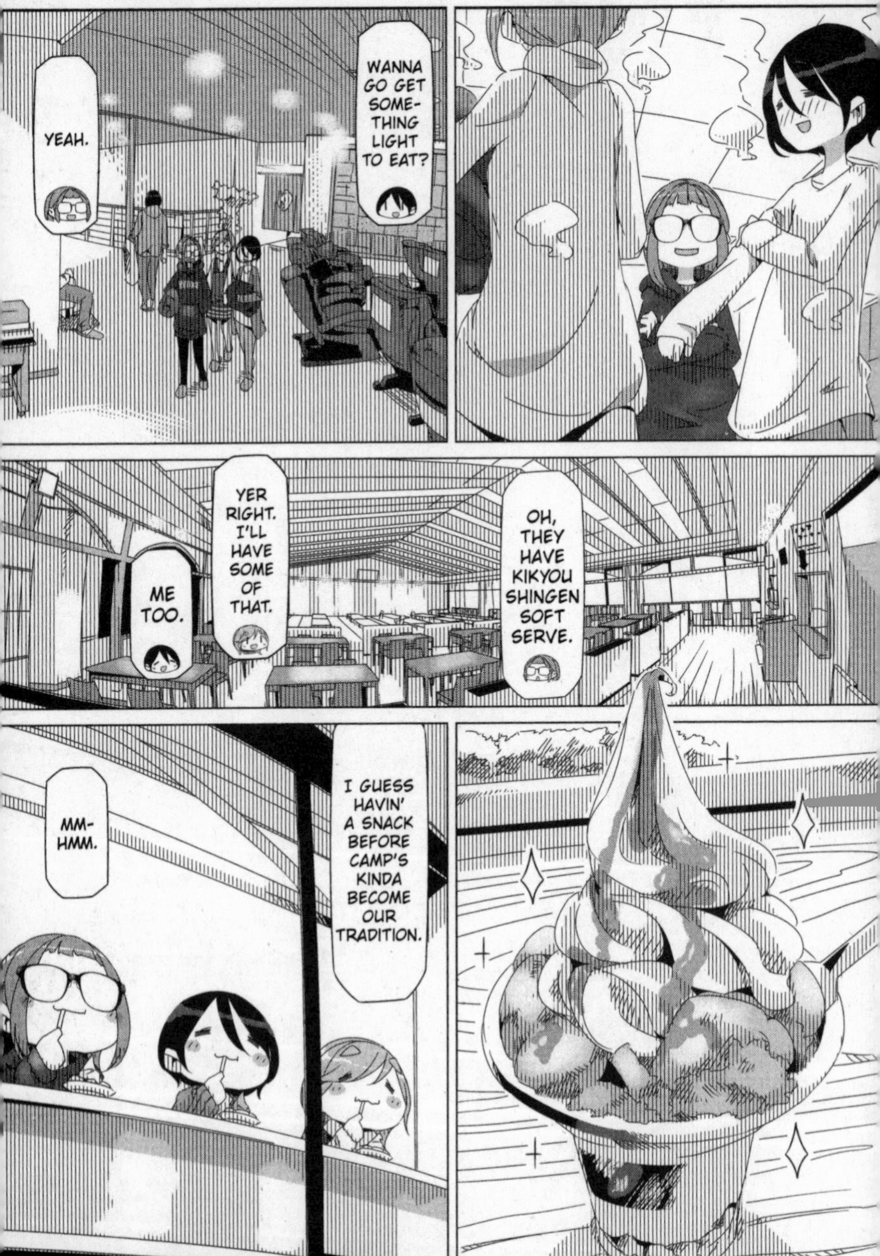
WANNA GO GET SOME-THING LIGHT TO EAT?
YEAH.
OH, THEY HAVE KIKYOU SHINGEN SOFT SERVE.
YER RIGHT. I'LL HAVE SOME OF THAT.
ME TOO.
I GUESS HAVIN' A SNACK BEFORE CAMP'S KINDA BECOME OUR TRADITION.
MM-HMM.

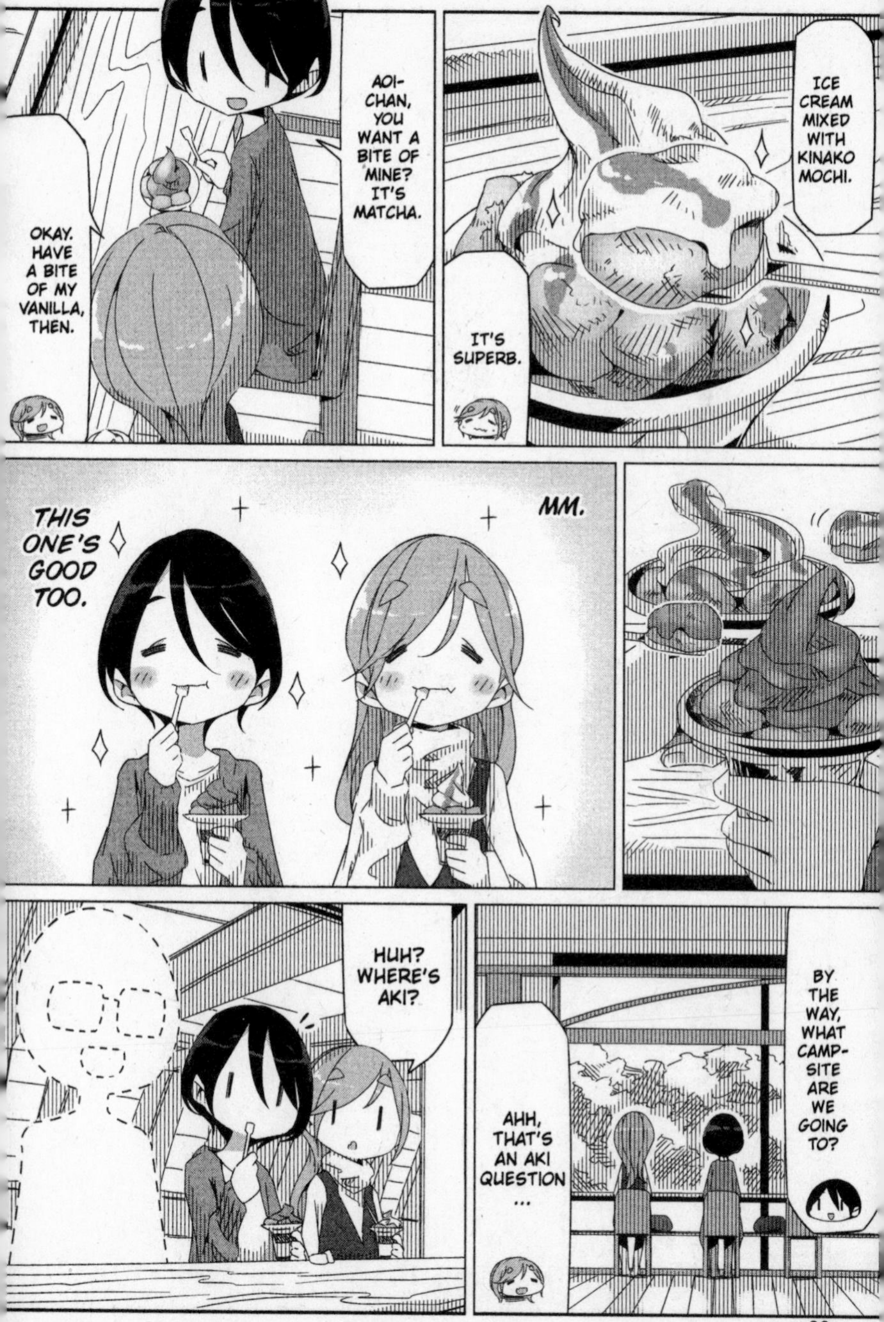
ICE CREAM MIXED WITH KINAKO MOCHI.
IT'S SUPERB.
AOI-CHAN, YOU WANT A BITE OF MINE? IT'S MATCHA.
OKAY. HAVE A BITE OF MY VANILLA, THEN.
MM.
THIS ONE'S GOOD TOO.
BY THE WAY, WHAT CAMPSITE ARE WE GOING TO?
AHH, THAT'S AN AKI QUESTION ...
HUH? WHERE'S AKI?

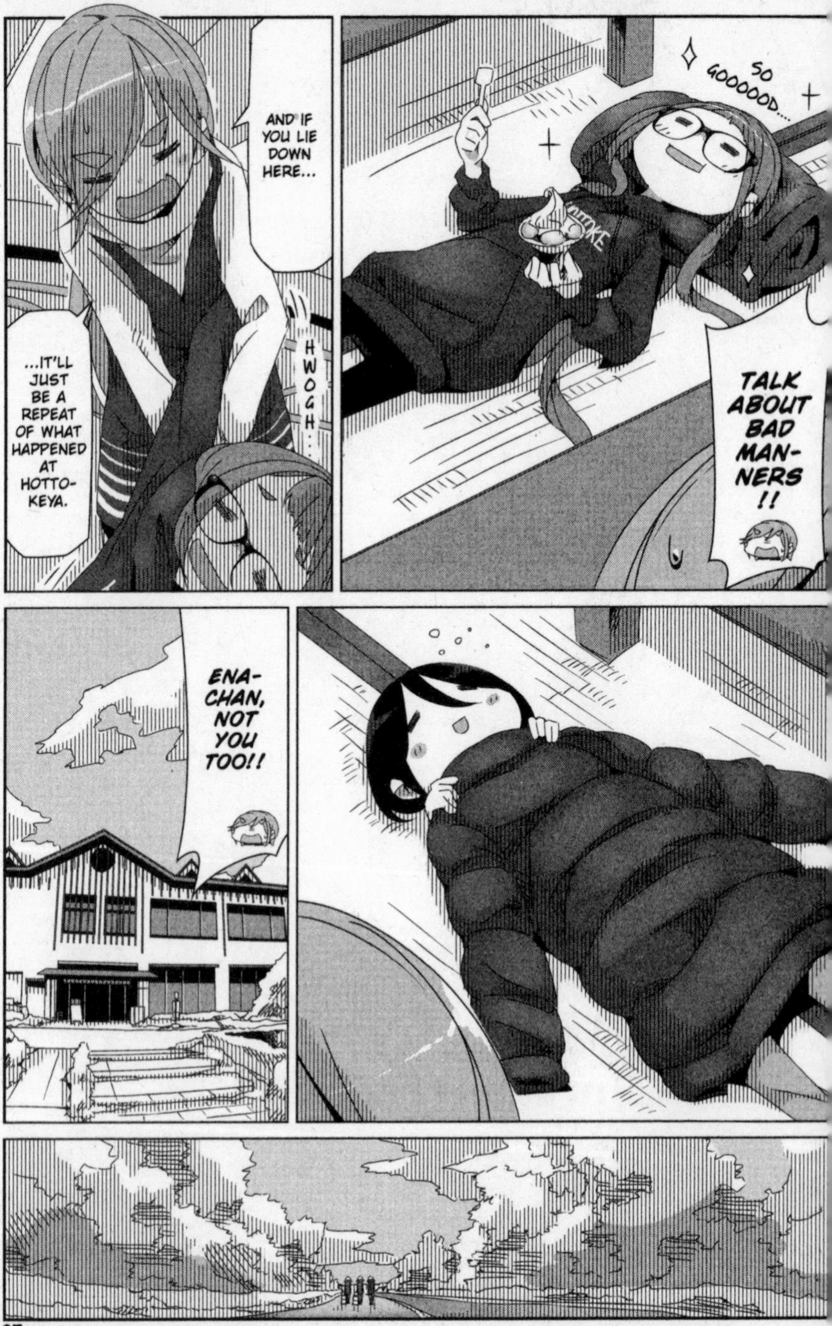
SO GOOOOOD....
TALK ABOUT BAD MAN-NERS!!
AND IF YOU LIE DOWN HERE...
HWOGH...
...IT'LL JUST BE A REPEAT OF WHAT HAPPENED AT HOTTO-KEYA.
ENA-CHAN, NOT YOU TOO!!

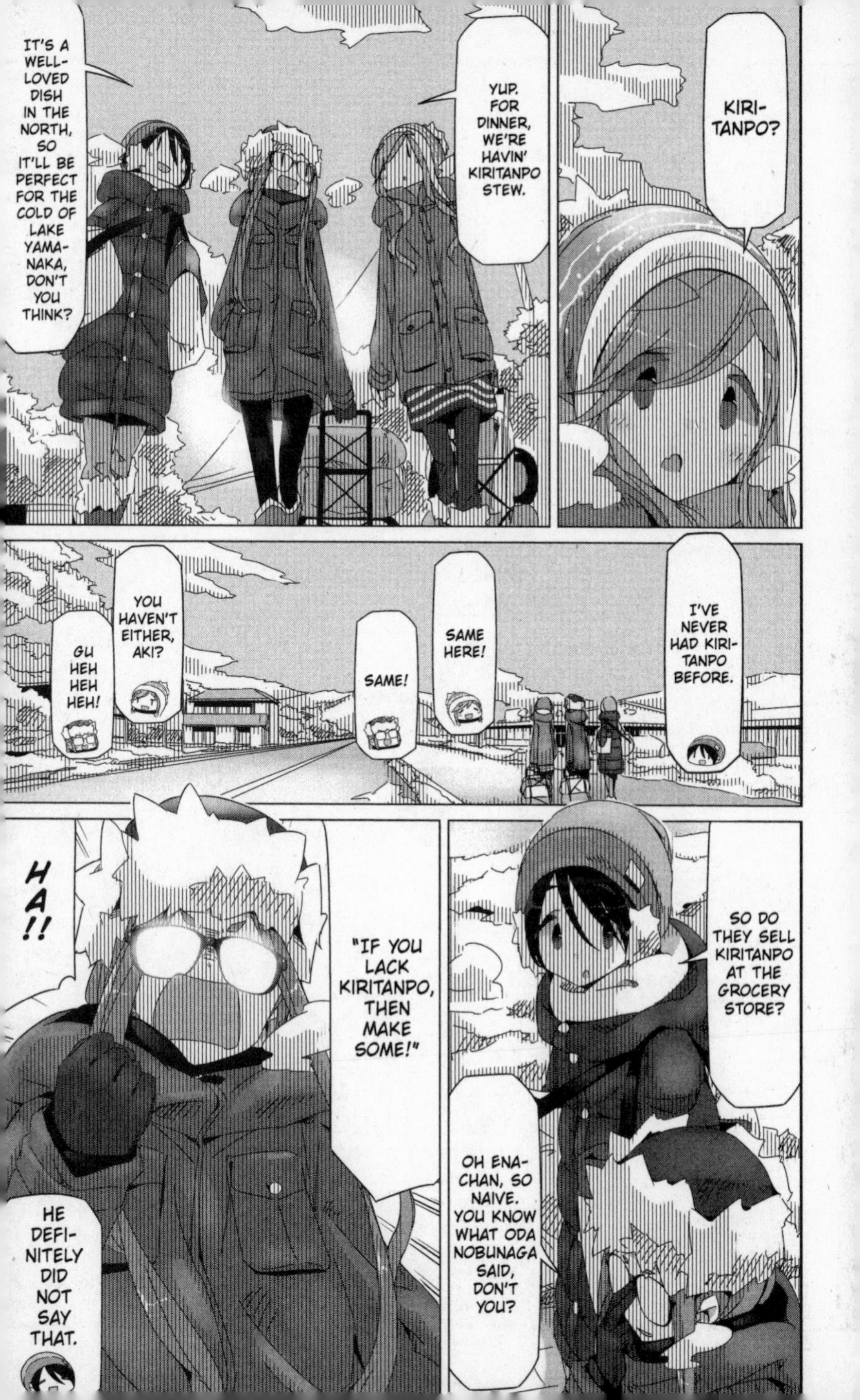
KIRI-TANPO?
YUP. FOR DINNER, WE'RE HAVIN' KIRITANPO STEW.
IT'S A WELL-LOVED DISH IN THE NORTH, SO IT'LL BE PERFECT FOR THE COLD OF LAKE YAMANAKA, DON'T YOU THINK?
I'VE NEVER HAD KIRI-TANPO BEFORE.
SAME HERE!
SAME!
YOU HAVEN'T EITHER, AKI?
GU HEH HEH HEH!
SO DO THEY SELL KIRITANPO AT THE GROCERY STORE?
OH ENA-CHAN, SO NAIVE. YOU KNOW WHAT ODA NOBUNAGA SAID, DON'T YOU?
"IF YOU LACK KIRITANPO, THEN MAKE SOME!"
HA!!
HE DEFINITELY DID NOT SAY THAT.

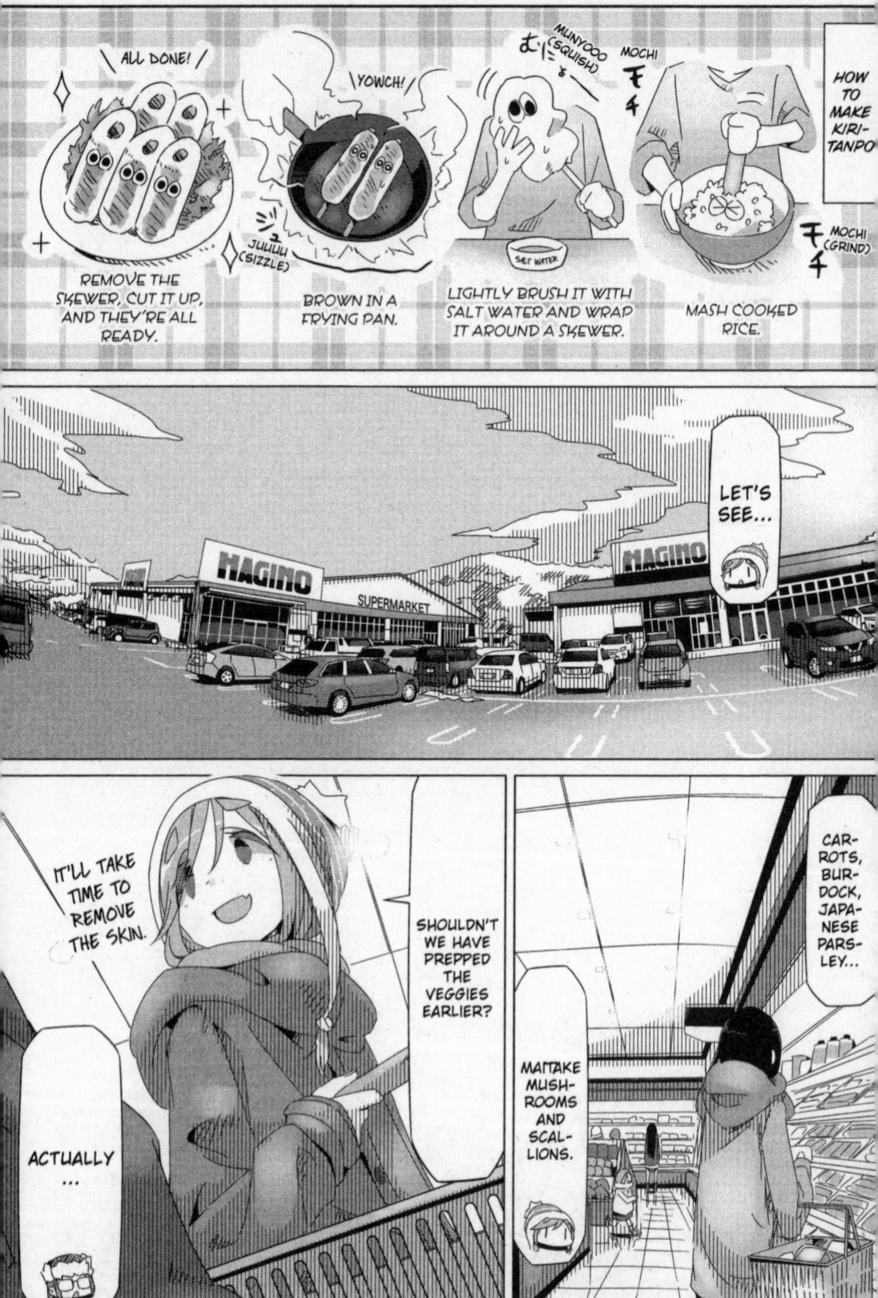
HOW TO MAKE KIRI-TANPO
MOCHI
MOCHI (GRIND)
MASH COOKED RICE.
MUNYOOO (SQUISH)
SALT WATER
LIGHTLY BRUSH IT WITH SALT WATER AND WRAP IT AROUND A SKEWER.
YOWCH!
JUUUU (SIZZLE)
BROWN IN A FRYING PAN.
ALL DONE!
REMOVE THE SKEWER, CUT IT UP, AND THEY'RE ALL READY.
LET'S SEE...
MAGINO
MAGINO
SUPERMARKET
CAR-ROTS, BUR-DOCK, JAPA-NESE PARS-LEY...
MAITAKE MUSH-ROOMS AND SCAL-LIONS.
SHOULDN'T WE HAVE PREPPED THE VEGGIES EARLIER?
IT'LL TAKE TIME TO REMOVE THE SKIN.
ACTUALLY...

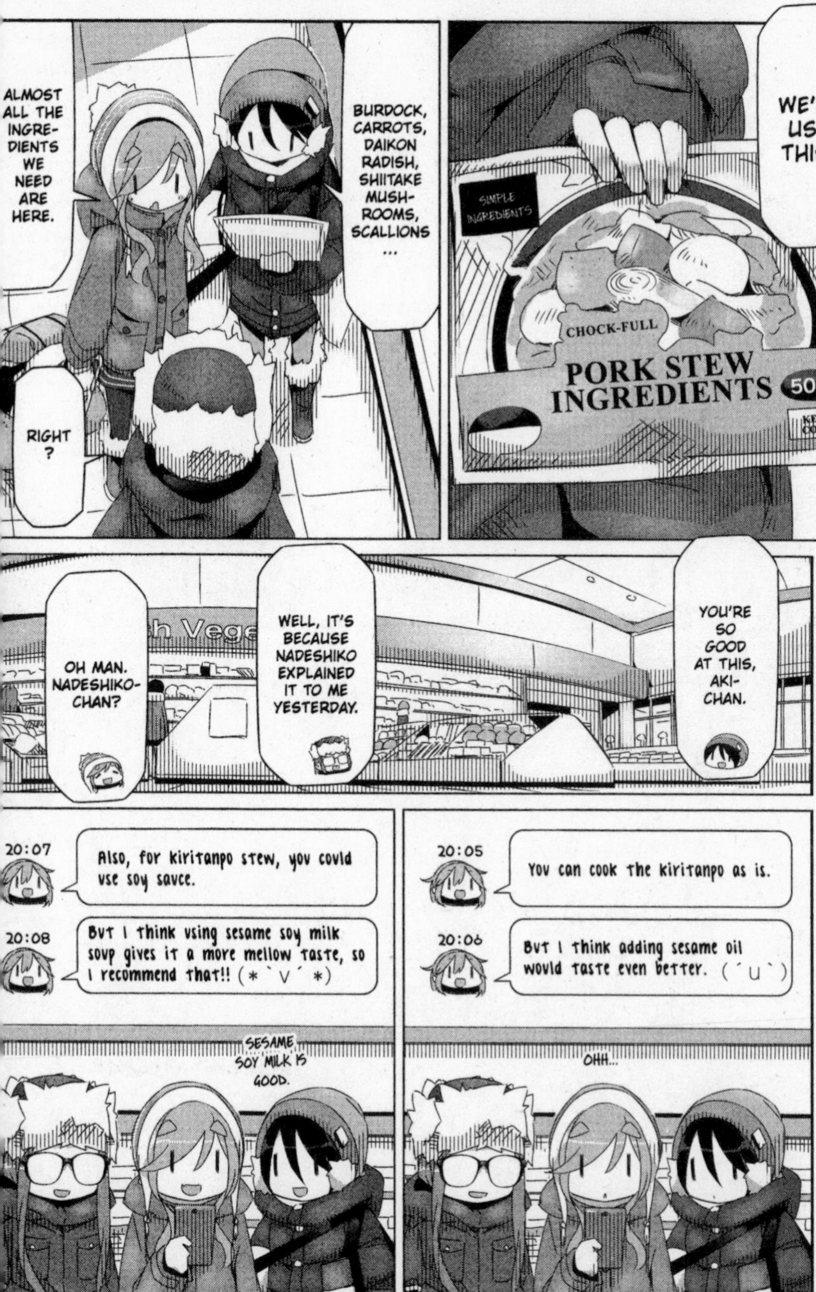
WE'LL USE THIS.
SIMPLE INGREDIENTS
CHOCK-FULL
PORK STEW INGREDIENTS
500g
KEEP COOL
BURDOCK, CARROTS, DAIKON RADISH, SHIITAKE MUSHROOMS, SCALLIONS...
ALMOST ALL THE INGREDIENTS WE NEED ARE HERE.
RIGHT?
YOU'RE SO GOOD AT THIS, AKI-CHAN.
WELL, IT'S BECAUSE NADESHIKO EXPLAINED IT TO ME YESTERDAY.
OH MAN. NADESHIKO-CHAN?
20:05
You can cook the kiritanpo as is.
20:06
But I think adding sesame oil would taste even better. (´u`)
20:07
Also, for kiritanpo stew, you could use soy sauce.
20:08
But I think using sesame soy milk soup gives it a more mellow taste, so I recommend that!! (*`v´*)
OHH...
SESAME SOY MILK IS GOOD.

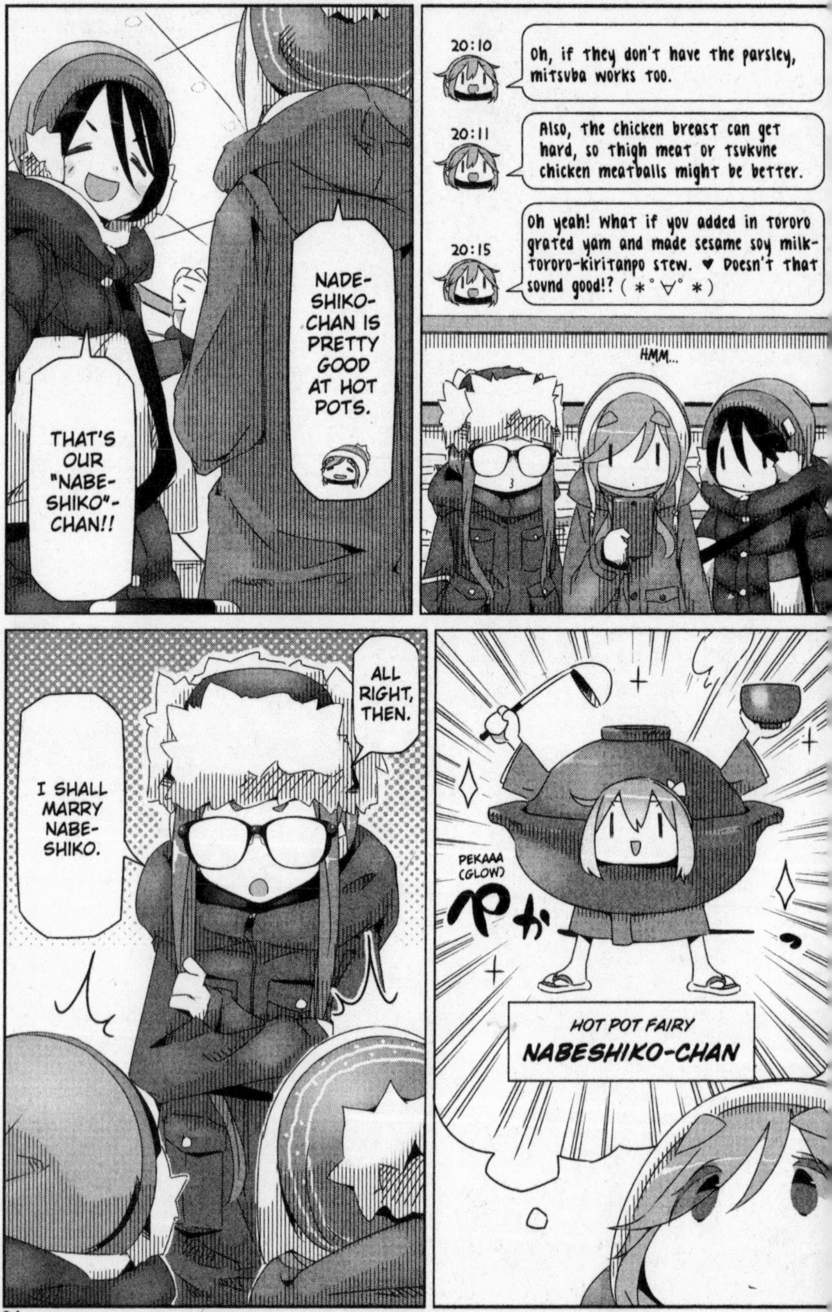
20:10
Oh, if they don't have the parsley, mitsuba works too.
20:11
Also, the chicken breast can get hard, so thigh meat or tsukune chicken meatballs might be better.
20:15
Oh yeah! What if you added in tororo grated yam and made sesame soy milk-tororo-kiritanpo stew. ♥ Doesn't that sound good!? (*°∀°*)
HMM...
NADE-SHIKO-CHAN IS PRETTY GOOD AT HOT POTS.
THAT'S OUR "NABE-SHIKO"-CHAN!!
PEKAAA (GLOW)
HOT POT FAIRY
NABESHIKO-CHAN
ALL RIGHT, THEN.
I SHALL MARRY NABE-SHIKO.

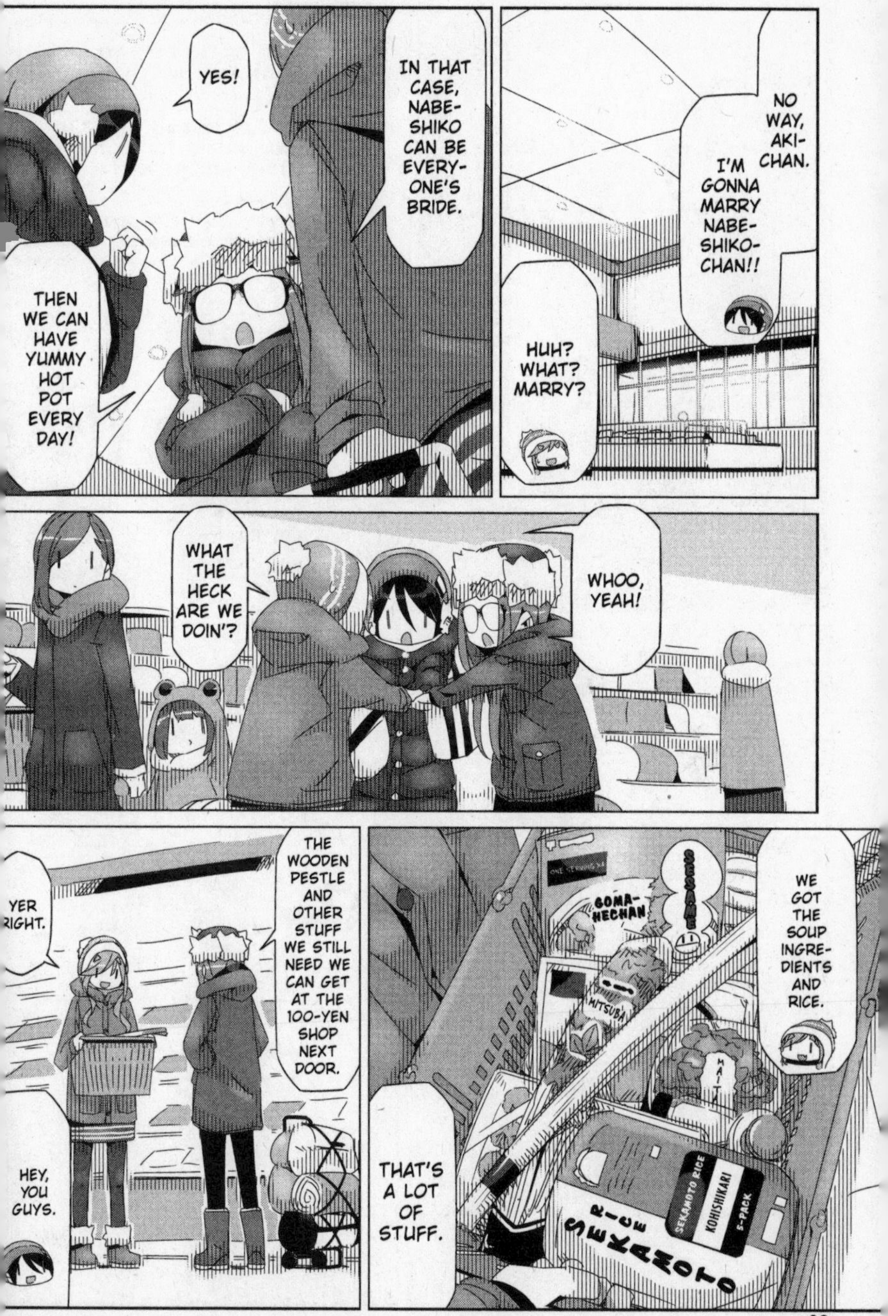

NO WAY, AKI-CHAN.
I'M GONNA MARRY NABE-SHIKO-CHAN!!
HUH? WHAT? MARRY?
IN THAT CASE, NABE-SHIKO CAN BE EVERY-ONE'S BRIDE.
YES!
THEN WE CAN HAVE YUMMY HOT POT EVERY DAY!
WHOO, YEAH!
WHAT THE HECK ARE WE DOIN'?
WE GOT THE SOUP INGRE-DIENTS AND RICE.
SESAME
GOMA-HECHAN
MITSUBA
SEKAMOTO RICE
KOHISHIKARI
5-PACK
RICE
SEKAMOTO
THAT'S A LOT OF STUFF.
THE WOODEN PESTLE AND OTHER STUFF WE STILL NEED WE CAN GET AT THE 100-YEN SHOP NEXT DOOR.
YER RIGHT.
HEY, YOU GUYS.

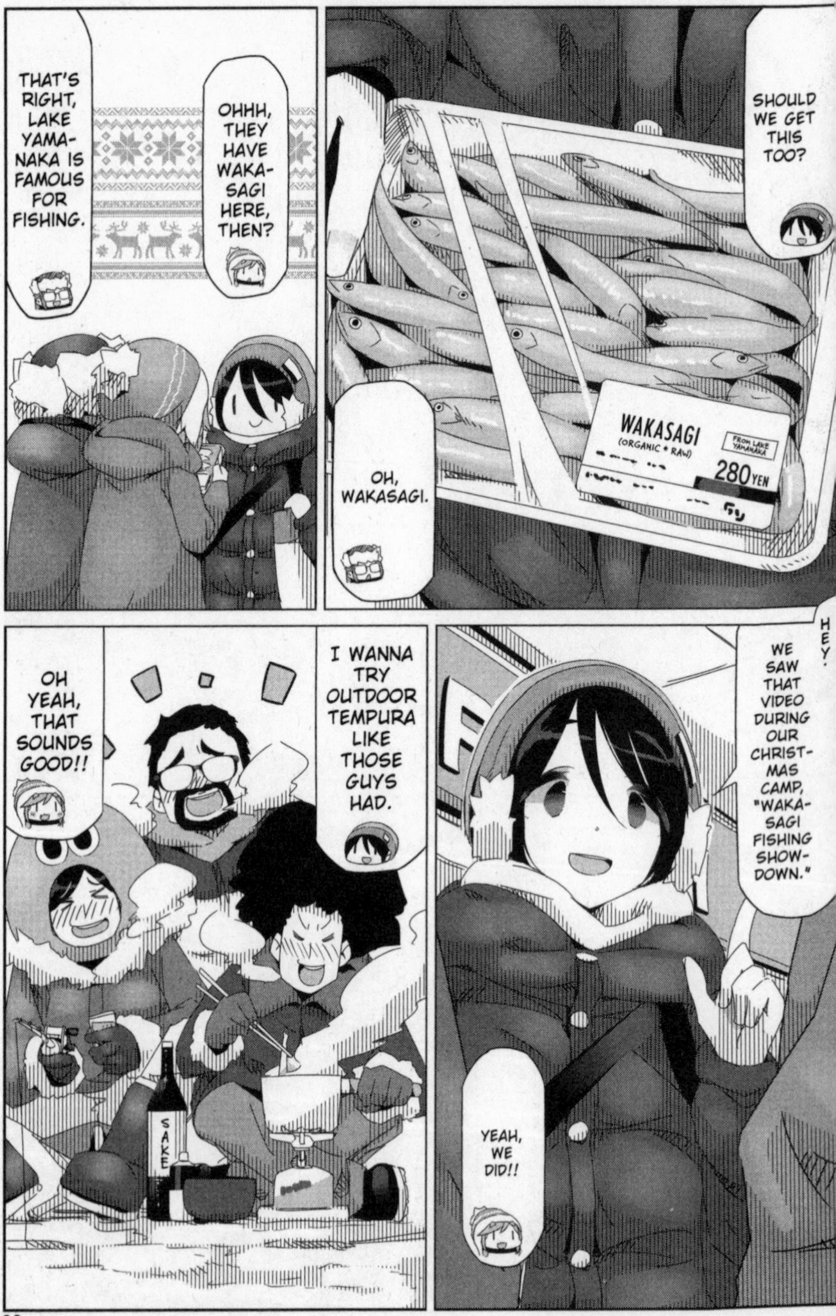
SHOULD WE GET THIS TOO?
WAKASAGI
(ORGANIC + RAW)
FROM LAKE YAMANAKA
280YEN
OH, WAKASAGI.
OHHH, THEY HAVE WAKASAGI HERE, THEN?
THAT'S RIGHT, LAKE YAMANAKA IS FAMOUS FOR FISHING.
HEY.
WE SAW THAT VIDEO DURING OUR CHRISTMAS CAMP, "WAKASAGI FISHING SHOWDOWN."
YEAH, WE DID!!
I WANNA TRY OUTDOOR TEMPURA LIKE THOSE GUYS HAD.
OH YEAH, THAT SOUNDS GOOD!!
SAKE

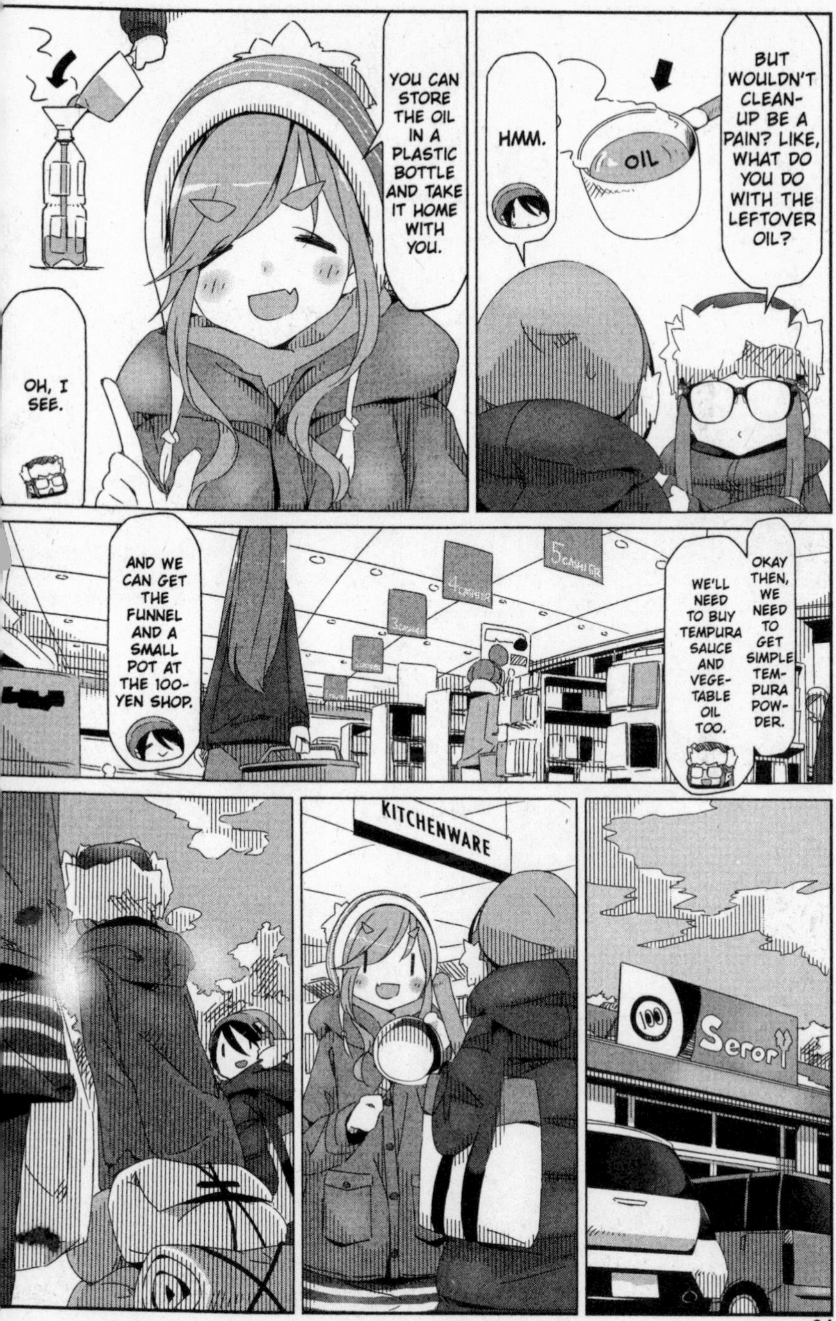
BUT WOULDN'T CLEAN-UP BE A PAIN? LIKE, WHAT DO YOU DO WITH THE LEFTOVER OIL?
OIL
HMM.
YOU CAN STORE THE OIL IN A PLASTIC BOTTLE AND TAKE IT HOME WITH YOU.
OH, I SEE.
OKAY THEN, WE NEED TO GET SIMPLE TEMPURA POWDER.
WE'LL NEED TO BUY TEMPURA SAUCE AND VEGETABLE OIL TOO.
AND WE CAN GET THE FUNNEL AND A SMALL POT AT THE 100-YEN SHOP.
100
KITCHENWARE

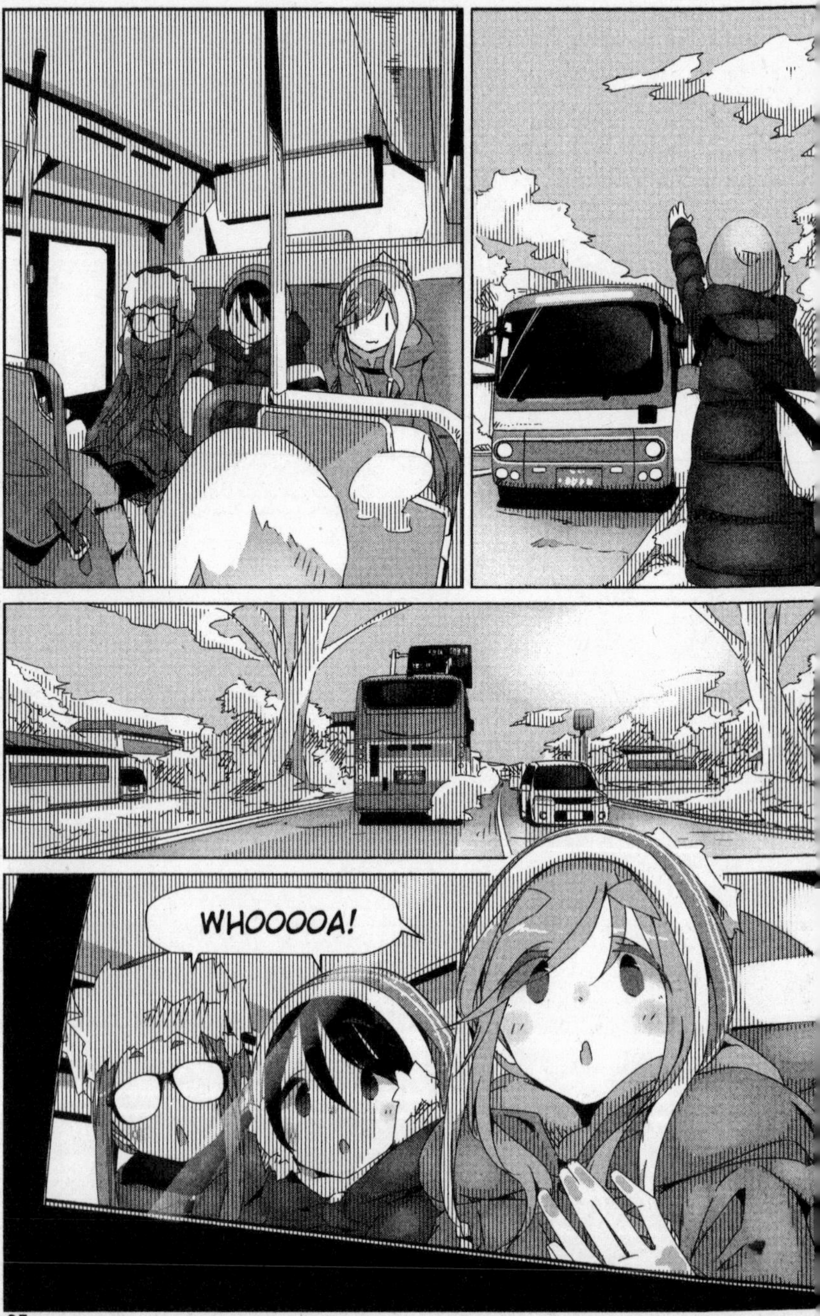
WHOOOOA!

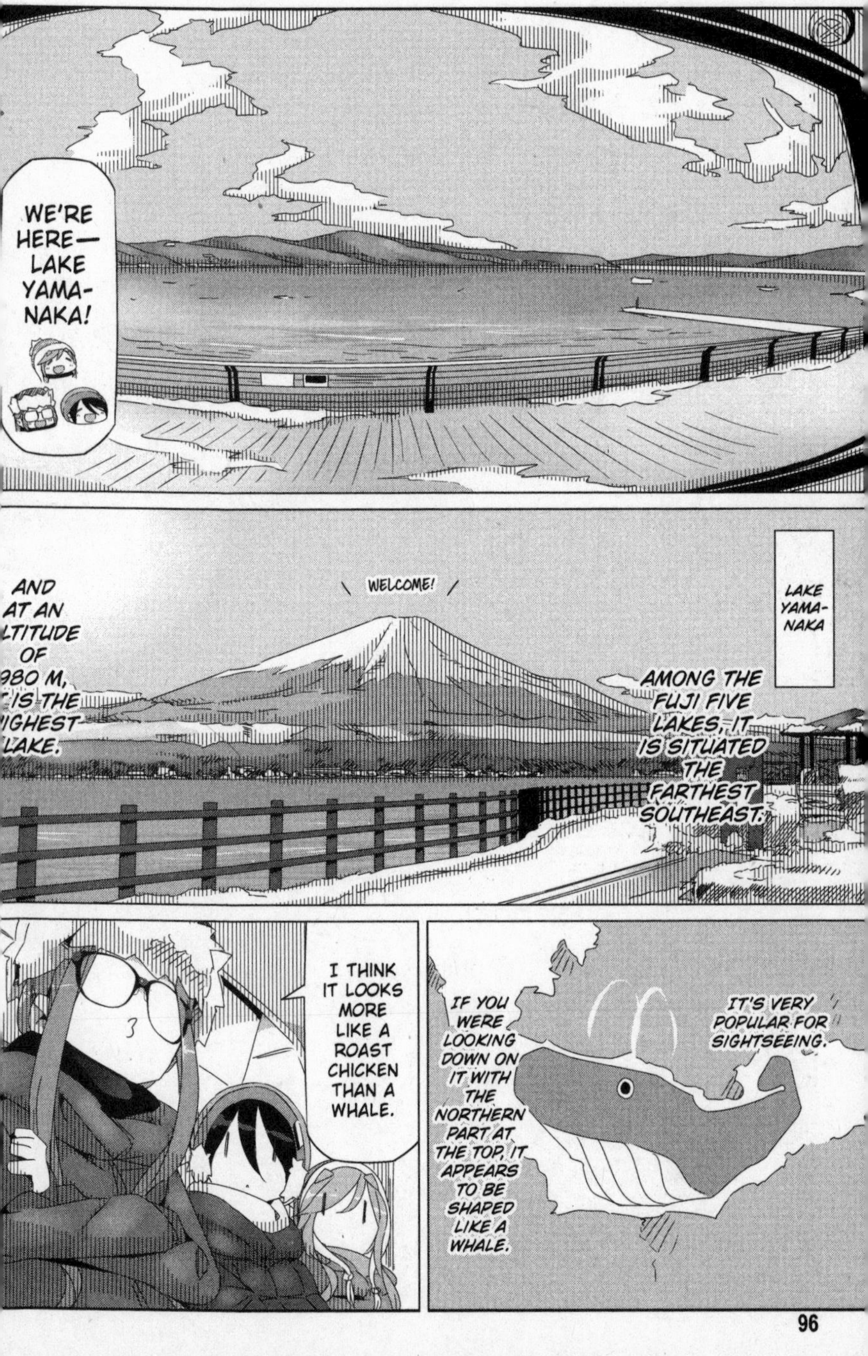
WE'RE HERE—LAKE YAMANAKA!
LAKE YAMANAKA
AMONG THE FUJI FIVE LAKES, IT IS SITUATED THE FARTHEST SOUTHEAST.
WELCOME!
AND AT AN LTITUDE OF 980 M, T IS THE IGHEST LAKE.
IT'S VERY POPULAR FOR SIGHTSEEING.
IF YOU WERE LOOKING DOWN ON IT WITH THE NORTHERN PART AT THE TOP, IT APPEARS TO BE SHAPED LIKE A WHALE.
I THINK IT LOOKS MORE LIKE A ROAST CHICKEN THAN A WHALE.

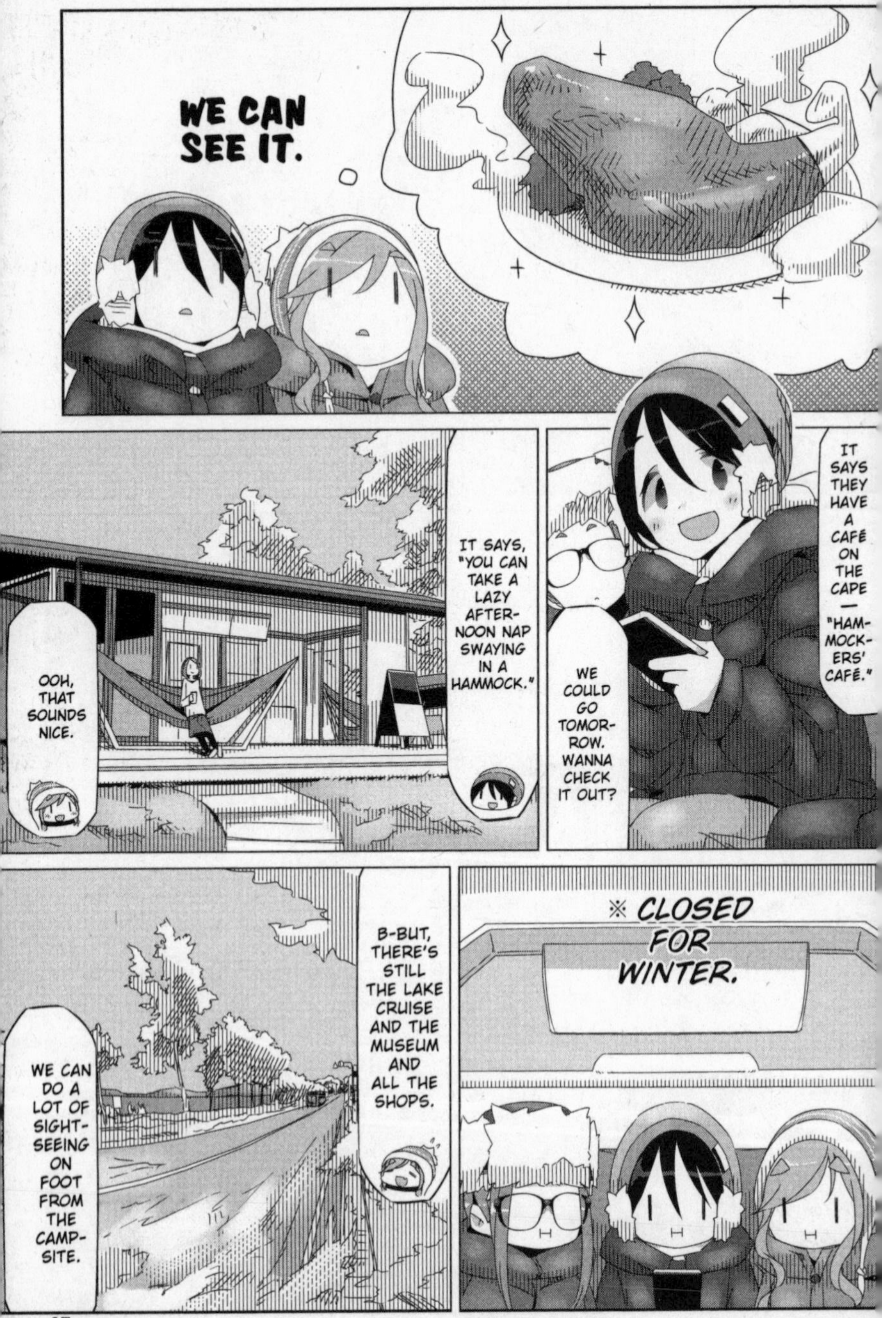
WE CAN SEE IT.
IT SAYS THEY HAVE A CAFÉ ON THE CAPE — "HAMMOCKERS' CAFÉ."
WE COULD GO TOMORROW. WANNA CHECK IT OUT?
IT SAYS, "YOU CAN TAKE A LAZY AFTERNOON NAP SWAYING IN A HAMMOCK."
OOH, THAT SOUNDS NICE.
※ CLOSED FOR WINTER.
B-BUT, THERE'S STILL THE LAKE CRUISE AND THE MUSEUM AND ALL THE SHOPS.
WE CAN DO A LOT OF SIGHTSEEING ON FOOT FROM THE CAMPSITE.

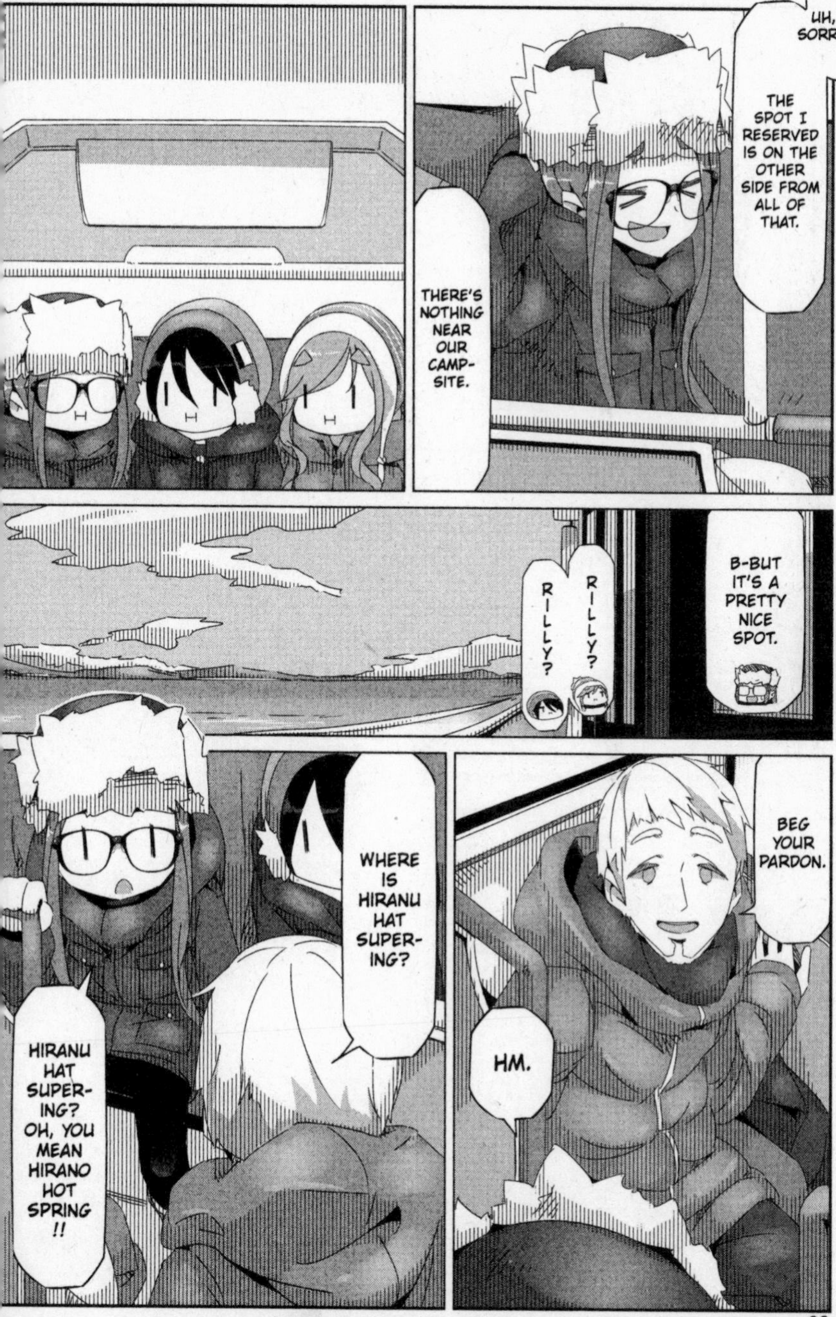
UH, SORRY.
THE SPOT I RESERVED IS ON THE OTHER SIDE FROM ALL OF THAT.
THERE'S NOTHING NEAR OUR CAMP-SITE.
B-BUT IT'S A PRETTY NICE SPOT.
RILLY?
RILLY?
BEG YOUR PARDON.
HM.
WHERE IS HIRANU HAT SUPER-ING?
HIRANU HAT SUPER-ING? OH, YOU MEAN HIRANO HOT SPRING!!

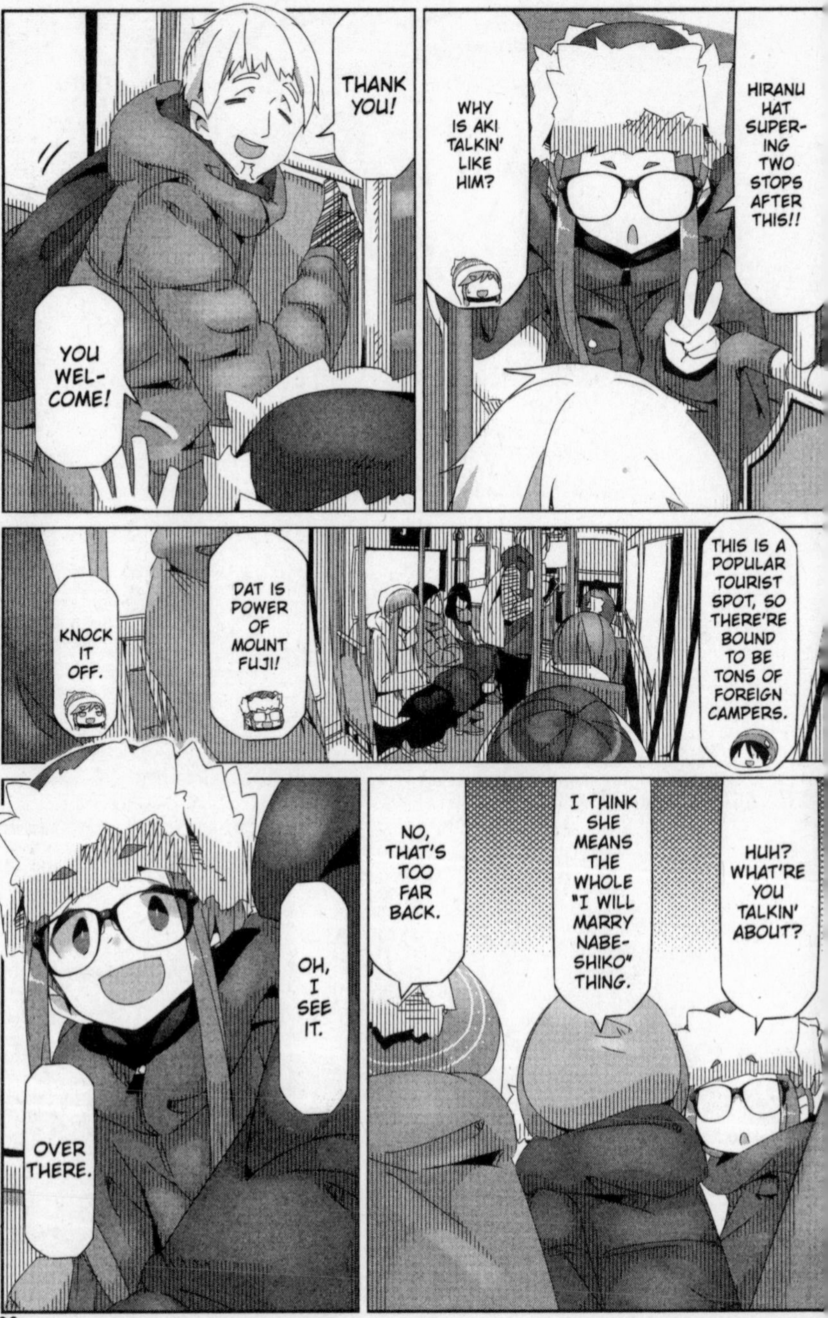
HIRANU HAT SUPER-ING TWO STOPS AFTER THIS!!
WHY IS AKI TALKIN' LIKE HIM?
THANK YOU!
YOU WEL-COME!
THIS IS A POPULAR TOURIST SPOT, SO THERE'RE BOUND TO BE TONS OF FOREIGN CAMPERS.
DAT IS POWER OF MOUNT FUJI!
KNOCK IT OFF.
HUH? WHAT'RE YOU TALKIN' ABOUT?
I THINK SHE MEANS THE WHOLE "I WILL MARRY NABE-SHIKO" THING.
NO, THAT'S TOO FAR BACK.
OH, I SEE IT.
OVER THERE.

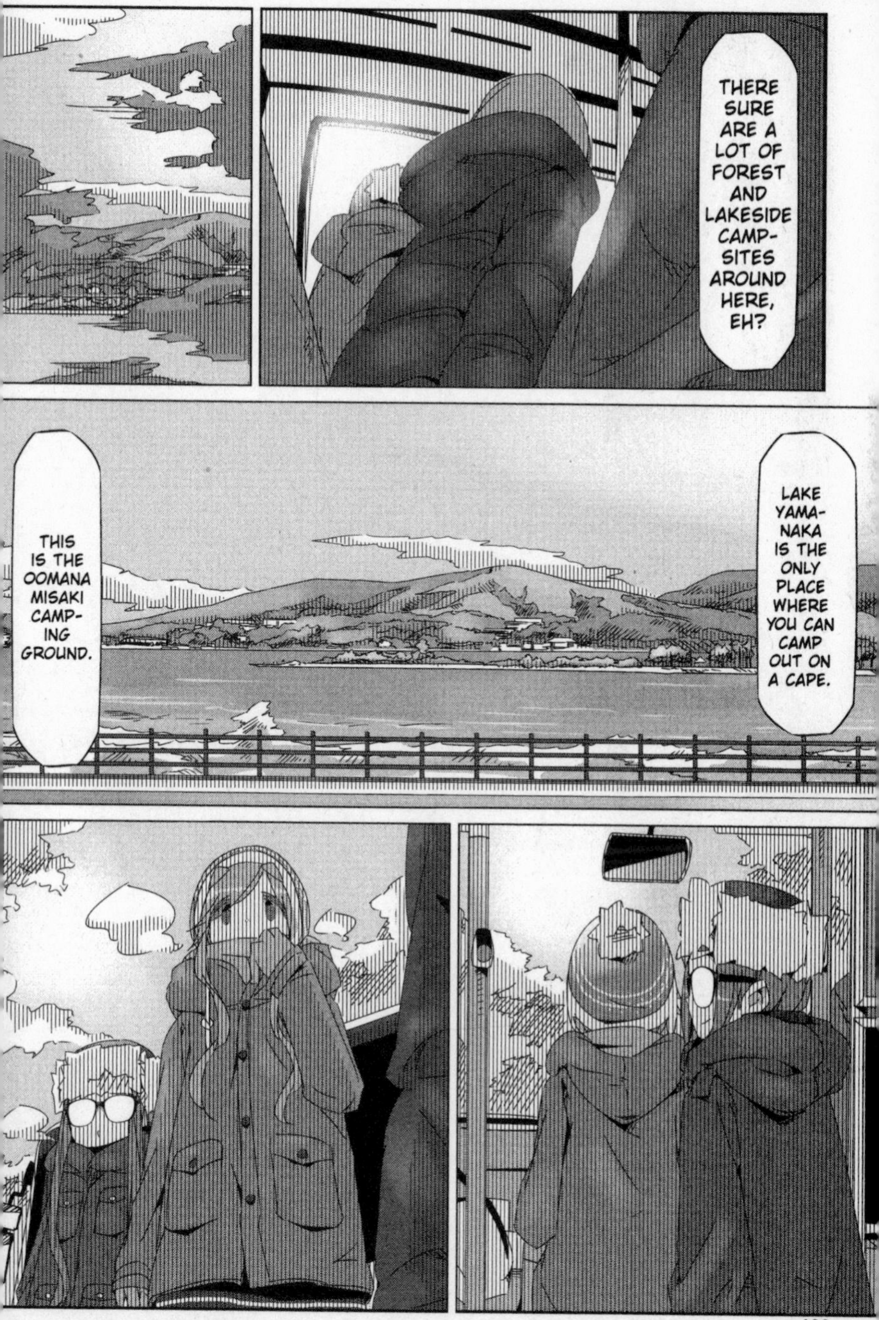
THERE SURE ARE A LOT OF FOREST AND LAKESIDE CAMP-SITES AROUND HERE, EH?
LAKE YAMA-NAKA IS THE ONLY PLACE WHERE YOU CAN CAMP OUT ON A CAPE.
THIS IS THE OOMANA MISAKI CAMP-ING GROUND.

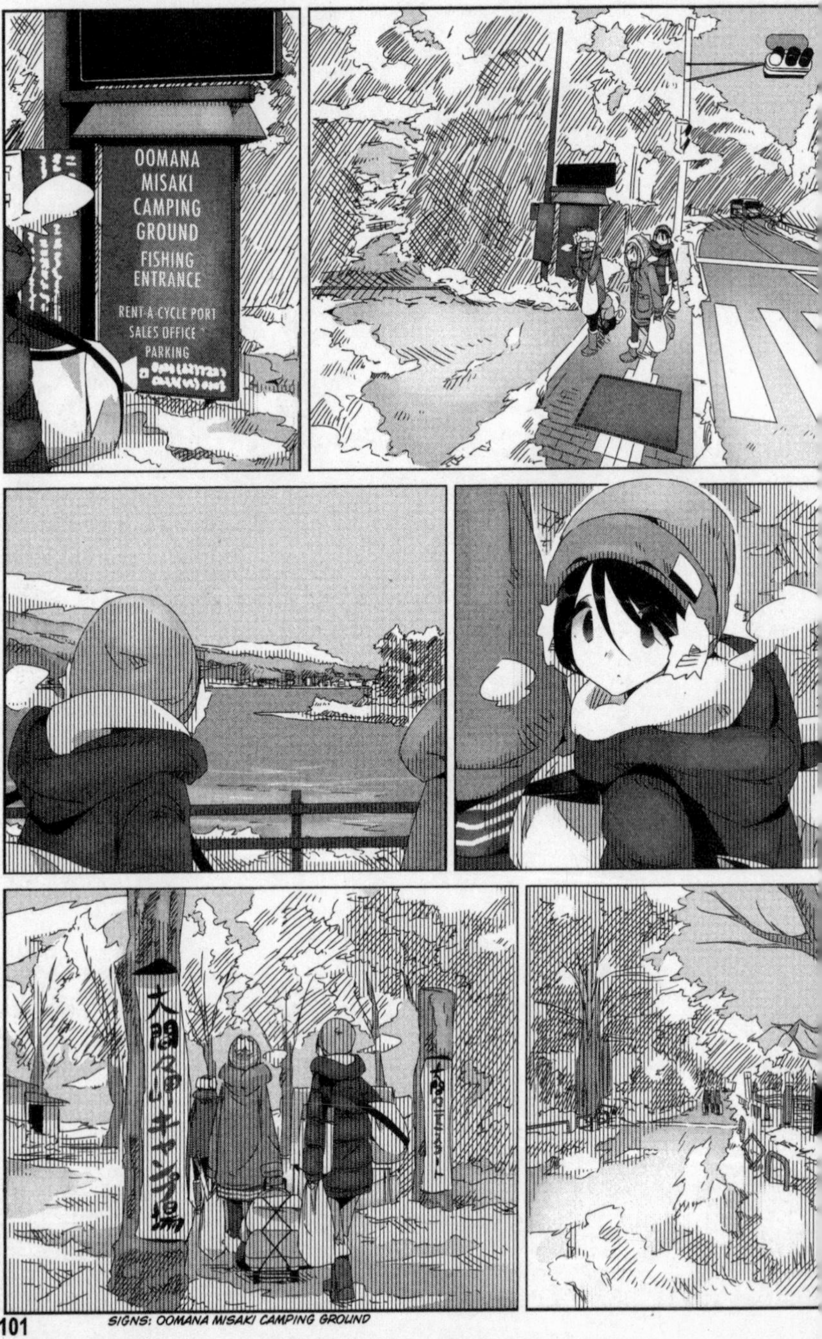
OOMANA
MISAKI
CAMPING
GROUND
FISHING
ENTRANCE
RENT-A-CYCLE PORT
SALES OFFICE
PARKING

SIGNS: OOMANA MISAKI CAMPING GROUND

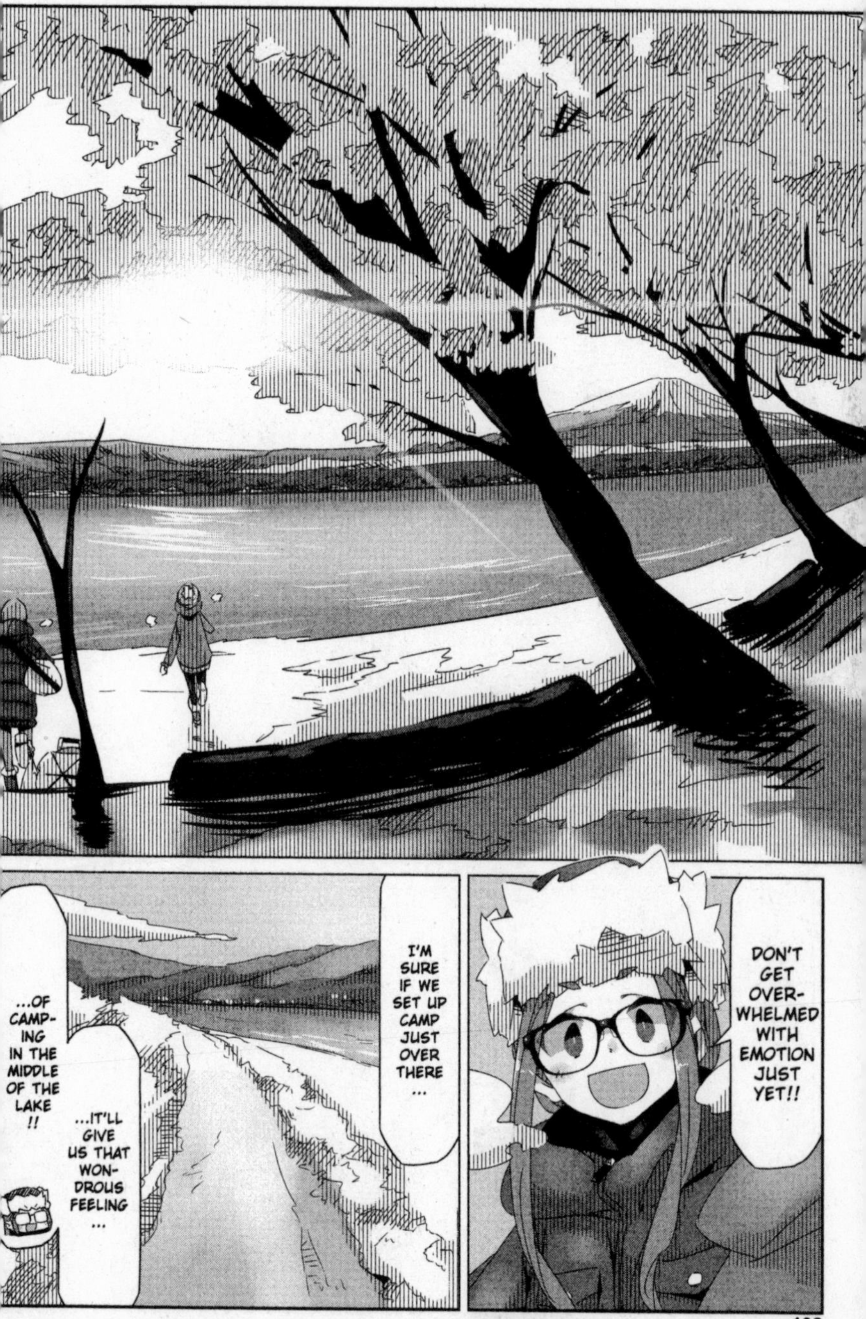
DON'T GET OVER-WHELMED WITH EMOTION JUST YET!!
I'M SURE IF WE SET UP CAMP JUST OVER THERE...
...IT'LL GIVE US THAT WON-DROUS FEELING...
...OF CAMP-ING IN THE MIDDLE OF THE LAKE!!

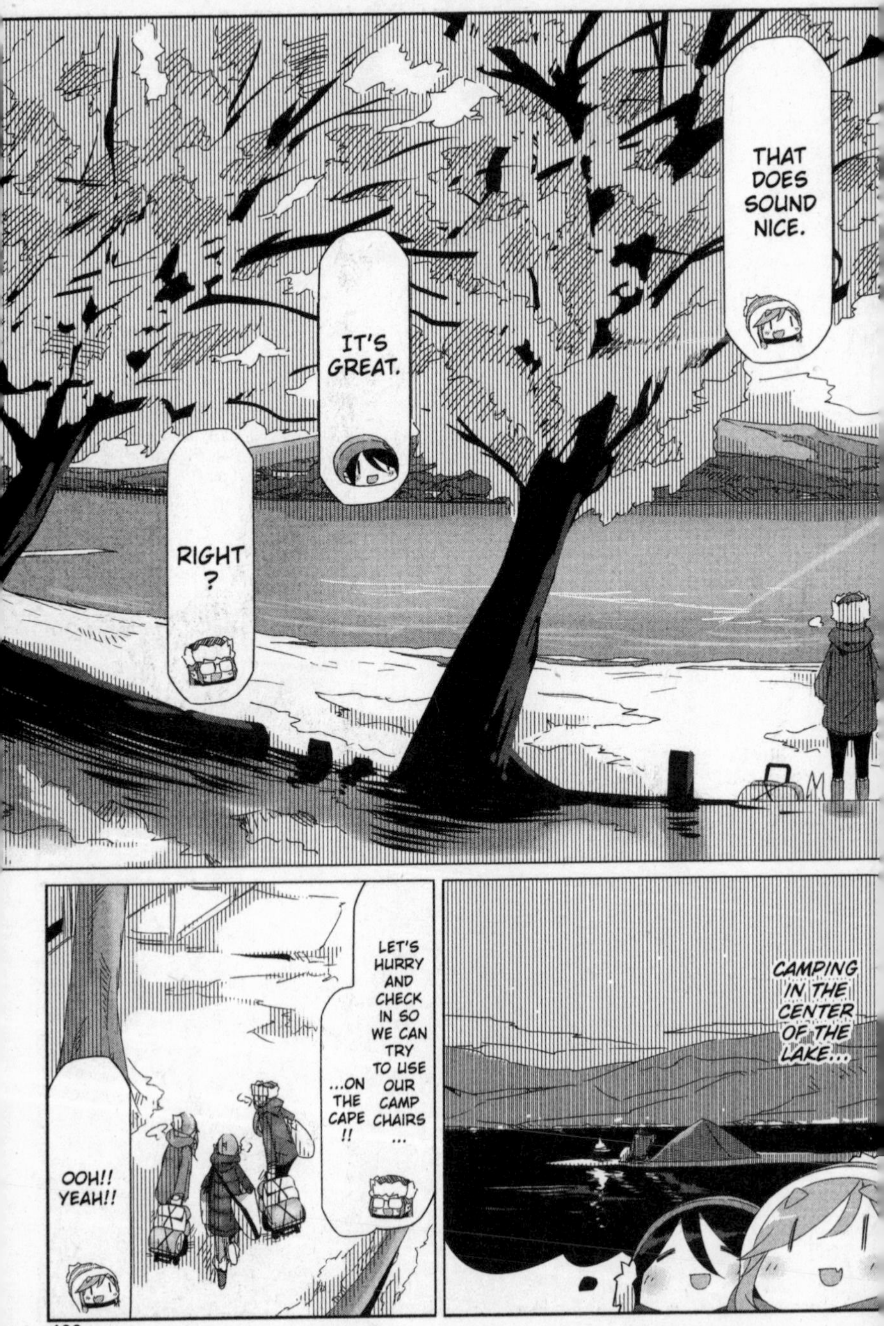
THAT DOES SOUND NICE.
IT'S GREAT.
RIGHT?
CAMPING IN THE CENTER OF THE LAKE...
LET'S HURRY AND CHECK IN SO WE CAN TRY TO USE OUR CAMP CHAIRS...
...ON THE CAPE!!
OOH!! YEAH!!

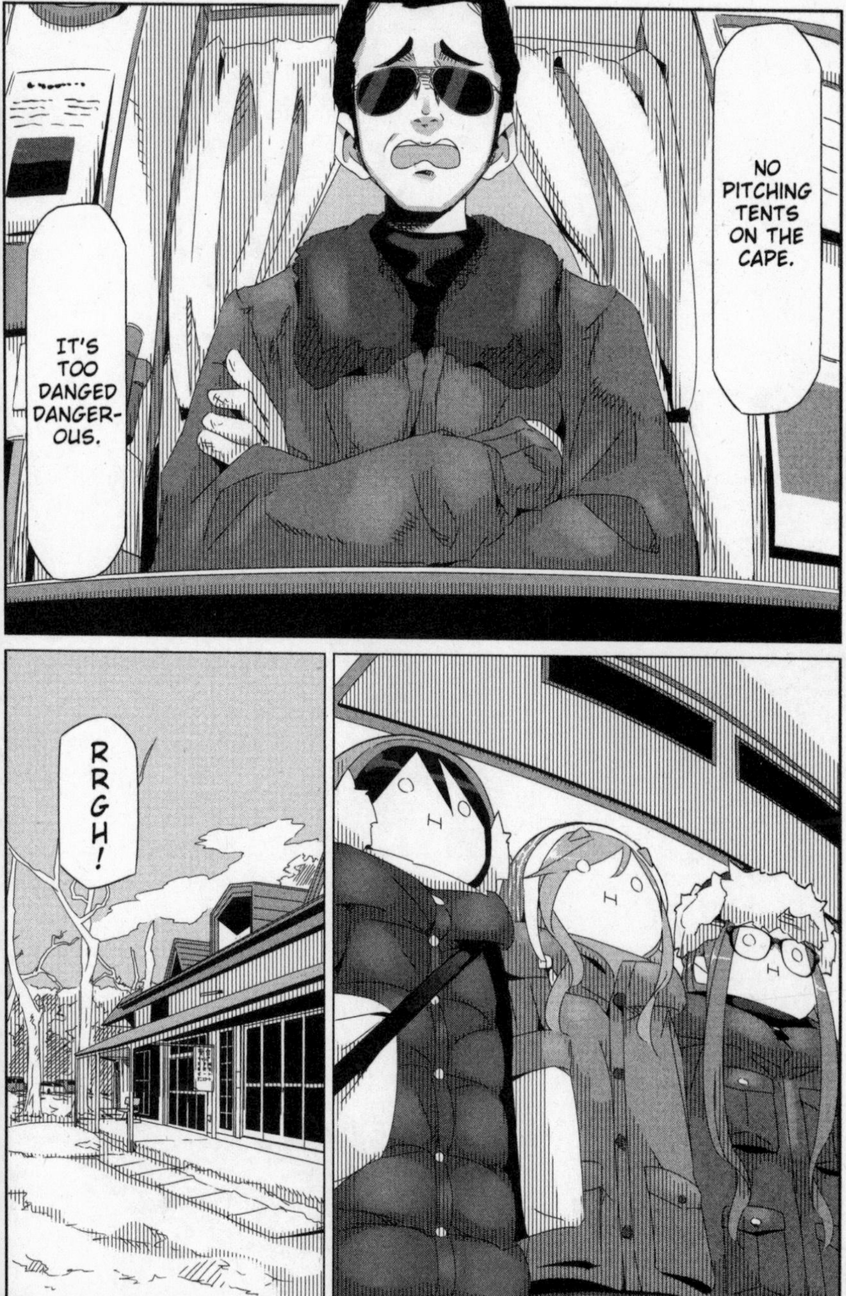
NO PITCHING TENTS ON THE CAPE.
IT'S TOO DANGED DANGER-OUS.
RRGH!

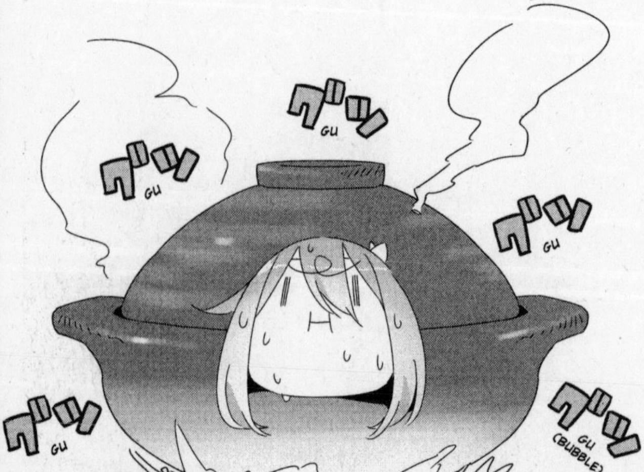
グツ
GU
グツ
GU
グツ
GU
グツ
GU
(BUBBLE)
グツ
GU

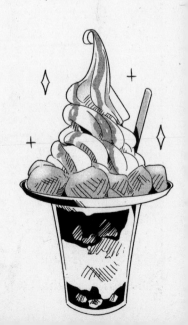

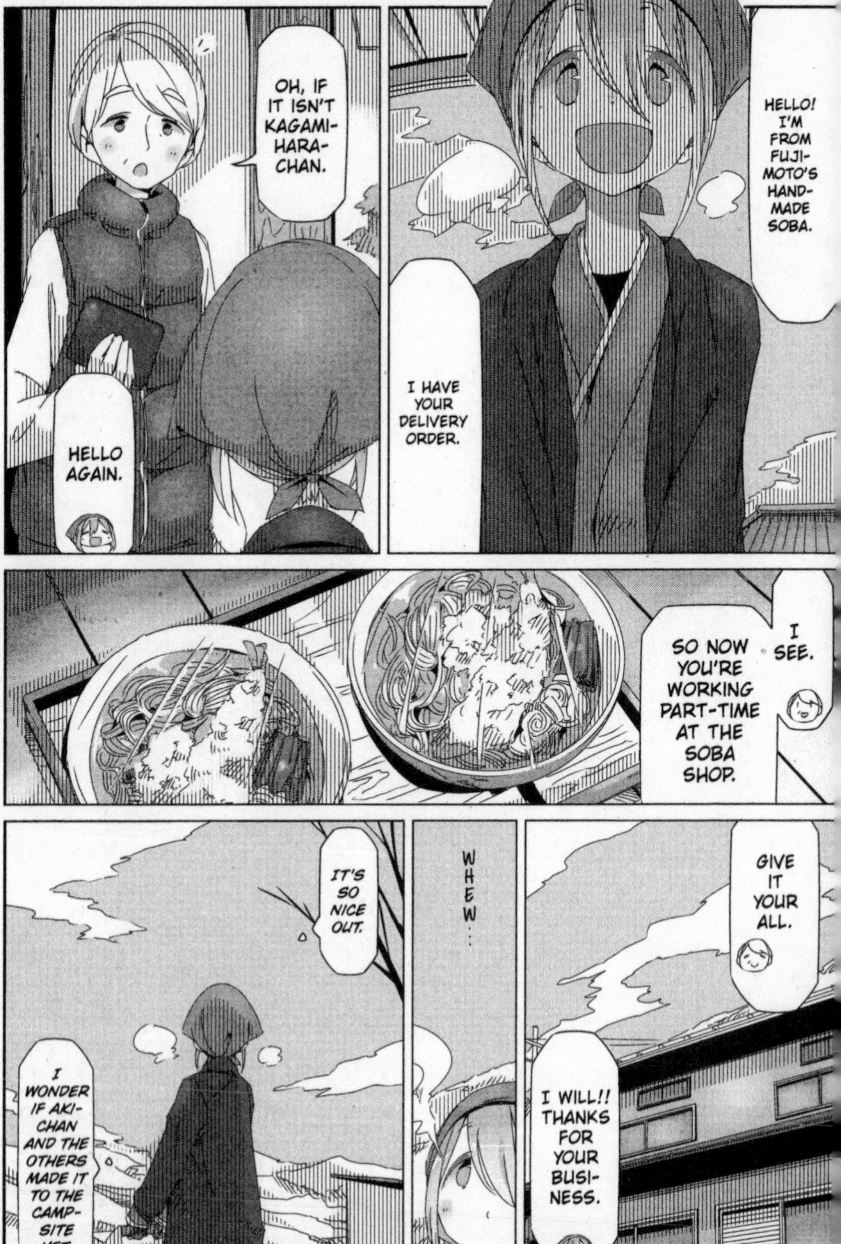
HELLO! I'M FROM FUJIMOTO'S HANDMADE SOBA.
I HAVE YOUR DELIVERY ORDER.
OH, IF IT ISN'T KAGAMIHARA-CHAN.
HELLO AGAIN.
I SEE.
SO NOW YOU'RE WORKING PART-TIME AT THE SOBA SHOP.
GIVE IT YOUR ALL.
I WILL!! THANKS FOR YOUR BUSINESS.
WHEW...
IT'S SO NICE OUT.
I WONDER IF AKI-CHAN AND THE OTHERS MADE IT TO THE CAMPSITE YET.

CHAPTER 33 WINTER AT OOMANA MISAKI

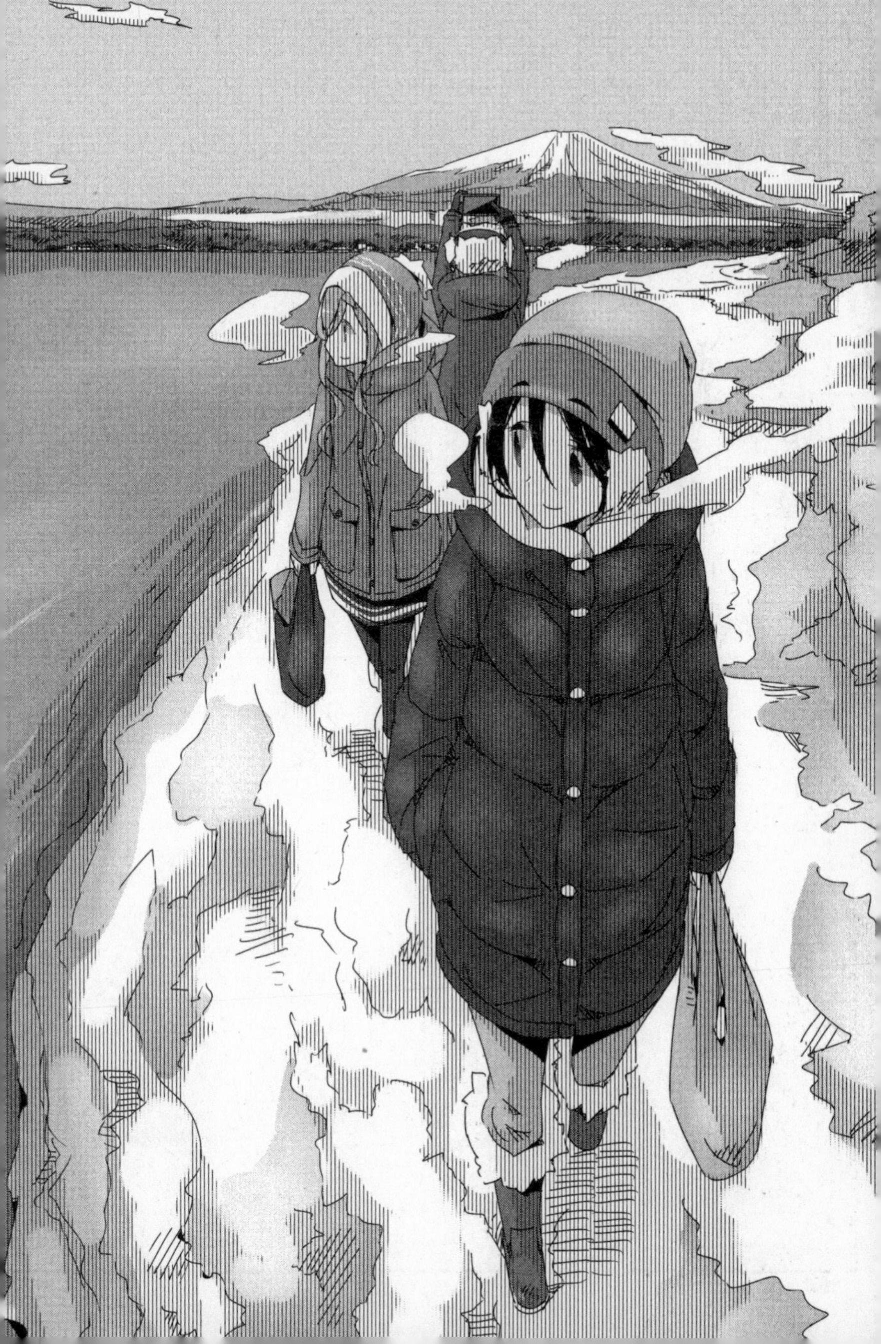

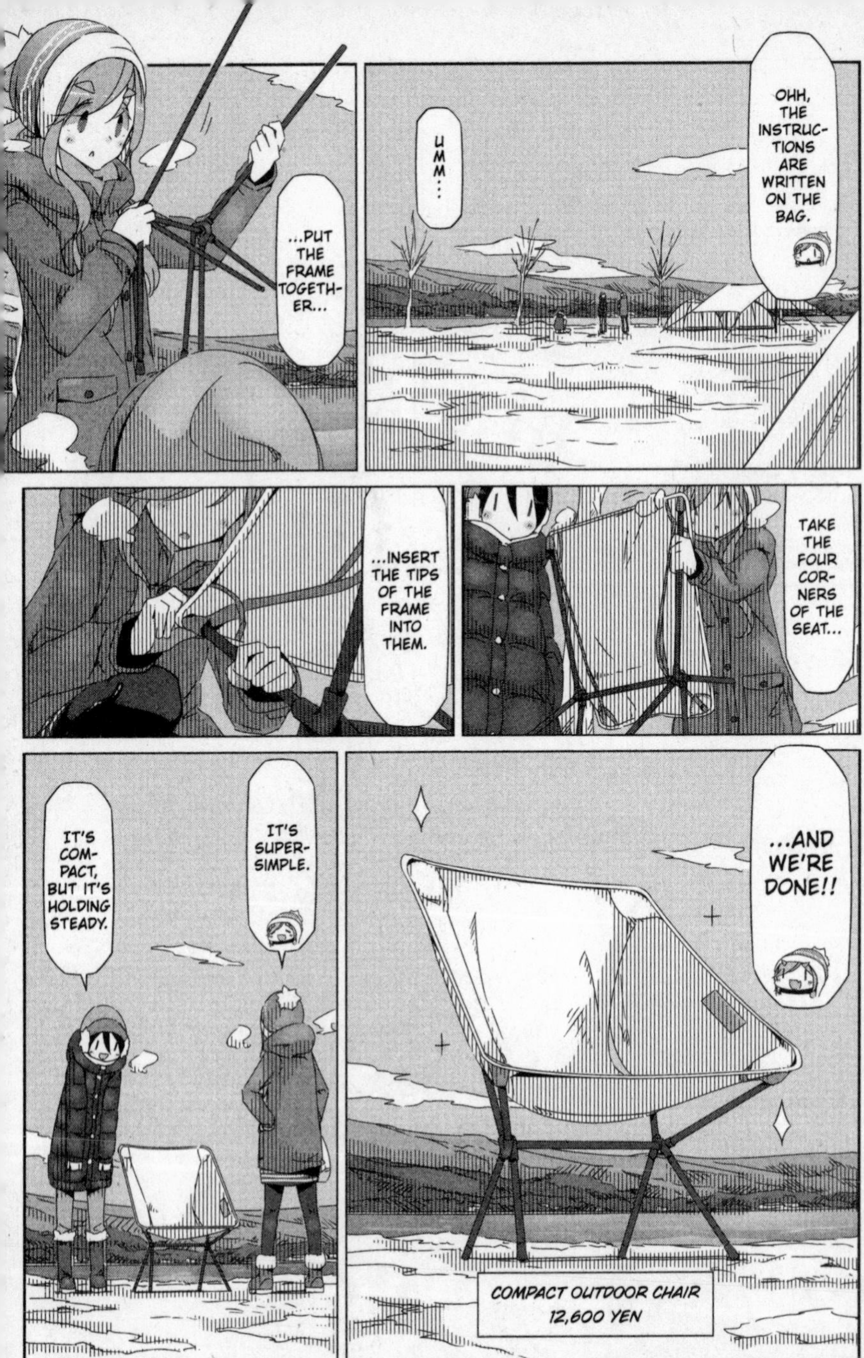
OHH, THE INSTRUCTIONS ARE WRITTEN ON THE BAG.
UMM...
...PUT THE FRAME TOGETHER...
TAKE THE FOUR CORNERS OF THE SEAT...
...INSERT THE TIPS OF THE FRAME INTO THEM.
...AND WE'RE DONE!!
COMPACT OUTDOOR CHAIR
12,600 YEN
IT'S SUPER-SIMPLE.
IT'S COMPACT, BUT IT'S HOLDING STEADY.

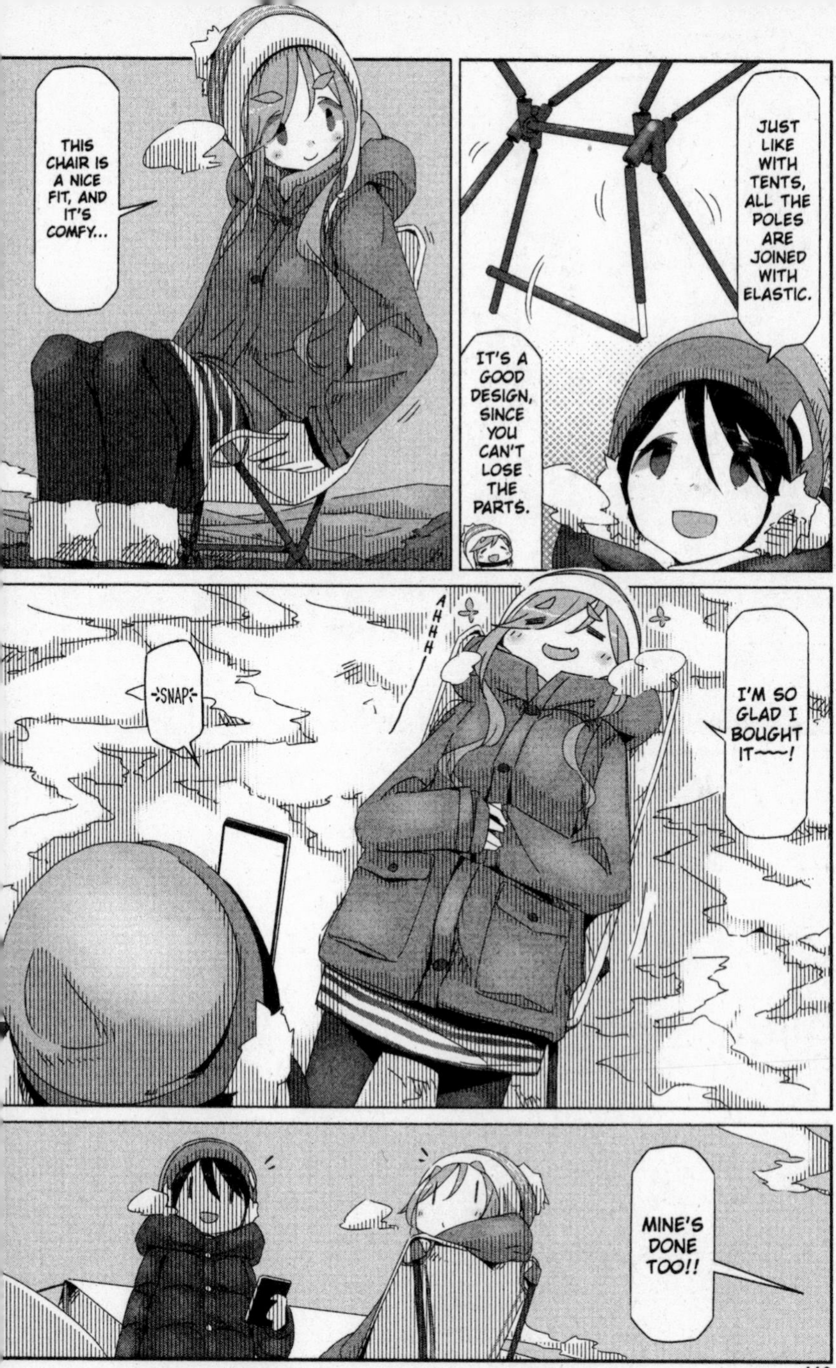
JUST LIKE WITH TENTS, ALL THE POLES ARE JOINED WITH ELASTIC.
IT'S A GOOD DESIGN, SINCE YOU CAN'T LOSE THE PARTS.
THIS CHAIR IS A NICE FIT, AND IT'S COMFY...
I'M SO GLAD I BOUGHT IT~~~!
AHHH
SNAP
MINE'S DONE TOO!!

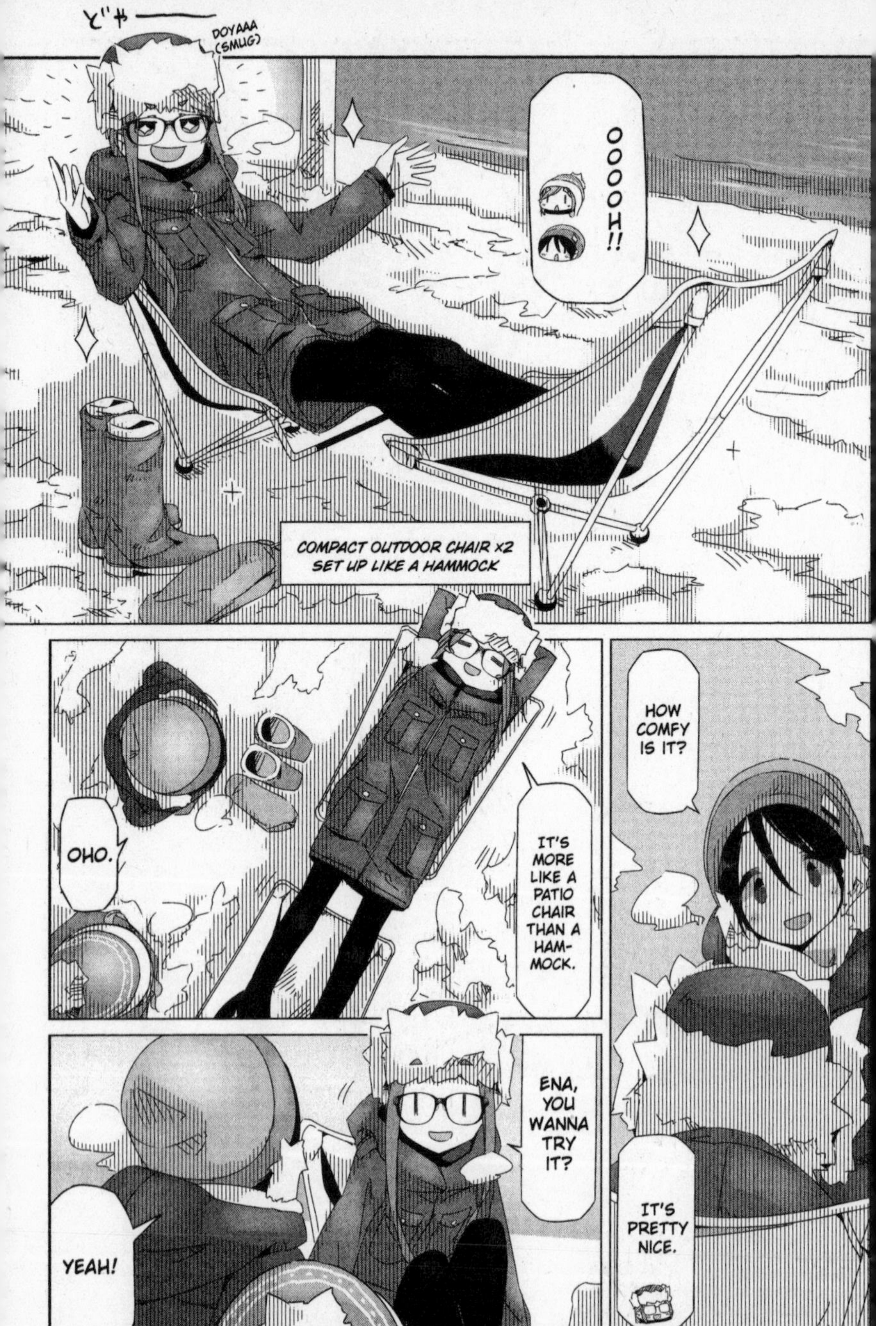
どや——
DOYAAA (SMUG)
OOOOH!!
COMPACT OUTDOOR CHAIR x2 SET UP LIKE A HAMMOCK
HOW COMFY IS IT?
IT'S PRETTY NICE.
IT'S MORE LIKE A PATIO CHAIR THAN A HAM-MOCK.
OHO.
ENA, YOU WANNA TRY IT?
YEAH!

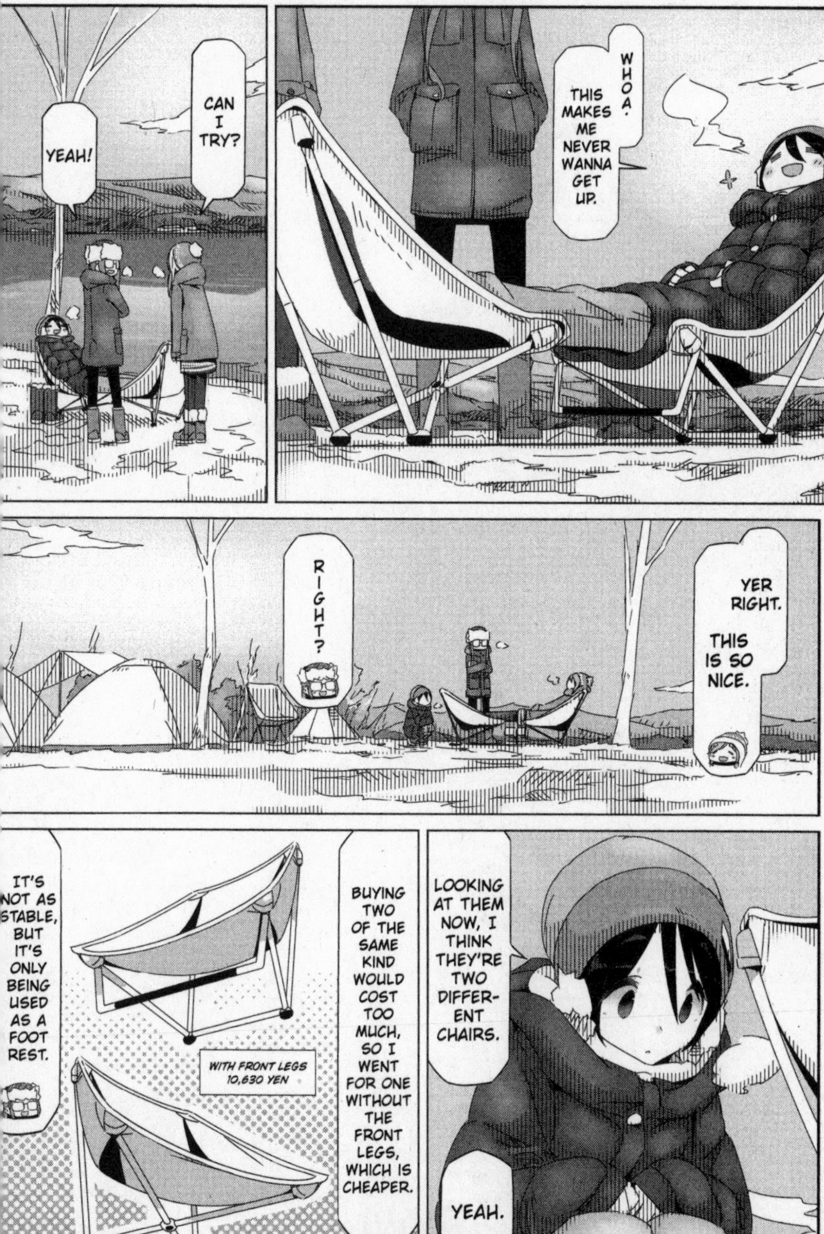
WHOA. THIS MAKES ME NEVER WANNA GET UP.
CAN I TRY?
YEAH!
YER RIGHT.
THIS IS SO NICE.
RIGHT?
LOOKING AT THEM NOW, I THINK THEY'RE TWO DIFFER-ENT CHAIRS.
YEAH.
BUYING TWO OF THE SAME KIND WOULD COST TOO MUCH, SO I WENT FOR ONE WITHOUT THE FRONT LEGS, WHICH IS CHEAPER.
IT'S NOT AS STABLE, BUT IT'S ONLY BEING USED AS A FOOT REST.
WITH FRONT LEGS 10,630 YEN
WITHOUT FRONT LEGS 7,700 YEN

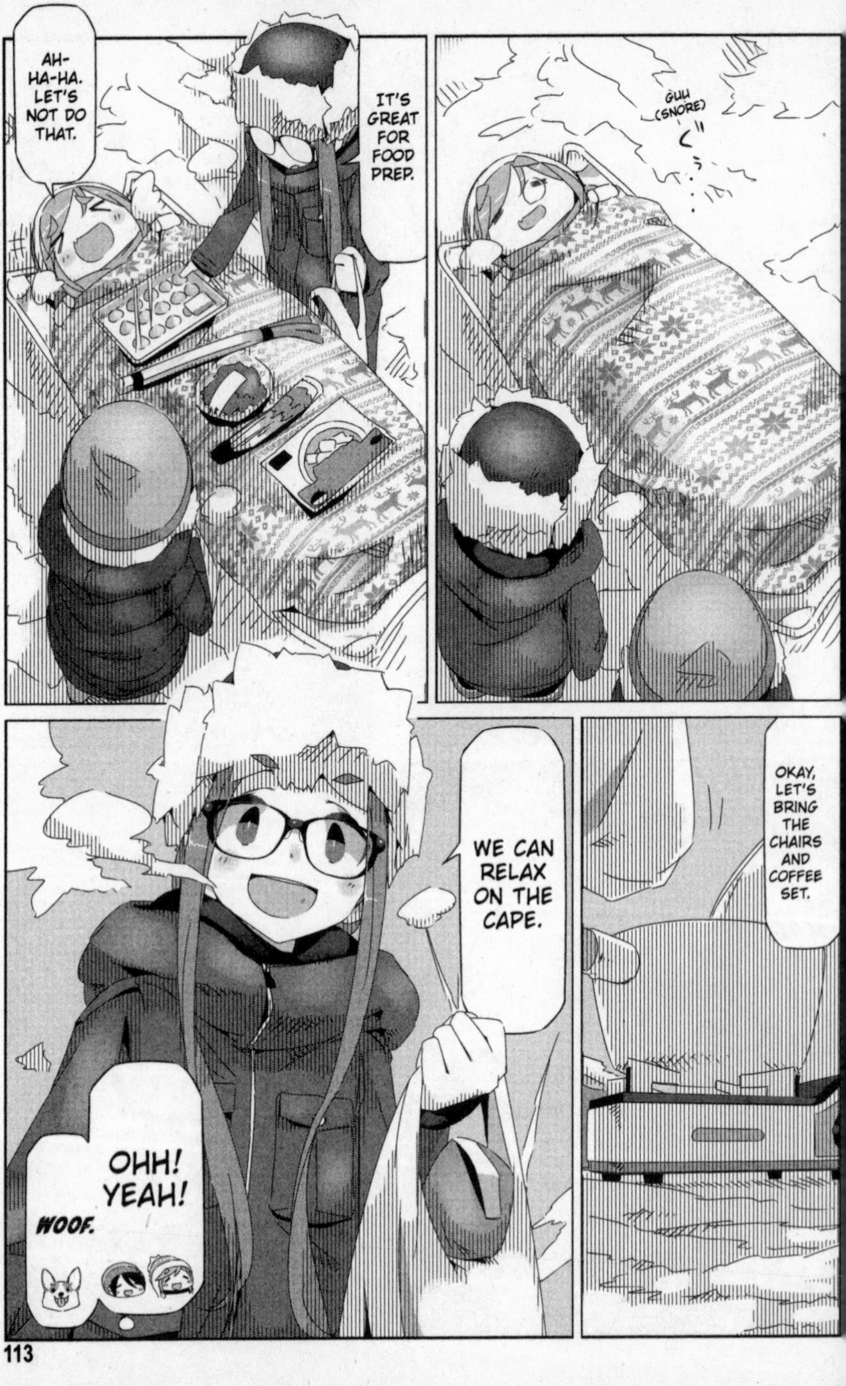
GUU (SNORE)
IT'S GREAT FOR FOOD PREP.
AH-HA-HA. LET'S NOT DO THAT.
OKAY, LET'S BRING THE CHAIRS AND COFFEE SET.
WE CAN RELAX ON THE CAPE.
OHH! YEAH!
WOOF.

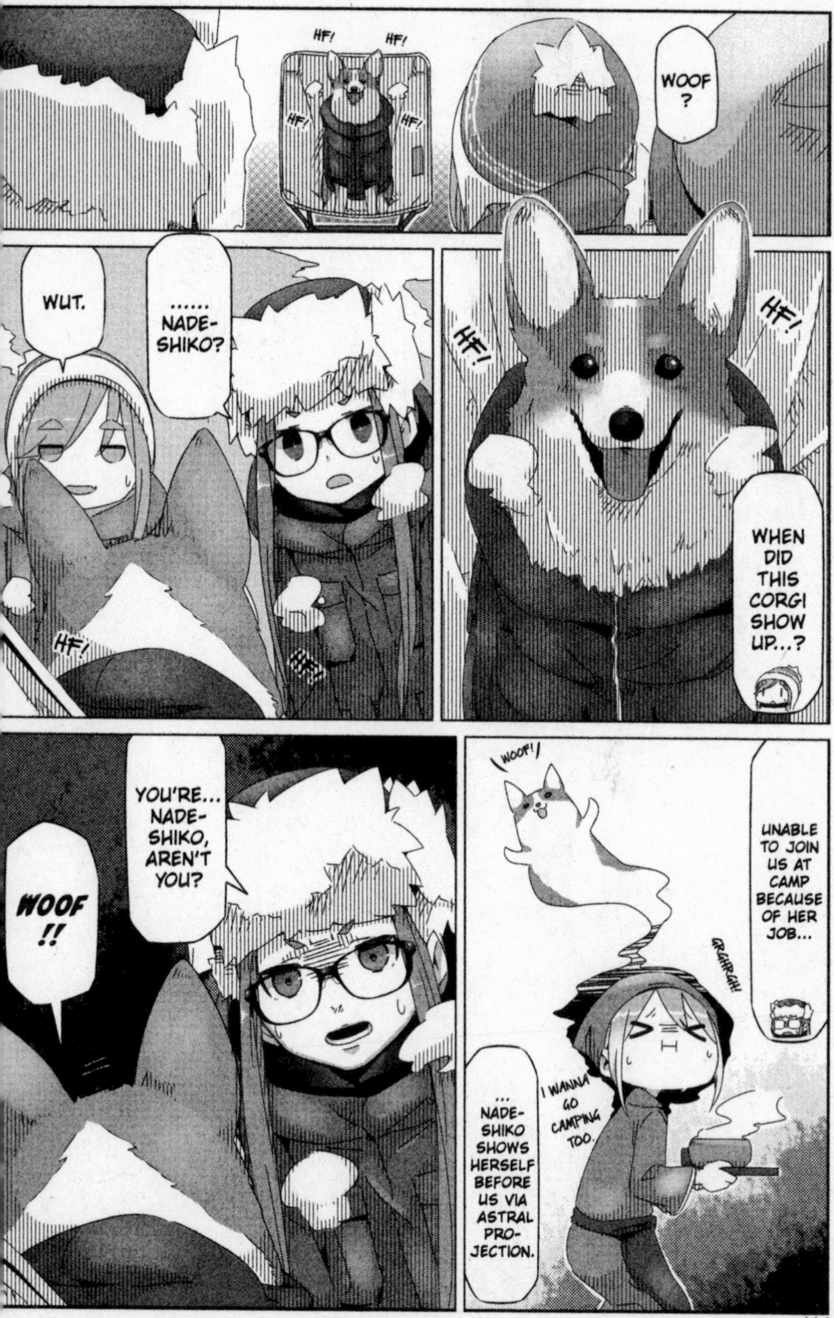
WOOF ?
HF!
HF!
HF!
HF!
HF!
HF!
WHEN DID THIS CORGI SHOW UP...?
......NADE-SHIKO?
WUT.
HF!
UNABLE TO JOIN US AT CAMP BECAUSE OF HER JOB...
WOOF!
GRGHRGH!
I WANNA GO CAMPING TOO.
...NADE-SHIKO SHOWS HERSELF BEFORE US VIA ASTRAL PRO-JECTION.
YOU'RE... NADE-SHIKO, AREN'T YOU?
WOOF !!

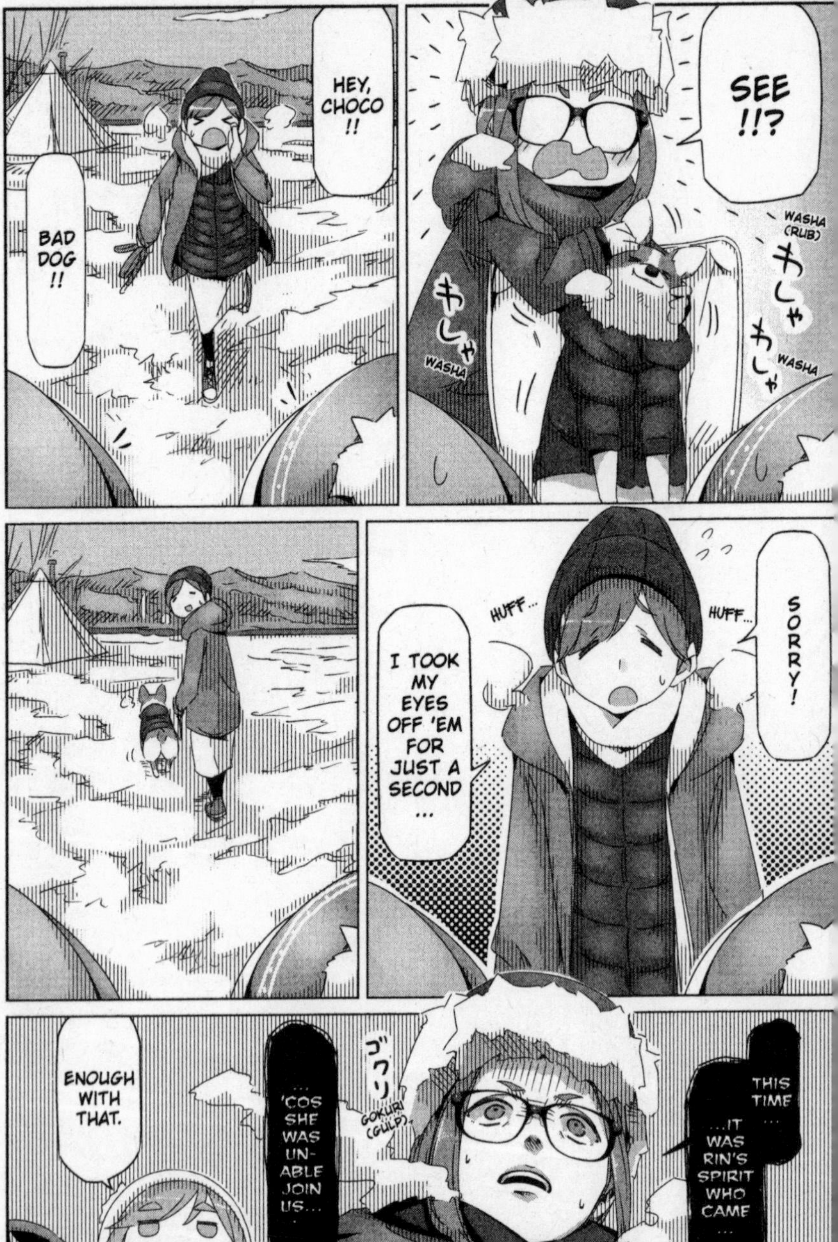
SEE !!?
WASHA (RUB) わしゃ わしゃ WASHA
わしゃ WASHA
HEY, CHOCO !!
BAD DOG !!
SORRY!
HUFF...
HUFF...
I TOOK MY EYES OFF 'EM FOR JUST A SECOND ...
THIS TIME ...
...IT WAS RIN'S SPIRIT WHO CAME ...
ゴクリ GOKURI (GULP)
... 'COS SHE WAS UN-ABLE JOIN US... .
ENOUGH WITH THAT.

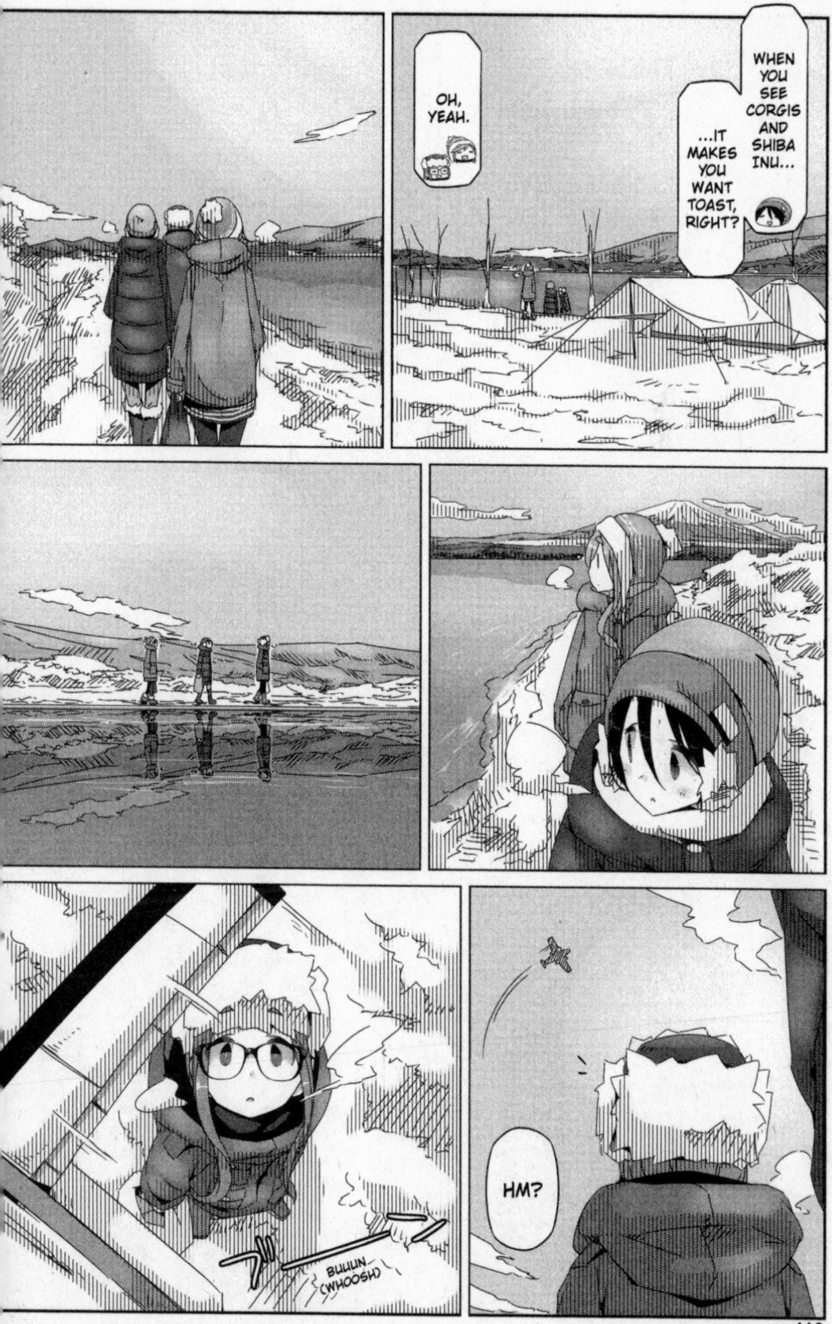
WHEN YOU SEE CORGIS AND SHIBA INU...
...IT MAKES YOU WANT TOAST, RIGHT?
OH, YEAH.
HM?
BUUUN (WHOOSH)

BUUUN
DRONES?
WAIT. AREN'T THOSE RC?
MUST BE THEIR HOBBY ...
'KAY, WE'RE HERE.

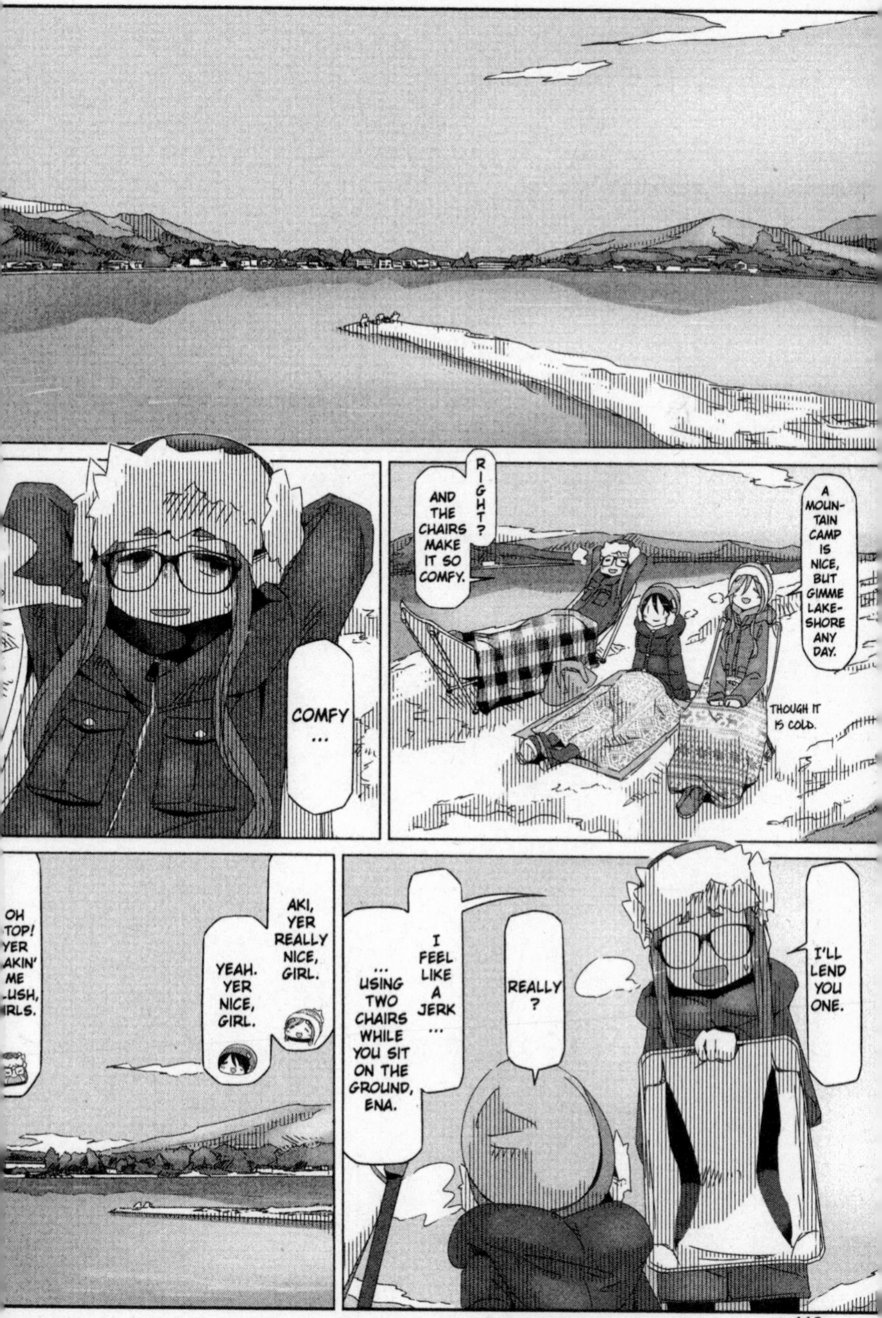
A MOUNTAIN CAMP IS NICE, BUT GIMME LAKESHORE ANY DAY.
THOUGH IT IS COLD.
RIGHT?
AND THE CHAIRS MAKE IT SO COMFY.
COMFY ...
I'LL LEND YOU ONE.
REALLY?
I FEEL LIKE A JERK ...
... USING TWO CHAIRS WHILE YOU SIT ON THE GROUND, ENA.
AKI, YER REALLY NICE, GIRL.
YEAH. YER NICE, GIRL.
OH TOP! YER AKIN' ME LUSH, IRLS.

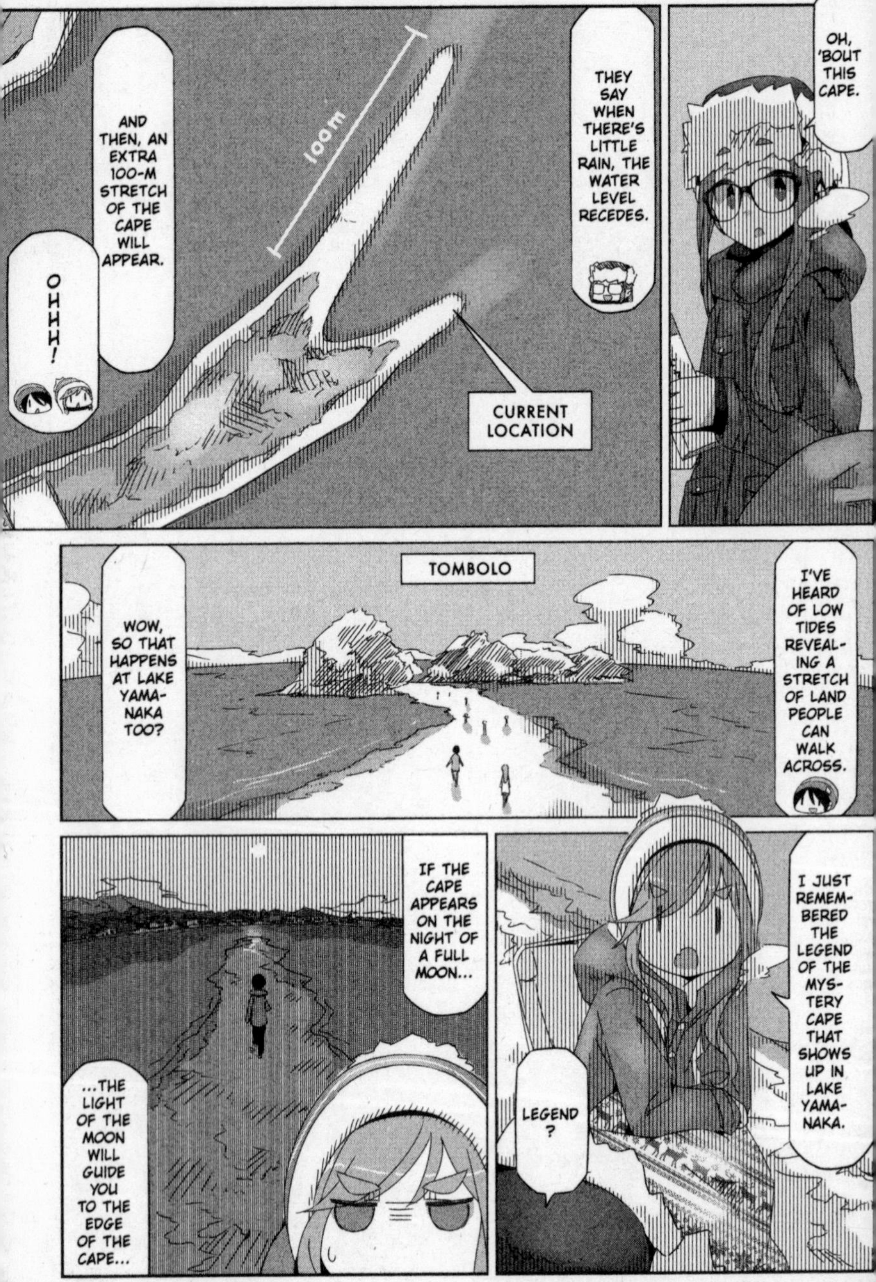
OH, 'BOUT THIS CAPE.
THEY SAY WHEN THERE'S LITTLE RAIN, THE WATER LEVEL RECEDES.
CURRENT LOCATION
100m
AND THEN, AN EXTRA 100-M STRETCH OF THE CAPE WILL APPEAR.
OHHH!
TOMBOLO
I'VE HEARD OF LOW TIDES REVEALING A STRETCH OF LAND PEOPLE CAN WALK ACROSS.
WOW, SO THAT HAPPENS AT LAKE YAMANAKA TOO?
I JUST REMEMBERED THE LEGEND OF THE MYSTERY CAPE THAT SHOWS UP IN LAKE YAMANAKA.
LEGEND?
IF THE CAPE APPEARS ON THE NIGHT OF A FULL MOON...
...THE LIGHT OF THE MOON WILL GUIDE YOU TO THE EDGE OF THE CAPE...

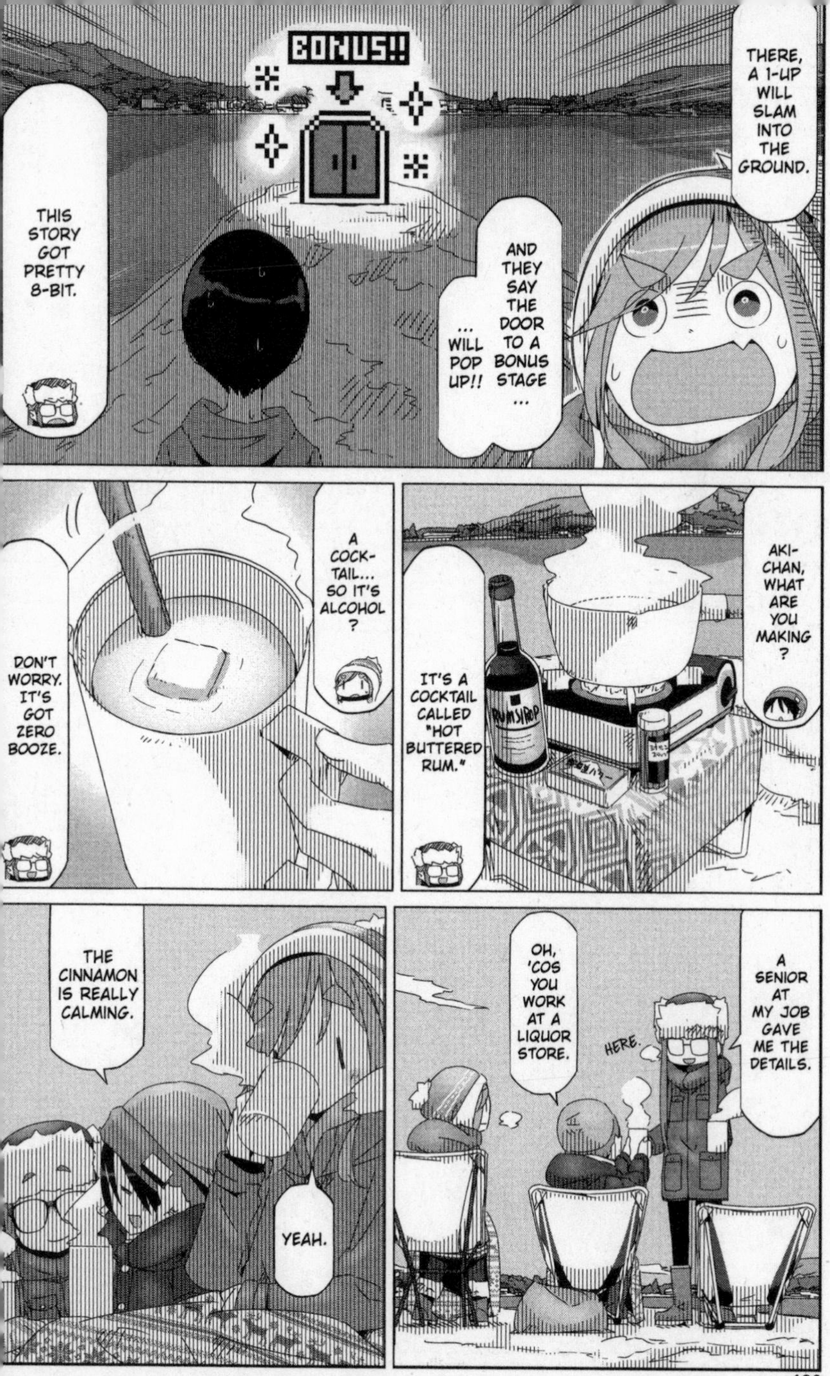
THERE, A 1-UP WILL SLAM INTO THE GROUND.
AND THEY SAY THE DOOR TO A BONUS STAGE ...
... WILL POP UP!!
BONUS!!
THIS STORY GOT PRETTY 8-BIT.
AKI-CHAN, WHAT ARE YOU MAKING?
IT'S A COCKTAIL CALLED "HOT BUTTERED RUM."
RUM SYRUP
A COCK-TAIL... SO IT'S ALCOHOL?
DON'T WORRY. IT'S GOT ZERO BOOZE.
A SENIOR AT MY JOB GAVE ME THE DETAILS.
HERE.
OH, 'COS YOU WORK AT A LIQUOR STORE.
THE CINNAMON IS REALLY CALMING.
YEAH.

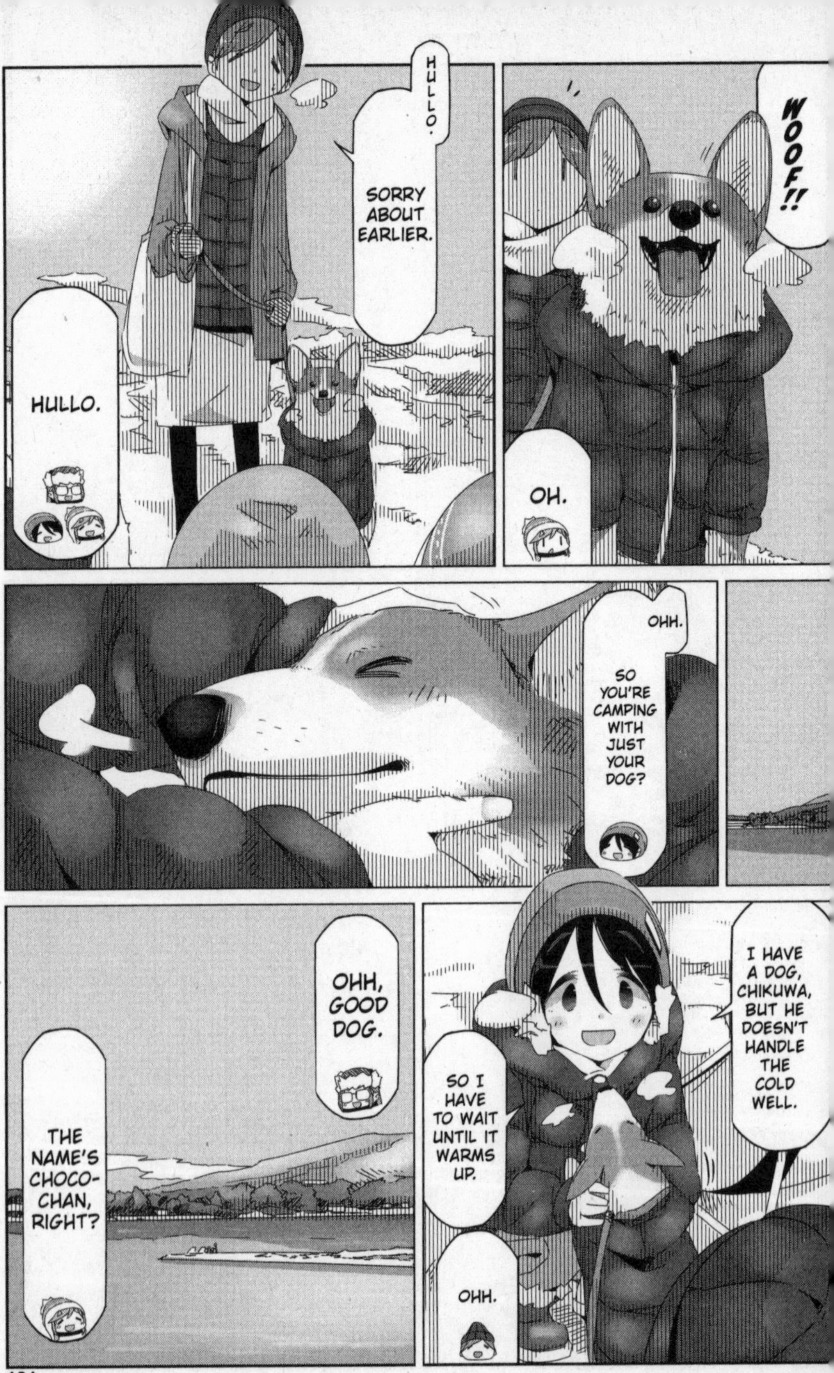
WOOF!!
OH.
HULLO.
SORRY ABOUT EARLIER.
HULLO.
OHH.
SO YOU'RE CAMPING WITH JUST YOUR DOG?
I HAVE A DOG, CHIKUWA, BUT HE DOESN'T HANDLE THE COLD WELL.
SO I HAVE TO WAIT UNTIL IT WARMS UP.
OHH.
OHH, GOOD DOG.
THE NAME'S CHOCO-CHAN, RIGHT?

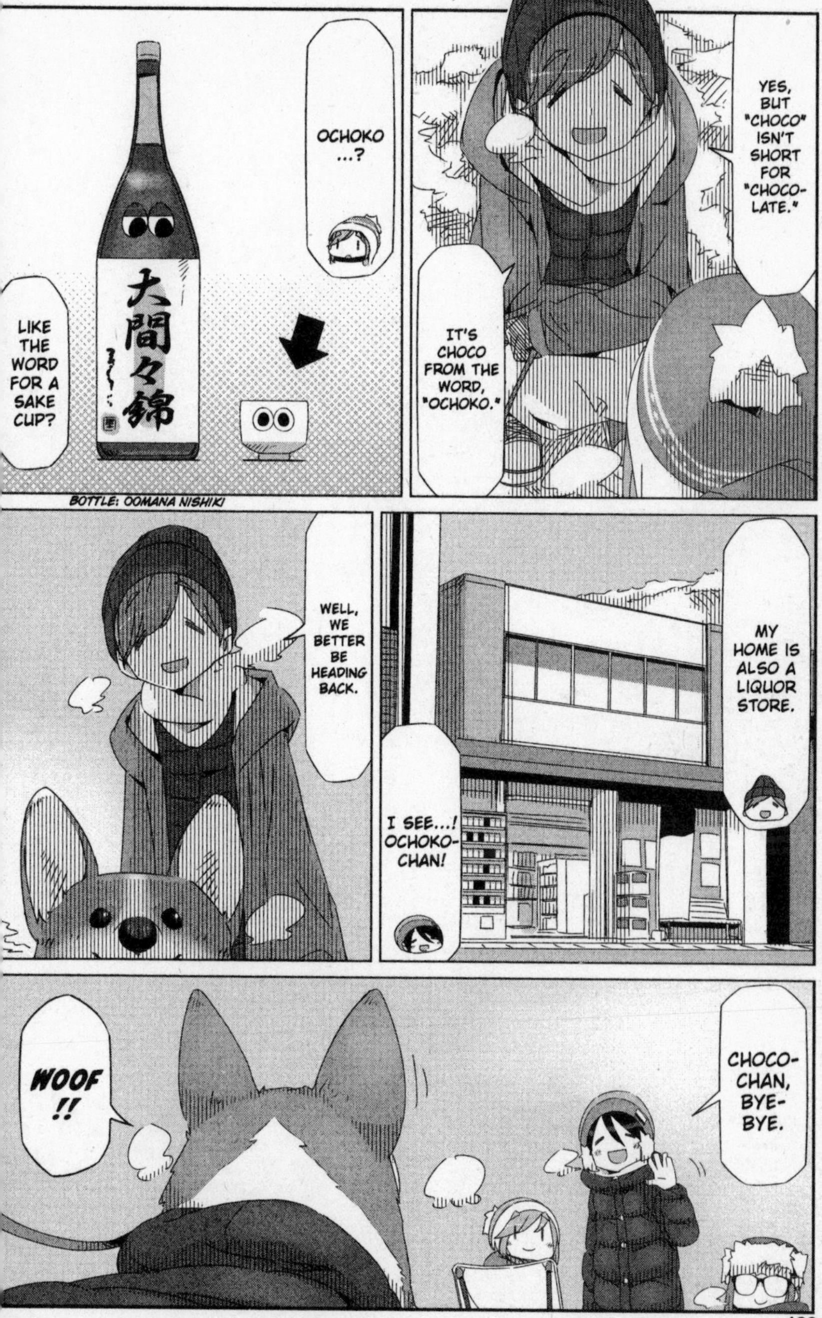
YES, BUT "CHOCO" ISN'T SHORT FOR "CHOCOLATE."
IT'S CHOCO FROM THE WORD, "OCHOKO."
OCHOKO ...?
LIKE THE WORD FOR A SAKE CUP?
大間々錦
BOTTLE: OOMANA NISHIKI
MY HOME IS ALSO A LIQUOR STORE.
I SEE...! OCHOKO-CHAN!
WELL, WE BETTER BE HEADING BACK.
CHOCO-CHAN, BYE-BYE.
WOOF!!

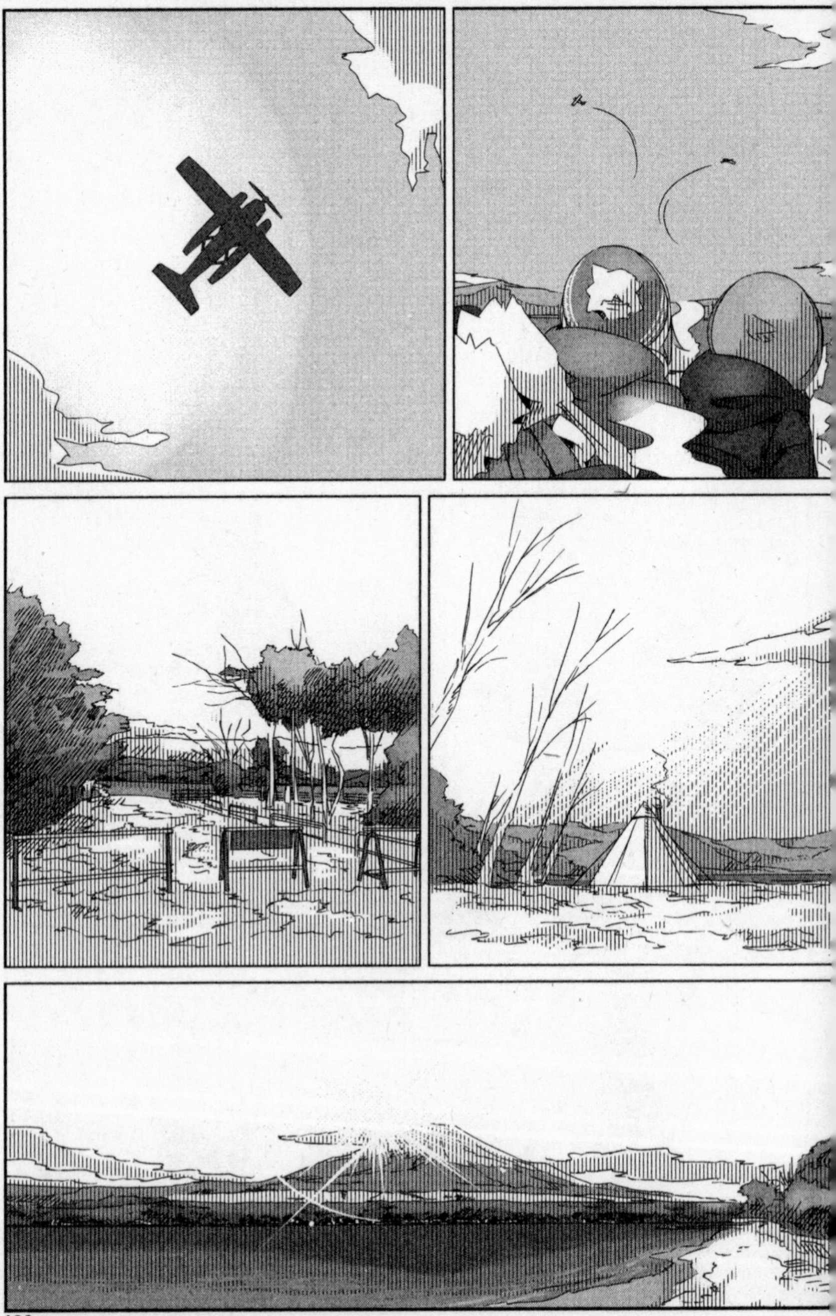

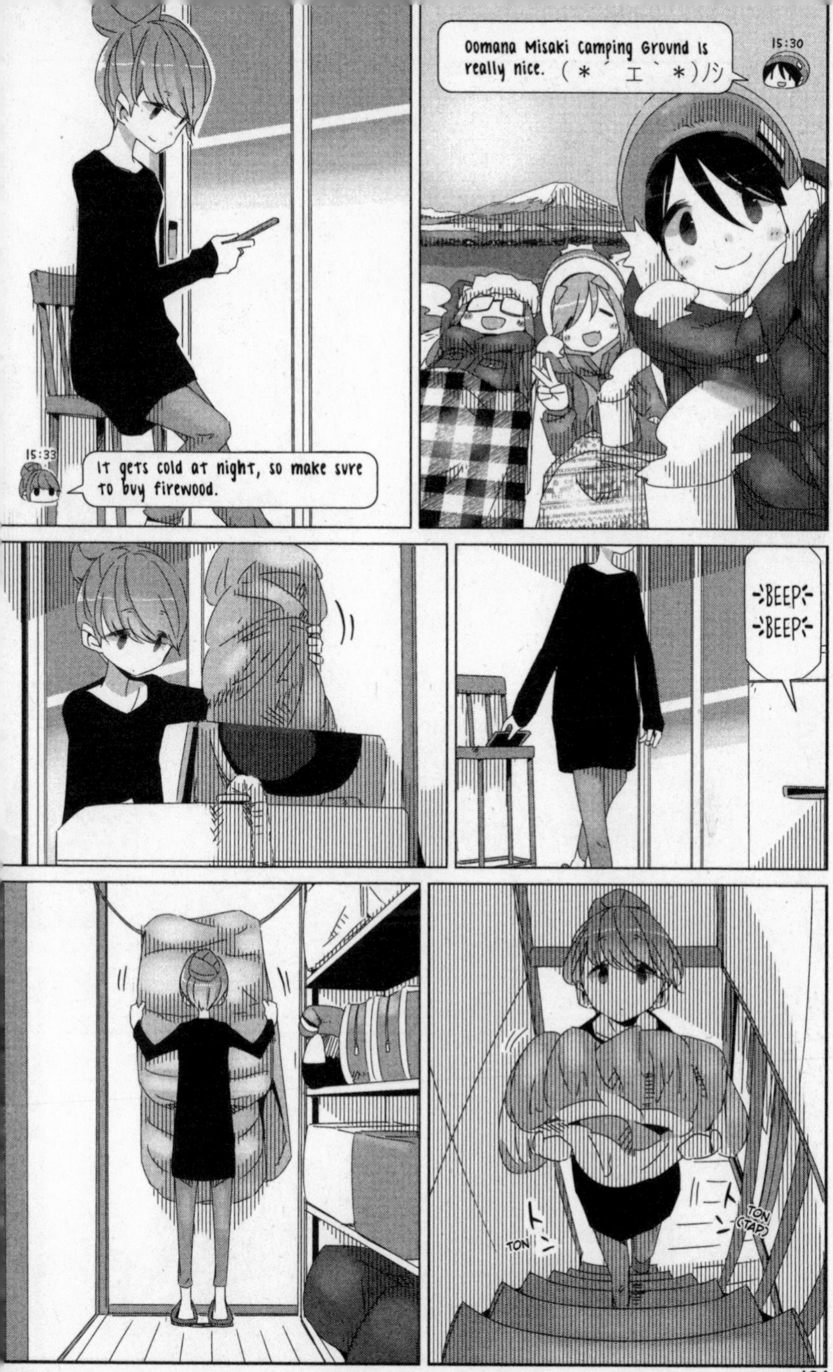

15:30
Oomana Misaki Camping Ground is really nice. (*´エ`*)ノシ
15:33
It gets cold at night, so make sure to buy firewood.
BEEP
BEEP
TON (TAP)
TON

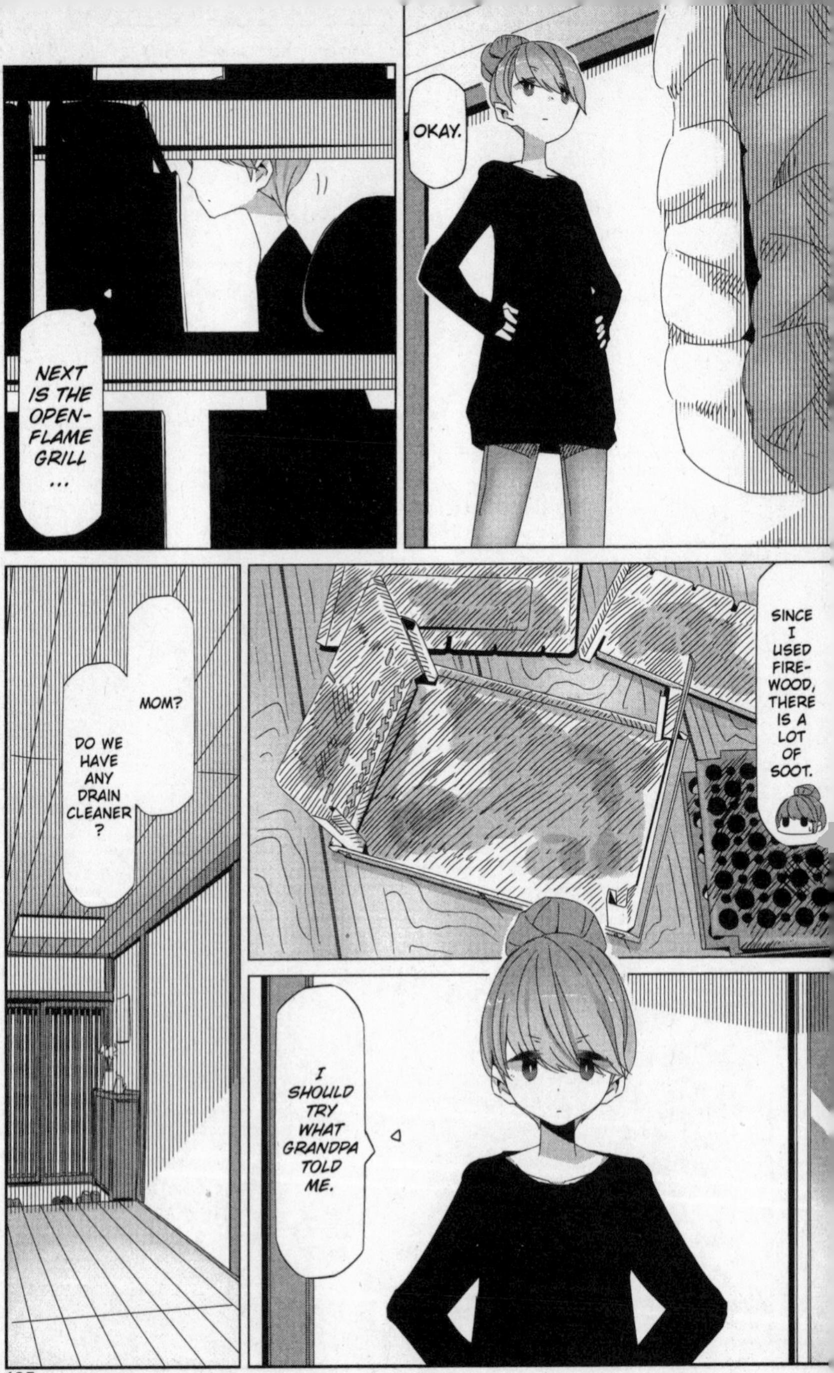
OKAY.
NEXT IS THE OPEN-FLAME GRILL...
SINCE I USED FIRE-WOOD, THERE IS A LOT OF SOOT.
I SHOULD TRY WHAT GRANDPA TOLD ME.
MOM?
DO WE HAVE ANY DRAIN CLEANER?

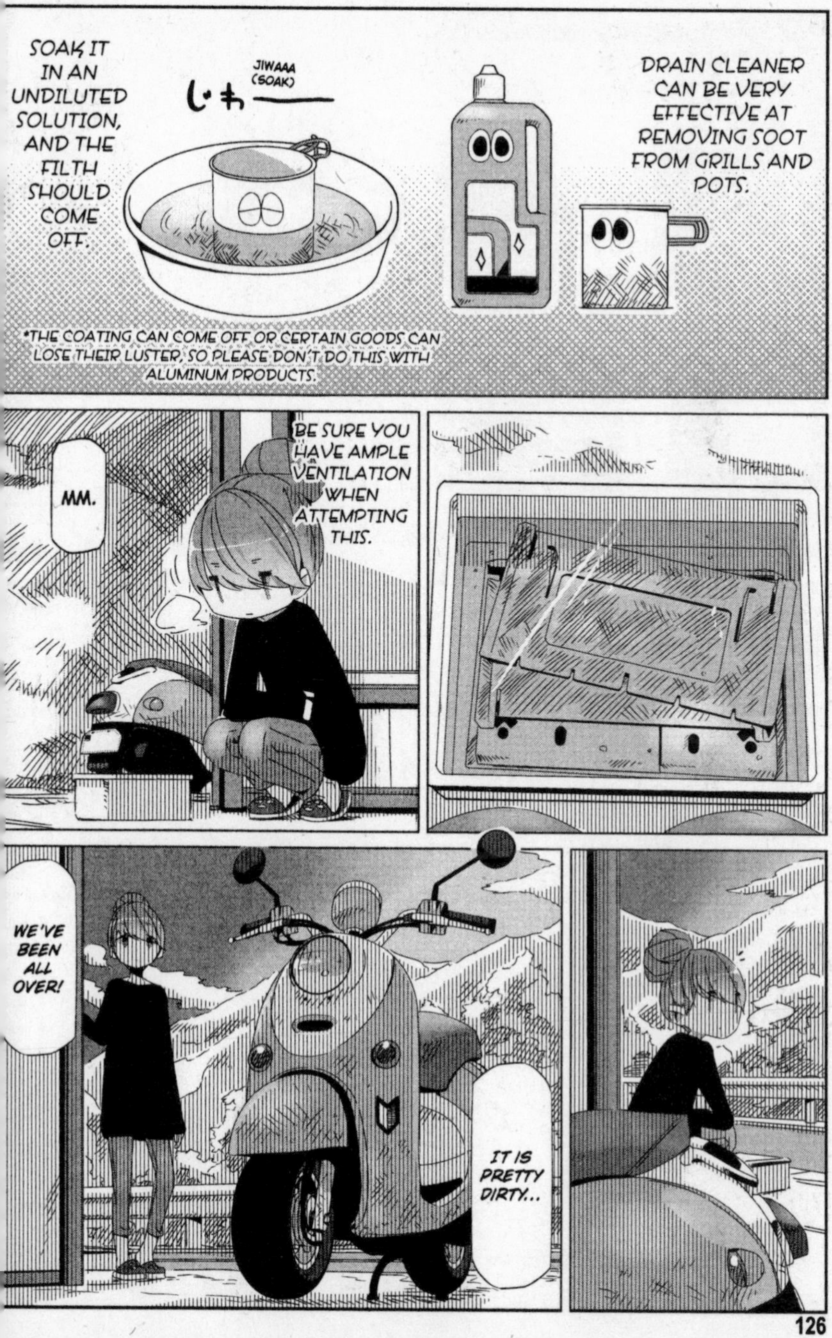
DRAIN CLEANER CAN BE VERY EFFECTIVE AT REMOVING SOOT FROM GRILLS AND POTS.
JIWAAA (SOAK)
じわ——
SOAK IT IN AN UNDILUTED SOLUTION, AND THE FILTH SHOULD COME OFF.
*THE COATING CAN COME OFF OR CERTAIN GOODS CAN LOSE THEIR LUSTER, SO PLEASE DON'T DO THIS WITH ALUMINUM PRODUCTS.
BE SURE YOU HAVE AMPLE VENTILATION WHEN ATTEMPTING THIS.
MM.
IT IS PRETTY DIRTY...
WE'VE BEEN ALL OVER!

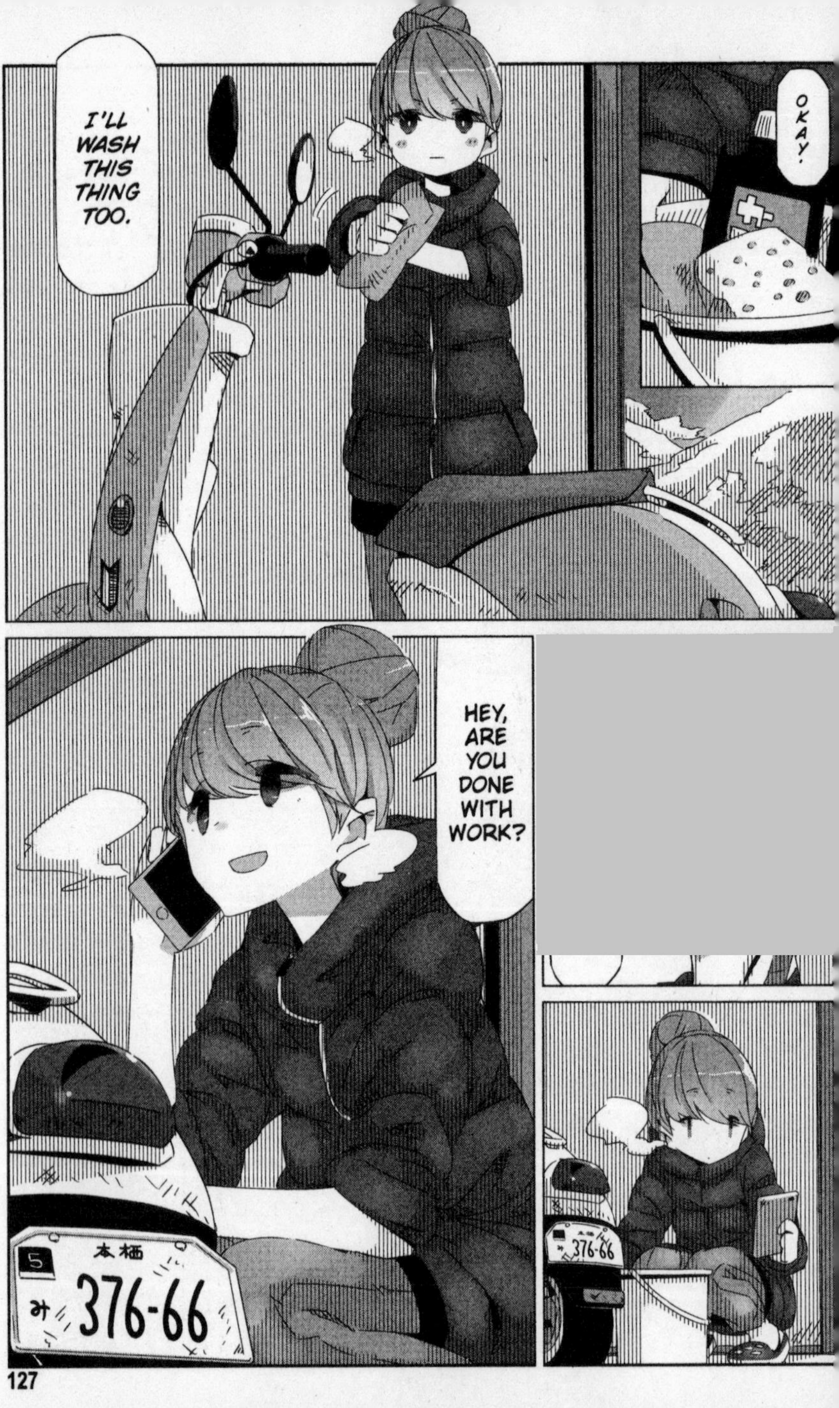
OKAY.
I'LL WASH THIS THING TOO.
HEY, ARE YOU DONE WITH WORK?
5 本栖
み 376-66

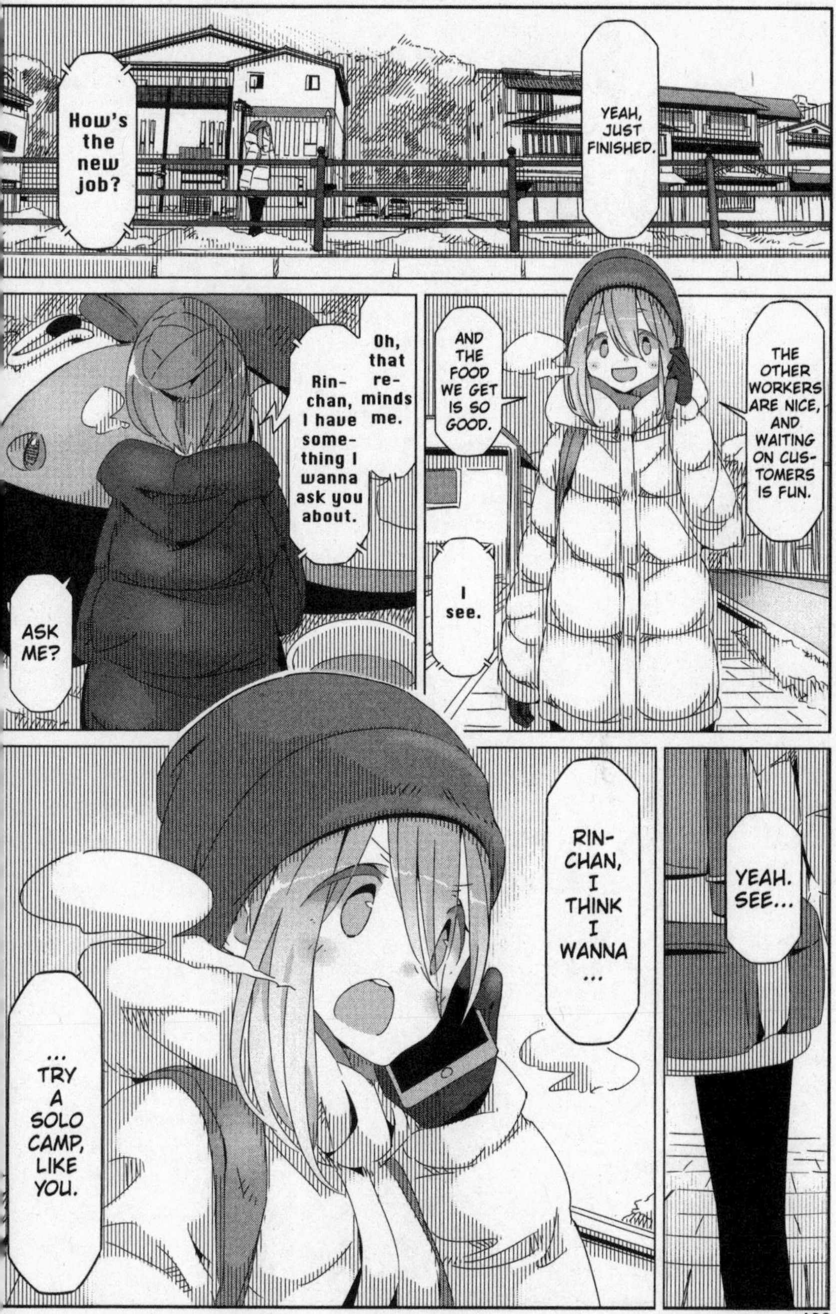
YEAH, JUST FINISHED.
How's the new job?
THE OTHER WORKERS ARE NICE, AND WAITING ON CUSTOMERS IS FUN.
AND THE FOOD WE GET IS SO GOOD.
I see.
Oh, that reminds me.
Rin-chan, I have something I wanna ask you about.
ASK ME?
YEAH. SEE...
RIN-CHAN, I THINK I WANNA...
...TRY A SOLO CAMP, LIKE YOU.

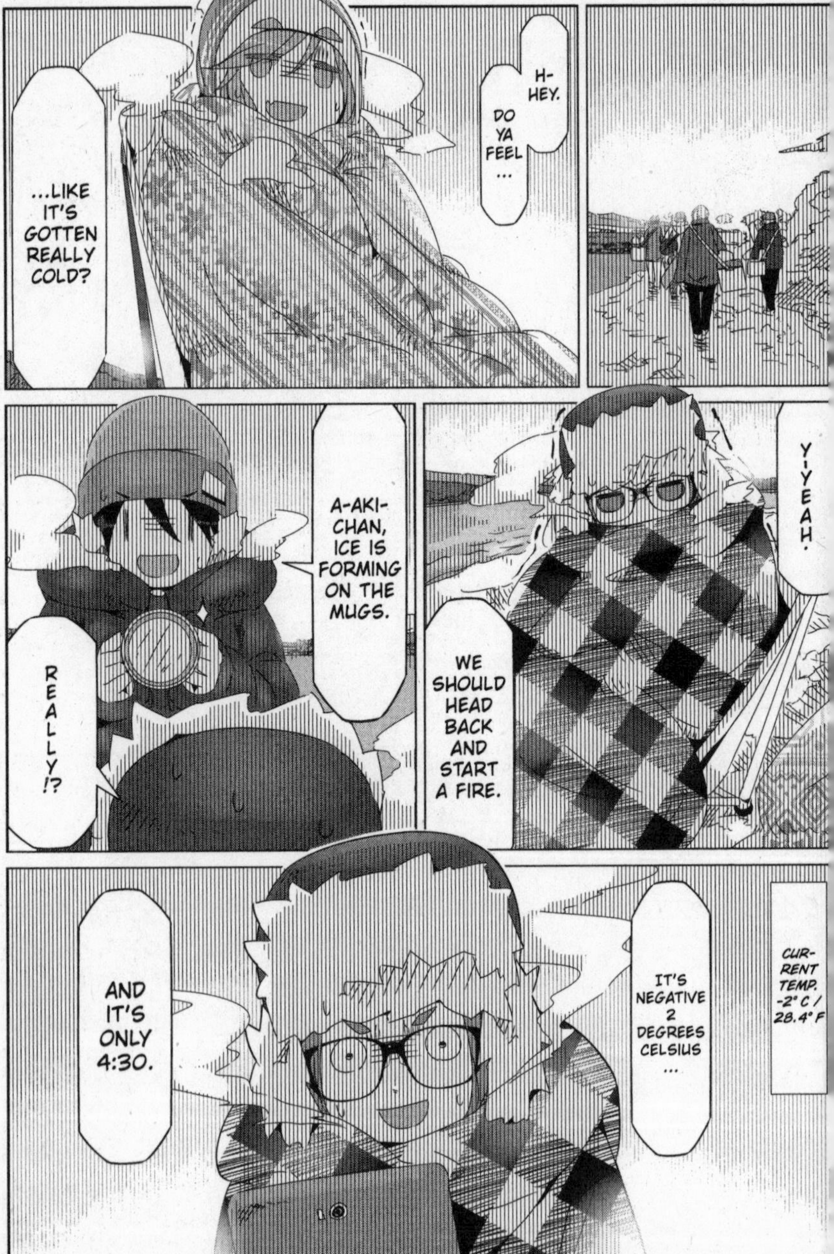
H-HEY. DO YA FEEL ...
...LIKE IT'S GOTTEN REALLY COLD?
Y-YEAH.
WE SHOULD HEAD BACK AND START A FIRE.
A-AKI-CHAN, ICE IS FORMING ON THE MUGS.
REALLY!?
CUR-RENT TEMP. -2° C / 28.4° F
IT'S NEGATIVE 2 DEGREES CELSIUS ...
AND IT'S ONLY 4:30.

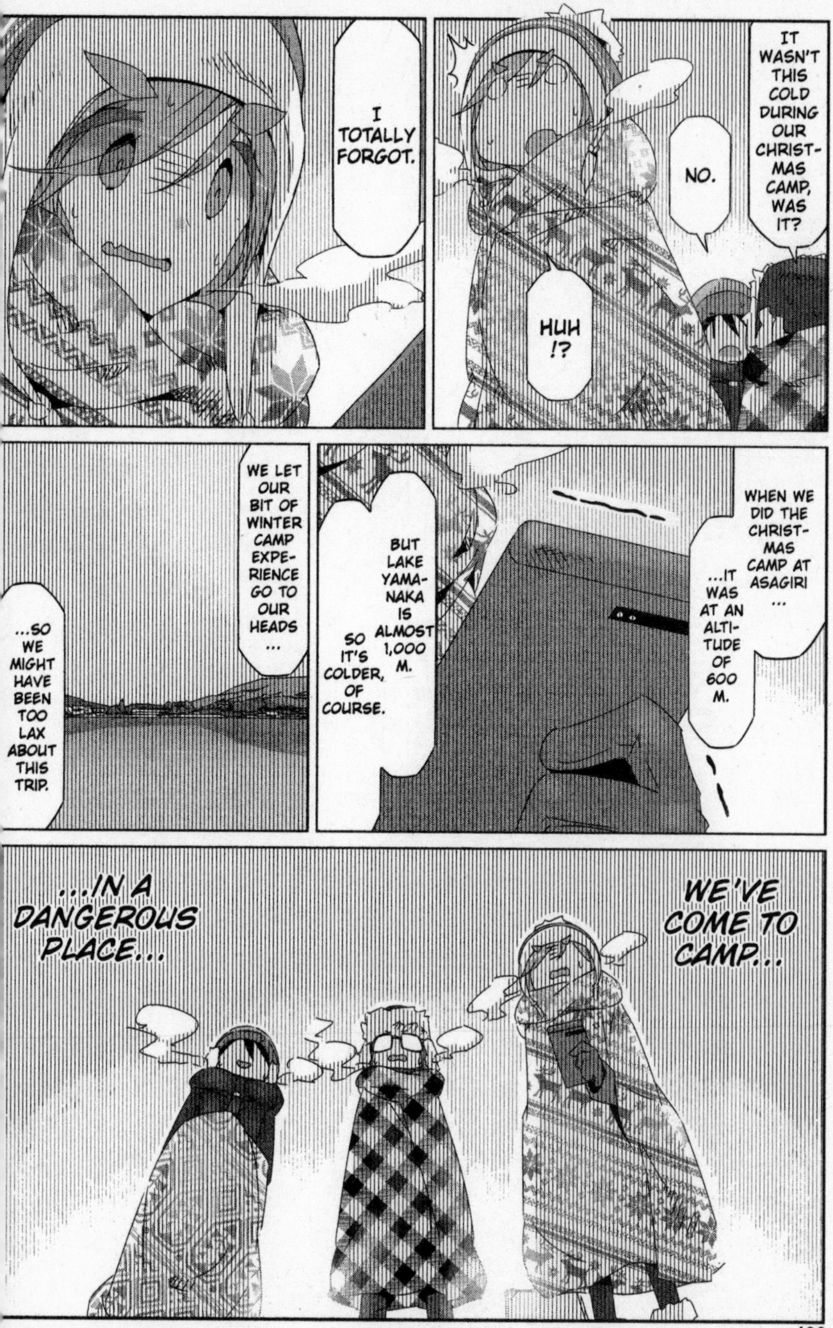
IT WASN'T THIS COLD DURING OUR CHRISTMAS CAMP, WAS IT?
NO.
HUH!?
I TOTALLY FORGOT.
WHEN WE DID THE CHRISTMAS CAMP AT ASAGIRI...
...IT WAS AT AN ALTITUDE OF 600 M.
BUT LAKE YAMANAKA IS ALMOST 1,000 M.
SO IT'S COLDER, OF COURSE.
WE LET OUR BIT OF WINTER CAMP EXPERIENCE GO TO OUR HEADS...
...SO WE MIGHT HAVE BEEN TOO LAX ABOUT THIS TRIP.
WE'VE COME TO CAMP...
...IN A DANGEROUS PLACE...

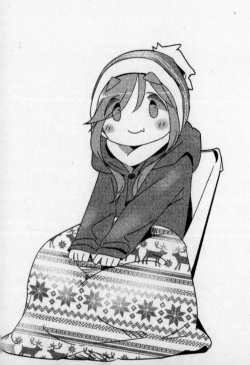

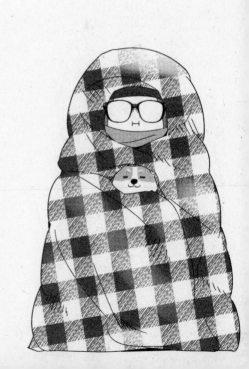

I CAME UP WITH IDEAS TO FIGHT THE COLD TO-NIGHT.
FIRST, WE EAT THE STEW AND WARM OUR BODIES FROM THE INSIDE.
THEN, BE-FORE OUR BODIES COOL...
...WE STICK TONS OF THESE HIGH-ALTITUDE HEAT PACKS INTO OUR SLEEPING BAGS AND CLIMB IN.
HIGH-ALTITUDE HEAT PACKS
KACHI-KACHI YAMA
THEN, WE ADD COATS AND BLAN-KETS ON TOP.
むぎゅっ
MUGYUU (SNUG)
AND THEN, WE SNUGGLE UP TIGHT AND GO TO SLEEP!!
WE CAN MAKE IT!!
WITH THIS, WE CAN SURVIVE THIS INTENSELY COLD NIGHT!!
CAN WE, THOUGH...?
CURRENT TEMPERATURE: -2° C / 28.4° F

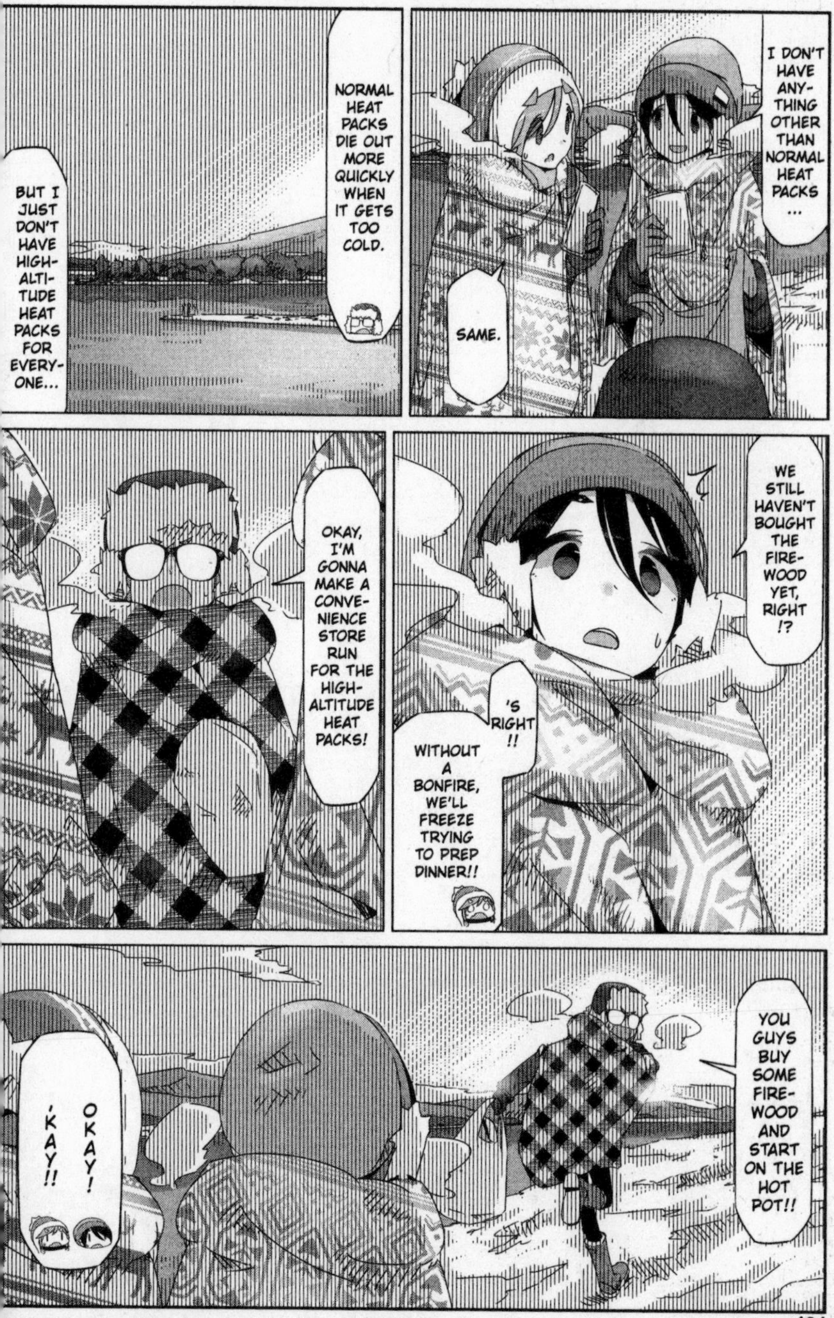
I DON'T HAVE ANYTHING OTHER THAN NORMAL HEAT PACKS...
SAME.
NORMAL HEAT PACKS DIE OUT MORE QUICKLY WHEN IT GETS TOO COLD.
BUT I JUST DON'T HAVE HIGH-ALTITUDE HEAT PACKS FOR EVERYONE...
WE STILL HAVEN'T BOUGHT THE FIREWOOD YET, RIGHT!?
'S RIGHT!!
WITHOUT A BONFIRE, WE'LL FREEZE TRYING TO PREP DINNER!!
OKAY, I'M GONNA MAKE A CONVENIENCE STORE RUN FOR THE HIGH-ALTITUDE HEAT PACKS!
YOU GUYS BUY SOME FIREWOOD AND START ON THE HOT POT!!
OKAY!
'KAY!!

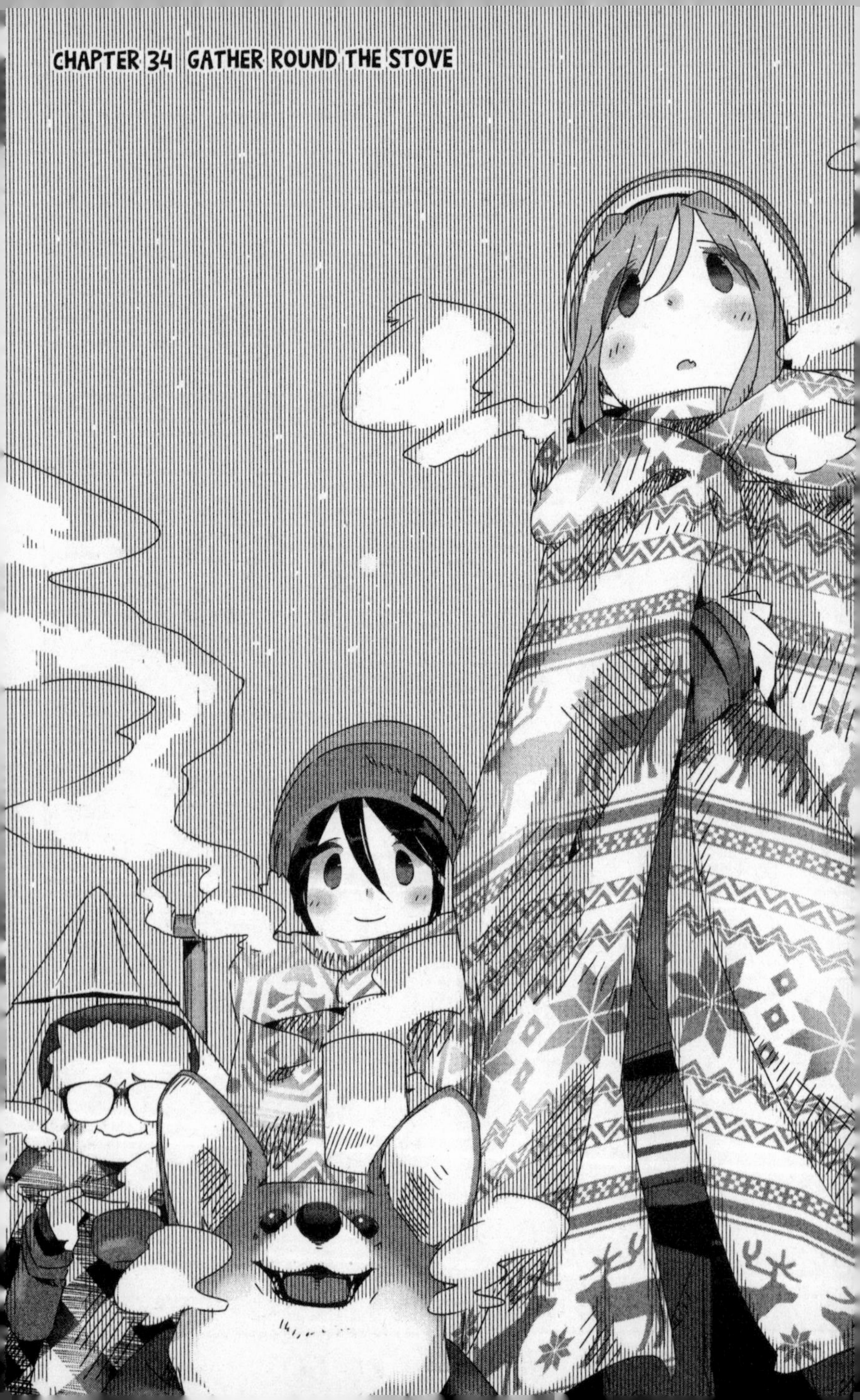
CHAPTER 34 GATHER ROUND THE STOVE

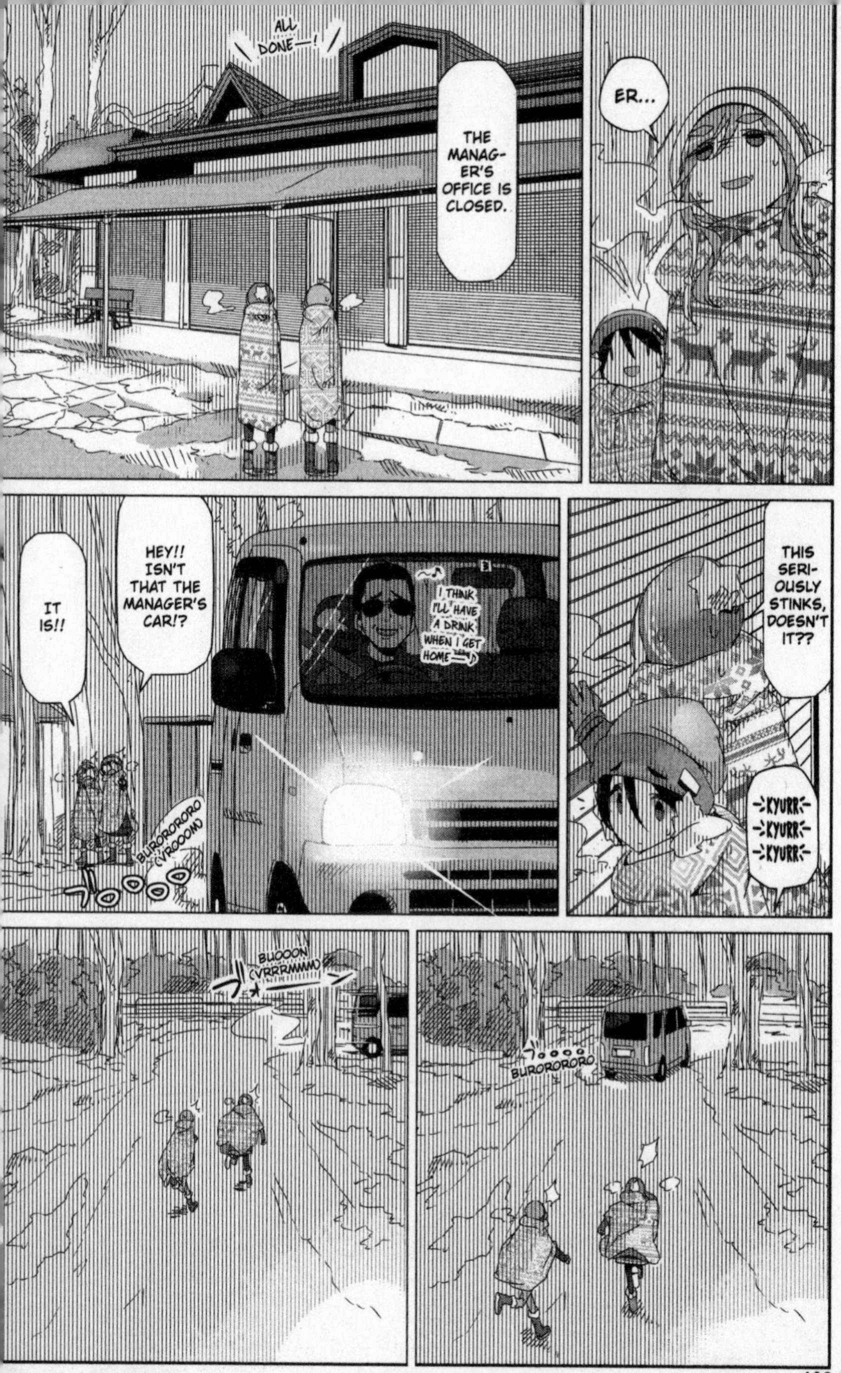
ER...
ALL DONE—!
THE MANAGER'S OFFICE IS CLOSED.
THIS SERIOUSLY STINKS, DOESN'T IT??
KYURR
KYURR
KYURR
I THINK I'LL HAVE A DRINK WHEN I GET HOME—♪
HEY!! ISN'T THAT THE MANAGER'S CAR!?
IT IS!!
BURORORORO (VROOOM)
BURORORO
BUOOON (VRRRMMM)

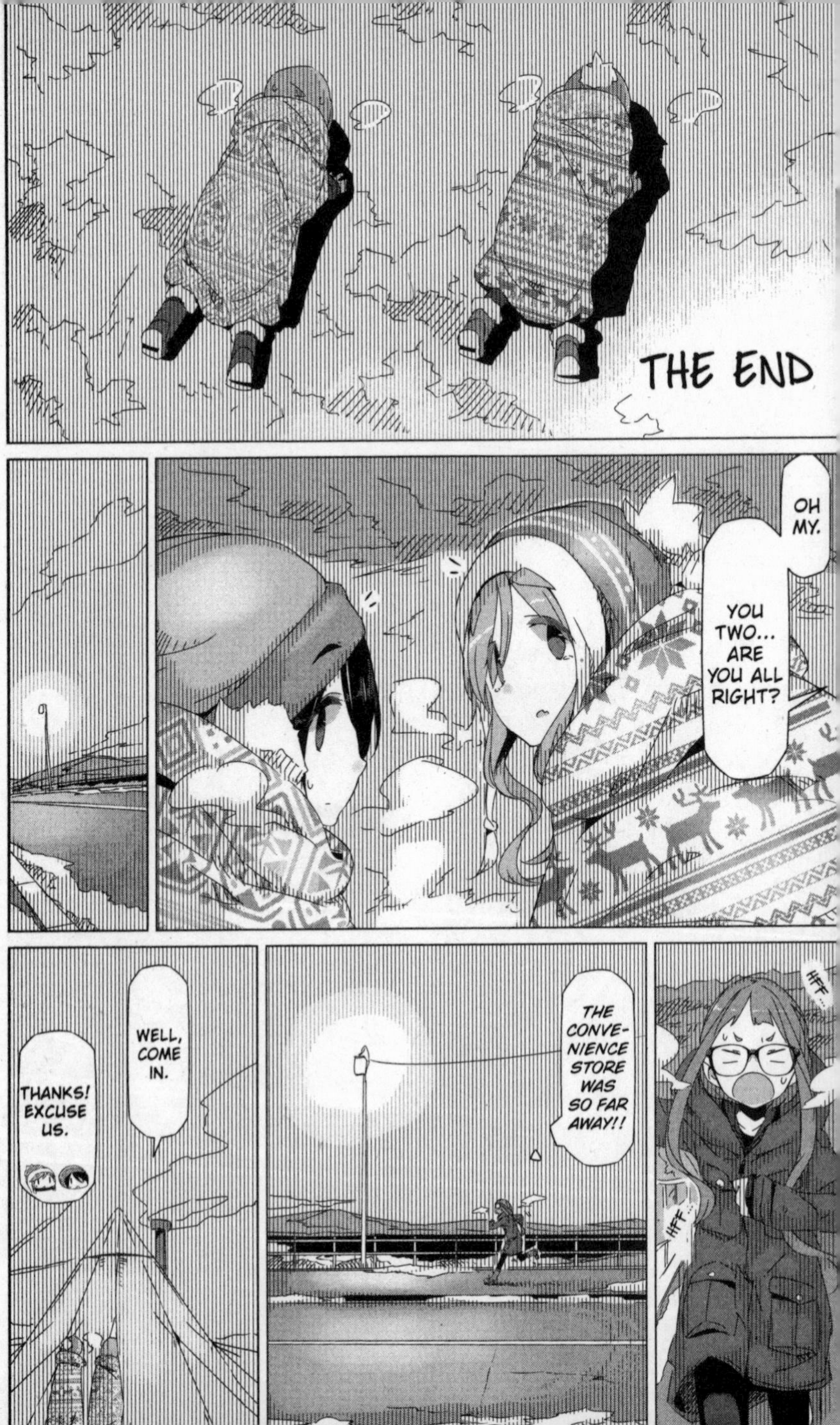
THE END
OH MY.
YOU TWO... ARE YOU ALL RIGHT?
HFF...
HFF...
THE CONVE-NIENCE STORE WAS SO FAR AWAY!!
WELL, COME IN.
THANKS! EXCUSE US.

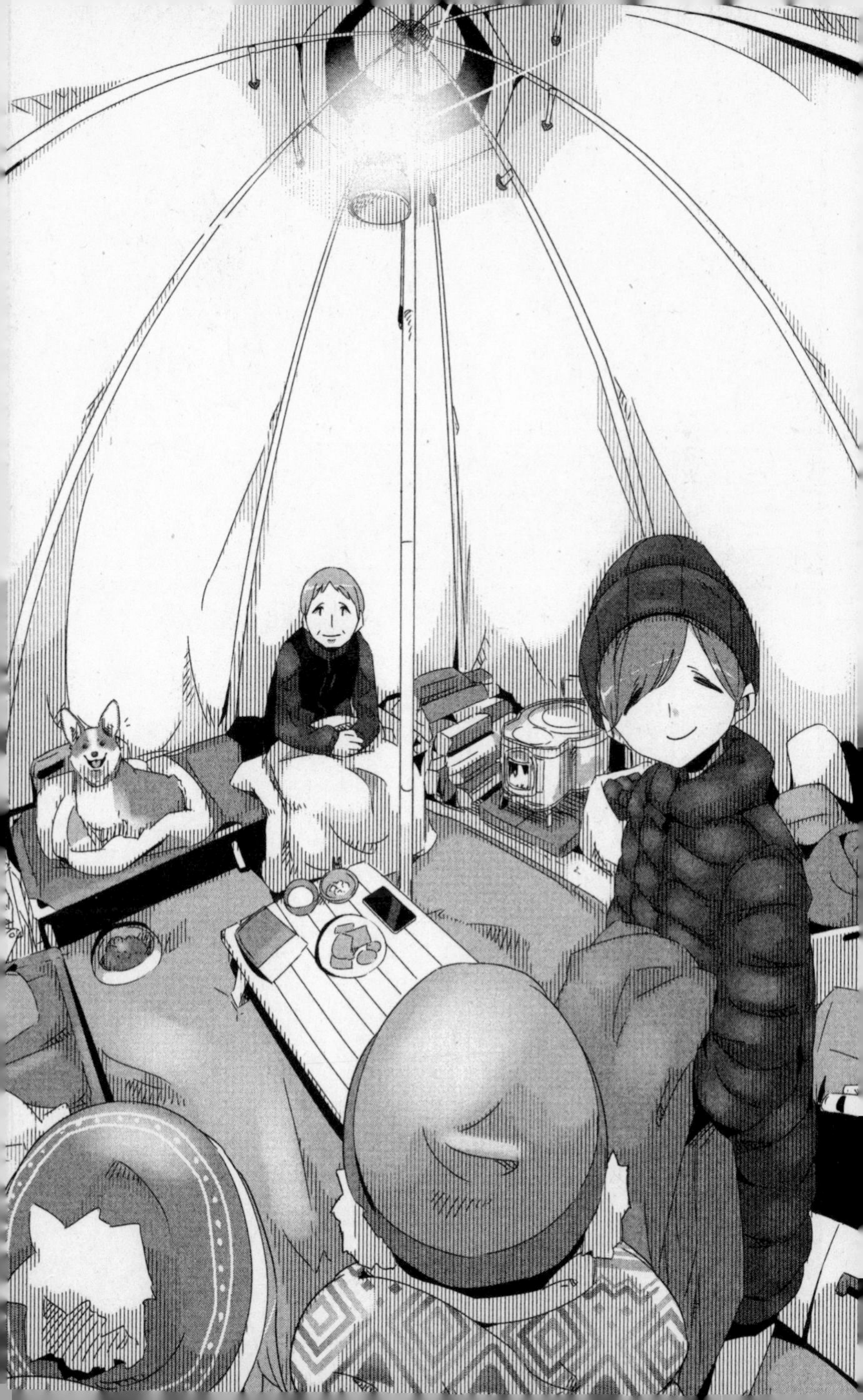

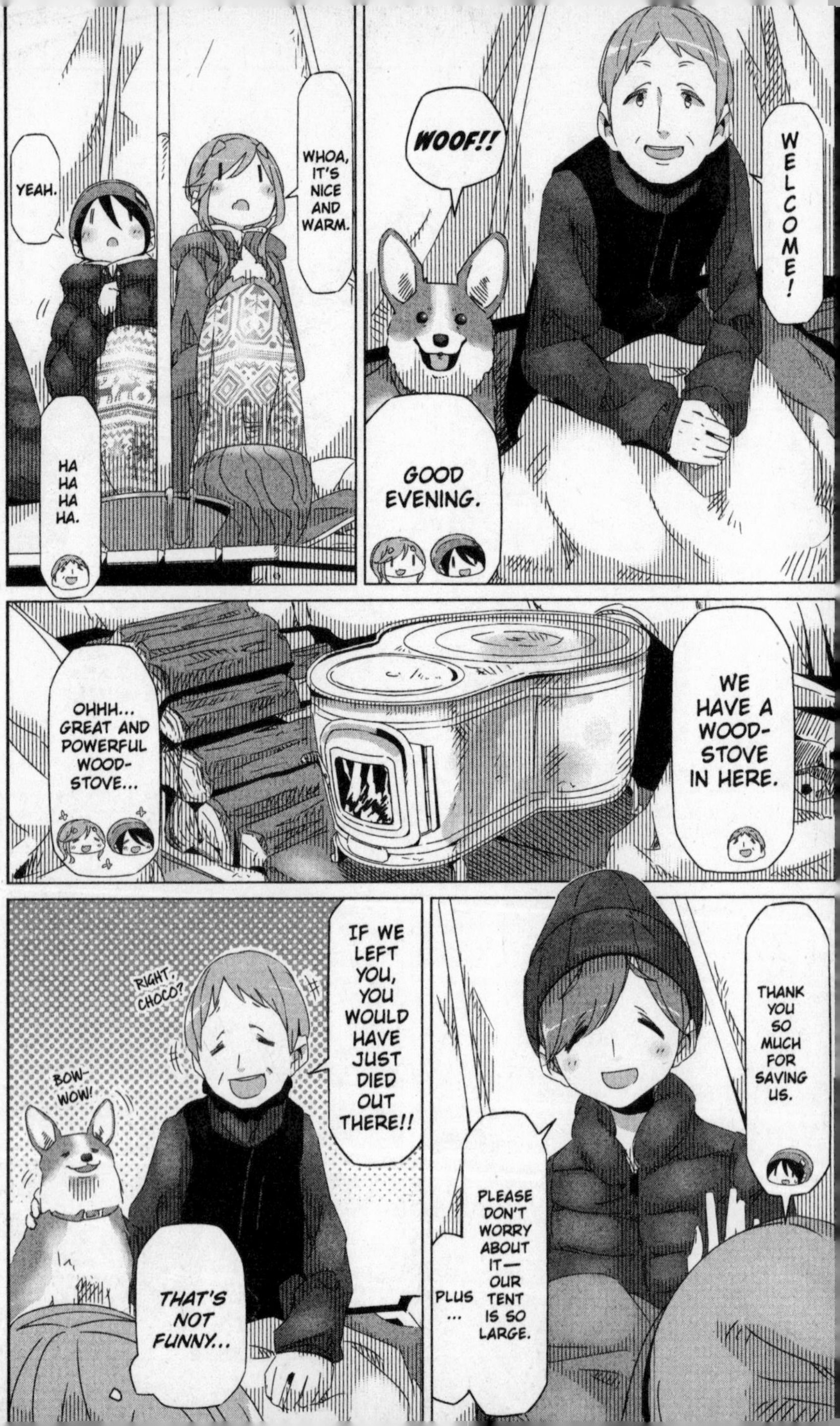
WELCOME!
WOOF!!
GOOD EVENING.
WHOA, IT'S NICE AND WARM.
YEAH.
HA HA HA HA.
WE HAVE A WOOD-STOVE IN HERE.
OHHH... GREAT AND POWERFUL WOOD-STOVE...
THANK YOU SO MUCH FOR SAVING US.
PLEASE DON'T WORRY ABOUT IT—OUR TENT IS SO LARGE.
PLUS...
IF WE LEFT YOU, YOU WOULD HAVE JUST DIED OUT THERE!!
RIGHT, CHOCO?
BOW-WOW!
THAT'S NOT FUNNY...

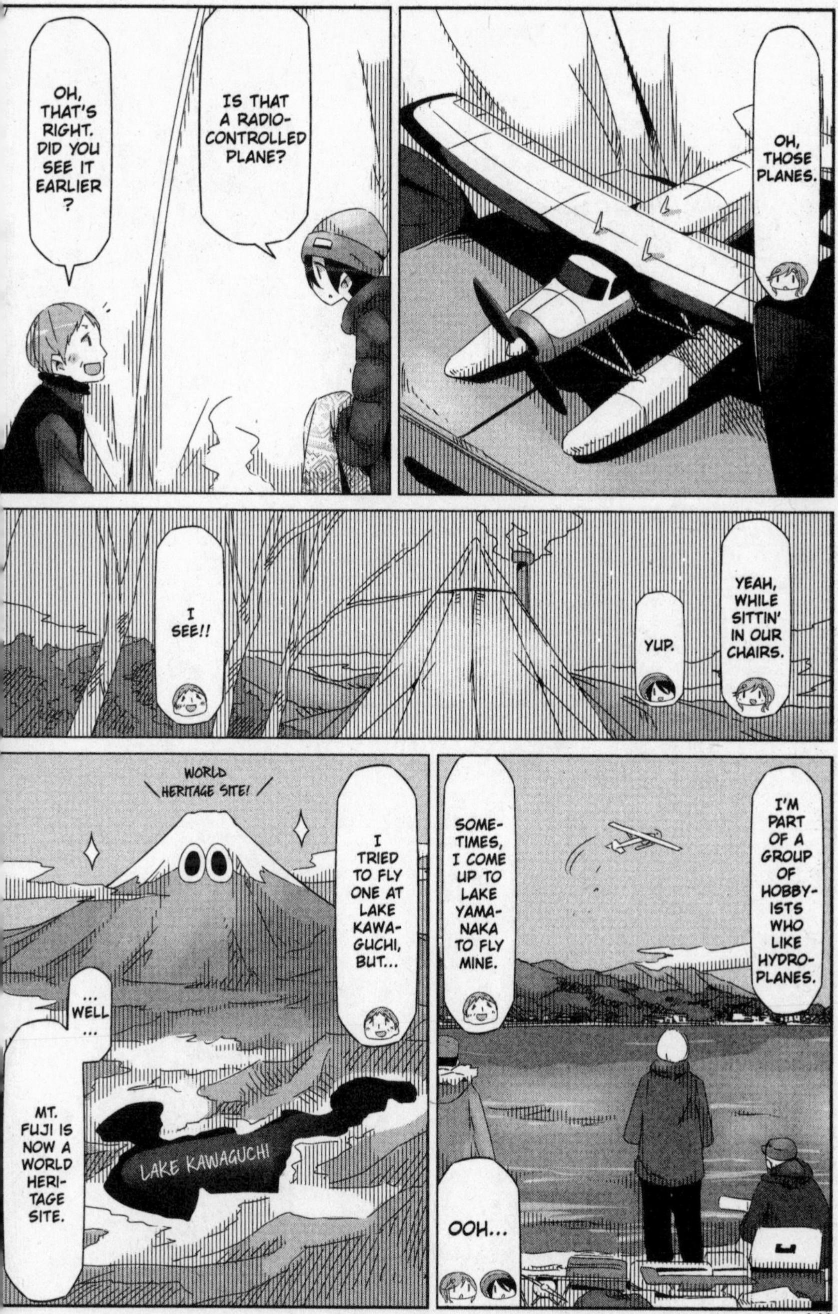
OH, THOSE PLANES.
IS THAT A RADIO-CONTROLLED PLANE?
OH, THAT'S RIGHT. DID YOU SEE IT EARLIER?
YEAH, WHILE SITTIN' IN OUR CHAIRS.
YUP.
I SEE!!
I'M PART OF A GROUP OF HOBBY-ISTS WHO LIKE HYDRO-PLANES.
SOME-TIMES, I COME UP TO LAKE YAMA-NAKA TO FLY MINE.
OOH...
I TRIED TO FLY ONE AT LAKE KAWA-GUCHI, BUT...
WORLD HERITAGE SITE!
...WELL...
MT. FUJI IS NOW A WORLD HERI-TAGE SITE.
LAKE KAWAGUCHI

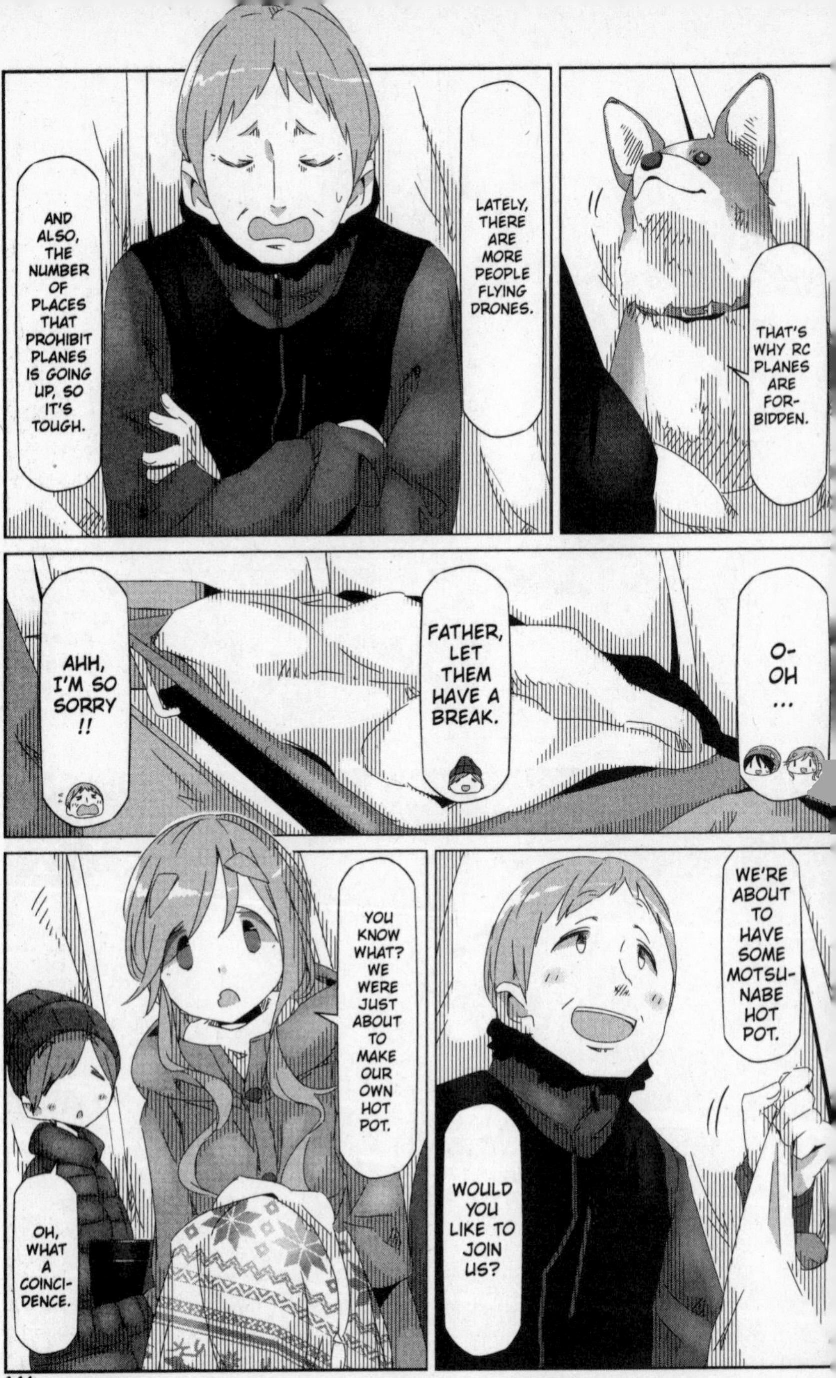
THAT'S WHY RC PLANES ARE FORBIDDEN.
LATELY, THERE ARE MORE PEOPLE FLYING DRONES.
AND ALSO, THE NUMBER OF PLACES THAT PROHIBIT PLANES IS GOING UP, SO IT'S TOUGH.
O-OH ...
FATHER, LET THEM HAVE A BREAK.
AHH, I'M SO SORRY !!
WE'RE ABOUT TO HAVE SOME MOTSU-NABE HOT POT.
WOULD YOU LIKE TO JOIN US?
YOU KNOW WHAT? WE WERE JUST ABOUT TO MAKE OUR OWN HOT POT.
OH, WHAT A COINCIDENCE.

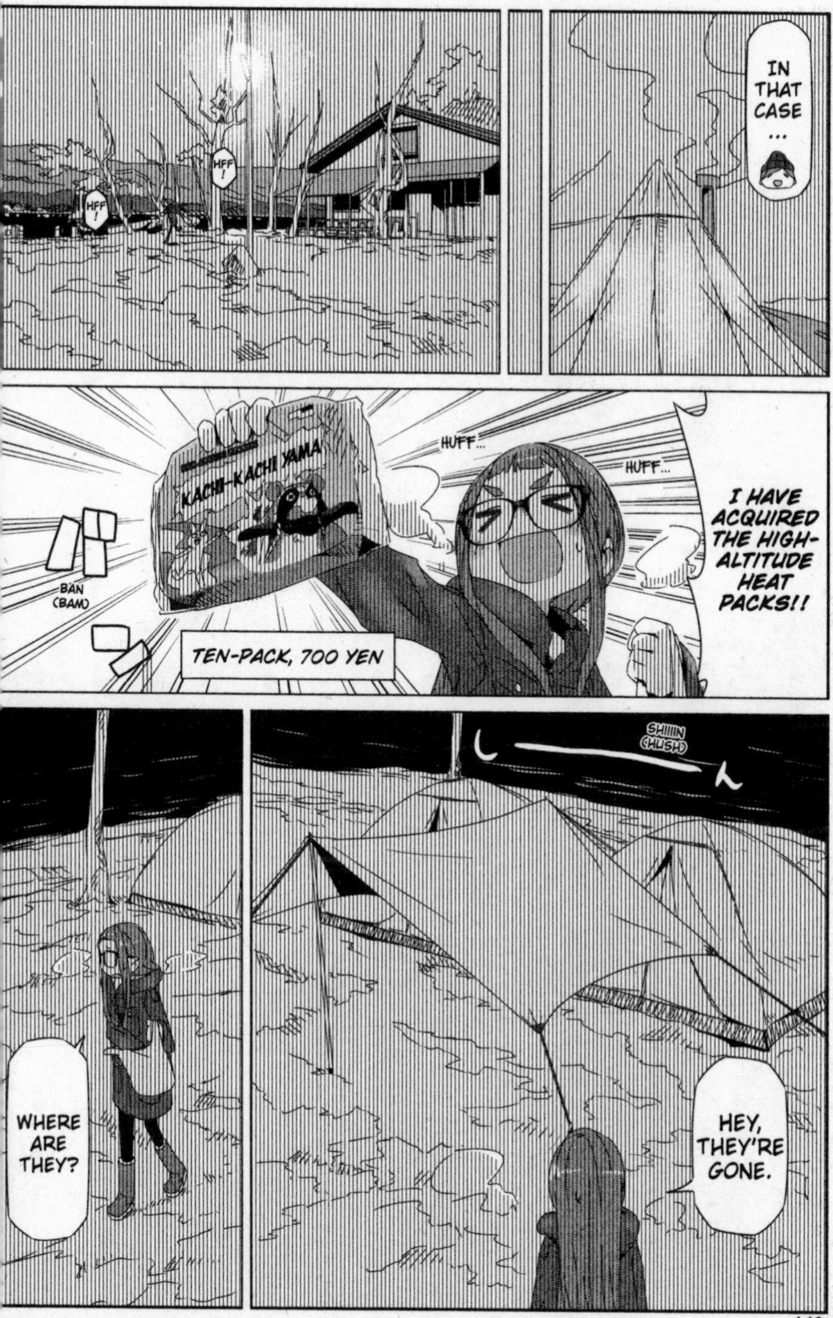
IN THAT CASE ...
HFF!
HFF!
I HAVE ACQUIRED THE HIGH-ALTITUDE HEAT PACKS!!
HUFF...
HUFF...
KACHI-KACHI YAMA
BAN (BAM)
TEN-PACK, 700 YEN
SHIIIIN (HUSH)
HEY, THEY'RE GONE.
WHERE ARE THEY?

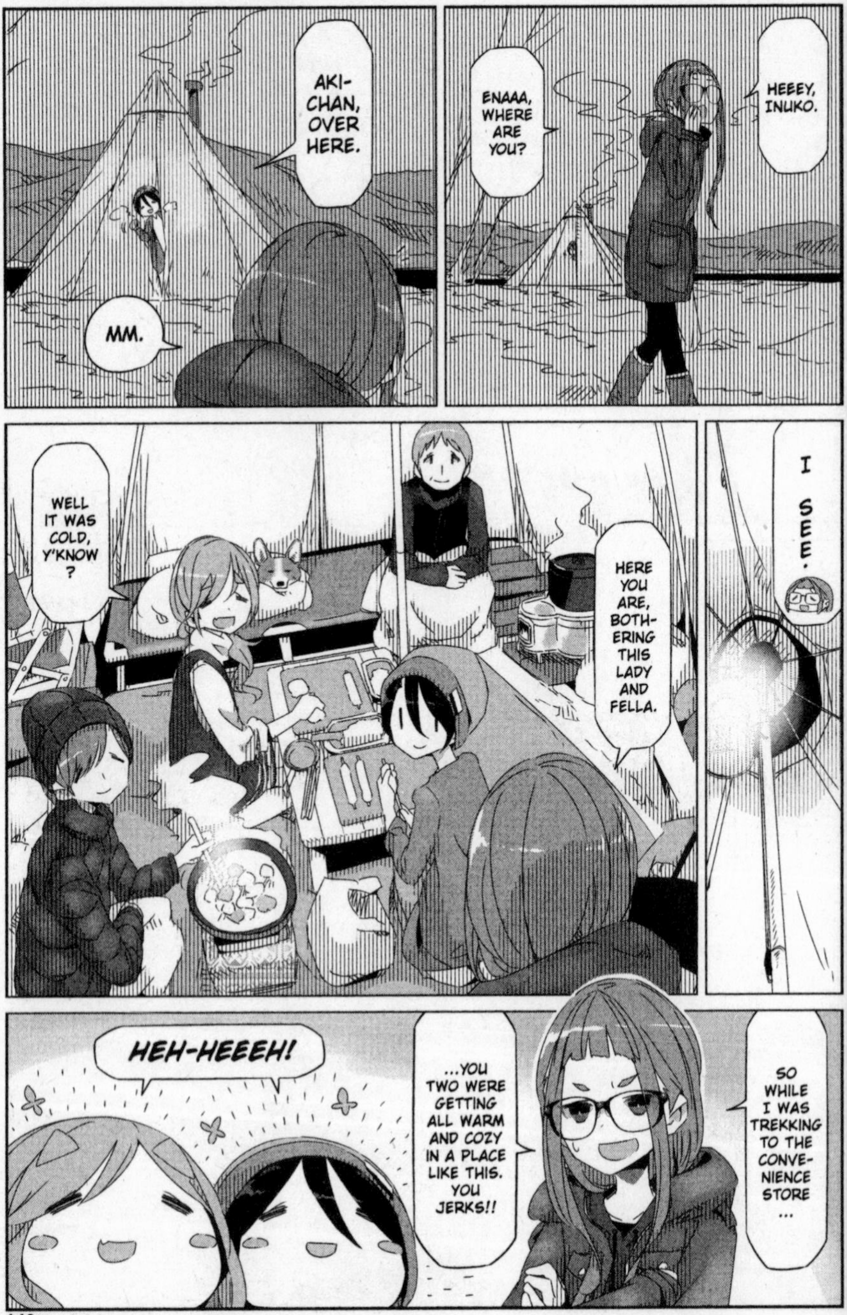
HEEEY, INUKO.
ENAAA, WHERE ARE YOU?
AKI-CHAN, OVER HERE.
MM.
I SEE.
HERE YOU ARE, BOTHERING THIS LADY AND FELLA.
WELL IT WAS COLD, Y'KNOW?
SO WHILE I WAS TREKKING TO THE CONVENIENCE STORE...
...YOU TWO WERE GETTING ALL WARM AND COZY IN A PLACE LIKE THIS. YOU JERKS!!
HEH-HEEEH!

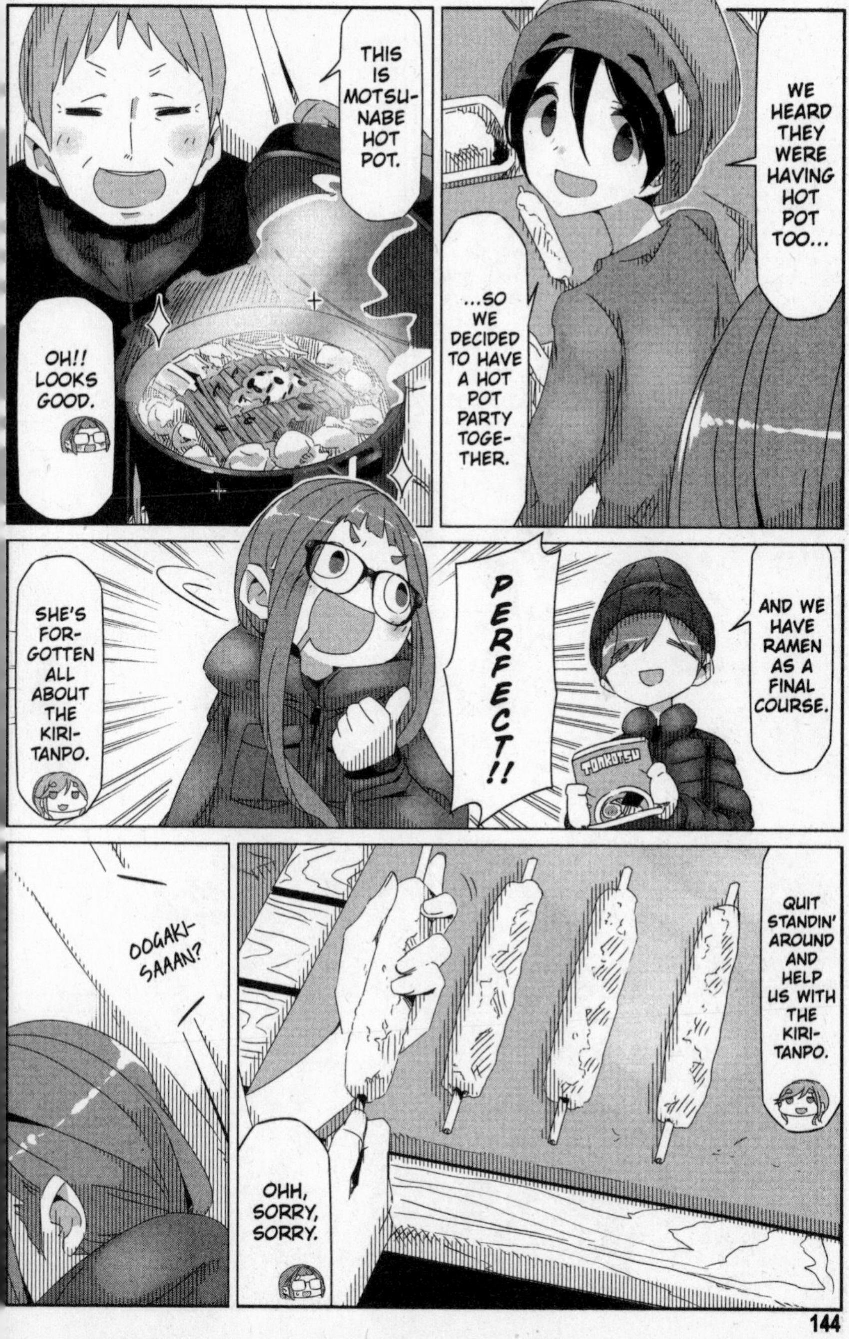
WE HEARD THEY WERE HAVING HOT POT TOO...
...SO WE DECIDED TO HAVE A HOT POT PARTY TOGETHER.
THIS IS MOTSUNABE HOT POT.
OH!! LOOKS GOOD.
AND WE HAVE RAMEN AS A FINAL COURSE.
TONKOTSU
PERFECT!!
SHE'S FORGOTTEN ALL ABOUT THE KIRITANPO.
QUIT STANDIN' AROUND AND HELP US WITH THE KIRITANPO.
OHH, SORRY, SORRY.
OOGAKI-SAAAN?

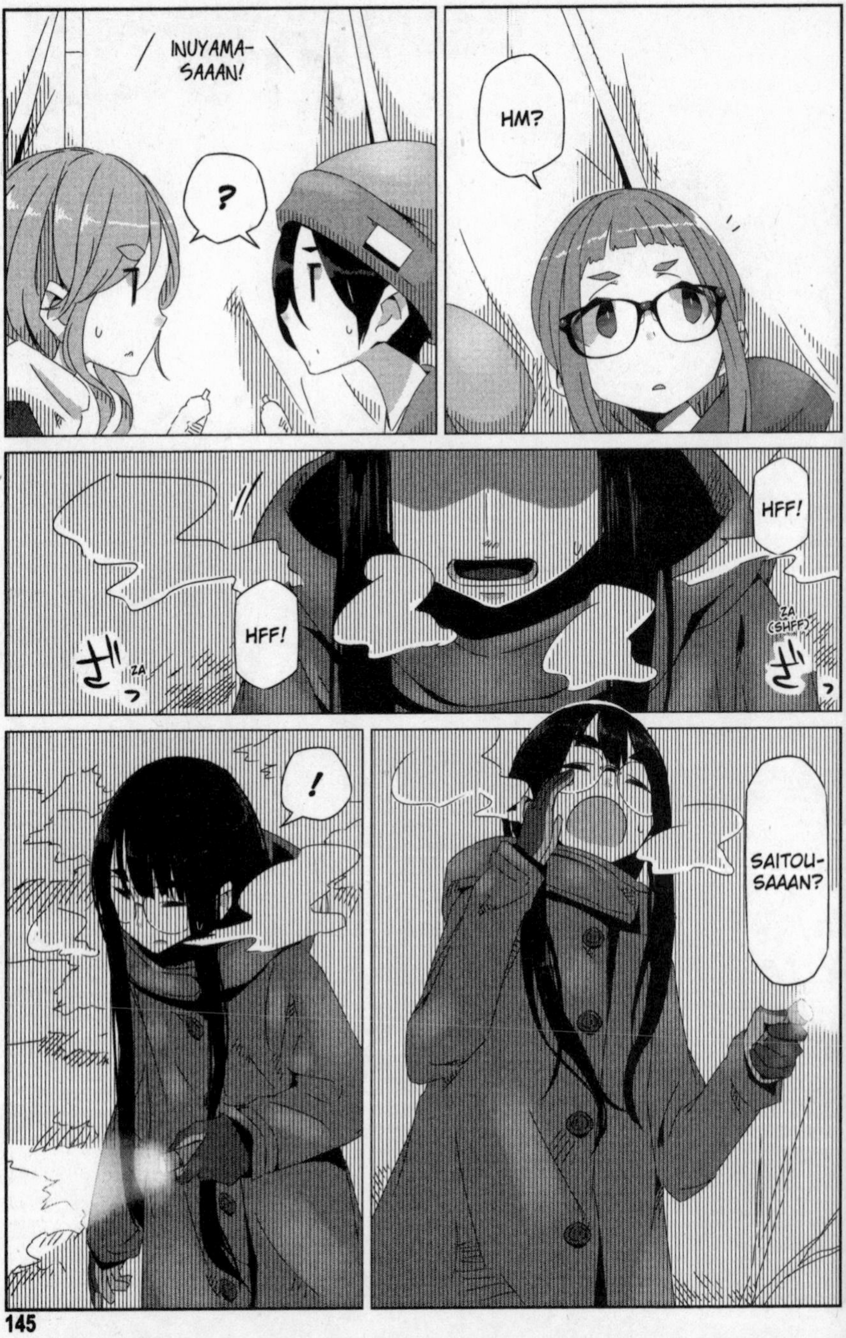
HM?
INUYAMA-SAAAN!
?
HFF!
ZA (SHFF)
ざっ
HFF!
ざっ
ZA
SAITOU-SAAAN?
!

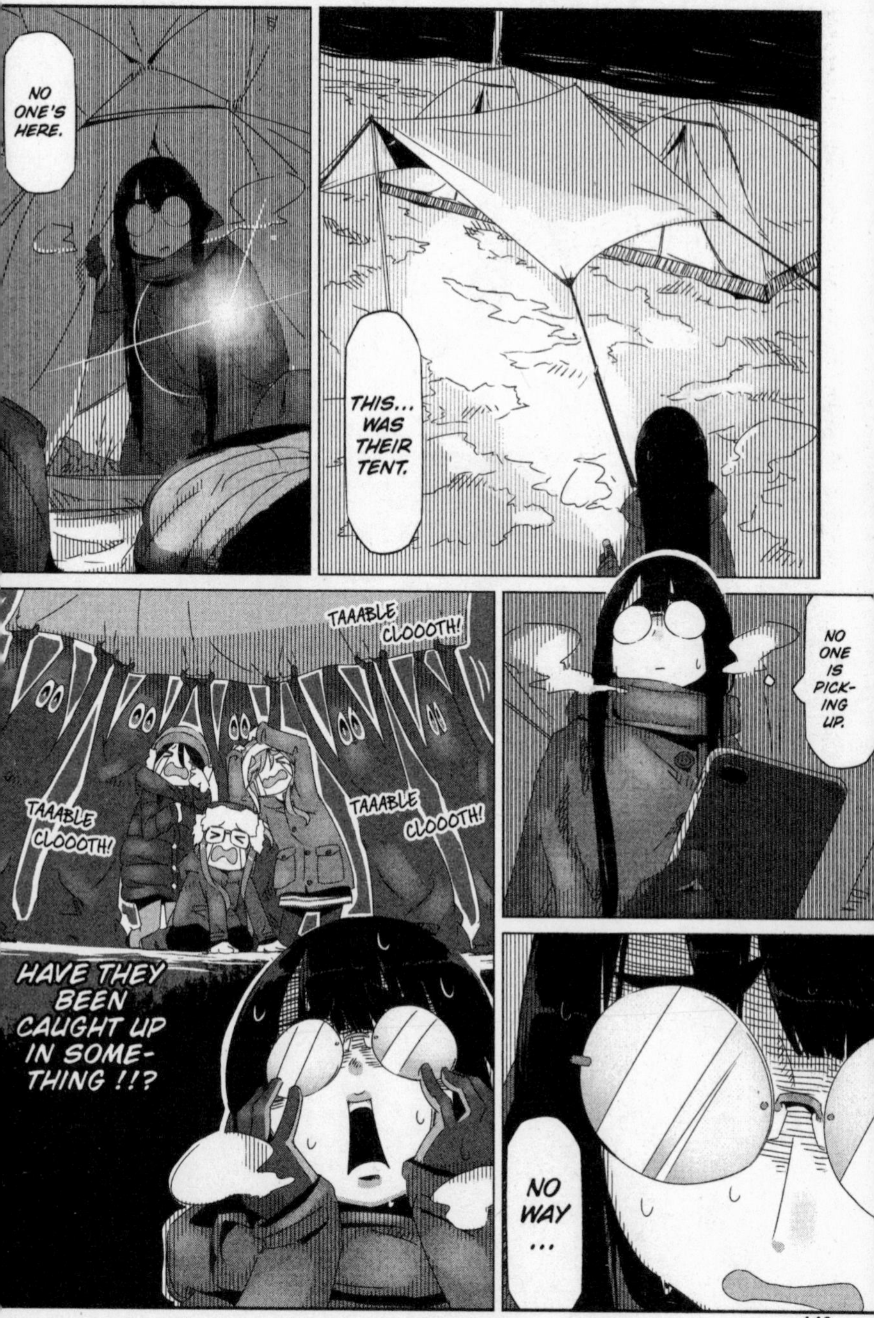
THIS... WAS THEIR TENT.
NO ONE'S HERE.
NO ONE IS PICK-ING UP.
TAAABLE CLOOOTH!
TAAABLE CLOOOTH!
TAAABLE CLOOOTH!
NO WAY ...
HAVE THEY BEEN CAUGHT UP IN SOME-THING !!?

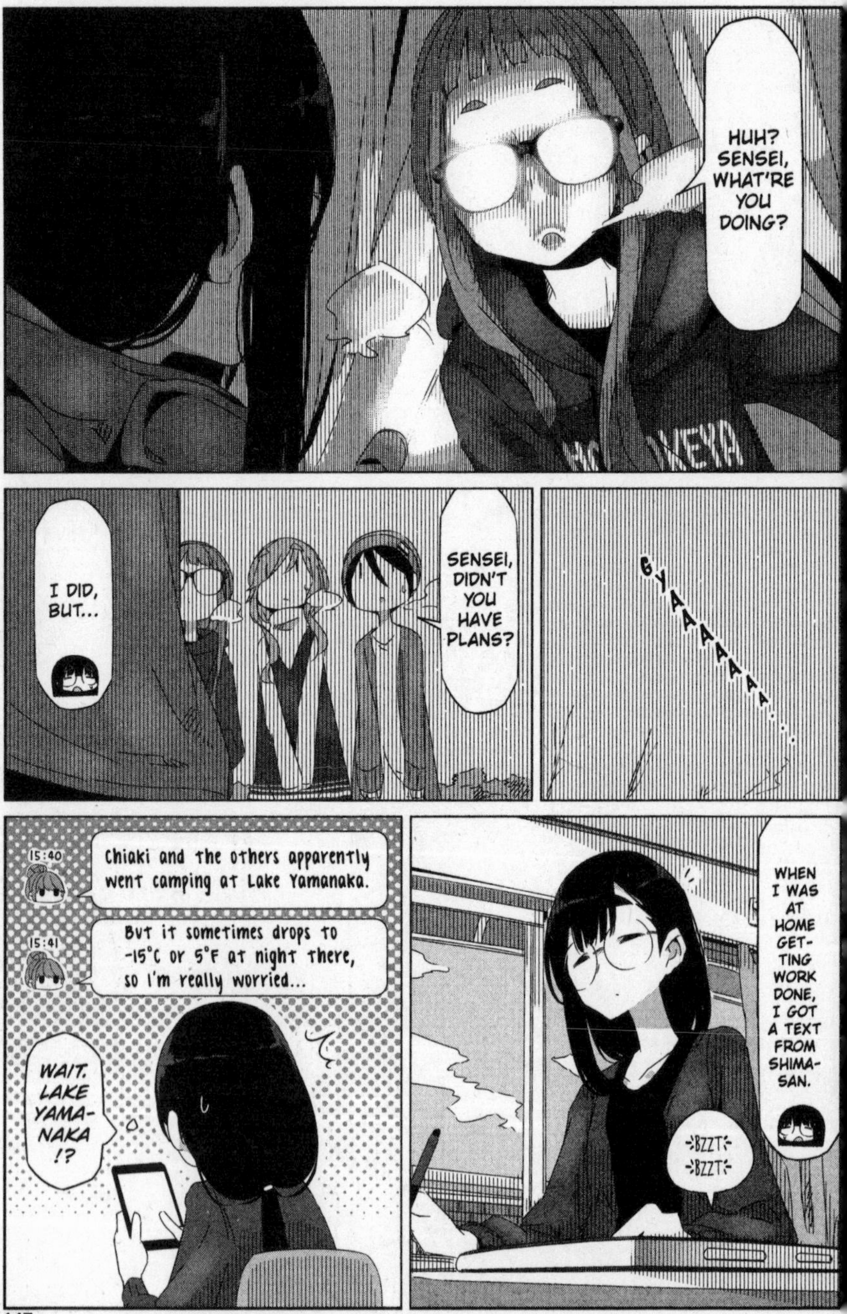
HUH? SENSEI, WHAT'RE YOU DOING?
GYAAAAAAAA...
SENSEI, DIDN'T YOU HAVE PLANS?
I DID, BUT...
WHEN I WAS AT HOME GETTING WORK DONE, I GOT A TEXT FROM SHIMA-SAN.
BZZT BZZT
15:40
Chiaki and the others apparently went camping at Lake Yamanaka.
15:41
But it sometimes drops to -15°C or 5°F at night there, so I'm really worried...
WAIT. LAKE YAMANAKA!?

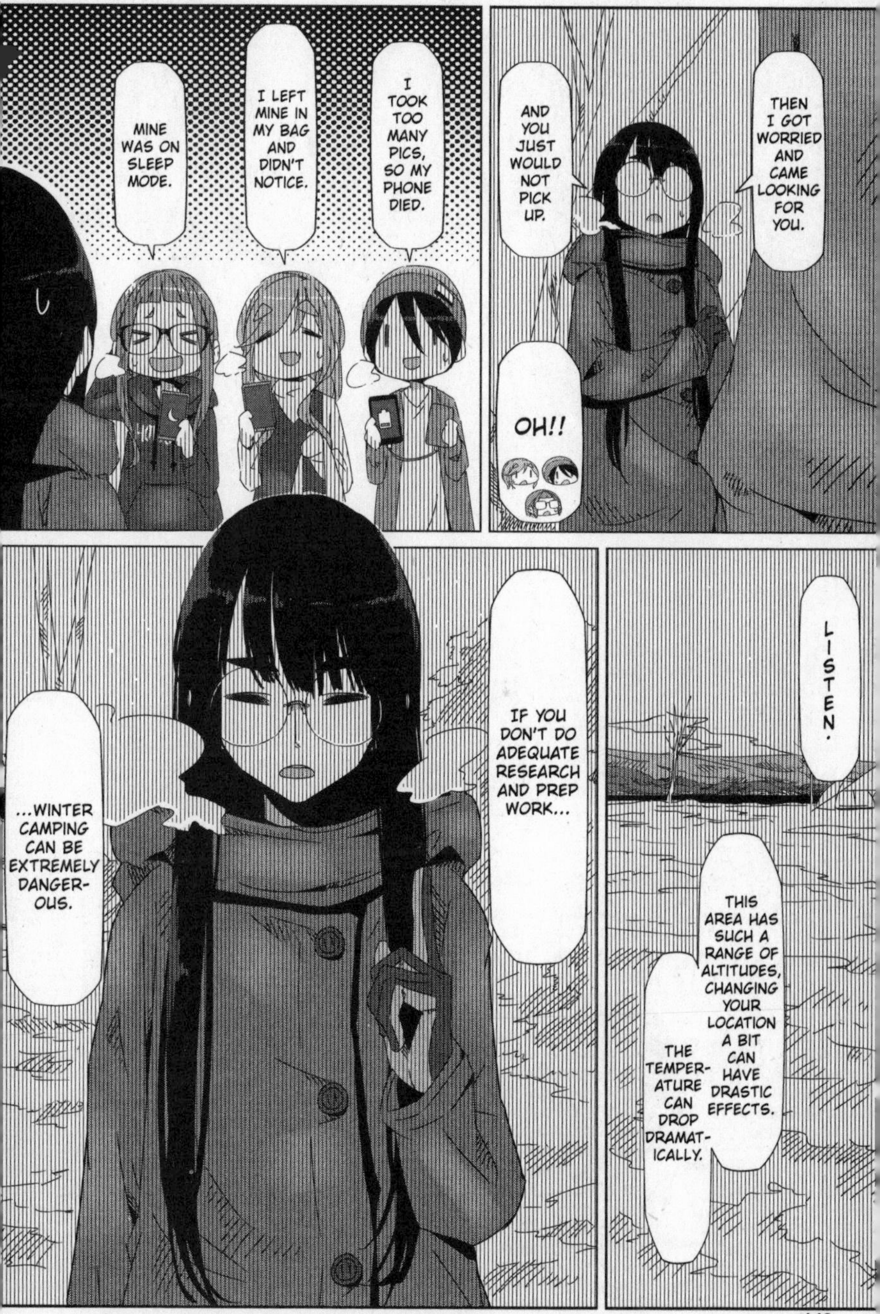
THEN I GOT WORRIED AND CAME LOOKING FOR YOU.
AND YOU JUST WOULD NOT PICK UP.
OH!!
I TOOK TOO MANY PICS, SO MY PHONE DIED.
I LEFT MINE IN MY BAG AND DIDN'T NOTICE.
MINE WAS ON SLEEP MODE.
LISTEN.
THIS AREA HAS SUCH A RANGE OF ALTITUDES, CHANGING YOUR LOCATION A BIT CAN HAVE DRASTIC EFFECTS.
THE TEMPER-ATURE CAN DROP DRAMAT-ICALLY.
IF YOU DON'T DO ADEQUATE RESEARCH AND PREP WORK...
...WINTER CAMPING CAN BE EXTREMELY DANGER-OUS.

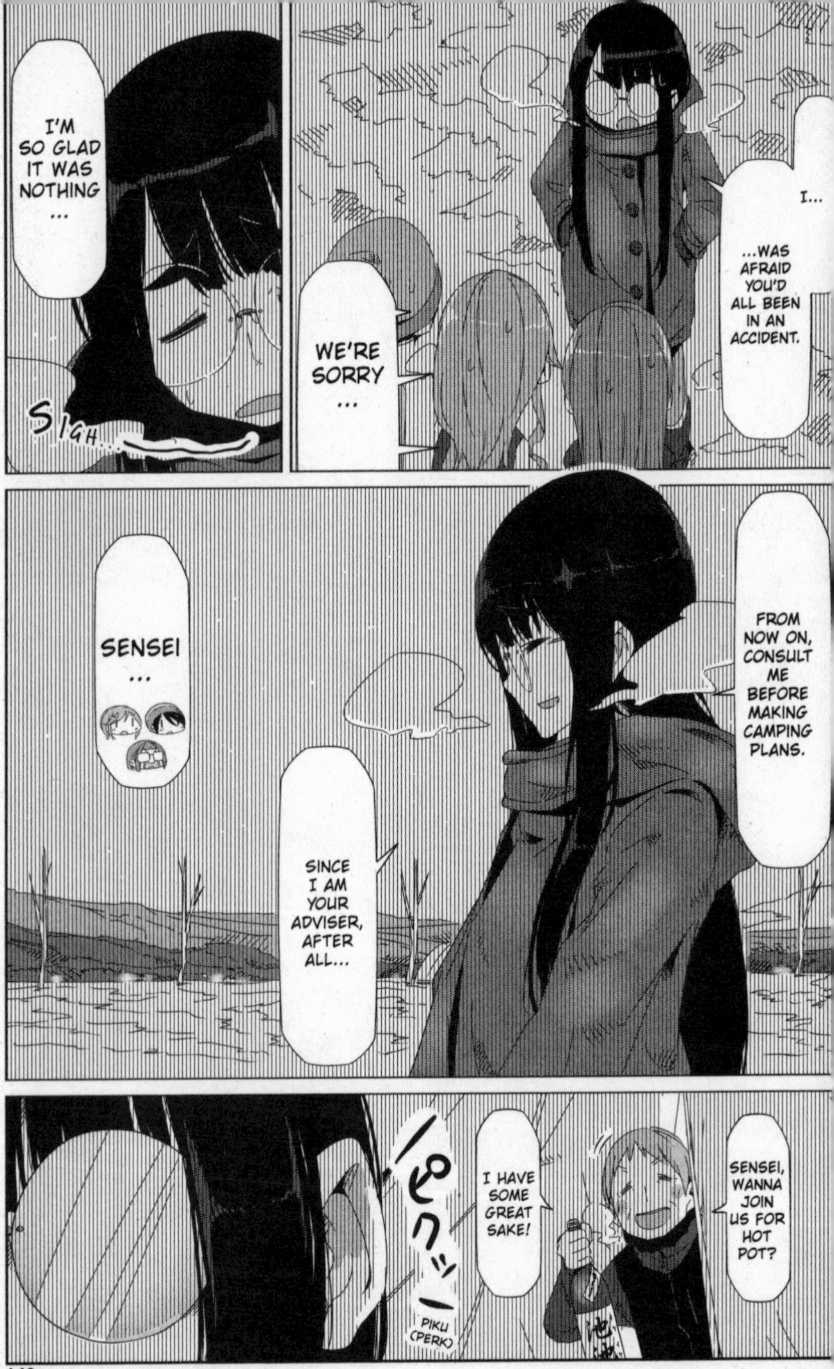
I...
...WAS AFRAID YOU'D ALL BEEN IN AN ACCIDENT.
WE'RE SORRY...
I'M SO GLAD IT WAS NOTHING...
SIGH...
FROM NOW ON, CONSULT ME BEFORE MAKING CAMPING PLANS.
SINCE I AM YOUR ADVISER, AFTER ALL...
SENSEI...
SENSEI, WANNA JOIN US FOR HOT POT?
I HAVE SOME GREAT SAKE!
ピクッ
PIKU (PERK)

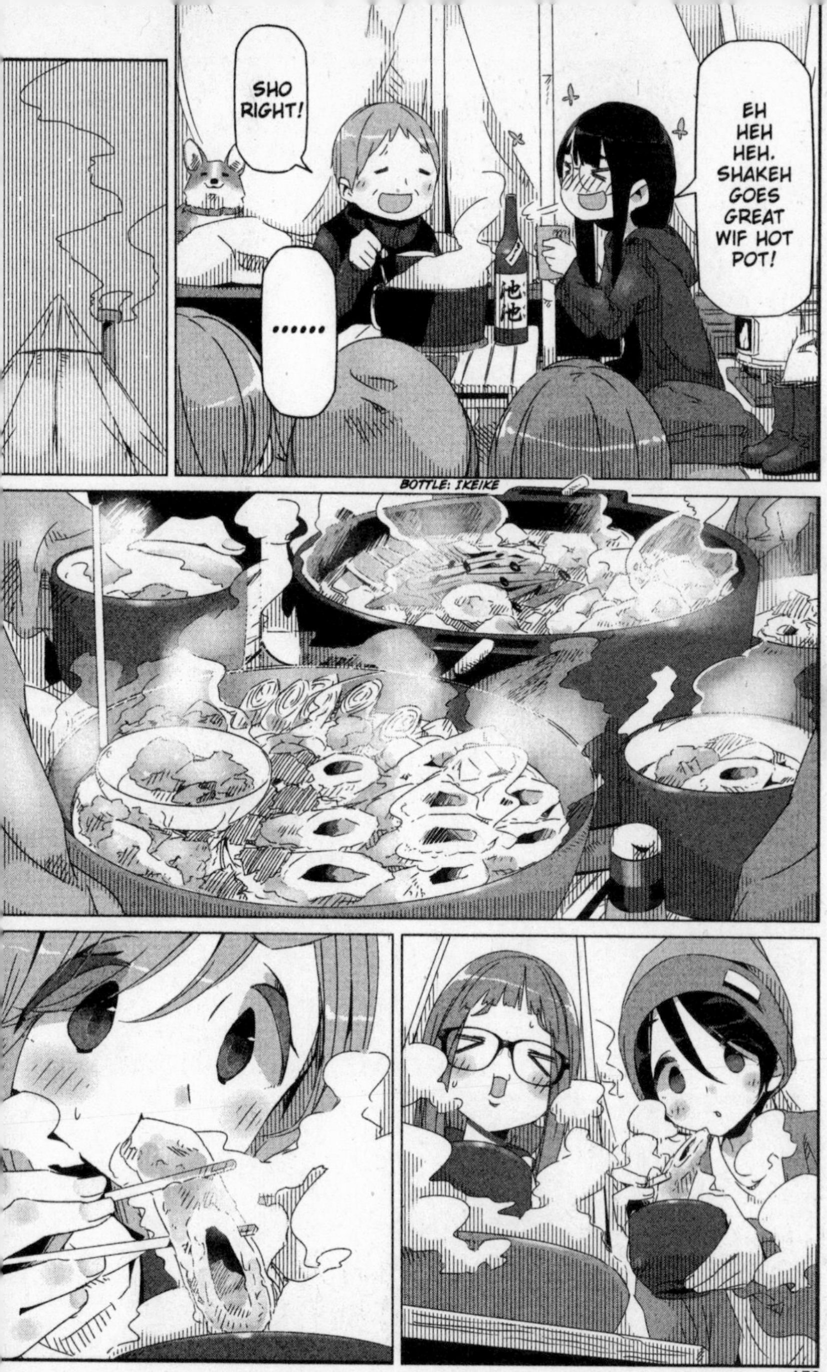
EH HEH HEH. SHAKEH GOES GREAT WIF HOT POT!
池池
SHO RIGHT!
......
BOTTLE: IKEIKE

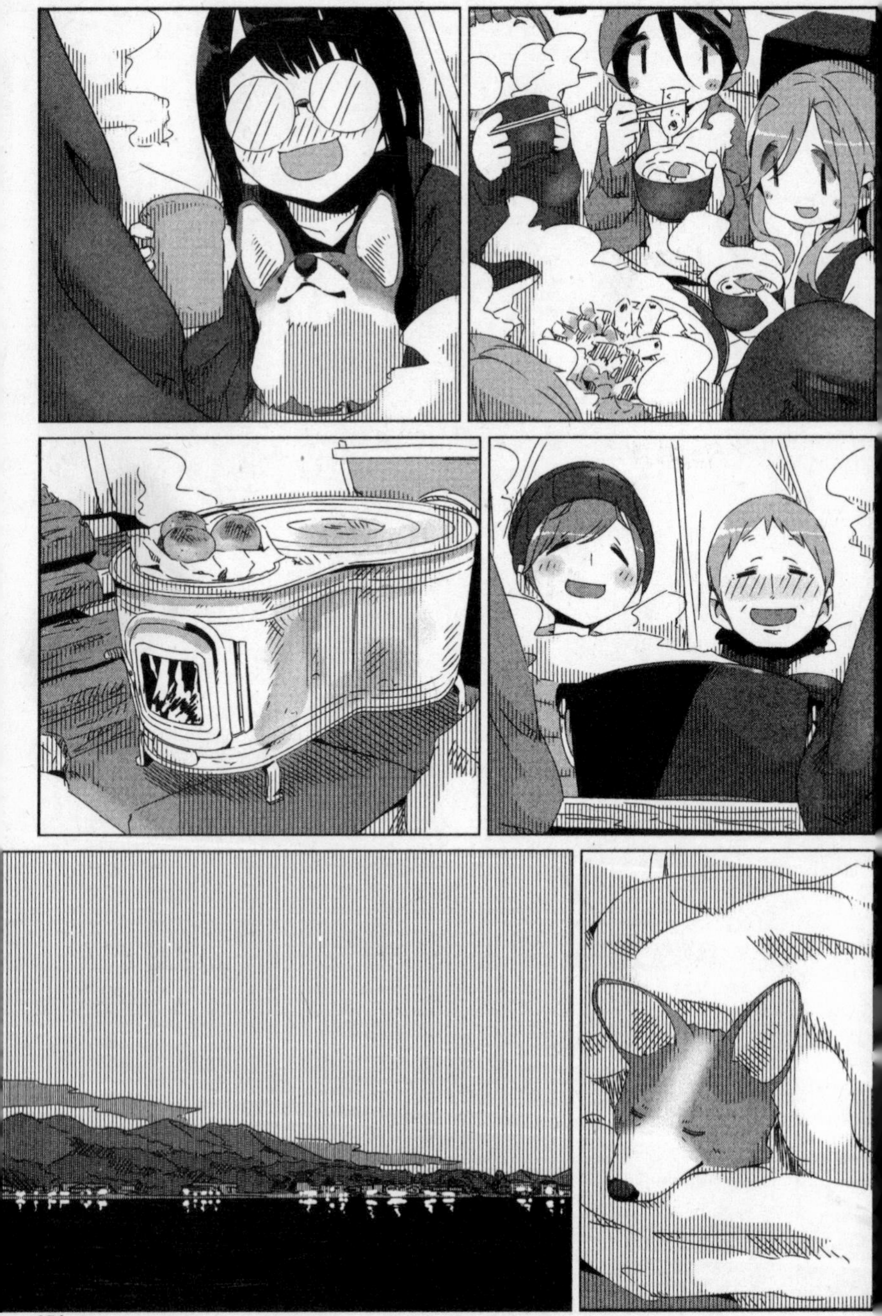

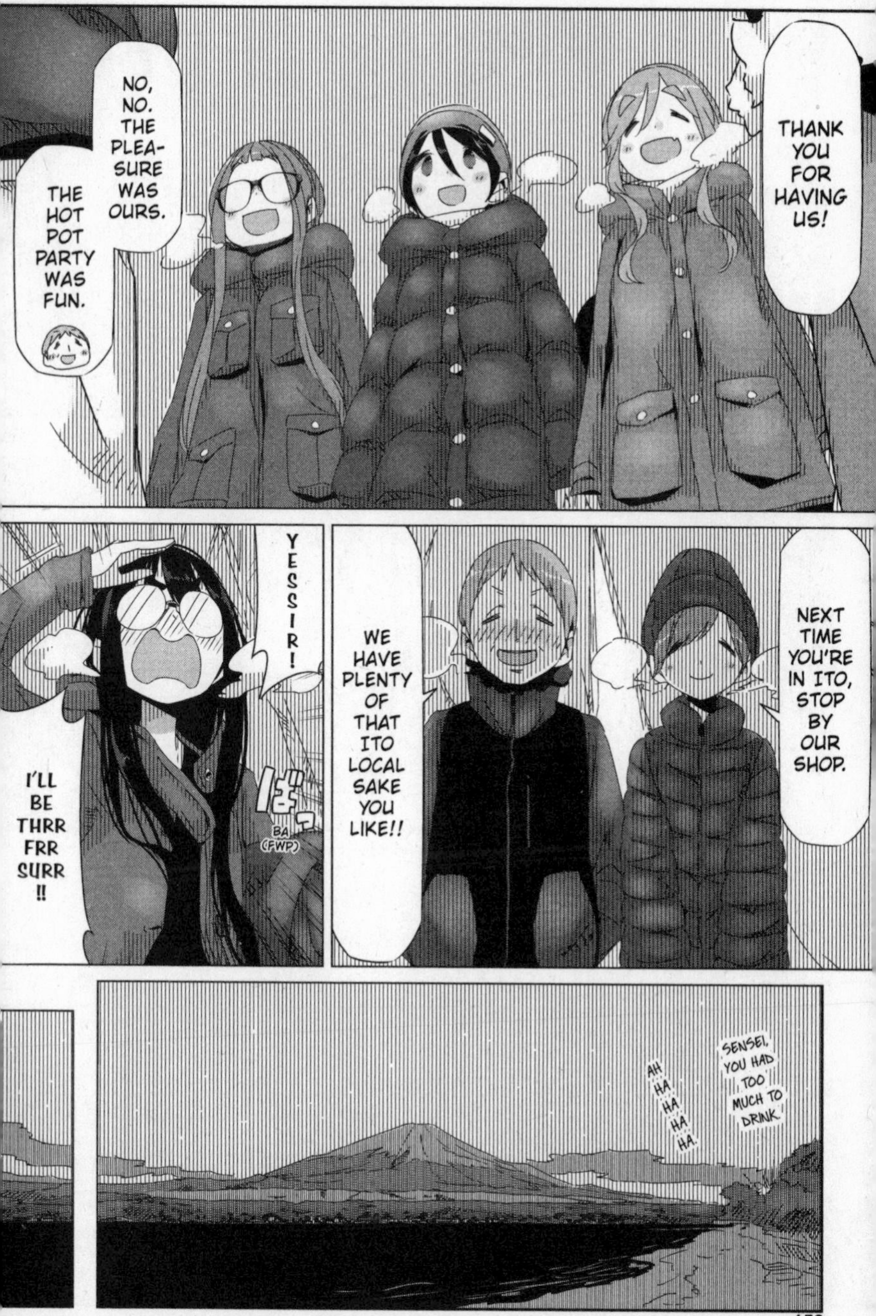
THANK YOU FOR HAVING US!
NO, NO. THE PLEA-SURE WAS OURS.
THE HOT POT PARTY WAS FUN.
NEXT TIME YOU'RE IN ITO, STOP BY OUR SHOP.
WE HAVE PLENTY OF THAT ITO LOCAL SAKE YOU LIKE!!
YESSIR!
BA (FWP)
I'LL BE THRR FRR SURR!!
SENSEI, YOU HAD TOO MUCH TO DRINK.
AH HA HA HA HA HA.

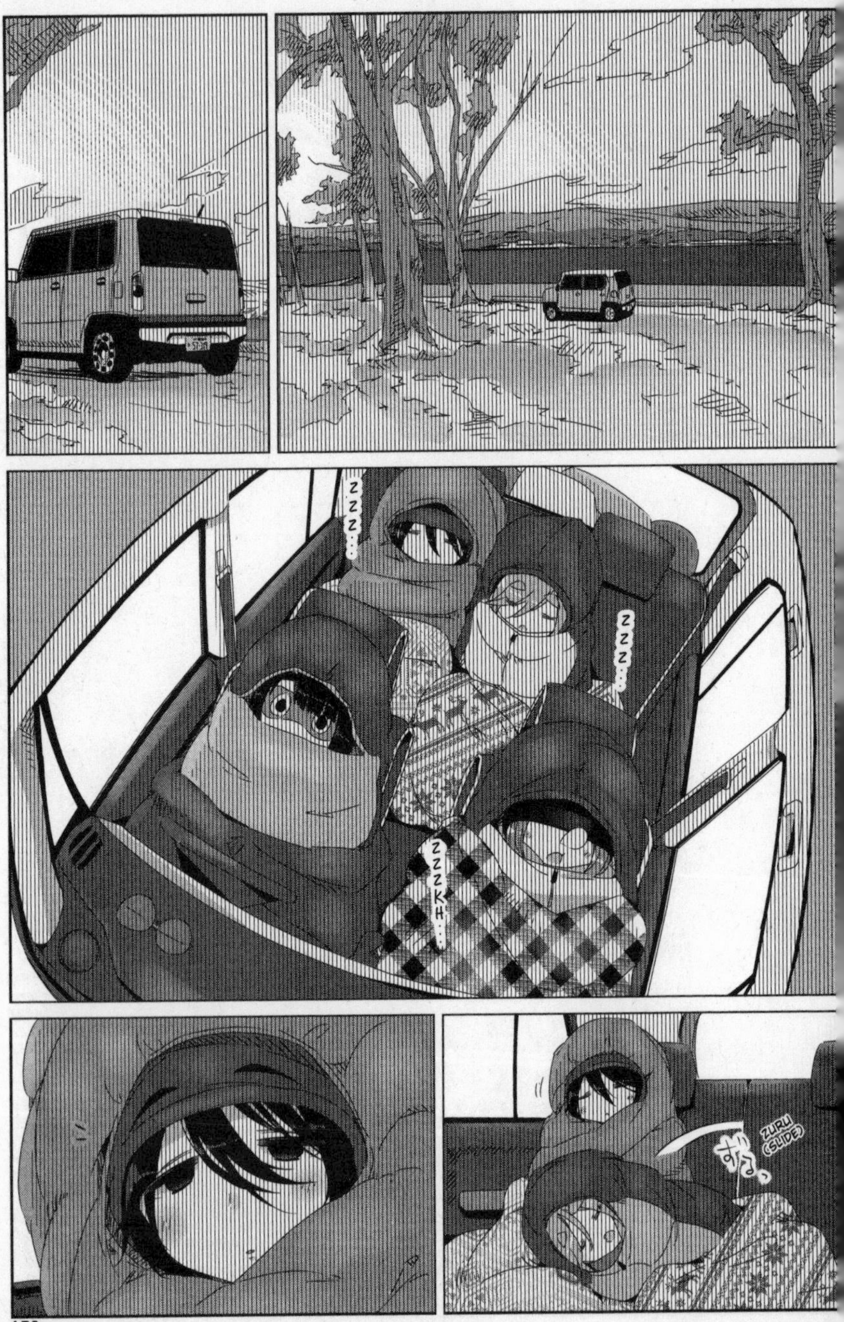
Z Z Z . . .
Z Z Z . . .
Z Z Z K H . . .
ZURU (SLIDE)

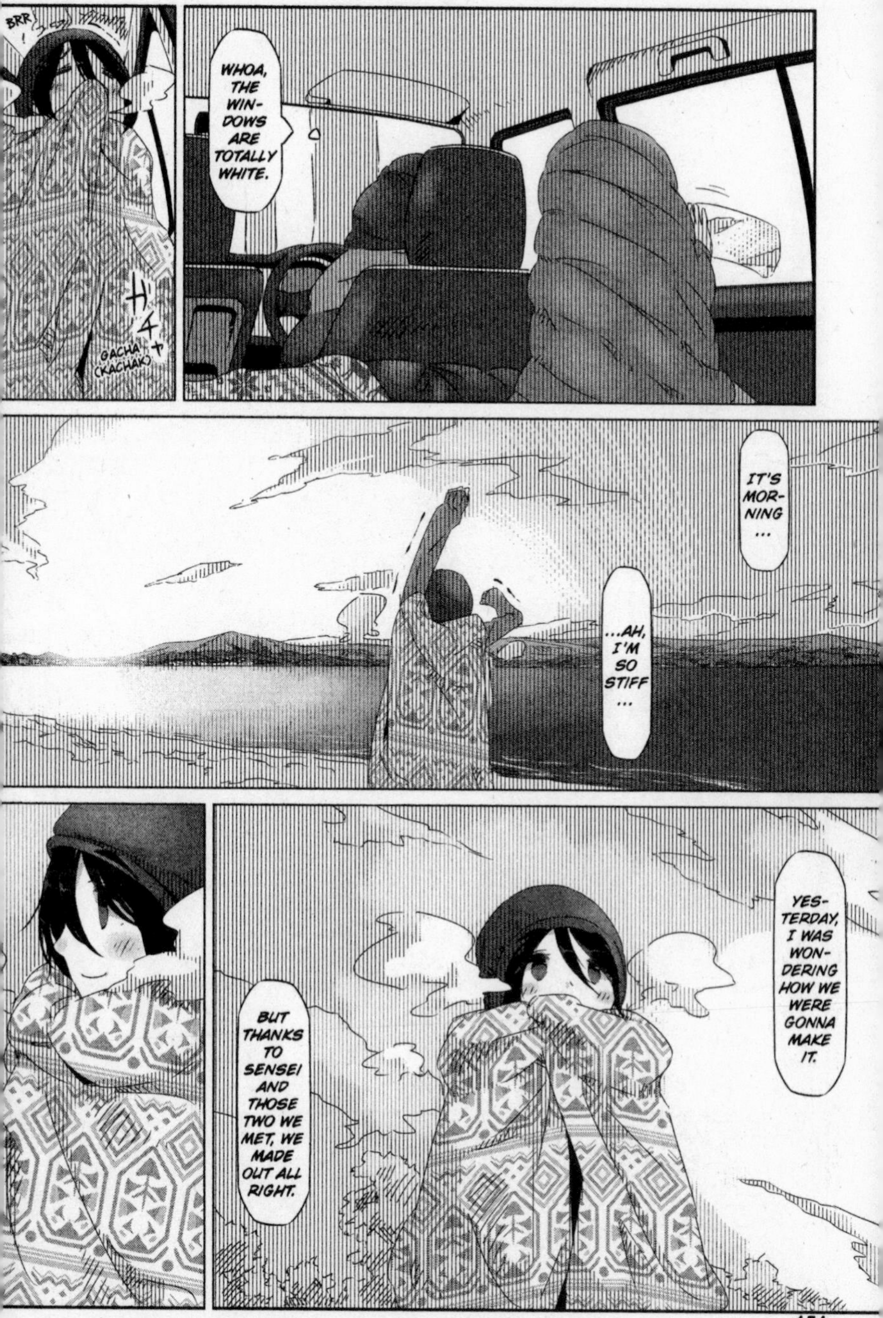
WHOA, THE WIN-DOWS ARE TOTALLY WHITE.
BRR!
ガチャ
GACHA (KACHAK)
IT'S MOR-NING...
...AH, I'M SO STIFF...
YES-TERDAY, I WAS WON-DERING HOW WE WERE GONNA MAKE IT.
BUT THANKS TO SENSEI AND THOSE TWO WE MET, WE MADE OUT ALL RIGHT.

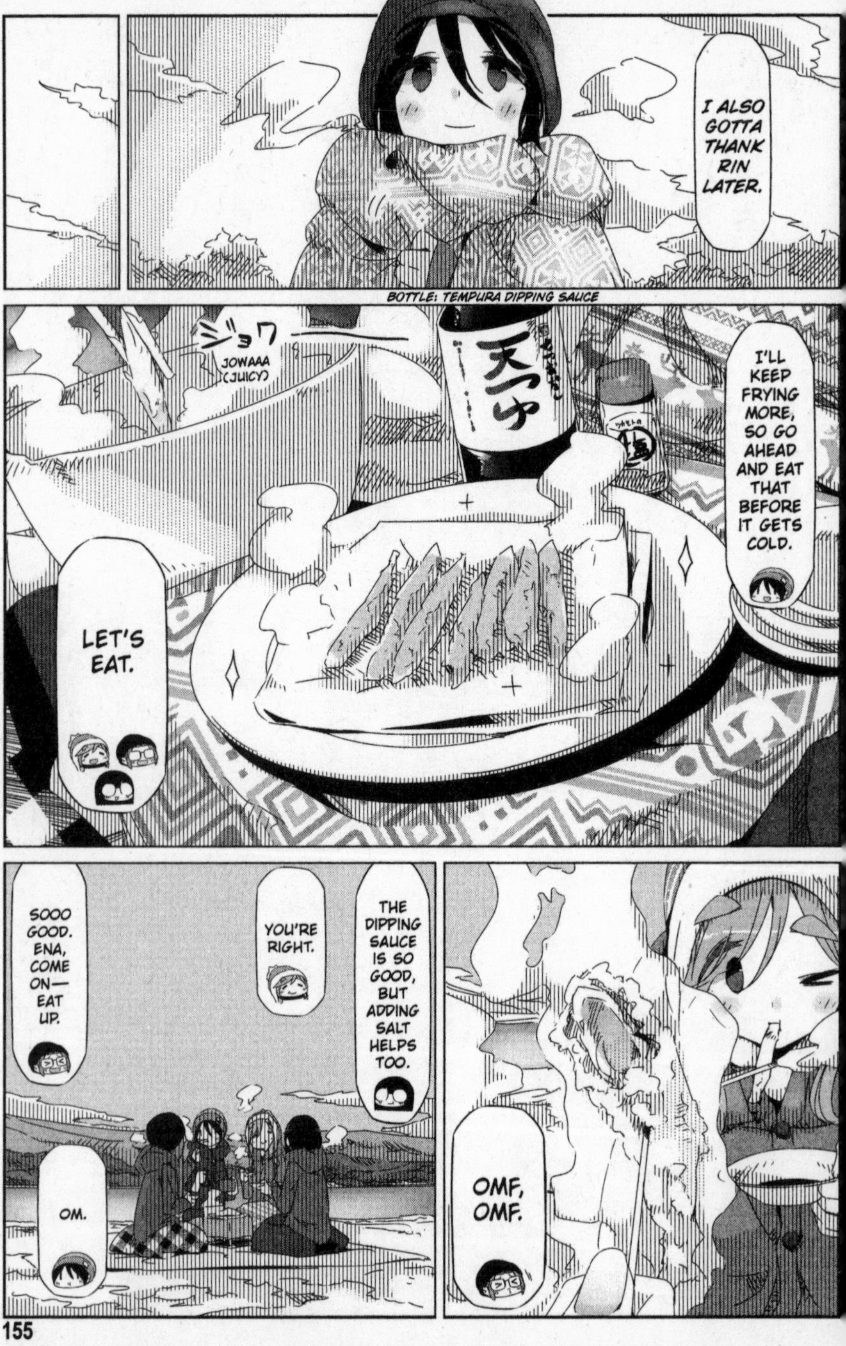
I ALSO GOTTA THANK RIN LATER.
BOTTLE: TEMPURA DIPPING SAUCE
I'LL KEEP FRYING MORE, SO GO AHEAD AND EAT THAT BEFORE IT GETS COLD.
ジョワ—
JOWAAA (JUICY)
天つゆ
LET'S EAT.
OMF, OMF.
THE DIPPING SAUCE IS SO GOOD, BUT ADDING SALT HELPS TOO.
YOU'RE RIGHT.
SOOO GOOD. ENA, COME ON— EAT UP.
OM.

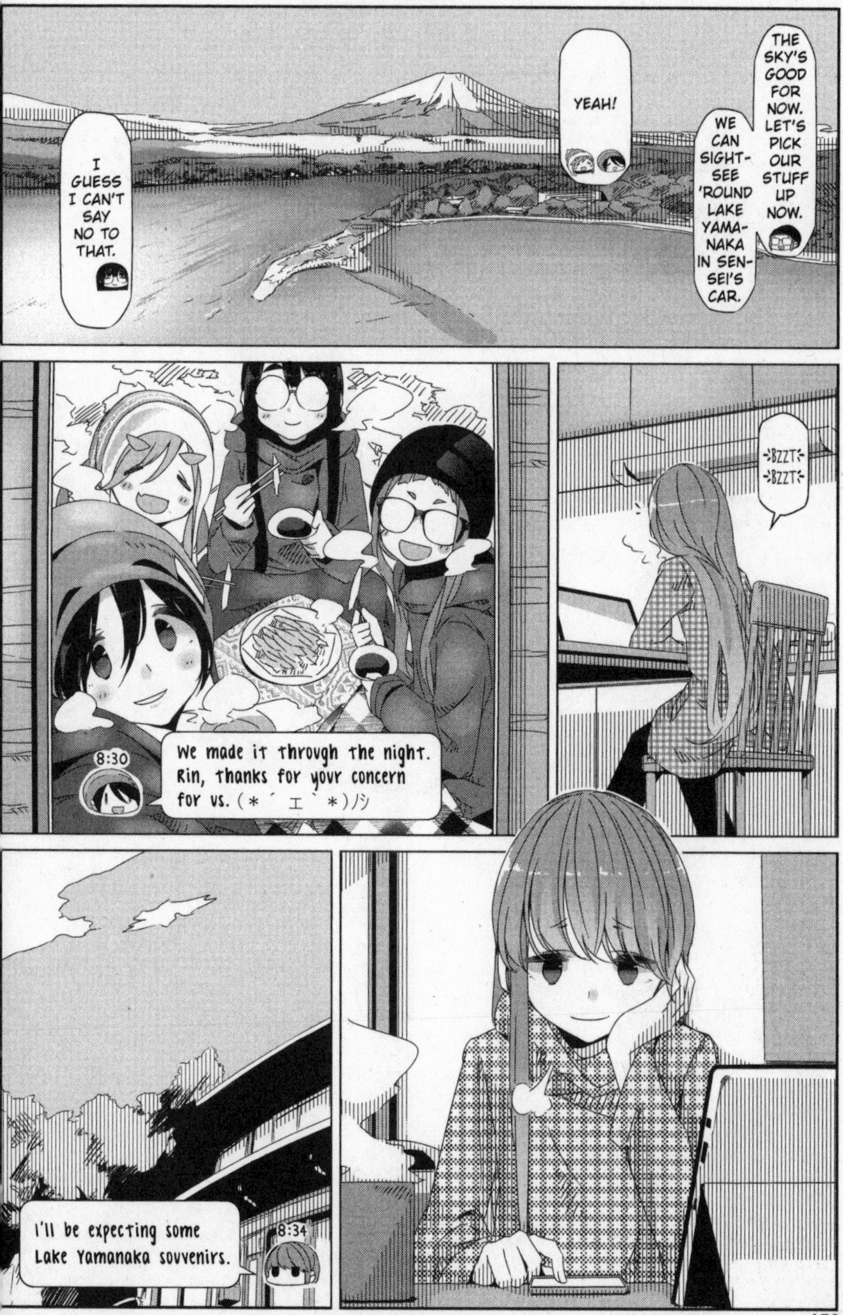
THE SKY'S GOOD FOR NOW. LET'S PICK OUR STUFF UP NOW.
WE CAN SIGHT-SEE 'ROUND LAKE YAMANAKA IN SEN-SEI'S CAR.
YEAH!
I GUESS I CAN'T SAY NO TO THAT.
-BZZT- -BZZT-
8:30
We made it through the night. Rin, thanks for your concern for us. (*´エ`*)ノシ
8:34
I'll be expecting some Lake Yamanaka souvenirs.

TRANSLATION NOTES

COMMON HONORIFICS

no honorific: Indicates familiarity or closeness; if used without permission or reason, addressing someone in this manner would constitute an insult.

-san: The Japanese equivalent of Mr./Mrs./Miss. If a situation calls for politeness, this is the fail-safe honorific.

-kun: Used most often when referring to boys, this indicates affection or familiarity. Occasionally used by older men among their peers, but it may also be used by anyone referring to a person of lower standing.

-chan: An affectionate honorific indicating familiarity used mostly in reference to girls; also used in reference to cute persons or animals of either gender.

-sensei: A respectful term for teachers, artists, or high-level professionals.

(o)nee: Japanese equivalent to "older sis."

(o)nii: Japanese equivalent to "older bro."

100 yen is approximately $1 USD.

PAGE 3
Kurikinton: Mashed potatoes blended with mashed chestnuts.

PAGE 4
Suppon Biscuit: Based on a similar real-life product called Suppon Sablé, a shortbread cookie made to resemble a soft-shelled turtle (*suppon*). There is no actual turtle (or turtle flavoring) inside the cookie.

PAGE 7
The End: This logo is a spoof of the ending logo that appears in NHK (Japan Broadcasting Corporation) broadcasts.

PAGE 30
Hagino: A parody of the Japanese supermarket chain Ogino.

PAGE 34
Cards: The game Nadeshiko is playing is called *e-awase karuta*. Typically, players must touch the correct card based on information given, and whoever has the most cards wins. It's most commonly played using poetry.

PAGE 36
Lake Yamanaka: One of the Mt. Fuji five lakes and the one highest in elevation.

PAGE 39
Tempura: A dish where vegetables, seafood, or other ingredients are deep-fried in a light batter.

Donburi: A dish where ingredients such as meat, vegetables, or fish are simmered together in sauce and served over rice.

PAGES 44
Nadeshiko's face: Her expression, especially in the eyes, resembles the typical look of a 1970s *shoujo* manga heroine.

PAGES 63
Mt. Fuji Radar Dome: A now-out-of-use weather observation center that has since become an exhibition facility dedicated to promoting the science of weather observation.

TRANSLATION NOTES (continued)

PAGES 85
Kikyou shingen: *Shingen mochi* (chewy rice balls covered in *kinako*, or soybean flour powder, and black molasses) from the confectionary maker Kikyouya.

PAGE 88
Kiritanpo: Mashed rice used for dumplings and soups.

Nobunaga Oda: A feudal lord famous for his attempt to unify Japan during the Sengoku period in the 16th century. As far as notable leaders in Japanese history go, he's one of the biggest.

PAGE 91
Mitsuba: Japanese parsley.

Nabe: Commonly translated as "hot pot," it comprises a variety of stews and soups prepared and served in a single pot.

PAGE 92
Kobishikari: A spoof on *koshihikari*, the quintessential cultivar of Japanese rice.

PAGE 93
Wakasagi: Japanese pond smelt.

PAGE 116
Corgis, Shiba Inu, toast: Viewed from behind, corgis and Shiba Inu kind of look like loaves of bread.

PAGE 119
Tombolo: An Italian word, meaning a piece of narrow land joined connecting an island to a larger landform.

PAGE 133
Kachi-Kachi-Yama: *Kachi-kachi* is the sound a crackling fire makes. This product name comes from a Japanese folktale in which a rabbit repeatedly punishes a *tanuki* who killed the wife of a farmer, whom the rabbit was friends with. In one instance, the rabbit sets fire to some kindling the *tanuki* is carrying.

PAGE 140
World Heritage Site: UNESCO World Heritage Sites are designated by the United Nations Educational, Scientific and Cultural Organization as significant landmarks to be preserved.

PAGE 141
Motsunabe: A hot pot dish made with beef or pork offal as its primary ingredient.

PAGE 159
Wabi-sabi: A Japanese aesthetic tradition heavily ingrained in the culture, it emphasizes finding beauty in imperfection, melancholy, and ephemerality.

Taro stew udon: Known as *imoni udon* in Japanese, it's a noodle-soup dish made with a potato-like vegetable called taro and a variety of other ingredients.

INSIDE COVER
Koinu Inuko: Inuko's name, if written backwards in Japanese, becomes *koinu*, or "puppy," hence the title of the book.

◁ SIDE STORIES BEGIN ON THE NEXT PAGE ◁

AFTER-SCHOOL 43 WABI-SABI

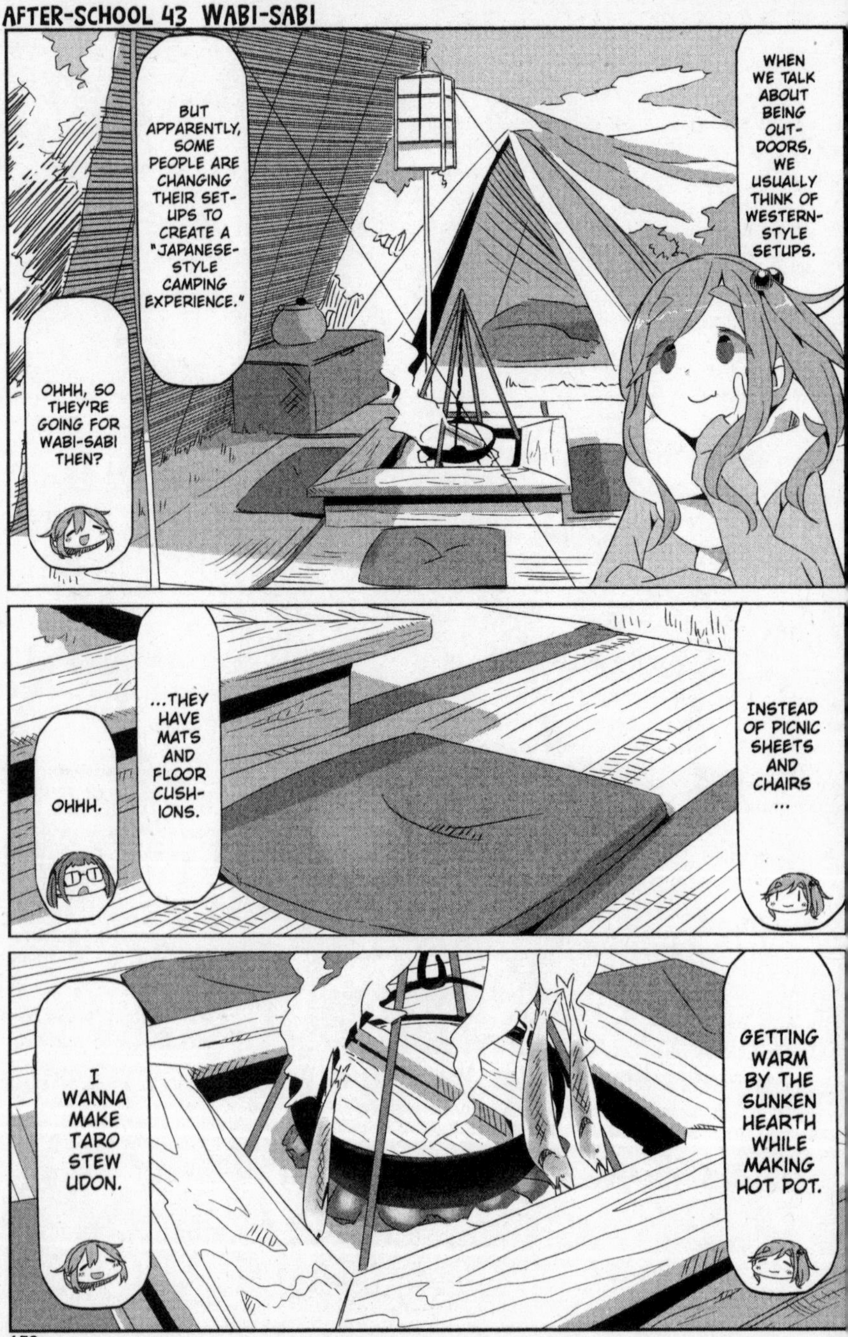
WHEN WE TALK ABOUT BEING OUT-DOORS, WE USUALLY THINK OF WESTERN-STYLE SETUPS.
BUT APPARENTLY, SOME PEOPLE ARE CHANGING THEIR SET-UPS TO CREATE A "JAPANESE-STYLE CAMPING EXPERIENCE."
OHHH, SO THEY'RE GOING FOR WABI-SABI THEN?
INSTEAD OF PICNIC SHEETS AND CHAIRS...
...THEY HAVE MATS AND FLOOR CUSH-IONS.
OHHH.
GETTING WARM BY THE SUNKEN HEARTH WHILE MAKING HOT POT.
I WANNA MAKE TARO STEW UDON.

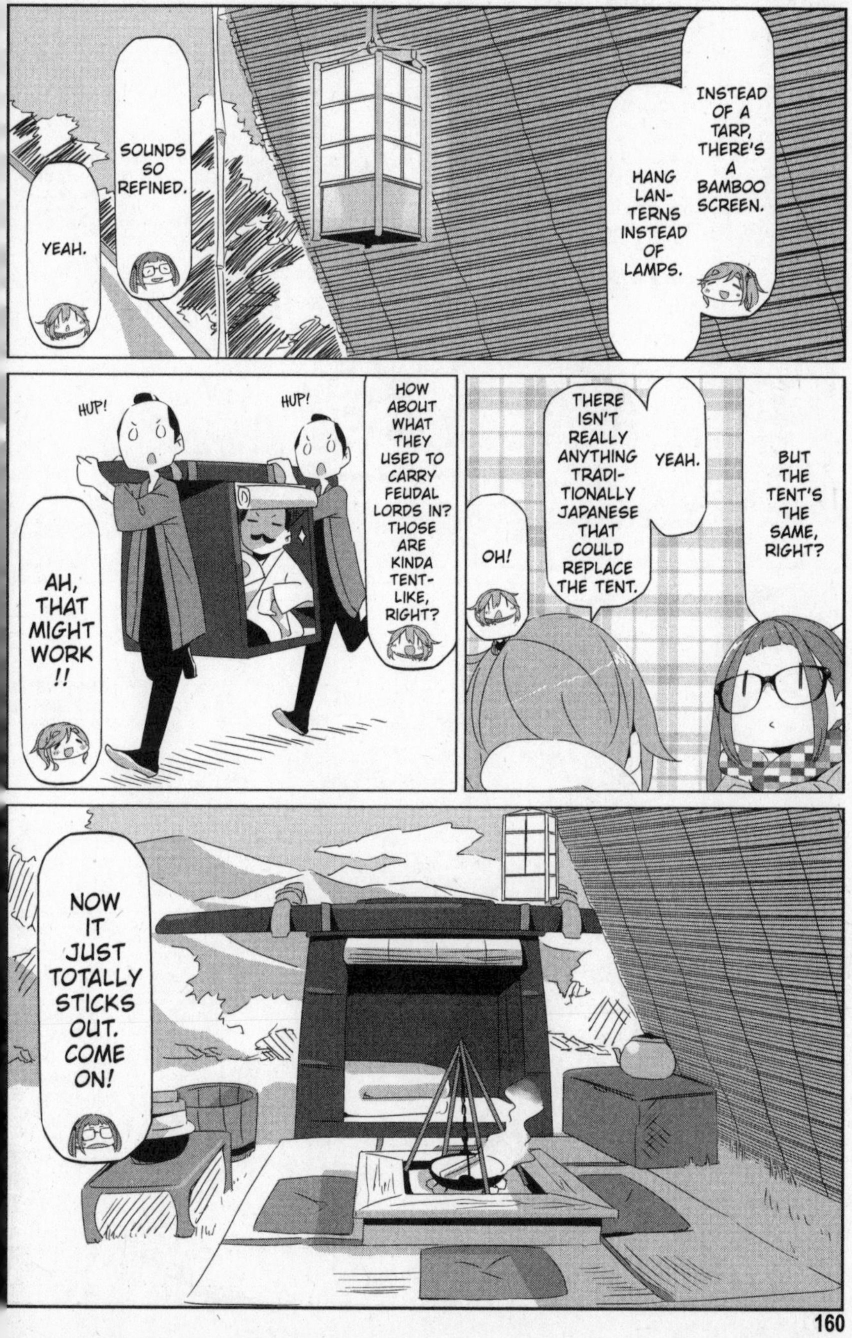
INSTEAD OF A TARP, THERE'S A BAMBOO SCREEN.
HANG LANTERNS INSTEAD OF LAMPS.
SOUNDS SO REFINED.
YEAH.
BUT THE TENT'S THE SAME, RIGHT?
YEAH.
THERE ISN'T REALLY ANYTHING TRADITIONALLY JAPANESE THAT COULD REPLACE THE TENT.
OH!
HOW ABOUT WHAT THEY USED TO CARRY FEUDAL LORDS IN? THOSE ARE KINDA TENT-LIKE, RIGHT?
HUP!
HUP!
AH, THAT MIGHT WORK!!
NOW IT JUST TOTALLY STICKS OUT. COME ON!

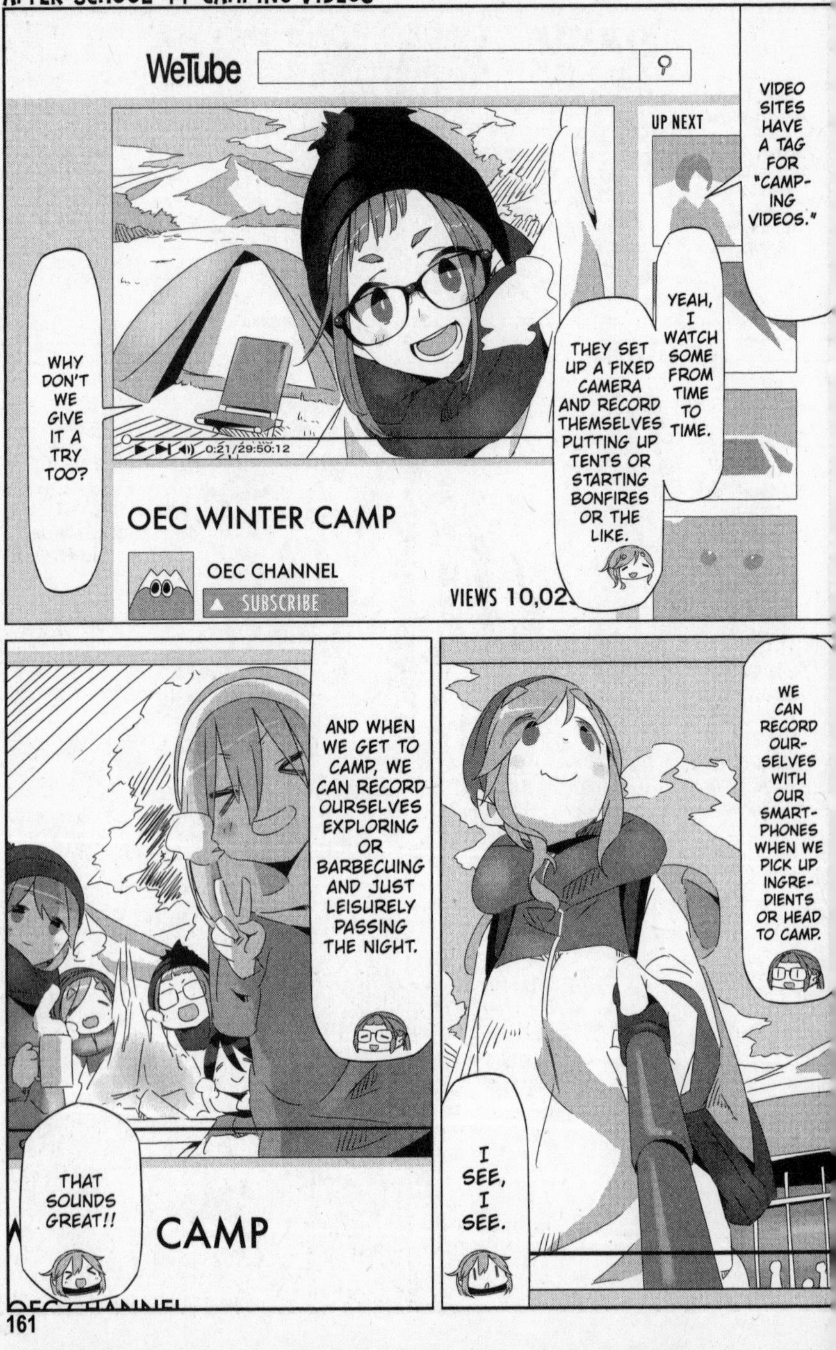
WeTube
UP NEXT
VIDEO SITES HAVE A TAG FOR "CAMPING VIDEOS."
YEAH, I WATCH SOME FROM TIME TO TIME.
THEY SET UP A FIXED CAMERA AND RECORD THEMSELVES PUTTING UP TENTS OR STARTING BONFIRES OR THE LIKE.
0:21/29:50:12
WHY DON'T WE GIVE IT A TRY TOO?
OEC WINTER CAMP
OEC CHANNEL
SUBSCRIBE
VIEWS 10,02
WE CAN RECORD OURSELVES WITH OUR SMARTPHONES WHEN WE PICK UP INGREDIENTS OR HEAD TO CAMP.
I SEE, I SEE.
AND WHEN WE GET TO CAMP, WE CAN RECORD OURSELVES EXPLORING OR BARBECUING AND JUST LEISURELY PASSING THE NIGHT.
CAMP
THAT SOUNDS GREAT!!

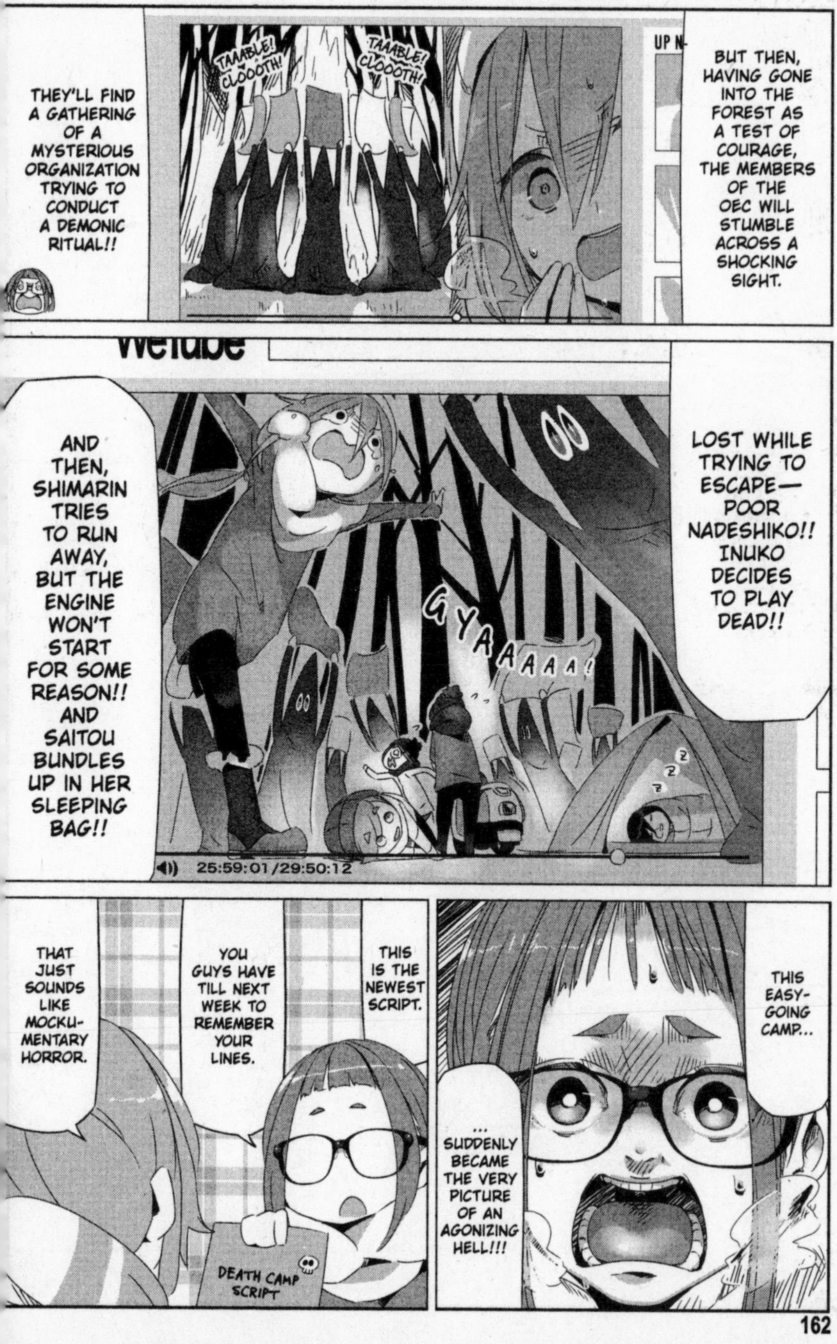

BUT THEN, HAVING GONE INTO THE FOREST AS A TEST OF COURAGE, THE MEMBERS OF THE OEC WILL STUMBLE ACROSS A SHOCKING SIGHT.
UP N-
TAAABLE! CLOOOTH!
TAAABLE! CLOOOTH!
THEY'LL FIND A GATHERING OF A MYSTERIOUS ORGANIZATION TRYING TO CONDUCT A DEMONIC RITUAL!!
LOST WHILE TRYING TO ESCAPE—POOR NADESHIKO!! INUKO DECIDES TO PLAY DEAD!!
GYAAAAAAA!
AND THEN, SHIMARIN TRIES TO RUN AWAY, BUT THE ENGINE WON'T START FOR SOME REASON!! AND SAITOU BUNDLES UP IN HER SLEEPING BAG!!
25:59:01/29:50:12
THIS EASY-GOING CAMP...
...SUDDENLY BECAME THE VERY PICTURE OF AN AGONIZING HELL!!!
THIS IS THE NEWEST SCRIPT.
YOU GUYS HAVE TILL NEXT WEEK TO REMEMBER YOUR LINES.
THAT JUST SOUNDS LIKE MOCKUMENTARY HORROR.
DEATH CAMP SCRIPT

AFTER-SCHOOL 45 CHIKUWA AND THE FRISBEE

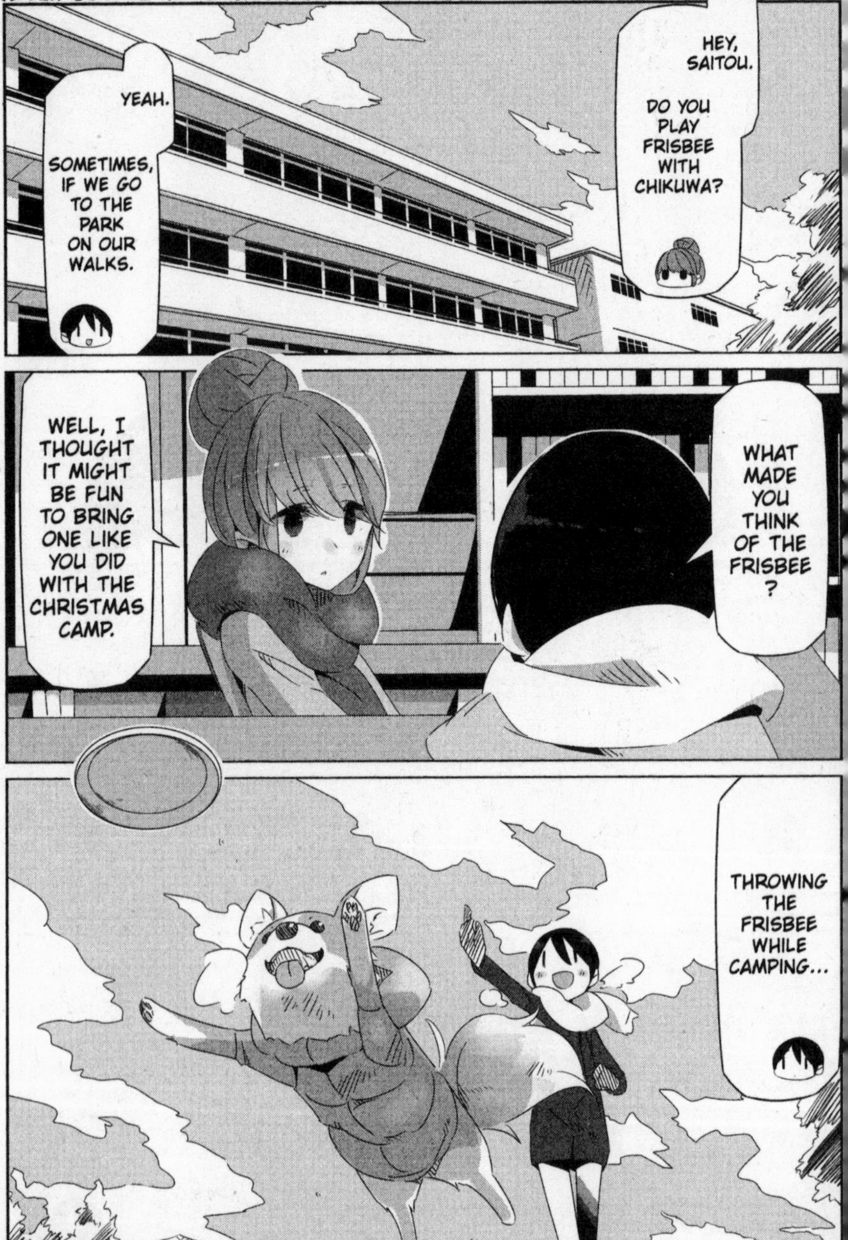
HEY, SAITOU. DO YOU PLAY FRISBEE WITH CHIKUWA?
YEAH. SOMETIMES, IF WE GO TO THE PARK ON OUR WALKS.
WHAT MADE YOU THINK OF THE FRISBEE?
WELL, I THOUGHT IT MIGHT BE FUN TO BRING ONE LIKE YOU DID WITH THE CHRISTMAS CAMP.
THROWING THE FRISBEE WHILE CAMPING...

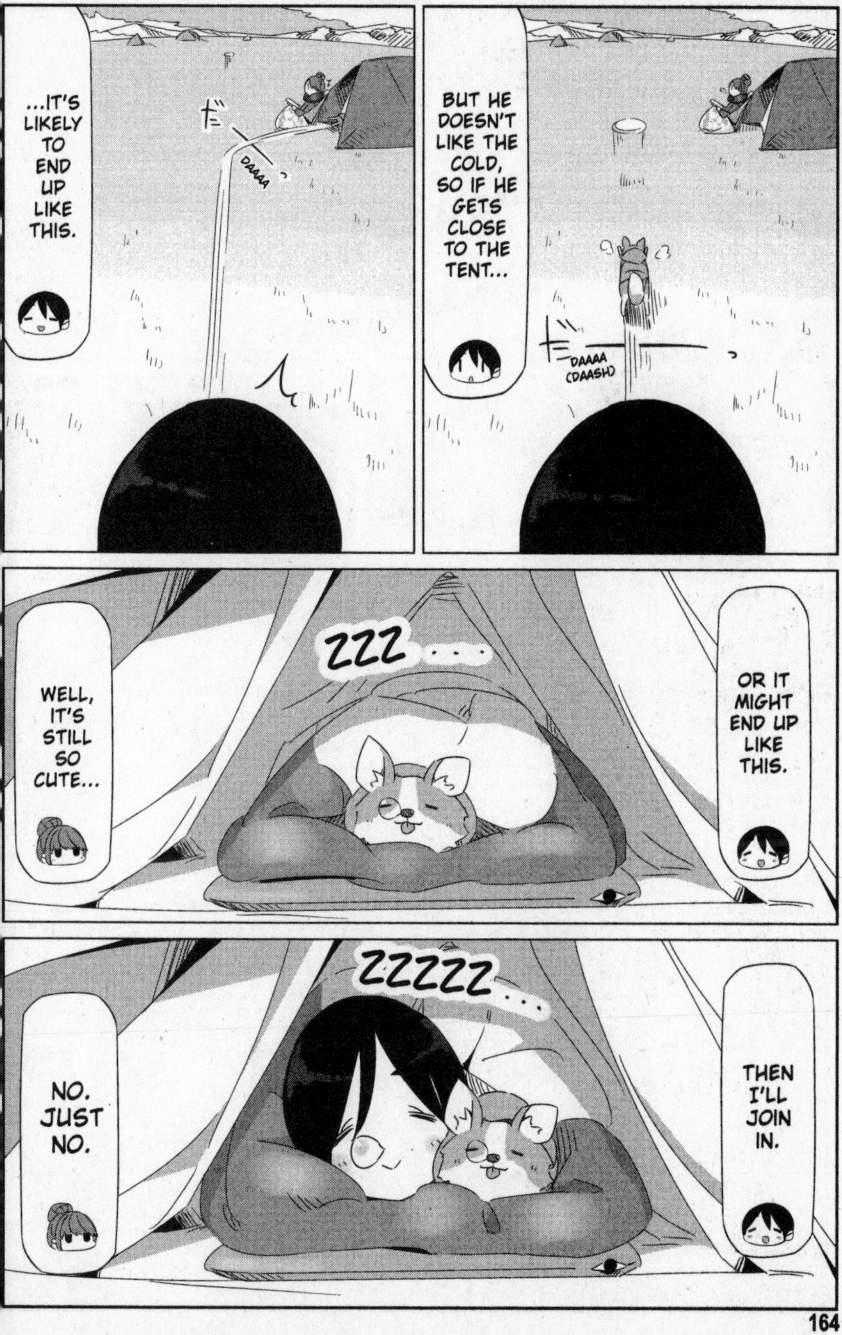
BUT HE DOESN'T LIKE THE COLD, SO IF HE GETS CLOSE TO THE TENT...
DAAAA (DAASH)
...IT'S LIKELY TO END UP LIKE THIS.
DAAAA
OR IT MIGHT END UP LIKE THIS.
ZZZ...
WELL, IT'S STILL SO CUTE...
THEN I'LL JOIN IN.
ZZZZZ...
NO. JUST NO.

AFTER-SCHOOL 46 LAX CAMP

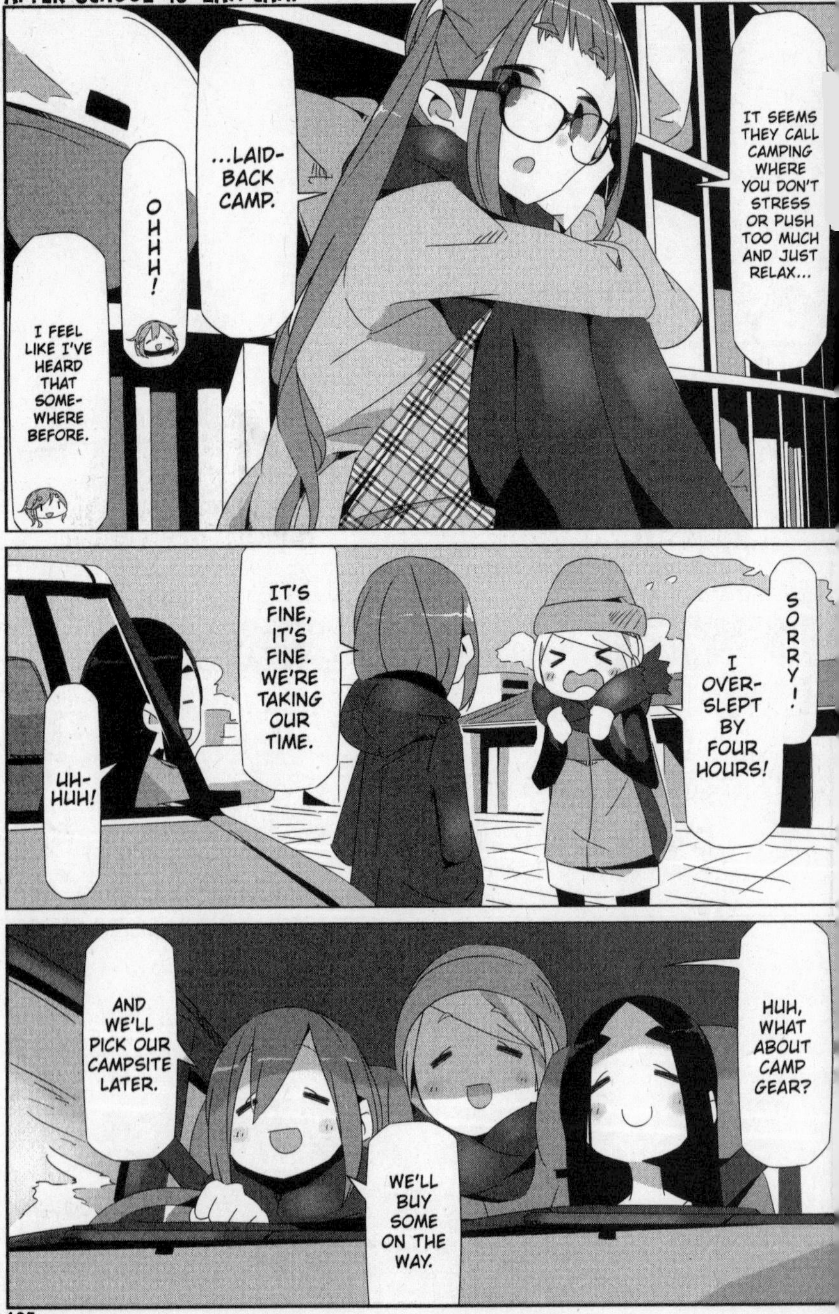
IT SEEMS THEY CALL CAMPING WHERE YOU DON'T STRESS OR PUSH TOO MUCH AND JUST RELAX...
...LAID-BACK CAMP.
OHHH!
I FEEL LIKE I'VE HEARD THAT SOME-WHERE BEFORE.
SORRY! I OVER-SLEPT BY FOUR HOURS!
IT'S FINE, IT'S FINE. WE'RE TAKING OUR TIME.
UH-HUH!
HUH, WHAT ABOUT CAMP GEAR?
WE'LL BUY SOME ON THE WAY.
AND WE'LL PICK OUR CAMPSITE LATER.

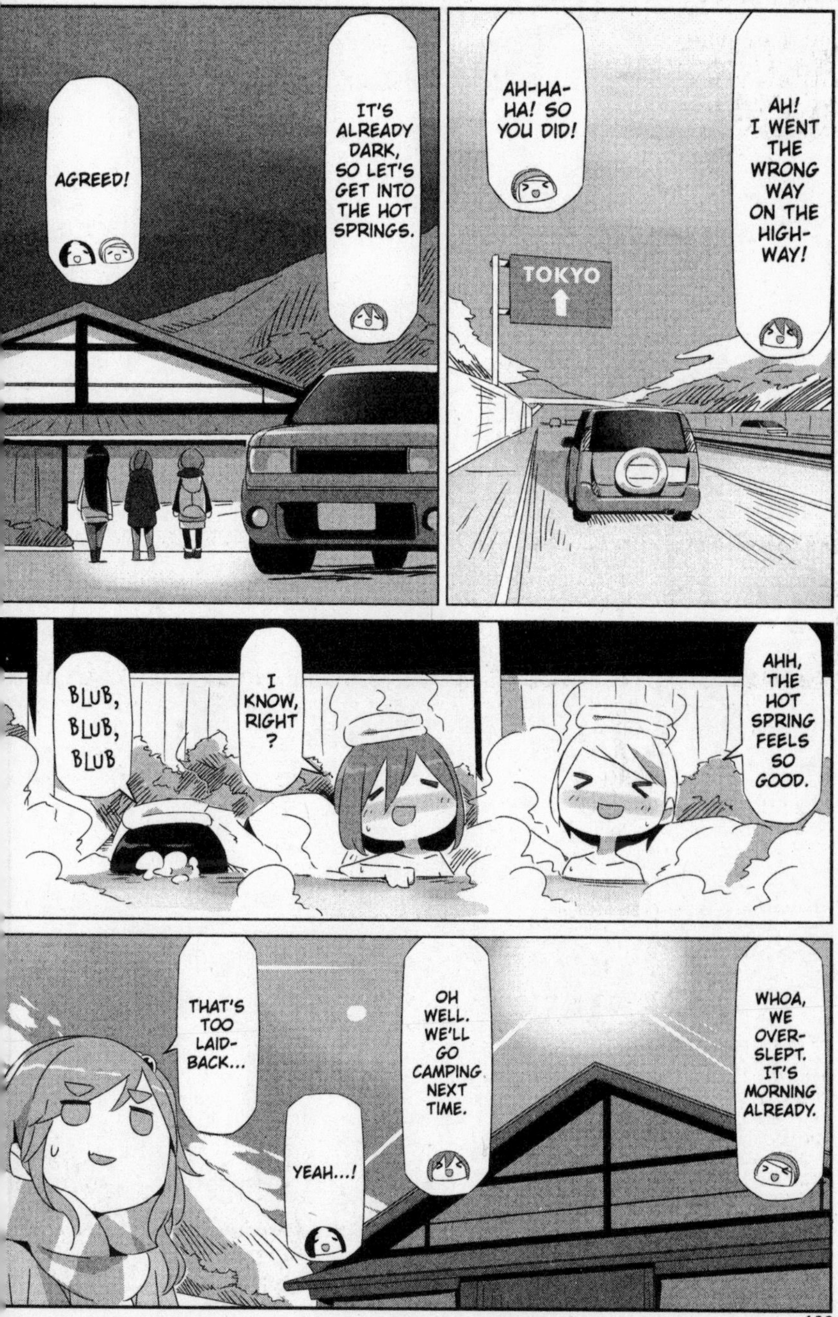

AH! I WENT THE WRONG WAY ON THE HIGH-WAY!
AH-HA-HA! SO YOU DID!
TOKYO
IT'S ALREADY DARK, SO LET'S GET INTO THE HOT SPRINGS.
AGREED!
AHH, THE HOT SPRING FEELS SO GOOD.
I KNOW, RIGHT?
BLUB, BLUB, BLUB
WHOA, WE OVER-SLEPT. IT'S MORNING ALREADY.
OH WELL. WE'LL GO CAMPING NEXT TIME.
YEAH...!
THAT'S TOO LAID-BACK...

AFTER-SCHOOL 47 LET'S LOOK AT CAMPING FROM ABOVE

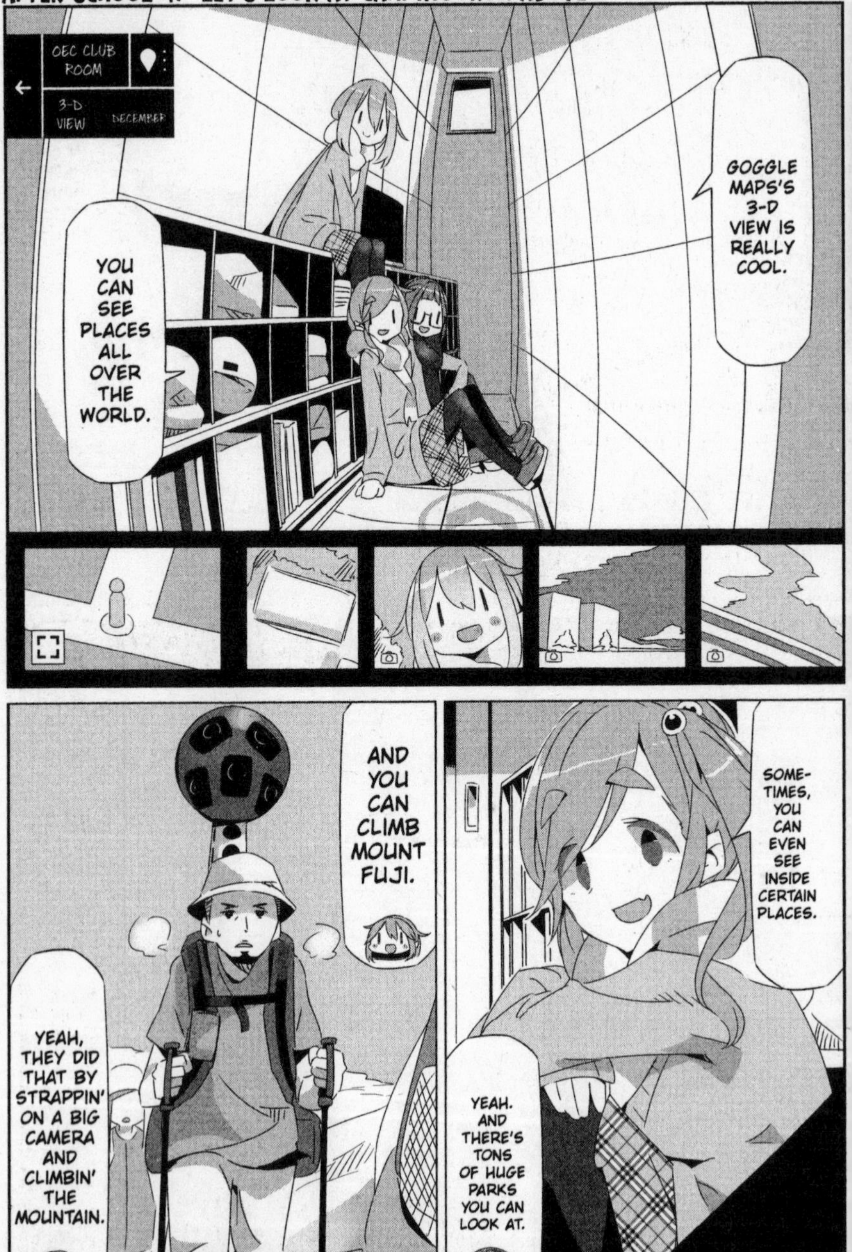
OEC CLUB ROOM
3-D VIEW
DECEMBER
GOGGLE MAPS'S 3-D VIEW IS REALLY COOL.
YOU CAN SEE PLACES ALL OVER THE WORLD.
SOME-TIMES, YOU CAN EVEN SEE INSIDE CERTAIN PLACES.
YEAH. AND THERE'S TONS OF HUGE PARKS YOU CAN LOOK AT.
AND YOU CAN CLIMB MOUNT FUJI.
YEAH, THEY DID THAT BY STRAPPIN' ON A BIG CAMERA AND CLIMBIN' THE MOUNTAIN.

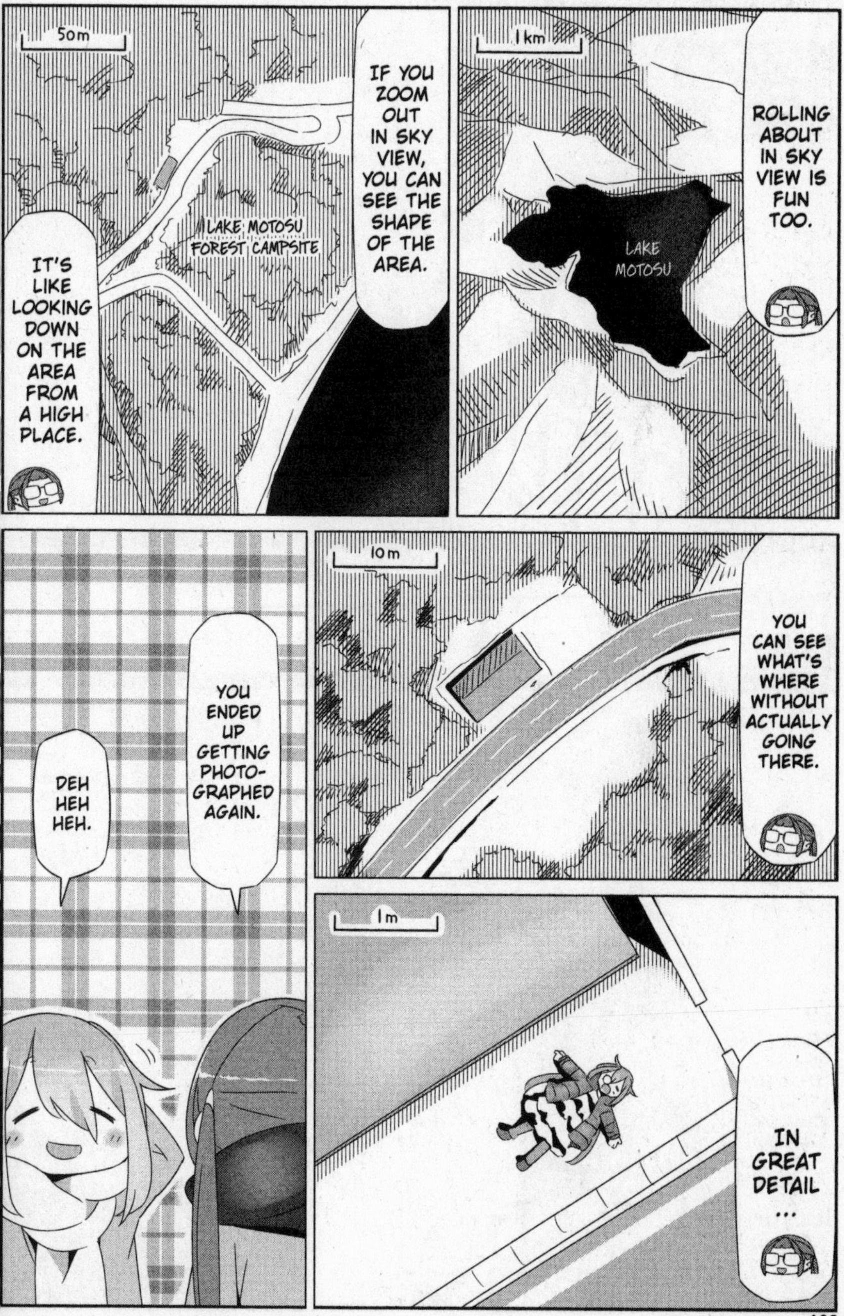
1 km
ROLLING ABOUT IN SKY VIEW IS FUN TOO.
LAKE MOTOSU
IF YOU ZOOM OUT IN SKY VIEW, YOU CAN SEE THE SHAPE OF THE AREA.
50m
LAKE MOTOSU FOREST CAMPSITE
IT'S LIKE LOOKING DOWN ON THE AREA FROM A HIGH PLACE.
10m
YOU CAN SEE WHAT'S WHERE WITHOUT ACTUALLY GOING THERE.
1m
IN GREAT DETAIL...
YOU ENDED UP GETTING PHOTOGRAPHED AGAIN.
DEH HEH HEH.

AFTER-SCHOOL 48 MAINTENANCE IS KEY

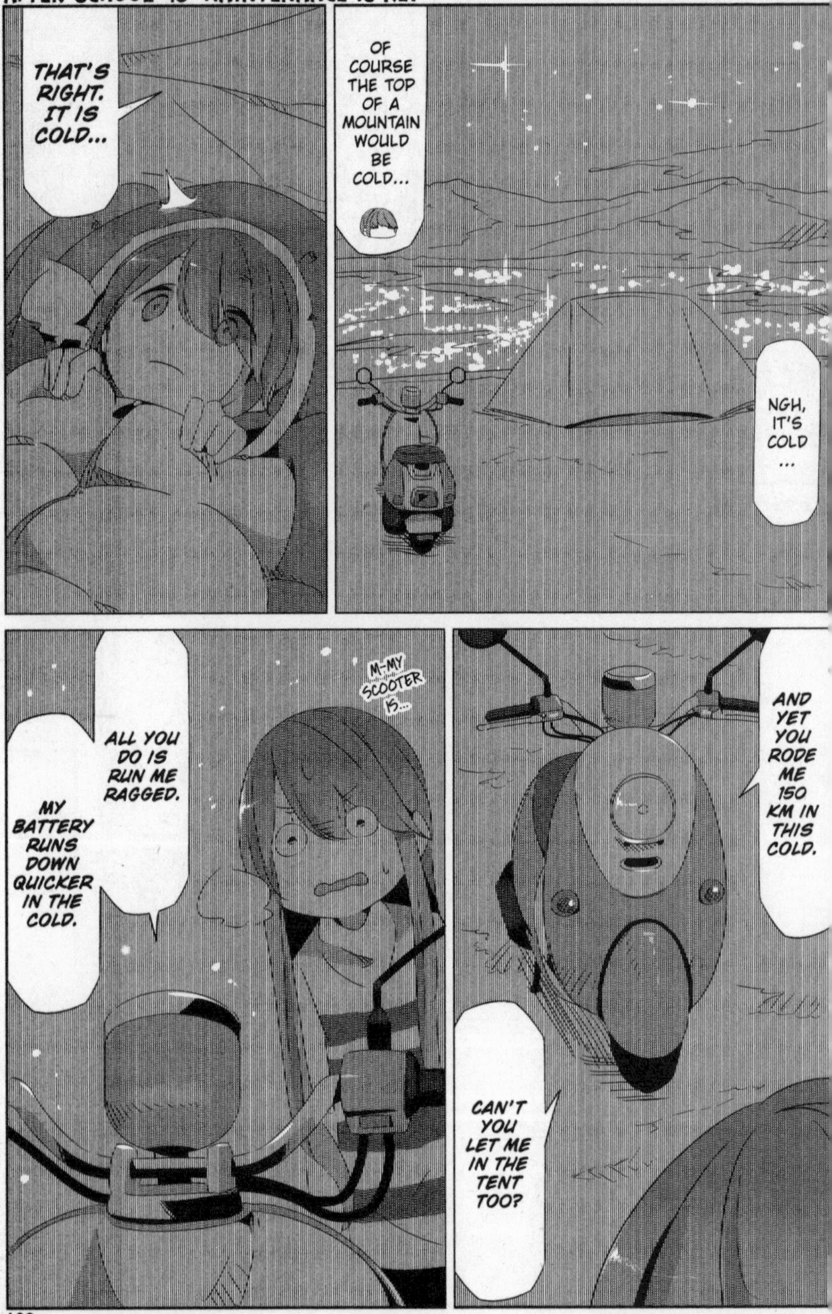
NGH, IT'S COLD ...
OF COURSE THE TOP OF A MOUNTAIN WOULD BE COLD...
THAT'S RIGHT. IT IS COLD...
AND YET YOU RODE ME 150 KM IN THIS COLD.
CAN'T YOU LET ME IN THE TENT TOO?
M-MY SCOOTER IS...
ALL YOU DO IS RUN ME RAGGED.
MY BATTERY RUNS DOWN QUICKER IN THE COLD.

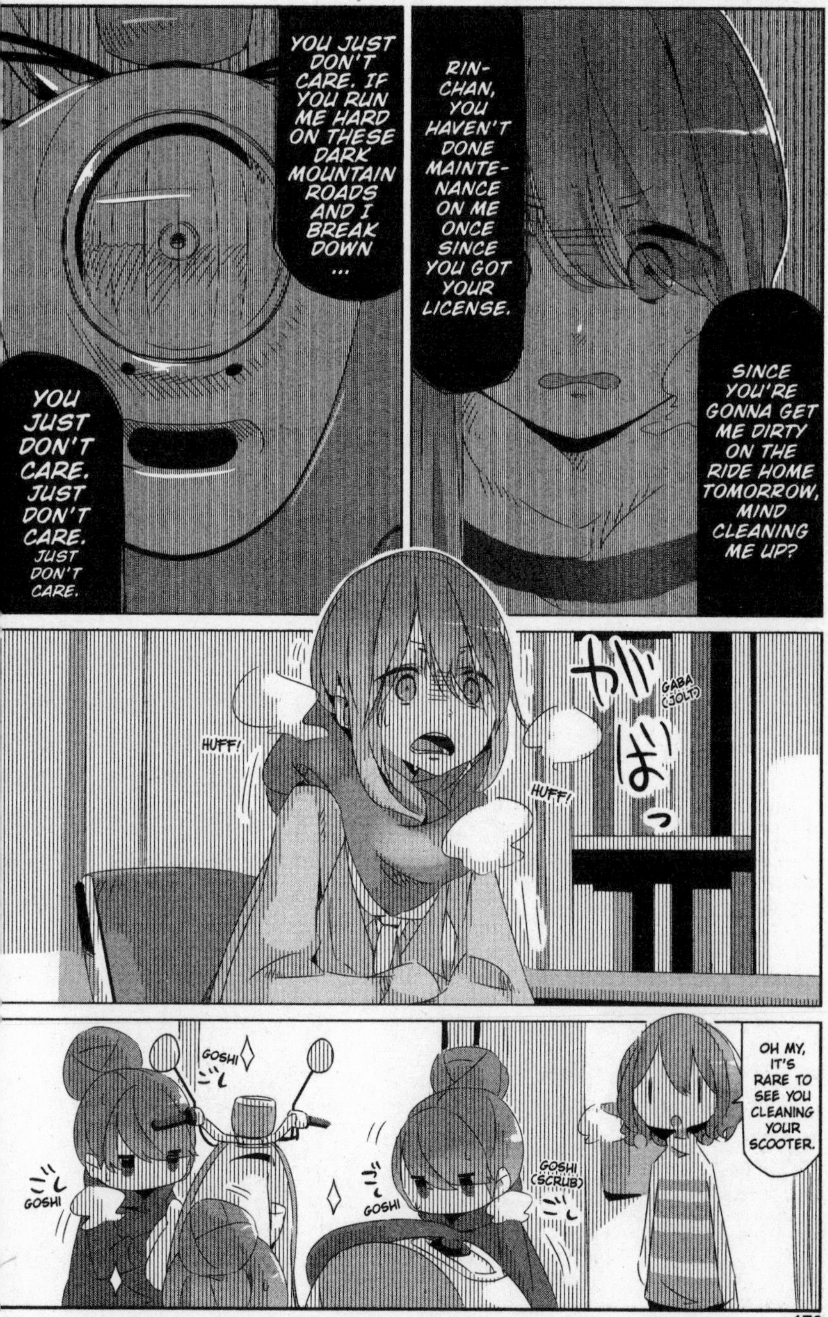
RIN-CHAN, YOU HAVEN'T DONE MAINTE-NANCE ON ME ONCE SINCE YOU GOT YOUR LICENSE.
SINCE YOU'RE GONNA GET ME DIRTY ON THE RIDE HOME TOMORROW, MIND CLEANING ME UP?
YOU JUST DON'T CARE. IF YOU RUN ME HARD ON THESE DARK MOUNTAIN ROADS AND I BREAK DOWN ...
YOU JUST DON'T CARE. JUST DON'T CARE. JUST DON'T CARE.
GABA (JOLT)
HUFF!
HUFF!
OH MY, IT'S RARE TO SEE YOU CLEANING YOUR SCOOTER.
GOSHI (SCRUB)
GOSHI
GOSHI
GOSHI

AFTER-SCHOOL 49 DISPOSABLE

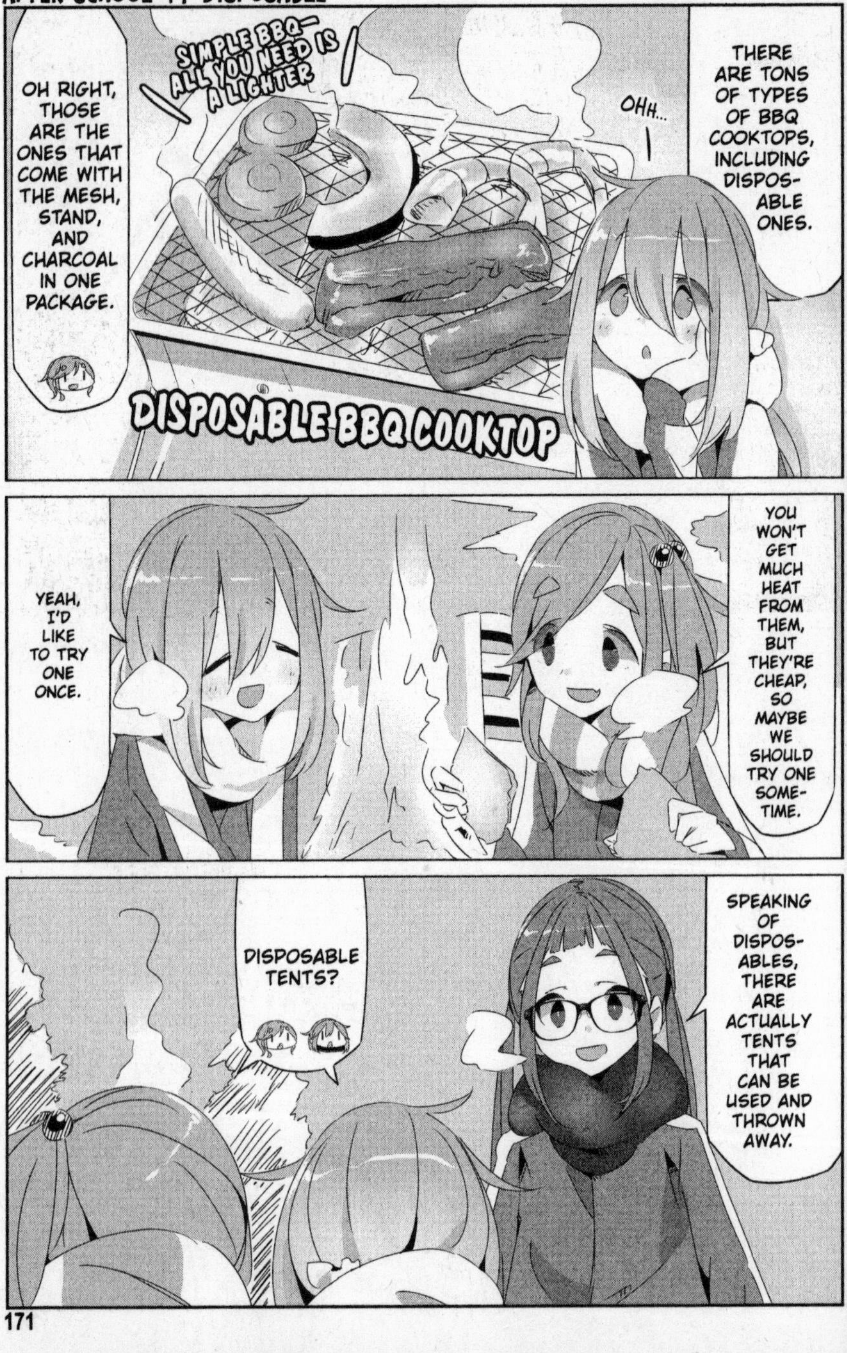
THERE ARE TONS OF TYPES OF BBQ COOKTOPS, INCLUDING DISPOS-ABLE ONES.
OHH...
SIMPLE BBQ— ALL YOU NEED IS A LIGHTER
OH RIGHT, THOSE ARE THE ONES THAT COME WITH THE MESH, STAND, AND CHARCOAL IN ONE PACKAGE.
DISPOSABLE BBQ COOKTOP
YOU WON'T GET MUCH HEAT FROM THEM, BUT THEY'RE CHEAP, SO MAYBE WE SHOULD TRY ONE SOME-TIME.
YEAH, I'D LIKE TO TRY ONE ONCE.
SPEAKING OF DISPOS-ABLES, THERE ARE ACTUALLY TENTS THAT CAN BE USED AND THROWN AWAY.
DISPOSABLE TENTS?

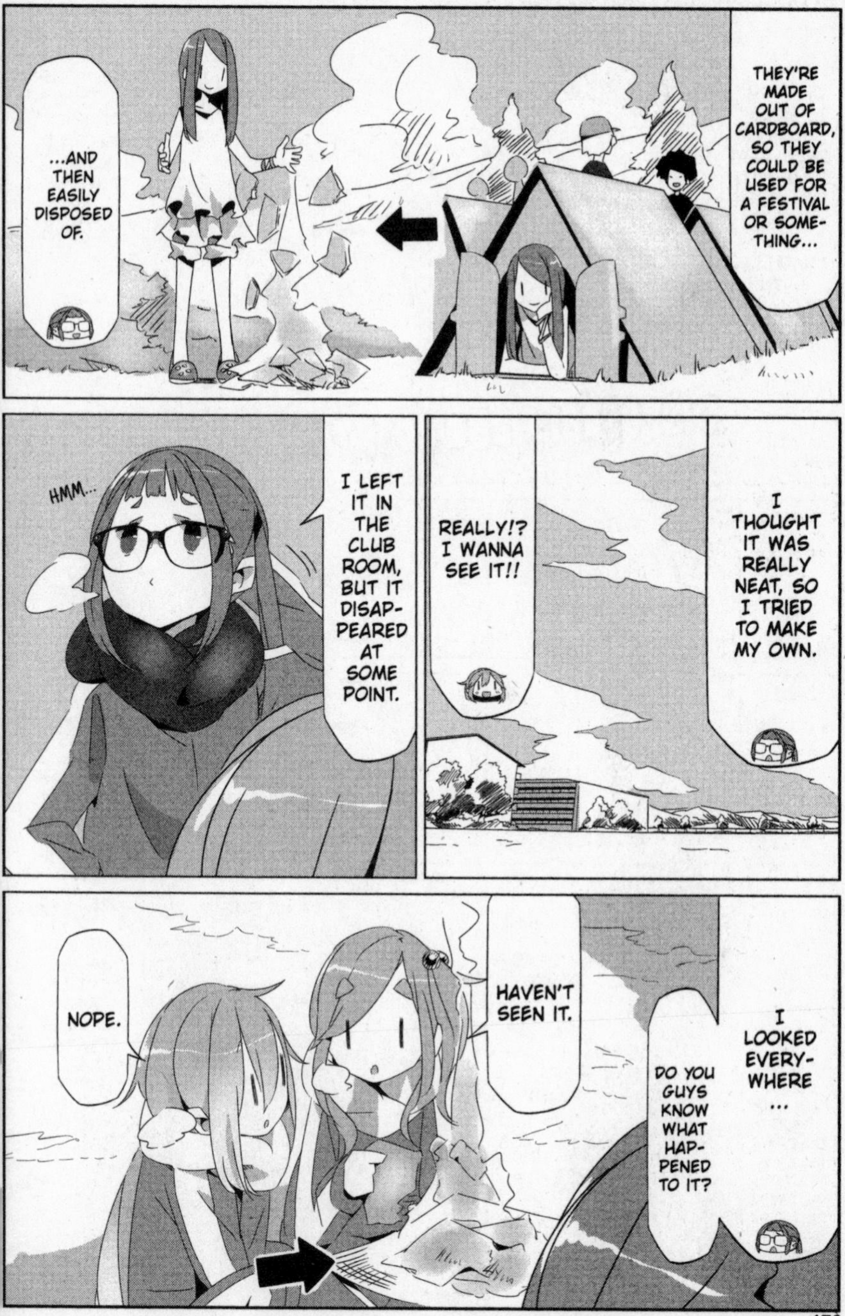
THEY'RE MADE OUT OF CARDBOARD, SO THEY COULD BE USED FOR A FESTIVAL OR SOME-THING...
...AND THEN EASILY DISPOSED OF.
I THOUGHT IT WAS REALLY NEAT, SO I TRIED TO MAKE MY OWN.
REALLY!? I WANNA SEE IT!!
I LEFT IT IN THE CLUB ROOM, BUT IT DISAP-PEARED AT SOME POINT.
HMM...
I LOOKED EVERY-WHERE...
DO YOU GUYS KNOW WHAT HAP-PENED TO IT?
HAVEN'T SEEN IT.
NOPE.

AFTER-SCHOOL 50 CONVENIENT OUTDOOR GOODS

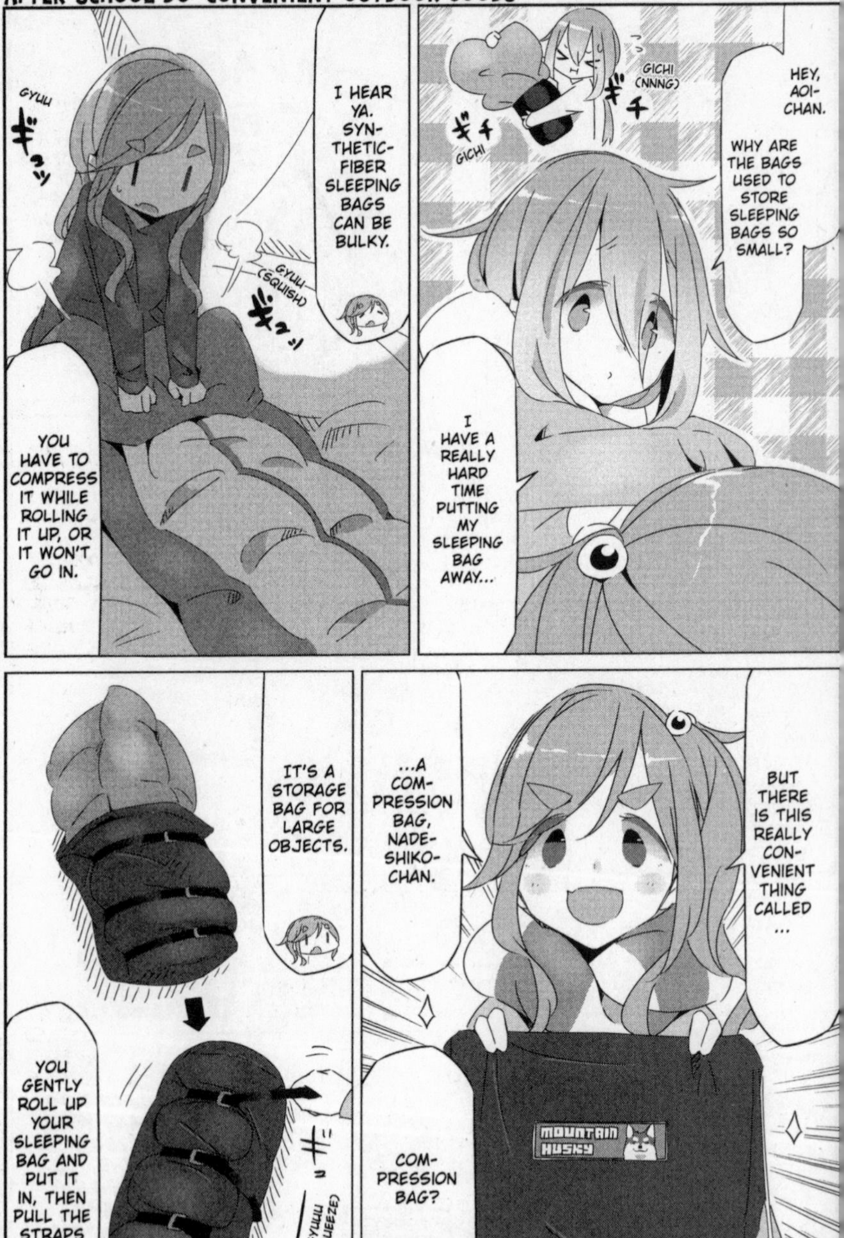
HEY, AOI-CHAN.
GICHI (NNNG)
GICHI
WHY ARE THE BAGS USED TO STORE SLEEPING BAGS SO SMALL?
I HAVE A REALLY HARD TIME PUTTING MY SLEEPING BAG AWAY...
I HEAR YA. SYNTHETIC-FIBER SLEEPING BAGS CAN BE BULKY.
GYUU
GYUU (SQUISH)
YOU HAVE TO COMPRESS IT WHILE ROLLING IT UP, OR IT WON'T GO IN.
BUT THERE IS THIS REALLY CONVENIENT THING CALLED...
...A COMPRESSION BAG, NADESHIKO-CHAN.
MOUNTAIN HUSKY
COMPRESSION BAG?
IT'S A STORAGE BAG FOR LARGE OBJECTS.
YOU GENTLY ROLL UP YOUR SLEEPING BAG AND PUT IT IN, THEN PULL THE STRAPS TIGHT.
GYUUU (SQUEEZE)

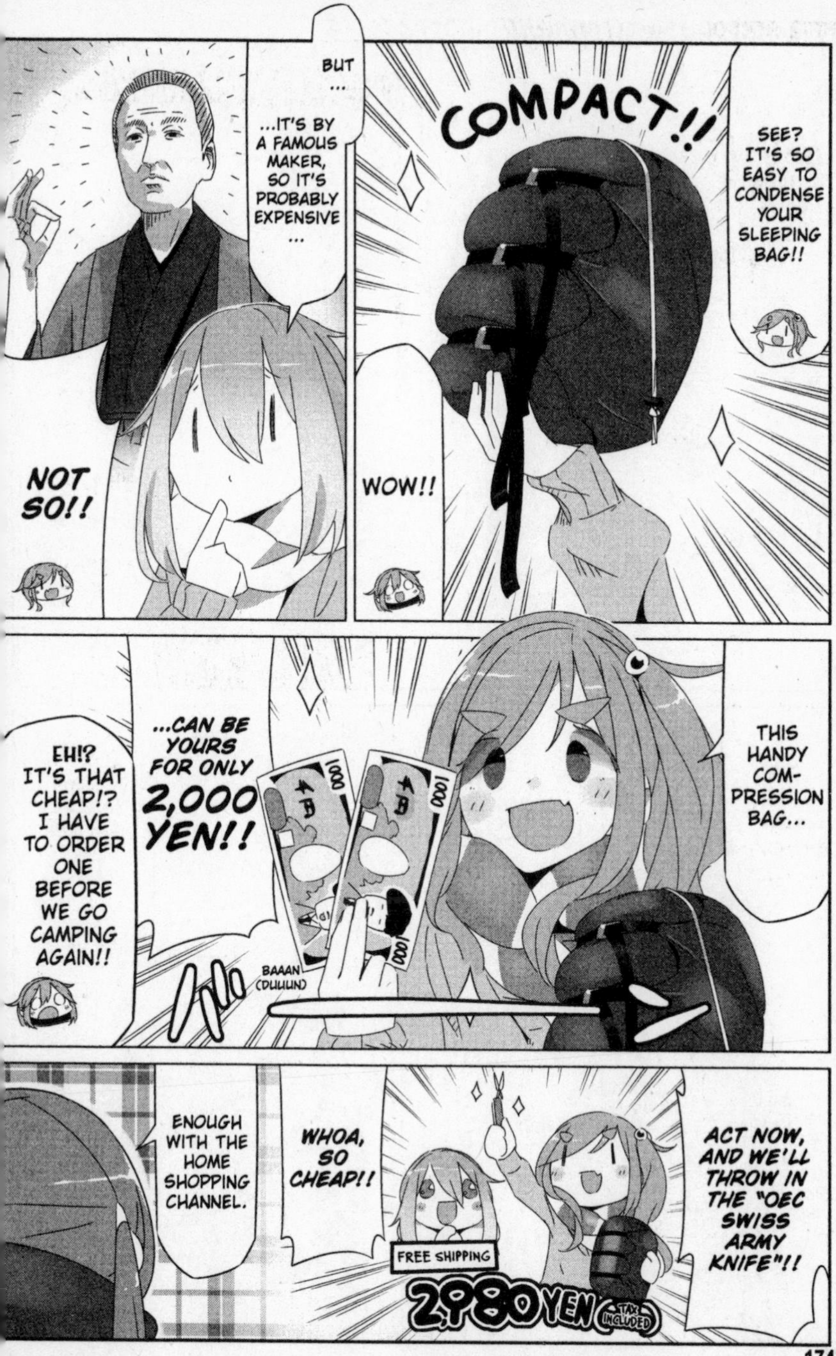
SEE? IT'S SO EASY TO CONDENSE YOUR SLEEPING BAG!!
COMPACT!!
WOW!!
BUT ...
...IT'S BY A FAMOUS MAKER, SO IT'S PROBABLY EXPENSIVE ...
NOT SO!!
THIS HANDY COM-PRESSION BAG...
...CAN BE YOURS FOR ONLY 2,000 YEN!!
BAAAN (DUUUN)
EH!? IT'S THAT CHEAP!? I HAVE TO ORDER ONE BEFORE WE GO CAMPING AGAIN!!
ACT NOW, AND WE'LL THROW IN THE "OEC SWISS ARMY KNIFE"!!
FREE SHIPPING
2,980 YEN (TAX INCLUDED)
WHOA, SO CHEAP!!
ENOUGH WITH THE HOME SHOPPING CHANNEL.

AFTER-SCHOOL 51 HOW TO DRAW

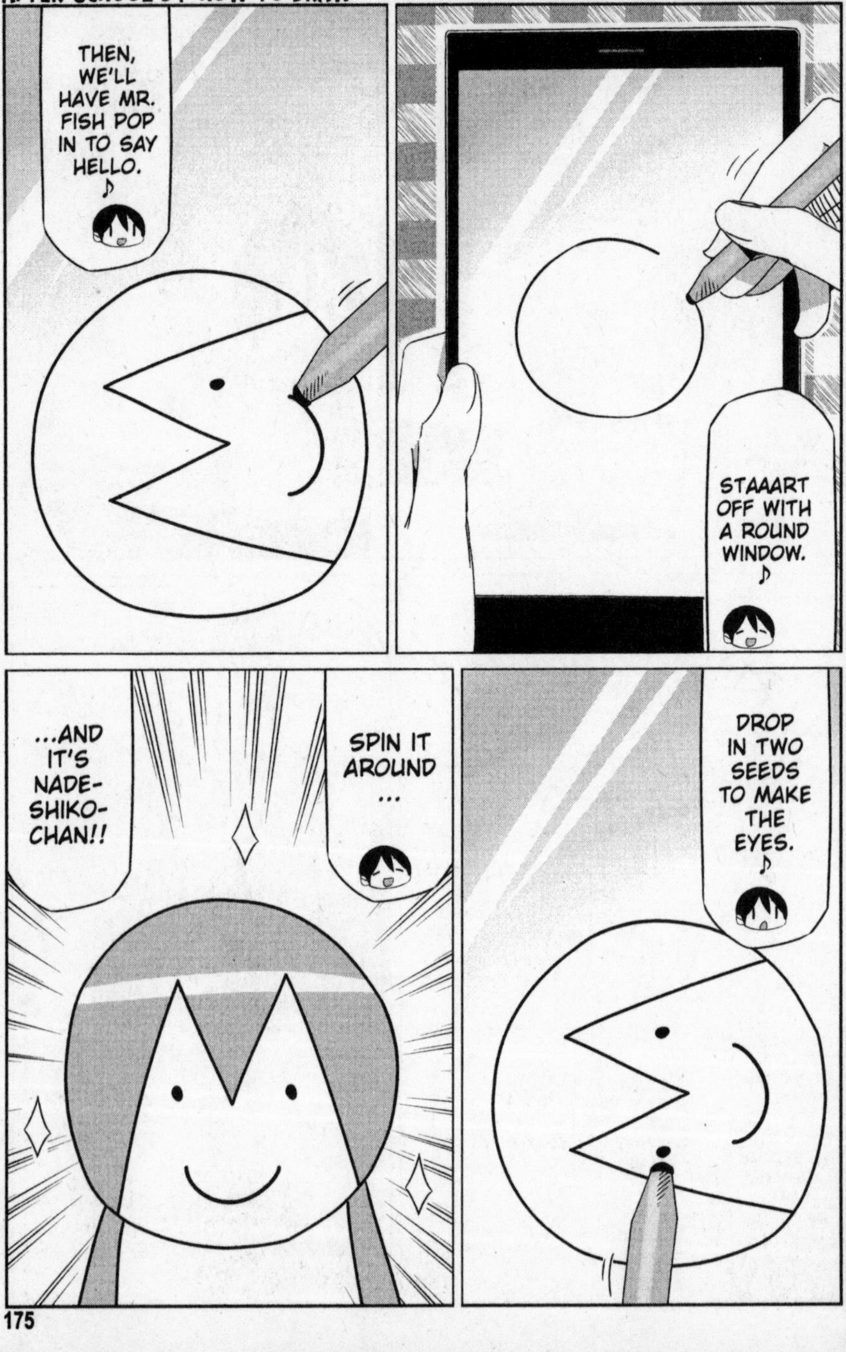
STAAART OFF WITH A ROUND WINDOW. ♪
THEN, WE'LL HAVE MR. FISH POP IN TO SAY HELLO. ♪
DROP IN TWO SEEDS TO MAKE THE EYES. ♪
SPIN IT AROUND...
...AND IT'S NADE-SHIKO-CHAN!!

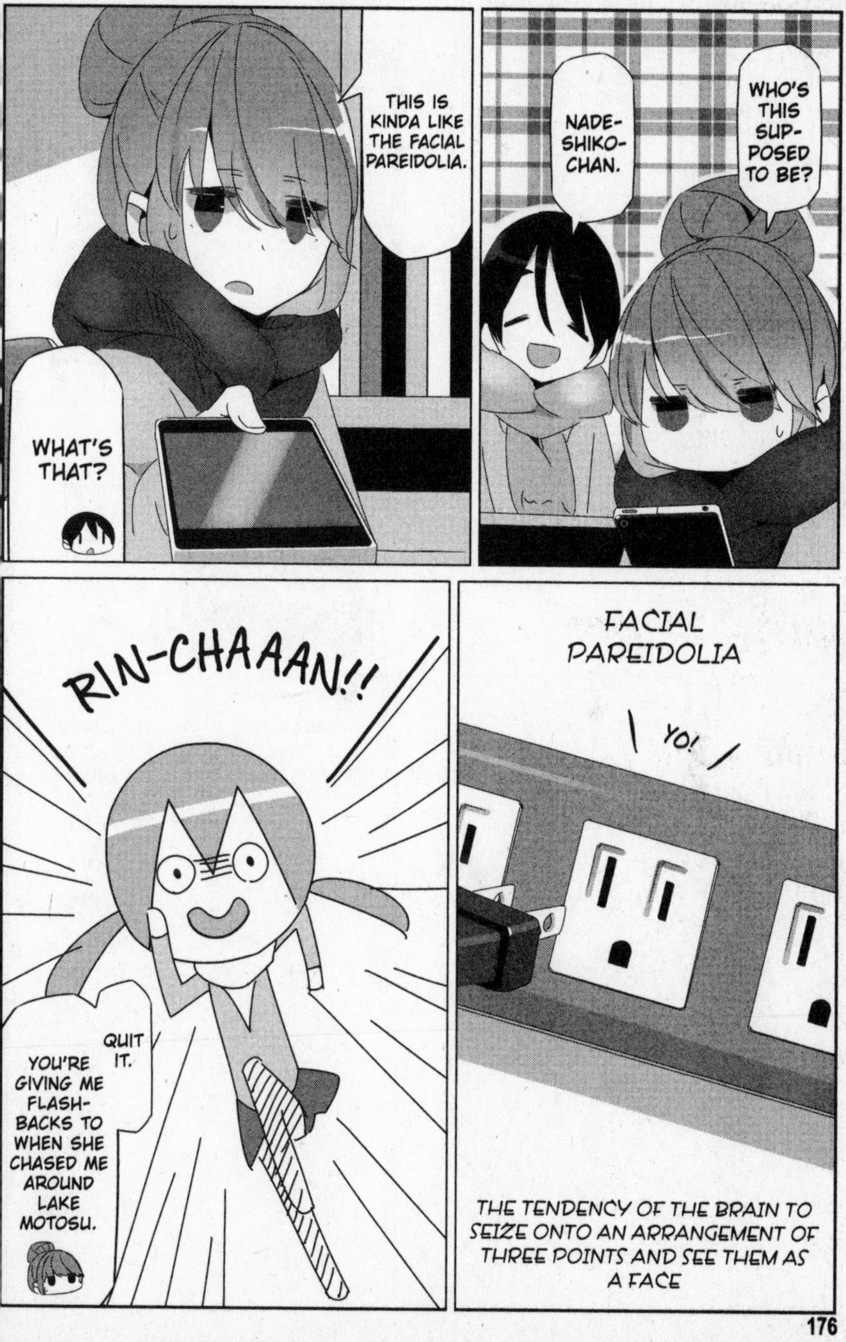
WHO'S THIS SUPPOSED TO BE?
NADESHIKO-CHAN.
THIS IS KINDA LIKE THE FACIAL PAREIDOLIA.
WHAT'S THAT?
FACIAL PAREIDOLIA
YO!
THE TENDENCY OF THE BRAIN TO SEIZE ONTO AN ARRANGEMENT OF THREE POINTS AND SEE THEM AS A FACE
RIN-CHAAAN!!
QUIT IT.
YOU'RE GIVING ME FLASHBACKS TO WHEN SHE CHASED ME AROUND LAKE MOTOSU.

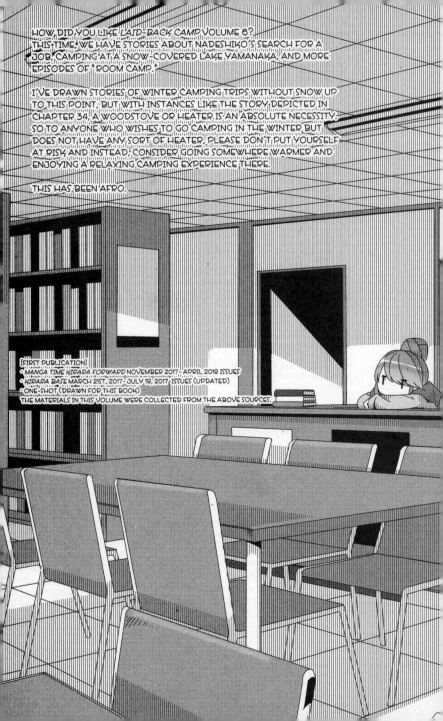

HOW DID YOU LIKE *LAID-BACK CAMP* VOLUME 6?
THIS TIME, WE HAVE STORIES ABOUT NADESHIKO'S SEARCH FOR A
JOB, CAMPING AT A SNOW-COVERED LAKE YAMANAKA, AND MORE
EPISODES OF "ROOM CAMP."

I'VE DRAWN STORIES OF WINTER CAMPING TRIPS WITHOUT SNOW UP
TO THIS POINT, BUT WITH INSTANCES LIKE THE STORY DEPICTED IN
CHAPTER 34, A WOODSTOVE OR HEATER IS AN ABSOLUTE NECESSITY.
SO TO ANYONE WHO WISHES TO GO CAMPING IN THE WINTER BUT
DOES NOT HAVE ANY SORT OF HEATER, PLEASE DON'T PUT YOURSELF
AT RISK AND INSTEAD, CONSIDER GOING SOMEWHERE WARMER AND
ENJOYING A RELAXING CAMPING EXPERIENCE THERE.

THIS HAS BEEN AFRO.

[FIRST PUBLICATION]
• *MANGA TIME KIRARA FORWARD* NOVEMBER 2017- APRIL 2019 ISSUES
• *KIRARA BASE* MARCH 21ST, 2017 - JULY 19, 2017 ISSUES (UPDATED)
• ONE-SHOT (DRAWN FOR THIS BOOK)
THE MATERIALS IN THIS VOLUME WERE COLLECTED FROM THE ABOVE SOURCES.

MRYA

LAID ✸ BACK CAMP ⑥
Afro

Translation: **Amber Tamosaitis** ✷ Lettering: **DK**

YURUCAMP Vol. 6
© 2018 afro. All rights reserved. First published in Japan in 2018 by HOUBUNSHA CO., LTD., Tokyo. English translation rights in United States, Canada, and United Kingdom arranged with HOUBUNSHA CO., LTD. through Tuttle-Mori Agency, Inc., Tokyo.

English translation © 2019 by Yen Press, LLC

Yen Press
1290 Avenue of the Americas
New York, NY 10104

Visit us at yenpress.com
facebook.com/yenpress
twitter.com/yenpress
yenpress.tumblr.com
instagram.com/yenpress

First Yen Press Edition: May 2019

Yen Press is an imprint of Yen Press, LLC.
The Yen Press name and logo are trademarks of Yen Press, LLC.

The publisher is not responsible for websites (or their content) that are not owned by the publisher.

Library of Congress Control Number: 2017959206

ISBNs: 978-1-9753-2863-4 (paperback)
       978-1-9753-2884-9 (ebook)

10 9 8 7 6 5 4 3 2 1

WOR

Printed in the United States of America